ROTATION
PLAN

Lee Langley is the author of novels, short stories, film and television screenplays. Born in Calcutta, of Scottish parents, she spent a nomadic childhood in India. She is a Fellow of the Royal Society of Literature and lives in London.

BUTTERFLY'S SHADOW

In Nagasaki, a fifteen-year-old tea-house girl prepares to welcome her client. Lieutenant Pinkerton approaches to find the female he's purchased for a few weeks. He sails away. She waits, aching for his return . . . In America with his father and new stepmother, Joey is torn between two cultures. Each one is haunted by that fateful day, by a secret that, once revealed, will change everything. They struggle towards self-discovery amid the shifting perspectives of the twentieth century — the Depression, Pearl Harbor, the havoc of war. And then time stops in Nagasaki . . . The deadly dust of the A-bomb settles and Joey finds his way back to the home of his memories, searching for traces of the mother who has for so long lived only in his dreams.

LEE LANGLEY

BUTTERFLY'S SHADOW

Complete and Unabridged

CHARNWOOD
Leicester

First published in Great Britain in 2010 by
Chatto & Windus
The Random House Group Limited, London

First Charnwood Edition
published 2011
by arrangement with
The Random House Group Limited, London

The quotation on page xi is from *Requiem for a Nun*
by William Faulkner, published by Chatto & Windus.
Reprinted by permission of
The Random House Group Limited

British Library CIP Data

Langley, Lee.
Butterfly's shadow.
1. Children of suicide victims- -Fiction.
2. Stepfamilies- -Fiction. 3. United States- -Social
conditions- -*1933 – 1945*- -Fiction. 4. United States- -
Social conditions- -*1918 – 1932*- -Fiction.
5. Large type books.
I. Title
823.9′14–dc22

ISBN 978–1–4448–0657–1

To Neil Vickers

Contents

The past is never dead, it's not even past.

William Faulkner

Nagasaki 1925

From the window Cho-Cho saw the rickshaw come to a stop at the bottom of the slope. Watched them climb out and start walking up towards the house, he in his white uniform, buttons catching the sun; she, yellow-haired, in a short dress printed with green leaves. They looked like an illustration in one of the foreign magazines she had seen: a perfect American couple.

At one point, when the blonde woman stumbled slightly in her unsuitable high heels he took her arm, but she disengaged, and continued to walk up the hill, unaided.

Kneeling by the low table the child was trying to master his new wooden spinning top, throwing it onto the lacquered surface to set the red and yellow bands whirling. Trying and failing. Trying again, lips thrust out in concentration. For this meeting she had dressed him with devious care in one of the few family heirlooms she had managed to hold on to: a tiny silk kimono, intricately hand-painted and embroidered in rich colours threaded with gold. On his feet, white socks with a separation for the big toe. A stiff silk bandeau circled his brow.

In a niche on the wall she had placed a scroll, the bold brushwork of the calligraphy glowing in the dimness of the alcove. Beneath it lay a neatly

1

folded length of dark silk, long and narrow, enveloping her father's ceremonial sword. In her head, her father's voice: *Bushido, the code of the samurai: to fight with honour. To die with honour when one can no longer live with honour.*

Honour was on her side today, she knew that. And she intended to fight. She touched the dark cloth, felt the steel within the silk; she must be like steel within her weak body. Her hands shook and she bent to stroke the child's head, as though touching a talisman.

★   ★   ★

Approaching the house, Pinkerton looked up as the door slid open. He heard Nancy give a small gasp of surprise.

Cho-Cho wore a gleaming white kimono swirling out at the hem, her hair intricately dressed, smooth ebony interwoven with pearls. Her face was whitened with make-up, her lips scarlet. The rims of her eyes were red, not from weeping, but outlined, according to tradition, with crimson. Framed by the doorway she glowed, as though lit from within. Next to him, Nancy, in her undersized frock and little hat seemed awkward, ungainly. He cut off the thought, guilty to be making such a comparison. Nancy was his fiancée; Cho-Cho a leftover from a regretted past.

Nancy sensed the tension in his body; she glanced up at him, and back at Cho-Cho. She dwelt on this vision, the woman in white,

2

gleaming like a marble statue, her neck frail as a flower stem. Oh, she's a clever one, she acknowledged with reluctant admiration. She tugged instinctively at her skimpy skirt, straightened her spine: back home she was considered the pretty one of the family.

When they reached the door, Cho-Cho bowed silently, motioned them inside.

'We should take off our shoes,' Pinkerton muttered.

Nancy silently kicked off her high sandals, her expression darkening. The instruction had the effect of linking him to the woman and the place, with Nancy a mere visitor ignorant of local custom.

The boy held out the wooden top to his father: '*Komo!*'

Pinkerton's stiff features creased into an uneasy grin. He took the top. '*Komo?*' he repeated, 'Right.'

As the two women watched, he squatted next to the lacquered table.

'Okay Joey, here we go!' He set the top spinning. The child clapped his hands, laughing, demanding more: '*Motto!*'

Only the clatter of wood on table surface broke the silence while Pinkerton repeatedly spun the top for his son. Mirrored in the lacquer, the sphere appeared to be balanced on its own tip as it twirled.

Nancy studied the child: the stiff band tied round his brow partly concealed the blond curls. In the richly patterned kimono he seemed very Japanese.

She said, formally, 'What a beautiful . . . outfit that is.' Adding, to fill the continuing silence, 'So colourful.'

Cho-Cho said, 'In a family, such a robe is passed from father to son.' She spoke slowly, spacing the syllables with care, aware of the pitfalls of this alien tongue, where consonants jostled each other disconcertingly, giving her words an odd inflection. 'It is called *takarabune*, treasure ship design. On the ship, if you look, there are ten precious ob-u-jects connected with happy marriage.'

Once again Nancy felt upstaged. Was this woman trying to make out that she had enjoyed a *happy marriage* with Ben? She felt anger building within her but her features remained as expressionless as Cho-Cho's mask-like face.

She touched Pinkerton's shoulder. 'Ben, will you leave us for a little. I want to speak to — the lady, in private.'

Pinkerton hesitated, but Cho-Cho decided the matter. She gave the tiniest of movements, a twitch, a turn of the head, and he got to his feet. He slipped on his shoes and the child followed him out into the patch of garden. Together they studied the plants, and Joey methodically identified them one by one, in Japanese, then in the English his mother had taught him.

A snail was slowly making its way across the path of moist earth in front of them, and the man and the boy watched, crouching to observe the steady progress of the creature, its antennae waving this way and that.

Pinkerton reached over and gently removed

4

the bandeau from around the boy's head; ruffled his hair, freeing the curls. From the dark rectangle of the doorway he heard the murmur of Nancy's voice. A silence. Cho-Cho responding, barely audible. Then Nancy. A longer silence. Nancy again, a murmuring stream. As his father watched, Joey picked up the snail and tilting back his head, held the shell and squirming body above his open mouth. Horrified, Pinkerton knocked it from the boy's hand, startling him. The small pink mouth curved into a downward arc.

'You don't eat a live snail, Joey!'

Pinkerton wondered queasily if perhaps they did. They ate fish with hearts still beating, and shrimps jumping on the plate.

The snail had moved on, leaving a shining trail. Pinkerton tried to think of something cheerful to say; he smiled at the boy but no words came. How long would the women go on talking?

The child was growing bored and fretful: he was hungry, he said, tugging at Pinkerton's sleeve. Then Nancy appeared in the doorway, and hurried over to them.

'Let's go!'

Pinkerton stood up, brushing his knees, and glanced questioningly towards the house.

Nancy said sharply, 'It's okay. Everything's settled.'

'Settled? What d'you mean? What's going on?'

She took the boy's hand and crouched beside him. She said, speaking with exaggerated care, 'Joey: you come. With us. Now.'

5

Pinkerton said, irritably, 'You don't have to speak so slow, he understands just fine.'

She leaned closer: 'You are coming on a visit with your daddy.'

Pinkerton could see no sign of Cho-Cho. Nancy stood up; she seemed very much in control of things.

'You're sure this is okay?'

Her nod was decisive. The child between them, each holding a hand, they set off, walking slowly down the hill away from the house, until, with an exclamation, the boy broke free, pulling away.

'*Koma!*' He ran back towards the house.

'Joey!' Nancy called. 'Wait!'

Pinkerton said, 'He forgot his spinning top.'

The small figure vanished through the door. A moment later they heard a howl from within.

Nancy, above the screaming, yelled, 'I'll deal with this,' and ran, leaving Pinkerton in the road. A moment later she reappeared, holding the child in her arms, his face against her breast. He was squirming, sobbing, and Pinkerton said loudly, 'Nancy? What in hell? We can't do this — '

'Let's go.'

She was already in the rickshaw. He climbed in after her, looking back, expecting Cho-Cho to appear at the door. He heard Nancy whispering, trying to soothe the child, saying how everything would be okay, would be just fine, would be great.

★　★　★

6

As the rickshaw rattled down the dirt road, Suzuki, trudging home from the market, saw them in the distance: the golden couple side by side. Between them was the child.

Nancy called to the rickshaw man to go faster. Neither she nor Pinkerton noticed that seeping from the sleeve of Joey's silk kimono into the green leaves of her dress a garish flower had begun to bloom: a bright red bloodstain.

★ ★ ★

Pinkerton, in a hurry, threads his way through the crowd towards the harbour where he is to meet Nancy, to say goodbye before she leaves.

He is late, and he sees her now, leaning on the rail of the liner, searching for him on the quayside, anxious, looking this way and that, and close beside her the child, dressed in a plain cotton outfit, staring down, eyes wide with fear, at the water widening between the harbour and the hull as the liner pulls away.

Pinkerton's ship will sail tomorrow, taking a different, longer route home. Their lives hang suspended in a floating no man's land and he feels a heaviness like a knot somewhere within him, a sensation he will learn to live with. Everything has moved so fast, there has been no time to alter course — or so he has convinced himself.

He turns away, and heads for the other end of the quay.

★ ★ ★

On the ship, Joey looks up, startled, alarmed, by a noise like the roaring of a wild beast. The lady with yellow hair laughs.

'That's just the horn, Joey.'

She tells him again that he is going on a visit to a place called America. His father will be there. He recalls his mother telling him stories about America, a place with tall buildings and bright flowers where one day they might live.

Clutching the rail he sees Nagasaki grow smaller, disappear, and he begins to cry again, calling for his mother, sobbing that his home is drowning in the sea. The lady seems to understand, and tells him that though he cannot see it, Nagasaki is still there.

'Look, Joey. Watch.'

Through a square hole in the deck she descends small wooden stairs, and slowly vanishes, first her feet, then her body, until all of her is invisible. Then her head pops up and she climbs on to the deck again.

'Okay, Joey? You couldn't see me, but I was always here.' She takes his hand. 'Now! Let's get you some ice cream. Did you ever eat ice cream?'

Later she shows him big fish she calls dolphins leaping high into the air alongside the ship, and after dark when his tears come again, she carries him up on deck, hushing him, rocking him in her arms, and he sees the foam around the boat glittering with a magic green light, the waves dancing as though lit by lanterns from beneath the water. She holds him close to the rail and a warm wind blows in his face and dries his tears.

'Look, Joey, phosphorus, isn't that great? Isn't that fun?'

★ ★ ★

Above the harbour, Suzuki watches the naval vessel sail between the lighthouses to the open sea beyond. Somewhere on board is Lieutenant Pinkerton. She murmurs bitter curses beneath her breath, calling down on him future suffering and a painful death.

She had never liked him, even before she saw him, hating the idea of the imperious American ordering a Japanese bride like someone calling for breakfast. The last time he left she suspected he would never return. How much better it would be had he stayed away.

Both ships have left now, cutting through the waves, needing no wind to guide them. How free they are, the visitors, coming and going, careless of what they leave behind, broken, or destroyed.

★ ★ ★

The harbour closes behind him and Pinkerton takes his last look at land, catching that moment, that heartbeat, a shadow between the flawless rim of sky and sea when the horizon is blurred; a moment that occurs both in leaving and arriving, which he had looked out for, that day three years before, when he sailed into Nagasaki for the first time.

PART ONE

1

The voyage had been rough, the seas high and vicious, the weather ugly. When he saw a smudge of land hazy on the sharp rim of the horizon he gave thanks. All day they had ploughed through the Japan Sea straits, progress slowed by storm damage to the hull. Close to land, there seemed to be no break in the low mountains, until they came to the narrow entrance of a round bay which opened into another, inner bay. From the map Pinkerton knew that around the shores of this inner harbour lay Nagasaki. He yearned for firm ground under his feet, looked forward to some comfort and, more important, pleasure.

Gliding silently through the narrow passages, they passed the sentinel lighthouses flashing port and starboard, the surrounding hills dark against the night sky. Around them the lights of small boats bobbed on the water, and then, in a semicircle, like an amphitheatre he had once seen in a schoolbook about ancient Greece, the lights of the city, glittering like fallen stars on the hillside, reflected in the black water. With luck Nagasaki would bring him what he required: a good meal, and a not-so-good woman. He'd ask Eddie what to do; Eddie had the experience. They were the same age, twenty-three last birthday, but Eddie seemed years older, and he knew the territory; he'd lay dollars to buttons Eddie would have the answers.

They went ashore next morning, early, in a sampan that set them down on the waterfront. The encircling hill was steep, in some places too steep for houses. Here and there it had been terraced for gardens that looked no bigger than a handkerchief and Pinkerton could see tiny figures bent low over whatever modest crop they were tending. When they stood upright, with their shallow straw hats and thin bodies, the figures looked like mushrooms growing in the green patches.

★　★　★

On shore Pinkerton and Eddie elbowed their way through rickshaw men calling out, plucking at the sailors' sleeves. Offering them a ride to a good time.

Eddie brushed them aside, as he did the pyjama-clad men smiling obsequiously and offering to escort them — 'right here, very quick' — to what Pinkerton guessed were whore-houses.

'We don't need them,' Eddie said reassuringly. 'Cat-houses are licensed by the government. Anything clean and decent will be in the centre of the city.'

'Are the people okay with that?'

'Sure. They're not like us, Ben. They're not *immoral* exactly, they just don't have morals.'

Ben and Eddie pushed their way through the crowd and into the market district, a maze of narrow streets lined with little shops. Then, as they turned the corner, the smell hit them: seafood and fish, an ammoniac tang so pungent that Pinkerton clamped his hand to his nostrils and tried to breathe through his fingers. The street smelled worse than a polecat. His stomach heaved and he thought longingly of sweet-smelling American fish: broiled red snapper, soft-shelled crabs, clam chowder . . .

But it was not only fish that hung in the air like an evil gas. The city stank. Open sewers ran down each side of the narrow streets, emptying into larger sewers further on. The stench was overpowering. Locals, in their wooden-soled sandals, were agile, even the women carrying babies strapped to their backs, avoiding the slippery edges of the sewers, deftly sidestepping rickshaws, bullock carts, horse-drawn wagons and bicycles. The two men, immaculate in their naval uniforms, trod carefully. Pinkerton's spirits dropped as he looked about him: what could anyone find to enjoy in surroundings so vile?

'*Eddie?*' He sounded desperate.

In the pandemonium he had to shout to be heard. He bawled questions into Eddie's ear about whore-houses and good-looking girls . . . But in truth the stink was blocking out all thought of pleasure as he pressed through the hubbub.

Eddie, an old hand, laughed away his doubts when they emerged into a quieter part of town and could talk. There was plenty of time to make themselves at home while the ship was repaired; to get a house in a nice neighbourhood, and a nice girl, a nice, clean Japanese wife provided by the local marriage broker. 'She'll be yours for as long as you need her.'

2

From the window of the little house on the side of the hill she could see foreign ships sitting on the water, fat and calm as swans. In the deep horseshoe of the harbour fishing boats were tied to the quay, the men working at their nets. The big ships were anchored further out, with tiny boats carrying men and supplies to and from the land. Not so long ago Cho-Cho would have walked along the sea path with her father, watching the fishermen, listening as he explained the intricacies of baiting and catching, scaling and slicing; this was his way, planting thoughts like seeds to grow inside her head, showing her things it could be useful to know. But now she waited fearfully for the unknown, and there was no father to explain anything.

She had been given certain information, but there were blank places and she had no experience to guide her. A man would arrive; a ceremony would follow. She would become a wife. Meanwhile she prepared herself; she concentrated on the surface of things, details: cloth, comb, sandals, sash.

A wedding kimono should be heavy silk, *shiromuku*, the whiteness denoting purity, woven to glow like *shogetsu* cherry blossom. What she wore on her body needed to be right in every respect, the ceremonial wig smooth as lacquer and over that the headdress shaped to conceal

16

possible horns of jealousy and selfishness. She had no knowledge of jealousy, but could she be guilty of selfishness, even without knowing it? The headdress would help to give her strength, as would the little purse, the mirror, the fan, and the *kaiken*, the delicate little knife with its tasselled sheath. She wondered why a bride should carry a defensive blade. As a talisman against bad luck perhaps? And a bride dishonoured would use a *kaiken*; the woman's traditional weapon.

She looked at the blossom beyond the window, and became aware of birdsong. Would she one day learn to recognise new and different birds? And what flowers would she see, would a different sort of sunlight fall on the green places, if she was lucky enough to be taken to America? What was an American garden? Not moss and shale and water, not stones set calmly in raked gravel. She pictured bright orange flowers and trees towering into a bright blue sky, houses taller than the trees, with windows that glittered — in the magazines she had seen, brought by visitors returning from their travels, the pictures sparkled: ice cream parlours and hot dog stands, the women's little dresses, their tilted hats, everything in America was brightly coloured.

She returned to the details that carried no uncertainty: a white nuptial gown and a scarlet kimono, its hem padded to swirl and trail. It should have long sleeves and a stiff obi sash. A sash tied in a *cho-cho* knot that resembled a butterfly — she must learn to tie the sash . . .

Slowly, as though her bones were melting, she

sank to the floor, resting her head against her knees. She could no longer hold back the tears that welled and spread, soaking the cloth of her garment.

She was shivering as if from a fever; her hands icy, although the air was not cold. The room was bare; no ceremonial costumes were spread out around her. She tried to hold on to the imagined bridal scene, doggedly listing the traditional items. She dwelt on silk, ivory, tortoiseshell. Pretty pictures. But she knew that in due course, when a wedding ceremony of sorts had taken place and the sliding *shoji* doors had closed against the outside world, she would be alone with a stranger who had purchased her body. He would expect her to remove the kimono and please him.

Shikata ga nai. The old expression said it all: *nothing to be done about it*.

But she was fifteen and she was afraid.

⋆　⋆　⋆

The curving path led up from the harbour, came into view at the headland, then vanished behind maple trees. She had been watching closely, but she must have glanced away and missed a moment, for she saw now that a man was walking towards the house and was already halfway up the hill. Dressed in white, the peak of his cap shading his face, until with a sudden movement he removed it to wipe what must be sweat from his brow, and revealed gleaming gold hair. She was

18

astonished: golden hair, so bright, so American!

He turned back and waited, and she saw that a second man was following him, a thin, dark, older man in a sombre suit: the consul, Sharpless-san. She had met him before; he knew her father. The two men continued up the hill, walking side by side, and to Cho-Cho watching them it seemed as though the bright shining American was accompanied by a man-shaped shadow.

3

Sharpless made the introduction: 'Lieutenant Benjamin Franklin Pinkerton, Cho-Cho-san . . . '

In the course of a working week the consul frequently found himself introducing strangers for one reason or another, though not usually to assist in selling a girl to a sailor. This exercise was distasteful, he would have preferred to withdraw, but he was needed, to translate, to lend a veneer of social normality to the transaction.

The formalities of arrival had been observed, the two men removing their shoes by the door. Now Pinkerton attempted a handshake just as Cho-Cho folded her body into a fluid bow, so that his knuckles collided glancingly with her cheekbone.

'Ah!' She recoiled, apologetic, feeling the mishap must be her fault.

'Shit! Sorry!' He waved his arms helplessly. In this fragile, papery room he felt huge and clumsy, at a loss.

The girl made a small, traditional speech of welcome and bowed again. Sharpless translated. Pinkerton nodded.

'Right.'

He tried to think of something more. There was a pause. He glanced at Sharpless for guidance. The pause lengthened into a silence, then a few words exchanged, in Japanese.

'She asks what religion you observe.'

20

'Oh! Right.' This was way beyond what he had been expecting. 'My family . . . we're Methodist. Not relevant here, I guess.'

Sharpless passed on as much information as he felt was helpful. She nodded. Another pause. More murmured words. Sharpless translated as the girl turned expectantly towards the lieutenant.

'She asks when you wish the ceremony to take place.'

'What ceremony?'

'The wedding.'

Pinkerton frowned and Sharpless added, 'I explained earlier — '

'Oh, sure, right. It's a marriage.' A note of impatience. 'I didn't think we needed an actual ceremony . . . ' Unspoken: to hire a hooker.

'In her eyes she will be your wife, lieutenant.'

To Pinkerton's growing irritation Sharpless went over the situation again: there would be formalities; the girl was not a prostitute.

'She expects a ceremony.'

Pinkerton was short of time, already due back on board for a duty watch. He reached into his back pocket and brought out a flask of bourbon. On a low side table were two tiny porcelain cups, and unscrewing the bottle he poured a measure into each. He handed one cup to Cho-Cho, and raised his own, encouragingly, in a toast.

She waited, the cup held lightly in her fingertips, eyes flicking from one man to the other, seeking guidance. Pinkerton's cheerfully expectant mood had sagged. He raised his porcelain cup again, attempting to revive the festive spirit.

'Bottoms up!'

She watched as he drained the cup.

'I now pronounce us man and wife.'

Pinkerton nodded at Sharpless. 'Can you tell her we just had the ceremony? Tell her it's the American way.'

He liked the phrase, he felt justified: you could say it was the American way under present circumstances. Sharpless kept repeating she wasn't a hooker, but what other kind of girl would sign up to a 'marriage' with a visiting sailor? She must know the ropes. If it was a case of keeping up appearances, he was prepared to go along with the game, though it wasn't cheap: the licence cost $4, the lease of the house $30, and there would be running expenses, food and so on. He had noticed a dumpy servant girl hovering outside the door; she'd probably need to be paid. Still: the place looked clean, and he could end up spending three or four weeks here. It was definitely preferable to a dubious Madam establishment in some backstreet in town.

'You will need to put your signature to the marriage contract,' Sharpless said, 'to observe the correct procedure — '

Pinkerton found his fellow countryman a bore, a real pen-pusher.

'Right. Just fix it.'

He felt the consul's eyes on him; cold yet fierce, the look a senior officer might hand out. Pinkerton found himself straightening up to attention. He adjusted his tone:

'Sir? Thanks for your help.'

To his dismay, the girl was now kneeling, her forehead touching the woven mat that covered the floor. What was he supposed to do here? Uncertain, he reached out and took her hands; raised her to her feet. For the first time they were close, touching, her face lifted to his. He was aware of the texture of her skin: smooth, not rosy like the girls back home, but pale, a sort of ivory, with a sheen like a peeled almond. And her eyes were almond-shaped, as he had heard them described, but shining, with the glow of an uncut gem. She was smiling up at him. Even though she stood very straight the top of her head was way below his shoulder. For a moment he was caught up, sensed an odd churning in his chest, and held on to her hands, the smooth fingertips cool against his palms. Did she guide his hand? He was momentarily confused, and to his surprise found himself raising her fingers briefly to his lips. He was relieved to see that Sharpless, glancing out of the window, had missed the embarrassing moment.

'Tell her I'll be back with my stuff.'

Pinkerton glanced around the bare room. No closets, no chests that he could see. What did these people do with their belongings? The houses were flimsy affairs made of wood and what looked like paper screens. And as for home comfort, forget it.

Sharpless had told him the word for goodbye: 'Sayonara.'

He pronounced it awkwardly in his flat American drawl. Then more awkwardness, as he put on

23

his shoes and slid open the flimsy door too forcefully, so that wood banged against wood.

* * *

The girl watched him go as he swung off down the hill back to the ship, saw his slouching ease, the way his body moved, the confident stride. In the sunlight he glittered white and gold. He glanced back and sketched a brief, good-humoured salute. She caught his smile: found herself smiling back. He looked younger when he smiled, almost a boy. She folded her hands into her kimono sleeves and squeezed her elbows nervously. Everything was different: what she had undertaken as an unpleasant duty, an obedient acceptance of fate, had changed its aspect. She continued to watch the American as he dwindled into the distance, then out of sight. She recalled his eyes that echoed the sea in the harbour; his hair that blazed like fresh wheat, his strong hands gripping hers, the shock of his lips on her fingertips. The way he towered over Sharpless-san, his head almost touching the ceiling. His smile. She saw that Lieutenant Pinkerton was beautiful.

The transaction was precarious; she was aware that the marriage was not intended to be permanent, but she could try and make it so. She could become useful, valuable, even. She could, perhaps, be taken back to America.

She said, diffidently, 'Would you say, Sharpless-san, that Lieutenant Pinkerton is a fine-looking man?'

24

She could not express the opinion herself; that would be *noroke*, quite inappropriate, but to seek his view was an acceptable way to suggest it.

He frowned. 'Many Americans have that appearance.'

He kept his voice deliberately neutral. When she had asked about the wedding ceremony, and received Pinkerton's curt response, Sharpless had observed her small, woebegone face.

What ceremony else? He felt there was indeed something Ophelia-like about Cho-Cho; a commodity to be traded by her family, an object to be desired by a man, and in due time discarded.

When he was promoted from vice-consul he found himself saddled with the only aspect of the job he had found unwelcome — a task he felt was hardly part of the diplomatic process.

The departing consul had shrugged. 'You can refuse, it's unofficial of course, and doesn't come up often — most of them go for the tea-house option. But when the ship's in port for a while . . . You have to ask yourself; would you want one of our boys to sail home with an unmentionable disease? It's a convenient system and it works. Everyone wins.' And so it had seemed, until it came to Pinkerton and Cho-Cho. But the girl wanted him here: he had known her father and she trusted him. He remained uneasy.

He had seen the way she watched Pinkerton. He wanted to say to her: leave now. Run away. Find work in a respectable tea-house, learn to sing and play an instrument; you don't have to do this. But of course she did have to do this.

The marriage broker had made it plain: with both parents dead — worse, a father ruined by debt, disgraced, redeemed only by his honourable suicide — the girl belonged to her uncle, and the uncle had entered into the contract on her behalf. She was a negotiable property.

The consul had listened to the story with dismay. 'And her own wishes?'

'She has no wishes,' the broker shrugged. 'She has no voice.'

Sharpless's mournful countenance and long muzzle did not easily crease into laughter, but the habitual grimness deepened as he glanced at Cho-Cho. She was still gazing out of the window, studying the now empty bend in the road as though it held an after-image of the man no longer visible. He found the sailor crude, ill-mannered. Luckily this liaison would be relatively brief; but he feared the girl would be bruised by it, her first such experience. He hoped that Pinkerton would be kind.

From across the room Cho-Cho was murmuring that she knew only a few words of this foreign tongue, gleaned from travellers calling on her father. She glanced again at the view from the window. She would like to acquire some American words; to speak, and to understand. She was known to be quick to learn. Could Sharpless-san do her the honour of giving her some help; perhaps there was a book she could study . . . ?

'I'm sure we have some books in the consulate library,' he said, and found himself adding, 'I

26

could give you a lesson or two. It is not a difficult language.'

'Not like Japanese, you mean?' He saw that the girl had a feeling for humour.

'In return,' he suggested, 'you can correct my mistakes.'

'Oh! Your Japanese is perfect, Sharpless-san.' She hesitated, and added, barely audibly, 'Almost.'

He watched her mouth curve into a smile, the bright glance she threw his way, and felt a pang, sweet yet painful. A paternal feeling? Or something less admissible? He bowed and moved briskly to the door. He reminded himself she was just a child.

4

The first night, after dinner, rising with aching knees from the floor cushion, Pinkerton made a mental note to bring in a couple of chairs and maybe a proper table. How uncomfortable did life have to be to qualify as 'traditional'? He had once visited an Amish family back home and had come to the conclusion then that anyone who refused the advantages of the modern world needed his head examining. His mother had had the good sense to get herself one of Mr Hoover's vacuum cleaners and declared herself tickled pink.

Dinner itself had been tricky, an array of mostly uneatable bits and pieces, but he managed a little rice and slices of something that might or might not have been pork. The sake was okay but he couldn't see it knocking bourbon off the market.

In fact the whole evening had hardly gone according to plan; somehow all this Japanese . . . ceremonial had sent him off course.

Now he intended to lead the girl swiftly to bed but before he could make a move she slid open the door and waved a hand at the sky. He looked up. Nodded.

'Right. Full moon.'

He waited. The waiting was getting him down. The silence was getting him down, the famous Japanese silences that, Sharpless told him, 'spoke

28

between the words'.

The consul had recited an old Japanese poem to him when they first met; something about a pond and a frog that jumps in. The last line was 'The sound of water.' The line, Pinkerton had commented, rang no poetical bells for him.

'Ah,' Sharpless said. 'We Americans might translate that line as 'Splash!' But for the Japanese there needs to be an awareness of the silence between the jump and the splash. They would wait to learn the sound from the silence. Hence, 'the sound of water'. That does it. Do you see?'

No he did not. For Pinkerton, a poem should make sense, describe something properly. And rhyme. At school they read Longfellow, learned verses by heart. You didn't need to hang around waiting for the silence to tell you what in hell Longfellow was driving at.

The girl was still looking up at the moon, he could see its light reflected in her eyes. Then she folded her hands and made a small bow, towards the sky, like a greeting. She turned her head slightly; now she seemed again to be waiting for something. He took a chance and inclined himself in a sort of bow in the general direction of the moon. She smiled.

In the bedroom he unwound her sash, lifted the kimono from her shoulders — the nape of her neck above the collar was as frail as a child's and for a moment he wondered just how young she was, nobody had mentioned her age, but too late to worry about that now. Pinkerton was not inexperienced, but something about this light, yielding body was unexpectedly arousing. In his urgency he ripped the fragile undergarment of white cotton and as the weight of his body crushed her against the mattress she gasped. Then she cried out.

The futon was as uncomfortable as he had feared and there were one or two misunderstandings and a few tears, but she took instruction well.

Afterwards she looked into his face and enquired, 'Nice?'

'Oh, sure. Nice.'

'Good.'

He was surprised. 'You speak English!'

She shook her head, serious. 'I learn.'

He laughed. That was cute and it was also true. She had much to learn, but she was learning fast.

★　★　★

Later, while Pinkerton slept, snoring gently, she explored her body, the silky folds he had pushed his way into so forcefully, still raw, so sore that even the touch of her tentative fingers caused her to cry out, softly. Her husband, stepping out of his white trousers, had revealed a startling body part, bright crimson, as thick as her wrist. Men could be rough, they had warned her in the tea-house, but no one had warned her of the pain, sharp as a knife blade, a burning flame between her legs that split her apart with each thrust. She slipped cautiously from the bed.

Among her few possessions was a doll, a

Cho-Cho doll, dressed in a kimono and obi sash, tied in the butterfly bow that gave her the name. She had sewn clothes for the doll, a kimono from a scrap of discarded silk, tiny beads binding the stiff black hair. But she had never undressed the doll completely. Now she removed the white underclothing and examined the pale body. Between the legs was nothing. Limbs flowed smoothly up to hips and waist. The doll could not be entered. The doll could feel no pain.

She washed away his stickiness, her blood. Applied a cooling ointment made from herbs. Summoned back to the futon, she was obedient, her small body pliable.

* * *

She was learning all the time. She no longer cried out, biting her lips as she flinched. She managed to smile, and learned that she was required to move in various ways, the better to accommodate him. There was still more she could learn, and did. And though sometimes she still wept, the tears trickling into her obediently smiling mouth, always she would enquire afterwards, anxiously,

'Nice?'

He was surprised, from the evidence of the sheet that first time, to discover she was a virgin. Or was she? These girls had ways of fooling you. All part of the game.

And she was learning fast.

'American way?' she would ask, nodding, when he showed her something new. She had an

31

admiration of things American that he found appealing. These people sat on the floor to eat and had some pretty funny ideas, but she was open to instruction, and not only in the bedroom.

As with the matter of the yard. He saw that her idea of a yard consisted of a few rocks, a bit of moss and a trickle of water. He showed her magazines from home and he could tell she picked up on the difference.

★　★　★

She walked down the hill and asked to see Sharpless.

'I was seeking guidance on a small matter . . .' She looked at his desk, piled with documents. 'Ah, but you are busy. Another time.'

He was swamped with applications from locals seeking work and a better life in America; there was much checking of dates and stamping of documents, but he waved her to a seat.

'Guidance?'

'Sharpless-san, I want to create . . .' She paused, moved into English, 'American garden.'

'Yes?'

'Please help me.' She paused and retreated into Japanese: 'I want you to tell me what I should plant.'

'It's not just a matter of what you plant. It's how you plant. There are gardens and gardens.'

'I want one that will be beautiful but not in the Japanese style.'

For Sharpless, growing ever closer to this

32

austere land with its culture of discretion, the desire seemed perverse. He smiled sadly.

'If that's what you want.'

He abandoned his desk and summoned a rickshaw.

'Where are we going?'

'You'll soon see.'

The rickshaw man grunted as he pulled them up the curving hillside path. Cho-Cho had never seen the harbour from the opposite side, and she looked about, noting the differences: the houses were larger, two-storeyed, built of stone and solid wood beams, with deep verandas. This was a district for affluent *gaijin*, a foreign enclave. But she could see no gardens of interest, until the rickshaw stopped outside a square stone structure with a wide, tiled roof.

'A man called Thomas Glover built this house.'

'An American?'

'He came from Aberdeen.'

'Is that in America?'

'Ah, not exactly — '

'But I want an American garden.'

'Trust me,' he said, and led her through the gates.

On either side of stone-paved paths the gardens spread out around them, huge beds of brilliant colour, circular or oval, interspersed with flowering trees.

'What are these called?' She pointed to a carpet of lush green leaves spiked with orange blooms.

'Marigolds,' Sharpless said with more confidence than he felt. 'I think those are marigolds.

The ones over there are roses. Some of them are fragrant.' He was on more secure ground with the roses, which the Japanese regarded as no more than bushes with thorns, their flowers banal.

He showed her the rest of the garden and she darted from bed to bed, hovering over the blooms like her namesake insect. As they moved on she fluttered ahead of him along the curving path into some shrubbery, her tiny figure glimpsed between the bushes. But when he caught up with her she was standing quite still, staring at a small statue of a woman in a kimono by the side of the path. Sharpless cursed silently. He had forgotten the statue.

'Who is she?'

'She was Mr Glover's wife.'

'Japanese.'

'Yes.'

The two figures confronted one another, both kimono-clad, one frozen in stone, spine gracefully curved, holding a fan, the other moving closer, backing away, pressing fingertips to face as though to confirm that indeed she too was Japanese and female.

Going home in the rickshaw she was silent for a while. Then she turned to Sharpless.

'I want to plant seeds, grow American flowers.'

'It will take some time,' he said cautiously.

'Oh, I have time! The lease of the house is nine hundred and ninety-nine years!' Her laugh was dangerously bright. 'My husband says the honeymoon may last longer than his lifetime!'

Sharpless was torn: he wanted to warn her, tell

34

her to beware of putting too much faith in a lifelong honeymoon; the lease could be cancelled in a day if Pinkerton decided to stop paying the rent. But it was not the Japanese way, to make bald statements. And did he have the right to intrude on the girl's happiness, to risk spoiling a story which, after all, might against all odds have a happy ending? When before her was visible evidence of a Nagasaki mixed marriage that had stood the test of time.

He ordered the seeds.

5

From the start Pinkerton had found the house cold, unwelcoming: no vases filled with flowers, no framed photographs, no shag rugs ... He searched for words, simple words that she would understand, to explain how he felt. Next day he came home to find her waiting, an expectant smile on her face, hands clasped. She had prepared a speech:

'Surprise for you, happy Pinkerton!'

He looked around, eyebrows raised, and glanced back at her, puzzled.

Her smile dimmed. She waved a small white hand at the wall. The scroll was one she treasured, it had belonged to her father and she had removed it from its crimson box and hung it in the small alcove at the centre of the wall, the *tokonoma*, the place of honour reserved for a precious object.

'From — my family.'

Pinkerton stared at the scroll, bemused; a few scribbled lines, dark grey on white, plus one red mark.

'Oh. Right. Nice.'

In his view the scroll didn't exactly light up the place; he thought the room still looked bleak.

And there was the matter of what they put into their mouths. Sharpless had warned him about the food: 'You eat raw things at home: think of it as a kind of salad.'

36

He was unpersuaded: 'Raw *fish*? Forget it!'

Next day he appeared with offerings from a sympathetic ship's cook, which he handed to Cho-Cho. She unwrapped the packages and looked doubtfully at the mysterious, curiously similar brown slabs.

Pointing at each in turn he identified them: 'Meat loaf. Hash brown potatoes. Apple pie like Momma makes.'

She broke off a morsel of meat loaf and placed it in her mouth. She did her best, nodding and smiling, but he noticed that she found it hard to swallow the small scrap.

'Okay, try this — apple pie.'

'Apple-u-pie,' she echoed, nibbling.

'Right!'

She continued to chew, cautiously.

'Good?'

'Good.'

No, she wanted to say, not good, horrible, but that would have been impolite. Instead she set out to win him over to real food.

He found himself watching her prepare the stuff, helped by the maid: kneeling, feet tucked beneath her, pale hands deft and swift, the blade slicing delicate fillets of fish into discs of almost transparent thinness, carving vegetables into fantastic flower shapes, moving small bowls of this and that from one low table to another. Finally she would turn her head, glance across at him with an encouraging smile.

'Try now.'

The tuna and swordfish, the vinegar-rice, grilled eel and fiery pickle proved easier to accept than he would have believed, and he even learned to manipulate the short, polished chopsticks, appreciate a good, aged sake.

He drew the line at horse mackerel, but grudgingly admitted that even the dishes he was unable to stomach were good to look at — you could put them in a glass case in a museum. Still, every now and then his taste buds sent unambiguous messages and he would bring home a parcel from the galley storeroom:

'Meatballs! Apple pie like Momma makes!'

★ ★ ★

His off-duty hours were agreeable; the girl constantly found new ways to please him and there were even times when — fleetingly — he felt a sense of uncertainty, of indecision. He floated on a sea of strangeness here; nothing in his life had prepared him for this unsettling blend of distance and closeness: she was obedient, totally subservient, yet within that servitude she found ways to make him feel like a beginner. His life had been a thing of broad brush-strokes, thoughtless pleasures; easy-come, easy-go. Here, where each action, each reaction entailed its history, he was reluctantly drawn into an acknowledgement of something more.

It was at moments like these, when Cho-Cho became aware of his blue eyes resting on her thoughtfully, that she felt most fiercely the hope of happiness. On days when he went swimming off the rocks she watched him from the shore, seeing the gleam of sunlight on his wet body as he rose from the surf like the sea god *Ryūjin*, who controlled the tides from his coral castle beneath the waves. He waved to her, sending drops of water flying through the air, sparkling like jewels being cast back into the foam. When he came ashore he would pull her from her perch like a boy prising a mollusc from a rock, and squeeze her with wet arms, soaking her cotton kimono until she squealed in mock protest.

The ship was almost ready; before long he would be leaving. But perhaps it would not end there. She persuaded herself that like two differently coloured threads entwined, as their bodies were so often entwined, they might form a strand that was strong enough to hold them together.

On his last night Cho-Cho prepared a special supper. She dismissed the maid, Suzuki, and did the whole meal herself. One dish was served, somewhat to Pinkerton's dismay, on an oval leaf plucked from a nearby tree. Given the choice, he preferred his food on a plate. She noted his bafflement.

'Tradition.'

'I should've guessed.'

'This — *tegashiwa* leaf.'

She had prepared her words, she wanted to tell him, as her father had explained to her that in the old days when a samurai left his home to follow his lord it was customary for his wife to serve him a farewell dish on a *tegashiwa* leaf. Afterwards, *otō-san* told her, the leaf was hung above the door to bring the departed samurai home safe.

'In old days,' she began, but she failed to find the words she needed. She smiled and shook her head; presented him with the leaf-dish.

'Tradition.'

When the meal was over, she washed and dried the leaf, and hung it above the door. She recalled *otō-san* saying that when the leaf, with its shape so like a human hand, was stirred by the wind it would wave up and down, the way a Japanese beckoned to a friend, a wife to her husband.

Pinkerton watched the procedure indulgently.

'Tradition?'

'Tradition.'

Early next morning, tucked together as close as two birds, they rested for the last time in the nest of the futon.

'You will come back, Pinkerton?'

He nodded sleepily.

'When?'

He tried to think of something vague enough not to tie him down but encouraging in a way she could accept. Outside the window he saw birds filling the sky, flying high, wing tips almost touching; tiny silhouettes speeding away from land.

'One day, after the birds come home.'

He was pleased with the reply; he felt it was a bit Japanese.

She followed his upward glance and watched the swallows darken the sky, wave after wave. Birds left. Birds came home. She nodded. She understood.

She curled up, into his shoulder, stroking the

golden hairs on his arms, delicately licking with the tip of her tongue first one nipple, then the other, as he had taught her. He groaned with pleasure, and a touch of sadness, momentarily sharing a sense of loss.

He would forget that fleeting twinge. It did not cross his mind that the pain would stay with her.

When the ship steamed out of the harbour Pinkerton was busy and failed to notice the moment when they slipped between the lighthouses and out to the open sea. As the wind sharpened and the waves creamed against the hull, he glanced back at the receding coastline and became aware of a sense of freedom, as though a fragile, yet unexpectedly powerful chain that had wound its way round him like a clinging ivy, had suddenly snapped.

★ ★ ★

Cho-Cho stood outside the house, watching the departing ship through the telescope he had brought her. Surely that was him, on deck, arm raised, waving? Behind her she heard a small sound and glanced round: in the morning breeze the hand-shaped *tegashiwa* leaf fluttered, up and down, waving farewell and beckoning, come back.

When the last trace of the ship was lost beyond the horizon she felt a chill as though the sun was covered by a sheet of ice and hurried into the house.

★ ★ ★

She planted the seeds and watered the ground. Small green shoots appeared and, to her delight, leaves and then buds that opened into flowers, bright and glowing. Where earlier she had watched for the cherry blossom, the plum, the chrysanthemums, now she hovered over these small saucers in colours she would once have considered too bright, too obvious. She was getting the garden ready for Pinkerton's return. For, of course, he would return.

And it was not only in the garden that new life was growing.

★   ★   ★

Calling on Cho-Cho one evening, Sharpless saw that she was busy at the far end of the garden, stooping to tie up a showy orange flower whose stalk was too fragile to stand without support. Suzuki showed him into the house and stood nearby, eyes lowered. In the weeks following Pinkerton's departure, he had seen how tenderly she cared for Cho-Cho, anticipating her needs, small, bright eyes following her mistress's every movement. But today her broad face was closed, she seemed distant.

'Suzuki? Is something wrong?'

'In one way, you could say so. In another, things could not be better.'

He knew enough of the form to wait.

'She is expecting a child.'

This was an appalling indiscretion, as they were both aware. But Suzuki, less naïve than her mistress, was also aware of the realities involved.

42

'If Lieutenant Pinkerton could be informed — '

But Cho-Cho was approaching, and the conversation ceased.

He should not have been surprised. Indeed, he was saddened rather than surprised. The girl's future had narrowed.

★ ★ ★

When the evidence was visible to all, Cho-Cho invited Sharpless to tea. She had not previously honoured him with the ceremony. Now he sat, legs folded under him, while she knelt, setting out the little cups, the scoop and powdered green tea and bowl; boiled the water, whisked and waited, concentrating on every movement.

Self-consciously he smoothed back his lank hair, almost Japanese in its darkness — not a grey hair to be seen though he was nudging forty-five. His scrawny, weightless body settled comfortably into a posture foreigners usually found painful. He folded his hands and watched her precise movements, the way she honoured each act in turn.

She had performed the tea ceremony for Pinkerton once, settling, as now, for the shorter version that lasted barely an hour, but it had not been one of their successes. He commented to Sharpless later, 'Pretty long wait for a mouthful of dishwater.'

Sharpless had tried to explain that the ceremony required years of training and practice: '*Chanoyu* is an art, a ritual of mystical significance which must be performed in a studied, graceful manner.'

He could enjoy it, he was enjoying it now, watching Cho-Cho's small hands lifting, pouring, whisking the liquid to a froth. The bowl she used was precious, one of her few possessions, a relic of a once-prosperous family. Black Oribe ceramic, it could be three or four hundred years old. He admired its lack of symmetry, the rustic surface. Still, he guiltily found himself acknowledging that the whole point of this extended ceremony, its arcane complexity, detail and importance, was, as Pinkerton had implied, the making and serving of a cup of tea.

After the ritual had been completed, the tea tasted, and the utensils carefully washed and dried and cleared away, Cho-Cho gave Sharpless her news. He offered his congratulations and told her he would write at once to inform Lieutenant Pinkerton that he was to be a father.

'A big surprise!' she said, smiling. 'It will bring him pleasure.'

Sharpless certainly agreed with the first statement. He was less sure about the second.

★   ★   ★

When the reply arrived, a brief scrawl, the large, untidy handwriting covering the page, it was accompanied by dollar bills in large denominations. Pinkerton wrote that he was sending more than enough to cover the expenses of the confinement and extend the rental of the house. Cho-Cho, he added, was a working girl in good health, and as for the child, under the

44

circumstances, who could know if it was even his? No personal message enclosed.

Sharpless sat for a long time at his desk, feeling a greyness settle over him; a sense of failure, of defeat, though who or what had defeated him he could not have said. Next day he called on Cho-Cho, and told her he had heard from Pinkerton. The lieutenant was, of course, delighted by the news. He had sent money to cover all expenses.

'And does he say when he will be returning?'

'It was a brief communication, between duties. He must be extremely busy.'

It was cowardly. It was also wrong, to continue to give her false hope. But he told himself that a woman expecting a child could not be expected also to handle news that would destroy all hope. Surely there would be a better time, a gentler way to lead her into reality?

★ ★ ★

When the child was born, Sharpless paid Cho-Cho a visit, bearing gifts.

She held out a tiny bundle, red-faced, snuffling. Sharpless saw that the infant had a fuzzy cap of pale gold hair; he stared out, unfocused, with small blue eyes. The Pinkerton genes were evident.

'Here he is, Sharpless-san. My *Kanashimi*.'

He looked startled: 'You're naming him Sorrow?'

'It also means Trouble.'

'Poor boy!'

45

She relented. 'It's a little joke among mothers. You tell him, Suzuki.'

'He is named *Kanashimi* meaning its opposite — *Sachio*.'

'It's to fend off the evil eye. If you're superstitious, it's a good idea to conceal the arrival of happiness,' Cho-Cho said. 'I'm not superstitious, of course, but . . . ' she laughed. 'Just in case.'

In due course, when the boy was older and less vulnerable, Sharpless was informed, he could address the child by his true name.

He paid a flowery tribute of admiration to the new arrival, presented appropriate gifts and left.

★ ★ ★

Alone, Cho-Cho leaned over the swaddled bundle, studying the tiny features. She must learn to play a new role: that of mother. But she must first grow accustomed to the very existence of a puzzling creature, one that had grown inside her — how unlikely that had seemed at the beginning, and then how natural. But now, escaping from her body, this small entity that had been part of her must be acknowledged as separate. She must learn to respect that separateness, while still feeling the two of them were one. She breathed in the odour of his body, as sweet as milk and rice, rested her palm on the crown of his head, feeling the faint pulse; lifted a tiny hand with its shrimp-like fingers that already could grip, the pink bud of a mouth that knew its way to her breast. Happiness. *Sachio*. Joy.

46

Sharpless was aware that the cash from Pinkerton must be running low. He tried to give Cho-Cho money he claimed had come from the absent husband. She handed it back. Whether she believed him or not he was unsure, but the response was exquisitely reasoned:

'I will wait until he returns; it is not . . . correct this way.'

Sharpless guessed she might feel that accepting an impersonal payout reduced the relationship to the level of commerce. She was a wife. Was she not?

Meanwhile she used her ingenuity to maintain independence. A zoologist friend of her father's had once told her that there was as much nourishment in the larvae of silk moths as in a domestic fowl. Her father had retorted drily that it would take a considerable number of larvae to equal a chicken breast. But to nourish a growing child she was prepared to try anything. Next to the house was a white mulberry tree; the cocoons were collected and split open; the silkworms cooked with appropriate seasoning. She dug up the garden and planted vegetables; what had once been flower beds were now pushing up food crops. She kept chickens. She learned to fish, baiting the hook with limpets pulled from rocks. She collected and cooked snails. But there was one aspect of reality that was not negotiable: she could no longer afford to employ Suzuki. Any object of value had been sold; the money had run out and ingenuity could not be stretched to cover the hole that yawned before her.

The difficulty was fundamental: how to arrive at a solution that would enable them to separate without embarrassment; without loss of face on either side.

Cho-Cho waited until the infant's bath time; a conveniently distracting moment, with both women concentrating on the baby. She began by expressing concern for Suzuki's possible state of mind: her own regret that they lived so quietly, spent such uneventful days.

'You must be growing restless in this small house; there is so little opportunity for you to exercise your talents. Really, Suzuki, I must apologise.'

She reached for the towel the maid held out. 'Sharpless-san was telling me about a family newly arrived from Italy; they have one of the big houses the other side of the harbour . . . '

The father was in the silk business and would be spending some time inspecting factories in the province. The Italian wife was looking for someone to help with two small children.

'Sharpless-san could provide an excellent reference for you. This could be a fine opportunity . . . ' And so forth.

The maid's smooth, square face remained expressionless. She nodded. Suzuki needed no lessons in the nuances of social deviousness. She expressed her gratitude to Cho-Cho-san, and indeed to Sharpless-san for his kindness in mentioning the Italian family.

'I will make enquiries without delay.' She broke off to take the baby and prepare him for sleep. She knew what her employer was really

48

saying, and Cho-Cho knew that she knew. But the form had been observed.

A few days later Suzuki announced that she had found work. Not with the Italian family, but in a silk-reeling factory on the outskirts of town. She was grateful to Sharpless-san: his mention of the Italians had been of help to her. This was an excellent opportunity; she was grateful to Cho-Cho-san for drawing her attention . . . And so forth.

Then, a hesitation; a diffidence: it would be a great kindness if Cho-Cho-san were to permit Suzuki to occupy her usual sleeping space at the back of the house — for a while.

'Luckily the factory shifts are quite long so I will not be in your way.' And so forth.

Cho-Cho knew what her maid was really saying and Suzuki knew that she knew. Nothing was spoken, all was understood, and the transition was made: Suzuki would continue to spread her futon in a corner of the house, and asked permission to make 'a trivial contribution' to the household expenses. Cho-Cho insisted that she must stay until she found more comfortable lodgings. It was, of course, they agreed, a temporary arrangement.

Next day, Suzuki put on her thick cotton work clothes and went out into the pre-dawn mist and the unknown territory of her new life.

After the silk farmers had gathered the bulging cocoons from mulberry trees stripped bare to feed the ravenous larvae, they took them to the factory. Suzuki joined the line of girls waiting to take charge of the loaded baskets and carry them

49

indoors to the cauldrons of boiling water, where the process began.

When she stumbled home from the factory long after dark, too exhausted to eat, an odd reversal of roles took place: it was Cho-Cho who persuaded her to nibble a few grains of rice; who undressed and washed the dazed girl and helped her to the futon spread out for her while, half asleep, she tried to describe her day.

'Poor worms! They work so hard, spinning threads, wrapping themselves in their fat cocoons, and then they're tipped into cauldrons and boiled alive. I have to pick out any that have become moths — '

'But why?'

'They crack open the cocoon, to get out. The thread is broken, useless.' She yawned, too tired to cover her mouth. 'When the cocoons are soft, we scoop them out of the water and very carefully start to wind the threads on to iron reels. They're beautiful, as fine as cobwebs.'

'It sounds difficult.'

'Yes,' she murmured. 'Difficult. I have acquired a skill.'

But when Suzuki spoke of the awesome size of the silk workshop; the long lines of tables where the women worked; the impressive quantity of thread produced — 'the thread from one cocoon can measure from the door to the shore' — she said nothing of the boiling vats that spilled over, scalding her arms, the fingertip testing of water temperature, the dangers of unstable machinery.

When she came home one night with bleeding

50

hands, she shrugged away Cho-Cho's alarmed questions.

'Machinery can break down. Girls are injured.'

Cho-Cho, distraught, spread healing ointment on the damaged fingers.

'You must take greater care.'

Together the two women clung to a precarious existence, and in the small house on the hillside Suzuki could still inhabit another world, one where a baby learned to crawl and then to walk. Where the air was fragrant with steaming rice and *shoyu* and where clean clothes flapped on the line outside the door. Alongside her at the workbench were girls who slept in cramped, airless dormitories, who had to line up for baths, moving from factory to sleeping quarters like prisoners. She pitied them; she considered herself blessed.

Occasionally Sharpless visited, bringing a tactful gift, small enough to be acceptable, slipping an additional offering to Suzuki, who could discreetly add it to the household store.

Cho-Cho welcomed his visits; he was a link with her father, with life as it had once been, and with Pinkerton. He trod warily, conscious of his privileged status, careful never to overstep the mark. He was behaving, he hoped, in a properly Japanese way. At least on the surface. But then, to the Japanese, he reminded himself, the surface was the reality. He felt reassured.

One day, as he was complimenting Cho-Cho on the precocious intelligence of her child, she committed the social indiscretion of cutting in, her voice barely above a whisper; attempting

51

English, as she often did with him, for practice.

'Sharpless-san, where is my husband?'

Where was Pinkerton? He had no idea, but he attempted a vague explanation of the difficulties of maritime life. The lieutenant could be anywhere.

'Ah. So I will wait.'

Sharpless learned to be devious. Back in town, he quietly arranged to extend again the lease of the house, telling the landlord that the money had been sent from America.

★　★　★

The marriage broker had been biding his time, keeping an eye on the house above the harbour. One morning he came knocking, all smiles, to tell Cho-Cho he had a proposition, a customer. She slid the *shoji* door closed without a word.

'Be realistic!' he called. Pinkerton was gone, swallowed into the ocean as far as they were all concerned.

'Luckily there are plenty more fish where he came from, you can pick and choose.'

But for Cho-Cho there was only Benjamin Franklin Pinkerton; she already had a husband.

'Obstinacy is not a virtue in a woman!' the broker exclaimed, exasperated.

He was heading for the road when the door opened and Cho-Cho called to him. Beaming, he hurried back.

'I have some good offers for you.'

But it was she who had an offer, for him.

'Young women in Nagasaki who 'marry' *gaijin*

will be more valued if they can speak a few words of English.'

She could give them lessons for a small fee. She could also teach them about American culture, which would please their temporary husbands.

The marriage broker felt he could be frank: vocabulary and culture were not uppermost in the minds of visiting foreign customers. Passing on social skills to other young potential 'wives' would not necessarily increase their charms. On the other hand, the charms she had to offer . . .

Cho-Cho closed the door.

Even when he returned a few days later to tell her a respectable elderly gentleman, a local merchant in need of an heir, was prepared to offer her a genuine marriage, a permanent arrangement, Cho-Cho remained unmoved. On his next visit Sharpless gently suggested she might consider this latest offer: the security was surely preferable to a future alone?

She turned to the window and looked out over the harbour. She gazed fiercely at the empty sea, as though through the force of her will she could create a ship, forge metal from water and draw it towards her over the curve of the horizon. And she repeated the familiar words: she knew her husband would return.

'One day, when the swallows nest again, his ship will be there in the harbour. He said so.'

* * *

As an act of faith she had held back one narrow strip of earth in the garden simply for decoration — 'my American flower bed!' Surrounded by the closely planted edible greenery the orange and pink blooms sang out, a banner of gaudy vividness.

But as time passed, as humid months gave way to fog and snow, as she warmed her hands at the little charcoal stove under the table; and the dark filigree of the swallows twice more filled the sky without his ship steaming into harbour, she grew thinner, and the flowers, untended, withered. The bright petals shrivelled, dying back into the dark soil.

6

When Pinkerton called at the consulate, Sharpless was not in his office.

Leaving a message to say he would look in again later, Pinkerton set off across town with a junior lieutenant on his first trip away from home, Pinkerton acting as guide and mentor to Jensen, just as Eddie had for him, three years before. Moving speedily through the pungent market district, Pinkerton remarked on signs of modernisation since his first visit:

'They got themselves a fire-truck! In my day it was a guy with a pole and a red paper lantern running ahead of a hose reel.'

He saw that some of the streets had been paved, some shops enlarged. But the stall where he had bought a bracelet one day as he passed was still as he remembered it. He glanced over silver and enamel jewellery spread out on a white cloth: *cloisonné*. She had taught him the name for it.

He drew the young officer to a stall selling sweetmeats. 'Jensen, you should try this: Nagasaki castella, sort of a Portuguese cake.'

Pinkerton was not given to self-searching: in his experience you took what life handed out, knocks included, and moved on. But as they wandered through the turmoil of the little town he felt unsettled; he felt stirrings: he realised with a shock of surprise that he had been happy here.

He wondered, with a twinge of guilt, how things had worked out for Cho-Cho. Not that he had anything to reproach himself with: she was a tea-house girl, it had been a commercial arrangement, but she was a sweet kid and he hoped she had found other protectors as generous as he had been. The existence of a child lurked at the back of his mind, but as a dim ghost of a thought; he pictured for a moment a sort of infant Cho-Cho, a tiny Japanese girl in a cute kimono such as he had seen in the market. There was little reality to the picture, and certainly he felt no sense of connection. The image that retained a hold on him was of Cho-Cho herself, clad in silk, a porcelain doll, the gentleness accompanied by a surprising passion. (Though, there again, he wondered whether 'passion' was something they taught the girls, a tool of their trade; a classy way to turn a trick.)

'It's a great place for a visit,' he told the new boy, and threw in a few facts: the system of the temporary wife, the house, 'home comforts'.

It was this mood of easy nostalgia that led him to the road round the harbour and up the hill, to take a look at the wood and paper house — if it still existed — where he had enjoyed sweet nights of pleasure on the futon, and learned to eat raw fish.

He was explaining the curious concept of a Japanese yard — 'a bunch of rocks, gravel and moss, basically' — as they rounded the last bend and came in sight of the house. To his surprise, the area around the house appeared to be filled edge to edge with green plants; vegetables, by the look of it. At the far end chickens pecked and clucked. The door of the house was open, and standing in the entrance they saw a small figure, thin, very upright, in a plain blue kimono. She called out, her voice clear and firm.

'Pinker-ton! *O-kaeri nasai!* Wel-u-come home!'

Sub-Lieutenant Jensen was confused: surely the so-called marriage had been a temporary affair? He glanced at his senior officer who was staring, aghast, at the woman in the doorway.

'I saw the ship,' she called, 'with your telescope. I knew it was you.'

She spoke English, surprising both men. Pinkerton was not often at a loss; he reckoned he knew how to handle a difficult situation. The problem here was that he was uncertain what situation he was confronting. Maybe the girl had prospered, had stayed on in the house, and was merely pleased to see an old client back in town. That must be it.

Then, almost invisible behind Cho-Cho, clutching at her knee, he saw the child; blue eyes fixed on his, blond hair bright in the dimness of the room. He was wearing a sailor suit. A living doll. And from the blurred jumble of images that occupied the inside of Pinkerton's head, one sharp memory emerged: himself as a child, posing for a snapshot, holding his mother's hand, on a visit to the State Fair. Staring at the child now, it all flooded back: the grinding music of the carousel, the crowd, the smell of hot dogs and the taste of cotton candy. The great treat, he recalled, had been for your dad to win a stuffed animal or a doll at the shooting range. A doll as big as a real live child. He recalled the snapshot, mounted in a leather-bound album rubbed at the corners, put away in some drawer. He had been wearing a sailor suit.

Cho-Cho drew the boy close and stood waiting, her hands on his shoulders, as the men approached.

'Here is your son. He is called Joy.'

Then, as the child darted forward and flung his arms round Pinkerton's knees, Cho-Cho knelt, touching her forehead to the ground. She rose to her feet, smiling.

'You can talk to him. He will understand. He is an American boy.'

★　★　★

Jensen saved the occasion. He stepped forward and introduced himself. The words flowed: he had heard so much about Japan, Lieutenant Pinkerton had told him what a great place Nagasaki was . . . He talked on, the soft Southern vowels filling the silence.

Years later, in command of his own ship, under enemy fire, Jensen recalled that occasion as the moment he recognised he possessed qualities of leadership. At the time, he was aware only that Pinkerton seemed frozen, incapable of speech.

★　★　★

Within the house, out of sight, Suzuki was about to leave for the late factory shift. She hovered by

58

the window and noted that an ocean liner was anchored in the harbour. She picked up Cho-Cho's telescope and looked more closely at the ship: the funnel, gleaming brass and pale deck. Leaning on the rail was a young woman wearing a yellow dress that ended at her knees, revealing legs in flesh-coloured stockings. Her hair too was yellow; cut short, barely visible beneath a tight hat that covered her head like a cooking basin. As Suzuki watched, a man climbed from a small boat on to the deck and approached the young woman. They embraced. The man was Sharpless-san.

7

For a few minutes, in the state of turbulence following his first sight of the boy, Pinkerton was incapable of anything more than a shocked recognition of paternity. He listened with astonishment as the child recited greetings, first in Japanese, then English.

Suzuki, emerging from the house, eyes downcast, mortified to be seen in her work clothes, did her best to remain invisible as she skirted the group. But Pinkerton called out, 'Hey, Suzuki! You're still here!'

She paused and bowed, still without looking up, trying to keep her factory-scarred hands out of sight, tucked into her sleeves. But Pinkerton, desperately seeking diversions from the calamity of this encounter, drew her aside and muttered that he needed a present for the boy — for Joey, as his Western ear had heard the name.

'You understand what I'm saying?'

Suzuki, who understood quite well what he was saying, cast a frantic glance in Cho-Cho's direction.

'Suzuki has work she must attend to — '

'Sure, just as soon as she's got me a little something for Joey, okay?'

He pressed bills into Suzuki's hand and pushed her cheerfully towards the path.

'I should be going,' Jensen said. 'I can find my own way back to the ship.'

Pinkerton, aware this would leave him stranded alone with Cho-Cho, waved away the suggestion:

'Heck no, you'll just get yourself lost. Enjoy the view, sniff that clean air.'

But the young lieutenant proved obstinate and set off to catch up with Suzuki, who could point out to him the best way back to the harbour.

* * *

On board the liner Sharpless greeted his niece affectionately.

'My dear Nancy, welcome to Japan!'

Mary was his favourite sister, and the girl had her mother's looks, the same way of wrinkling her nose when she laughed, a mannerism he found endearing. He smiled, taking pleasure in the look of her, the shiny hair, the quick smile, the sense she brought him of an outside world where people were open and direct and said what they thought. He had grown to love this complicated, unfathomable, coiled society; there was a poetry to social intercourse here that turned humdrum exchange into an art form, but just occasionally he yearned for simplicity, the calling of a spade a spade. The American world.

* * *

As they rode through town he made plans for her brief visit.

'You'll stay at the Methodist mission house, with Mrs Sinclair.'

Disappointed, Nancy murmured, 'Not with you?'

He shook his head, smiling.

'My quarters are hardly suitable. I think I should warn you: Nagasaki has made some progress — look at the paved streets — but conditions are unlikely to match American expectations.'

He did not add that it had been his own decision to choose a traditional Japanese house rather than westernised accommodation.

He asked for news from home, but as they rattled along the road he kept breaking in to point out an unusual building, or a view worth noting. She saw with some surprise the affection, even pride, with which he regarded this malodorous, primitive place.

Only when she was seated across the desk from him did he enquire why she had so suddenly decided to join the ship which brought her to Nagasaki. She gave a small, gleeful jiggle of the shoulders.

'I thought you'd never ask! The trip's horribly expensive, but Daddy said he never gave me a proper twenty-first birthday present, so this is it.'

An excited laugh and a wrinkling of her nose. 'My fiancé is here and it seemed a cute thing to do, to give him a surprise!'

'You're engaged! I didn't know — '

'It happened quite quickly.' She laughed again. 'He swept me off my feet!'

'And he's here in Nagasaki?'

A tray with tea and refreshments edged its way

round the half-open door, followed by a young servant. He bowed and placed a small salver with a scribbled note on the desk. Sharpless read it and glanced up at the youth: 'Lieutenant Pinkerton was here?'

He heard Nancy cry out in surprise and at once he understood everything. He felt a deadening sense of inevitability: he was about to watch a disaster take place, unable to influence or avert it.

'You are engaged to Lieutenant Pinkerton.'

She blushed. Sharpless was astonished that in this modern day American girls could still blush, but then he remembered that, despite the flapper dress and cloche hat he was familiar with from the American newspapers, Nancy was not a modern girl. She was the granddaughter of missionaries, the daughter of churchgoing folk, herself trained to be a teacher. She would, of course, have a sense of duty, he thought, and was not comforted.

Sharpless wondered later whether, had he been at his desk when Pinkerton called, he could have altered the course of events. But what would he — could he — have done? Momentum, once established, has its own imperative; the situation had moved beyond his power to affect it. There was no runaway horse to be mastered here, no vehicle out of control; just three people moving towards a calamitous impact. Sharpless was a quiet man, not given to emotional extravagance, but he found himself groaning as he contemplated the picture before him.

* ★ ★

In the house above the harbour, Pinkerton felt
time stretching like elastic, past and present
shifting disconcertingly: now, as on that first
time, he felt the ridged tatami mat beneath his
feet; saw the way light fell on paper walls; inhaled
the smell of sweet rice. Across the room, a
woman with almond white skin waited.

Seated cross-legged, he engaged his son in a
game, a sleight of hand in which an errant
thumb mysteriously vanished, then reappeared.
The child gurgled with delight as Cho-Cho
watched. At one point Pinkerton looked up and
caught her eye, but turned back immediately to
the game, putting off a conversation that could
only be painful. In this situation natural
behaviour felt unnatural.

'Pinker-ton' — she had never called him Ben
— 'I will prepare some refreshment for you.' A
hint of a reassuring smile. 'No tea ceremony!'

He was surprised by her grasp of English; she
had obviously been studying. And he knew that
what her words were really saying was, 'we must
talk', but she would never say that: it would be
too quick, too open, not the Japanese way.

He shook his head. 'I'm fine.'

When Suzuki hurried back with a small
package wrapped in thin purple paper, Pinkerton
handed it to the boy with a flourish:

'Here you go, Joey. Surprise!'

The boy had never before received a present,
and he held the rustling paper sphere cupped in
his hands, turning it, stroking the dark wrapping.

Impatient, Pinkerton tore the flimsy paper to reveal a wooden spinning top patterned in scarlet and yellow.

'*Koma!*' the boy exclaimed, clapping his hands.

'Thank *otō-san* for your present.'

'*Arigatou gozaimasu*,' he said obediently. 'Thank you, *otō-san*.'

Suzuki watched them for a moment. Outwardly they were a family engaged in a family game, but she saw how Cho-Cho's hands were clenched in her lap; the sheen of sweat that gleamed on Pinkerton's face although the day was cool. She backed out, bowing, and ran down the hill to the factory.

The woven reed-straw of the tatami mat was proving useless as a spinning surface. Pinkerton reached for the low table and set the top spinning smoothly on the gleaming lacquer. As it spun, the red and yellow painted rings seemed to rise and hover magically in the air above the twirling disc. Again and again the child handed the top back to his father —

'More!'

Another spin.

'*Motto!*'

Another chance to snatch in vain at the hovering rings.

Pinkerton ruffled the boy's fair curls, smiling. Then he got to his feet.

'I'm due back on the ship.'

There was awkwardness: he knew she was waiting to be drawn into his arms, embraced. Instead, Pinkerton scooped up the child and kissed him heartily on both cheeks, then handed him to his mother, so that the boy was between them, making an embrace impossible. He threw a quick, discomfited glance at Cho-Cho and consulted his watch.

'I better get back. I'll see you tomorrow.' He pinched the boy's cheek. 'So long, kid!' And then, remembering: '*Sayonara!*'

Pinkerton struggled to get his shoes on, hands and feet failing to co-ordinate. He left hastily, not looking back, feeling her eyes on him as he strode down the hill. In his white uniform he sweated, moisture crawling down his back, soaking his armpits. He took off his cap and wiped his brow, his brain a buzzing hive of bees.

★   ★   ★

From the house she saw him remove the naval cap; saw the way the sun glittered on his hair, the golden hair of her golden husband, who had not touched her since he arrived.

8

Pinkerton had seen on a market stall a woodcut of a Japanese dragon caught in a trap, its body writhing in panic. He walked through the Nagasaki streets now in a state of agitation no less panic-stricken, his thoughts twisting this way and that.

One: he had a son. Two: the mother was Japanese. Three: he had a career to consider. Four: he had a fiancée. Another man might have put these priorities in a different order. Again and again he ran through the situation, a dragon trapped in a pit, a rat trapped in a maze: a son, a woman he'd almost forgotten, a fiancée . . .

He had found his way without thinking to the consul's office, perhaps intending to ask his advice, but as he reached the entrance, a woman appeared in the doorway — a vision in yellow, an impossible sight: a girl who should be safely far away in Oregon stood before him as though materialising from his wild thoughts. She laughed delightedly at his astonishment.

'Surprise!' she cried, opening her arms wide like a self-presenting conjuror.

He folded her in an extravagant welcoming hug and saw, over her shoulder, Sharpless watching them, bleak-faced. Once again Pinkerton felt sweat break out on his body.

And Sharpless, seeing his niece flinging herself into the arms of a man he despised, felt incredulity melt into something like horror. Was Nancy, like Cho-Cho, to become a woman betrayed? He felt a sinking of the heart, a taste of the pain that lay ahead.

★ ★ ★

The afternoon aged into the evening and a tray of tea brought in by a servant was removed untouched, to be replaced by another, steaming hot, which cooled untouched in its turn. Nancy, huddled in the consul's oversized wooden chair, tried to make sense of what she was hearing. Pinkerton had finally run out of words and the silence lengthened. She looked at the two men appraisingly, as though considering their relative merits. Her uncle seemed to have shrunk into himself; he looked old, the long face gaunt and drawn; Pinkerton sat very straight, naval cap tucked under his arm, as though facing an examining board — which in a way he was.

Nancy said slowly, her voice drained of expression, 'So. You have a child.'

He nodded.

'Did you not know this before?'

'Not exactly . . .'

She frowned in puzzlement. 'How could you not know *exactly*, Ben? Either you know you have a child or you don't.'

He had been uncertain, he said. He tried to explain the difficulties: the naval life, moving about from place to place, communication chancy . . . It sounded thin, even to his ears.

Nancy attempted to keep to the facts that

68

could be established. The certainties of this messy affair.

'So the child's mother died.'

'Well, no.'

'No?'

Sharpless saw a steeliness enter his niece's face, an expression he had seen in his sister. She leaned forward, hands gripping the arms of her chair.

'You have a *wife*?'

Haltingly, he tried to build a picture for her of how it had been. A man, lonely, far from home. The local custom. A wife here was not for always. It was . . . what was it? The words filled his mouth like fur balls in a cat's throat; he coughed, tried to swallow. 'It was a mistake. But it happened.'

A spasm of disgust. She glanced carefully about the room, as though assessing the framed prints on the walls.

Pinkerton's ruddy complexion had drained into greyness. He looked and sounded like a sick man as he fumbled his way through a thicket of words: he knew it was impossible for Nancy to condone what had happened. He did not expect her to forgive him; nothing could make up for what he had done. He was the worst of men. All he could attempt now was to do what was right for the child. But he wanted her to know that she mattered more to him than the world —

Nancy stood up briskly.

'I'm going back to the ship now.' She addressed Sharpless, her voice as mechanical as a railroad station announcement:

'Will you get a rickshaw for me, please?'

'Wait!' It was almost a shout. Pinkerton added, quietly, 'Please. Hear me out.'

Sharpless stood up. 'I'll leave you — '

But Nancy, in a quiet, dead voice, asked him to stay.

And Pinkerton talked on, sentence after stumbling sentence, his words filling the room like a thickening gas.

He said desperately, 'It's not the kid's fault. He's my son and I can't just abandon him. I want to give him a life, I reckon it would be the Christian thing to do. It would be asking too much of you, I know that. But — can we talk? *Please?*'

After a while Sharpless found it hard to breathe. He reached for a fragile cup of cold tea and drained it. He sensed Nancy's hesitation. Should he speak? She was on a knife-edge and he could tilt her one way or the other. But which way should it be?

He was no Solomon; he wanted no part of a situation that was bound to end in tears. Pinkerton, backed into a corner, was reluctantly seeking what would be the right thing to do. Cho-Cho, he knew, remained wrapped in a protective garment of hope and illusion that prevented her from seeing the reality before her eyes. One day, she had always maintained, one fine day when the swallows returned, so would her husband. He had returned, but not as her husband, and despite the sunlight the day had taken on the chill of betrayal.

But he was getting ahead of himself: there

70

were three people involved here and the third was being introduced to circumstances bizarre beyond anything she could have imagined.

He expected anything from hysterics to fury, but when, after a long silence, Nancy spoke, she seemed oddly calm, seemed at first to be changing the subject.

'They told us on the ship that there's a special church here, an old wooden church.'

'That would be Oura Cathedral,' Sharpless said.

'Is it far?'

'Not really.' He felt unreality descending: were they actually having a conversation about a Gothic wooden church? Perhaps his niece was unable to face the truth of what she had heard and was retreating into a sanctuary of ignorance.

Nancy said, 'I would like to go there. Now. With Ben.'

'You are aware it is a Catholic cathedral,' Sharpless said cautiously.

'I think I can speak to God from a Catholic cathedral as directly as from a Methodist church, Uncle Henry.'

She rose and stood waiting. Sharpless marvelled at her composure, that a girl so young and innocent seemed of the three people in the room to be the one in charge.

He led the way to the street and put them into a rickshaw.

*   *   *

On the journey she remained silent, unreachable beyond an invisible wall, eyes fixed on some

71

point in the middle distance. Pinkerton, clammy in the heat, a babel of unspoken words filling his head, just once attempted to break through.

'Nance,' he began, 'if you could just let me try and explain — '

She held up a hand, cutting him off.

At the cathedral she walked ahead of him, went to a pew and knelt, head on folded hands. He seated himself at the back, close to the open door, and prayed, not for forgiveness or a solution, but for a breeze to cool his feverish skin. Time passed. The angle of the sun on the stained-glass windows shifted, throwing moving patches of colour on to the floor. Outside, from nearby trees, the relentless creaking of cicadas filled the air, a sound like rusty scissors, stabbing into his head. Shifting his weight, his uniform trousers damp beneath his buttocks, he waited until at last she rose, gave a brisk nod to the altar, and walked back down the aisle, passing him without a glance.

Nancy no longer looked troubled; indeed she seemed radiant. She had reached a decision, though she did not yet share it with her fianceé; she was human enough to enjoy letting him suffer for a while. She simply asked him to see her back on board the liner. She would talk to him, she said, at noon the next day, in her uncle's office.

★ ★ ★

In her cabin, brushing her hair, creaming her face, cleaning her teeth, she sifted through

Pinkerton's words, coming ever closer to the heart of it. She now understood how it had all happened. The way she saw it, a lonely and gullible man, stranded in a foreign port, had been battened on by a clever woman of ill repute who had managed to arouse his pity. From kindness had come something less honourable — Nancy did not flinch from the realities — and an innocent man had been trapped in a dangerous web of deceit. She liked the phrase and repeated it to herself: a dangerous web of deceit. She had heard similar stories from missionaries returning home from abroad. An American husband was the grail sought by women of this type. And what better way to trap a man than by presenting him with a child?

9

When Nancy arrived at the consulate early next morning she was dressed in a plain dark frock and a black hat with a veil. Her face was bare of powder or paint. Sharpless thought she looked as though she was on her way to a funeral. She strode into the office and requested that he take her to the house of 'that person'.

'Lieutenant Pinkerton's not here yet.'

'Ben will be along later. I mean to speak to her alone. With your help, uncle.'

Sharpless was startled: he demurred, he protested, he suggested that such a meeting would be not only irregular but embarrassing, indeed painful. Ten minutes later the two were on their way. Nancy, Sharpless realised, was as stubborn as her mother and had the force of youth on her side.

In the rickshaw she sat, eyes lowered, breathing deeply like someone preparing for a challenge. The rickshaw came to a halt some way short of the house, the slope too steep for them to be pulled further up the hill.

As they walked up the final stretch of road Sharpless saw Cho-Cho move away from the window. The *shoji* door slid open and she stood waiting, expressionless. Sharpless saw that she was studying with cat-like intentness the fair-haired stranger walking towards her. He called out,

'*Ohayō gozaimasu*, Cho-Cho-san!'

Her bow was tiny, just perceptible. She motioned them into the house and Sharpless made an awkward, brief introduction.

Inside, he automatically removed his shoes. Nancy, staring at Cho-Cho, failed to notice, and Sharpless for once decided to say nothing.

They stood by the door, the three of them, ill at ease, like models awaiting the arrival of an artist, a sculptor, to move them into a composition of harmony, of logic. Then the child ran into the room and buried his face in his mother's dark cotton kimono.

Nancy stared down at the small creature, at the back of his head, the golden Pinkerton curls, the thin neck, pale legs. He was dressed in light, washed-out cotton. She swayed slightly. Sharpless thought she might be about to faint, but she drew herself up very straight and said in an unexpectedly firm tone, 'Will you tell her I have come to discuss — '

'You may speak to me in English,' Cho-Cho cut in with her lapidary delivery. 'I will understand.'

Nancy had not anticipated a direct confrontation; the mediation of a well-disposed interpreter, one she could trust, had been part of the scene she had envisaged. Suddenly she was on her own. Sharpless had withdrawn into himself, his gaze turned inward, though he appeared to be looking out at the dull blue of the sea beyond the window.

She plunged: 'I want to speak plainly. I am not here as an enemy. I understand that at some time

75

in the past you entered into certain . . . arrangements with Lieutenant Pinkerton — '

'He became my husband.'

'Well. Perhaps there were misunderstandings. I am his fiancée. Perhaps you are unfamiliar with the word.'

'I know the word. It — means' — a calmly disdainful inflection — 'at some time you hope to become his wife.'

'We will be married in the eyes of God. And the State. There will be a wedding ceremony.'

What ceremony else? Sharpless recalled with a pang Cho-Cho's wedding: that graceless moment, Pinkerton impatiently draining his bourbon, '*Bottoms up! Tell her it's the American way.*'

He listened as Nancy talked on, her light voice carrying words through the air, words innocuous in themselves but deadly in their implications; she was laying out the route for a journey, and who was to embark on it: a father, a child and a destination. America.

Cho-Cho bent down and whispered to the boy. He looked at the visitors and wandered away, out through the door. A moment later they heard the alarmed squawk of a chicken and the sound of childish giggles.

His mother gazed incredulously at the pale woman.

'You want me to give you my son?'

'It is for his sake.'

Sharpless listened to his niece's voice: the words rehearsed, dead; lines from some social science textbook.

76

'In America he will have a better life. An education. Opportunities. What can you offer him here?'

For a moment he saw the room through Nancy's eyes: a bare, stark box, a place constructed of wood and paper. Straw matting on the floor, no furniture, no trace of comfort. Money clearly in short supply.

'With us, he will have a room of his own in a nice house, attend a fine school, go to college, make a career, be happy. I will be a mother to him — '

Cho-Cho's apparent calm cracked. She said harshly, 'You will not . . . be a mother to him. *I* am a mother to him.'

Nancy nodded, conceding the point.

'But he would be with his father. Can you deprive him of that? Can you condemn a father never to see his child?'

Sharpless thought Cho-Cho might well point out that in fact Pinkerton had never seen his son till yesterday, that he could hardly be wrenched apart from a child he had just encountered for the first time. She might reasonably add that he should make his future with his Japanese wife, his son's real mother; the three of them were already a family.

Cho-Cho remained silent. Then she made a small sideways movement of her head, as though checking for a half-heard sound. She said, barely above a whisper,

'Please. Go now.'

Nancy's hands were tightly clenched, as though in prayer.

She whispered, 'I beg you.'

Cho-Cho had turned away, smoothing a lock of hair behind an ear. Nancy watched and waited.

There was bargaining to be done here. Dare she offer money? Maybe later. There must be a way; some weakness to be found, used. Her thoughts whirled.

She moved to the door. 'We will come again tomorrow. Ben wants to see his son.'

★ ★ ★

Looking back later, trying to detach the possible from the achieved, separate what he witnessed from what he heard, Sharpless became confused; he saw that Nancy had changed; was no longer the fun-loving girl he remembered. And the following day, when she strode into his office, it became clear that from being a guiding figure he had been relegated to the role of onlooker.

She looked gaunt, sharp-featured. In her arms, his cheeks smeared with tears, was the child.

'We've come to say goodbye.' She sounded rushed.

He was startled. 'We?'

'I'm taking Joey with me.'

Sharpless said incredulously, 'Cho-Cho agreed?'

She gave a quick nod, and turned to the door: 'We haven't got much time; the ship's due to sail.'

It was as she turned that he noticed a dark red stain on the side of her dress, where Joey's sleeve had rested, a sleeve whose edge was dark with wet blood.

PART TWO

10

Nancy was the product of a good Methodist home: educated to obey her parents, fear God and do the right thing. The right thing on this occasion had surely been to rescue Ben's child from an immoral woman and an alien environment, restore him to his father and give him a good home.

She now acknowledged that to achieve those ends she had found herself capable of duplicity; she had been drawn into dark places of the soul. In the cause of the greater good she saw that she had been sucked into wickedness. It did not come easily to her, she had no experience of deception and — vulnerable — she succumbed to the long sickness that follows a fall from grace. Where she had secretly hoped for a sense of purpose, the moral glow of a sacrificial act — to care for another woman's child — she found that words could be more dangerous than blows, that nightmares can be experienced in waking hours, that one damn thing leads to another, though her mother would have told her to wash out her mouth for using such a word. She learned that guilt does not lessen with time.

Caring for the child was easy; giving him all the affection she could muster was more difficult. She told herself he was part of Ben, and she loved Ben, so she must also love his son, though there were moments when Joey turned his head to one side, when he flicked his eyes or turned down his mouth in a certain way that had nothing to do with Ben, when Nancy found herself fighting off disloyal thoughts.

But that was the least of it. The worm at the heart of her happiness, the barrier to her finding peace was the fact from which all the rest sprang: Nancy had lied. She watched herself as she talked and talked, spinning a lie that had seemed necessary at the time, a small transgression for the greater good. And then, faced with a situation beyond her imagining, she had lied to Ben.

Inside her head, over and over, she saw the paper house, the figure in a white robe, the child screaming. In true Methodist tradition she had felt herself to be embracing a good deed; words were her means to achieve the necessary end. But words led to action, and nothing was the way she had planned.

As a child she modelled herself on the good girls in *Little Women* but here she was, all grown, and she found she was living a story that was closer to Nathaniel Hawthorne. She was suffused with guilt.

★   ★   ★

Her parents met her at the dockside. Waving, smiling, they looked with interest at the child in her arms, a child who presumably belonged to someone on the boat. And then Nancy, reaching for words she had rehearsed, rewritten, reshaped, could find nothing more satisfactory than, 'Ma, Pa, this is Joey, Ben's boy.' She set him down on the dockside and took his hand.

A handful of everyday words which in one breath smashed the pretty picture — fairytale romance, white wedding, honeymoon — with the finality of a boot on a beetle. Her mother stared at the blue-eyed, blond child, silenced, bewildered. Her father was quicker off the mark.

'You taking him on?'

She nodded.

Louis looked down at the boy. 'So. You're Joey, right? Well, kid, I'm called Louis, but to you, I'm Gramps.'

He picked up the boy and turned to his wife: 'Mary, let's get these people home.'

What's done is done.

When Nancy was out of earshot he shook his head and told his wife that Ben had clearly got himself into a pretty mess.

'I hadn't figured that young man for a fool, but — '

'We can't be sure what happened.'

Louis tilted his head. 'Mark Twain said some circumstantial evidence is pretty strong, like for instance when you find a trout in the milk.' He looked out at Nancy introducing Joey to the unknown territory of an American yard.

'I guess we have the trout here.'

Mary called to the boy, 'Joey! D'you like lemonade?'

He looked up at her consideringly with blue

83

eyes that were, and were not, the same as Ben's.

'I don't know. What is it?'

'You'll find out, I'm about to make some. You can help me squeeze the lemons.'

'What is s-ukweeze?'

Louis murmured, 'Oh boy, this is gonna take a miracle.'

'No,' Mary said, 'just time.' She beckoned the boy. 'Okay, let's you and me squeeze.'

★　★　★

To Nancy's relief, her parents asked few questions. With old friends it was more difficult; there was the need to explain the presence of a child who looked too much like Ben for there to be any way around the fact of fatherhood. A story was devised — a tale of a faraway, long-ago romance, a marriage cut tragically short by death. 'Poor child!' people would murmur, looking at the boy with curiosity, such a serious child, and so silent. They would look again at Nancy, with pity: poor girl, taking on a widower, with a kid.

After a while she became incapable of reciting the 'facts' and left it to her parents to dress it up in whatever clothes fitted the occasion. The story varied, creating occasional social awkwardness. Meanwhile she waited for Ben to return from his tour of duty.

It would be their first meeting since that last day, racing down the hill in the rickshaw, they had shouted at one another over the head of the child, Ben puzzled, then alarmed.

84

'What in hell — '

'I'll explain. Later.'

Nancy urged the rickshaw on. But it was already too late to explain, just as it was too late to go back.

11

The ship nosed into the Oregon coastline, Ben came ashore and a brief ceremony replaced more ambitious wedding plans.

It was a subdued affair. The preacher took Nancy to one side and said in the low, convinced voice people use to comfort the afflicted, that the boy would be a blessing to her, an opportunity.

'The Lord tests us, Nancy, and like tempered steel we come through stronger for the testing.'

Amen, she said silently, adding a quick, secret prayer of her own that had become a companion.

From across the room a Pinkerton uncle was heading her way with a child; tall for his age, blond, blue-eyed: a boy with the Pinkerton looks.

'Nancy. This here's our youngest, Jack. I brought him along to keep Joey company.'

The two children stared at each other, Joey with his considering, sideways look, Jack without interest. Aged seven, he was already a world away from the toddler. He tugged his hand free of the paternal grip and pushed through the knot of adults until he found himself next to Ben, his grown-up cousin. He gazed at the naval uniform.

'How big is your ship?'

'Pretty big.'

'Do you drive it yourself?'

'Not exactly, Jack. But I help.'

'And do you always wear your uniform?'

'Oh, sure. That's how people know who we are.'

'When I grow up, I want to join the navy and go to sea.'

'Well why not? The wide blue ocean. Nothing but sky around you. Beats an office any day. Welcome aboard, Jack!'

He shook the boy's hand, smiling, unaware he was participating in a commitment ritual.

Ben's parents did not attend the wedding. Where Louis and Mary had seen the boy as an unexpected grandchild, the Pinkertons saw only an alien offspring. On the one occasion they met him, they watched Joey for signs of otherness. Okay, he had the Pinkerton colouring, but wasn't there something about the boy's eyes? Something different. Something . . . foreign? They noted his politeness, his graceful movements: he could sit cross-legged on the floor without difficulty. All these were signs of his Japanese blood, they told each other. Without drama, they withdrew. And in any case, Ben and Nancy were relocating, further away.

A new home in a new town meant making new friends. Neighbours were welcoming but Nancy felt alone. Here, it was taken for granted that Joey was her son. When tricky questions came up she grew skilled at covering the moment of hesitation, the beat while she reached for the 'right' answer. Nothing was simple any more.

This was brought home to her one morning over breakfast. As she poured the coffee she asked Ben if he had heard yet when he was due back on board for the next tour of duty.

Carefully he ladled maple syrup over a waffle. He said, 'Well now: you'll be seeing more of me in the future, Nance.'

He concentrated on chewing and swallowing. He picked up his coffee cup, studied it for a moment, and put it down.

'Here's the thing.'

It was difficult not to have it sound like a rehearsed speech: how he had realised it would be tricky for her to be alone, now. How it seemed like the right time for a change, what with the kid . . .

The kid. The problem. The burden. When he saw Nancy washing Joey's clothes, tidying away toys, cooking special stuff, he was swept with guilt. Here she was, stuck with the kid. His kid. At some future point they'd produce their own, of course, but at the right time, not now. The kid had changed everything. He said none of this to Nancy.

He said, 'I'm looking at a garage, showroom attached.'

'Can we afford that?'

'I'll get some help from the bank. You know what they say: the automobile is the future of America.' He laughed selfconsciously.

'Ben, that's wonderful.'

She tried to make her voice sound as it should, but it came out breathless, not quite the genuine article. Because she recalled how Ben used to talk about the navy, the freedom, the unbroken horizon, the moment when a hint of land blurred the rim, the way the sky blended into the sea at

88

night, the darkness seeming to turn the water to ink. It had stirred her, it was part of why she fell in love with him. Now it seemed he was brushing all that to one side.

'You're sure about this?'

'Oh, I'm sure!' Hearty.

Well. What was it the preacher had said a couple of weeks ago? A problem is just another name for an opportunity.

Ben said, 'It's an opportunity!'

She was aware that the horizon had shrunk for both of them. It was goodbye to a teaching career: she had a child to care for now. One who was special. He could kick a ball around; at first sight no different from the other youngsters. But difference there was: older than his years, he looked at things mindfully, with a curious intensity, as if searching for something. One day, walking in the park, he stopped beside a flowering shrub. He smiled with delight and touched a pale bloom with his fingertips.

'*Ajisai* flowers!' he exclaimed.

'No, Joey,' Nancy corrected him. 'Those are hydrangeas.'

Then she realised they probably were whatever it was he had called them, but in another place, another language, another life.

'Let's go!' she said brightly. 'We don't want to be late now.'

But when she glanced back he was still beside the hydrangea bush, his small hand cupping a bloom. He looked up at her questioningly.

'When can I see my mother?'

She stared at the child, head suddenly emptied

89

of words, excuses, possibilities.

'Well now, Joey. We'll talk about that.'

She took his hand.

★   ★   ★

She was a mother, a wife, a homemaker, and she worked at it, keeping the house shiny bright, her hair sleek and bouncy, and welcoming Ben home from work each day with a kiss.

She was working at it right now, reaching for the cookie jar, setting out plates in the afternoon hush as the gingham curtains blew in a breeze that carried the sound of a creaking swing-seat from a neighbour's garden: *crik-crik . . . criik-crik*. Saucers clattered on her new Formica worktop; the kitchen smelled of freshly baked cornmeal cake, and tears ran down her cheeks, dripping on to the golden crust as she took the cake from the oven. Oh, to turn back the clock. But to what hour and what day? And which decision?

She cleared her throat and called up the stairs to Joey to come down for his tea.

★   ★   ★

He heard her calling and stayed where he was, kneeling on the shag rug, rearranging the animals two by two outside his wooden Ark. Some of the animals had been new to him when he first got the Ark as a present for his sixth birthday — long-necked giraffes, stripy tigers, and there were others that Noah didn't want on board that Joey decided should be included, so he had created a pair of tiny origami cranes, two jumping frogs and a couple of dragonflies and set them down alongside the horses and the monkeys.

Shifting to reach for another animal he noticed that the strands of the rug had pressed into his knee, forming a pattern of deep lines. He ran his finger over the temporary scar, feeling ridges in his skin, almost like the tightly woven rushes of a tatami mat. He remembered walking along a seashore once long ago; he had stumbled on half-hidden rocks, their surface sharp as knives, but clinging to the rocks were tiny shells, satin-smooth, and seaweed like dark green lace. All those surfaces, those discoveries, were part of another way of life, like sleeping on a futon, not the soft American bed that sagged beneath him, softness he had now grown used to. Thick rugs instead of the tatami mat beneath his feet. What had seemed strange no longer surprised him.

But sometimes his head rang with words that turned into an endless song, words that added up to minutes, hours, days of a life that was growing fainter as he grew more at home in this huge, flat land planted with crops that people were always comparing to the colour of his hair. Sometimes, to keep the old life alive in his head, he drew pictures of rocks and waterfalls, of mist curling round pine trees like a white scarf; he drew snow cranes with scarlet crowns, and funny-looking chickens, different shapes and sizes.

Nancy kept chickens but they all looked the

same, round, plump, as though they had been built in a factory. Not like the chickens he recalled, some with long feathers cascading over their shoulders like the paper streamers in street parades here, others black as tar and scrawny, stretched tall, menacing. And so many colours, the feathers glowing bronze, ivory, gold.

There had been fishing trips by the shore, watching for the fish that hid themselves without concealment, taking on the colour of the water they swam in. He missed the smell of fish, and he missed the rain, sometimes no more than a fine spray that washed the leaves, then turning angry, hammering the hillside with such force it cut off the view like a curtain of steel rods.

Words and phrases filled his head, the past and the present jostling, the old familiar and the newly learned — baseball, *ikebana*, popcorn, *kamishibai*, movies, *onsen*, bubble gum, *sento*, Coca-Cola, *miso*, taffy, radio, steak, hot dogs, steak, hamburgers, steak . . . Meat. So much meat. In that fading, shadowy place inside his head he used to eat bean curd, rice, wild nettles, grass-shoots and dark *arame* harvested from the sea. Chopsticks transferred morsels from bowl to mouth. Here, meat covered the plate. People held a fork in their right hand and stabbed it into their food as though digging up plants from earth.

But beneath all the rest — the animals, the birds, the sound of the temple gong, the *kamishibai* man with his bicycle, handing out candies and telling stories of dragons and princes and demons who spirited children away from their homes — he endlessly circled the thing unmentioned, always unmentioned. He bunched the memories up close, tight, squeezing them together, and at the centre there was a blank, a hole, a gap, a nothingness where comfort and love and softness had been. He could draw this emptiness, this shape: a kimono, smooth hair, curved neck, but he kept the drawings in a box in the closet. Sometimes he took them out and held one up close to his face, trying to breathe in something, some hint of life, and then another sound took over — the sound of screaming — and he dropped the drawing and pressed his hands to his ears to shut out the noise, but of course it was there inside his head.

★　★　★

He tries, now, to remember how, long ago, in that shadow-time, he had been taken on to a big boat and told he was going on a visit to a place called America, to see his father. He thinks he remembers crying, but more and more he forgets — had he cried?

He recalls being pulled this way and that, to look at new things —

'Isn't this great? Isn't this fun?'

★　★　★

He would have fun in America, Nancy kept telling him, life was great in America. There was everything you could want. But when he got to America — *look, Joey, ice cream, look, cookies and roller skates* — what was missing was his mother. His dad arrived, and soon they were living in a house with an upstairs and a couch and a yard. But when he asked when he was going home they told him this was home now, his mother was dead. His dad didn't wear a white uniform any more, and they saw Charlie Chaplin at the movies, but nobody wanted to talk about a place called Nagasaki and the woman who took him walking by the shore.

★   ★   ★

It was the first time a friend from school had stayed overnight. Nancy brought in a folding cot and made up a bed for Frank, and they pestered Ben until he showed them how to calculate depth and distance on a sea chart, for Joey's school geography project. Frank was impressed with Joey's father and with Joey's train set, and the medal that had belonged to Ben's big brother Charlie who didn't come home from the war. They were allowed to stay up and listen to a broadcast on the new radio.

Later, in the bedroom, when Frank was looking at Joey's toys he picked up the red and yellow wooden spinning top — the paint now chipped and worn — and asked why Joey kept such a shabby old thing.

'It's from Japan,' Joey said.

'What's that?'

'A place. The other side of the ocean.'

'So, what, your dad brought it home for you?'

'No. I was there with him.'

'You went to *Japan*?'

'I was there already. That's where my mom was.' He could tell Frank was losing his way and added helpfully, 'Nancy isn't my real mom, she brought me back here from Nagasaki — from Japan.'

Nobody in Frank's family had been outside the state, let alone the country; the idea of some place the other side of the ocean and an extra mother was beyond his understanding.

'Okay,' he said. 'So the spinning top came from this . . . '

'Japan.'

'From there. Right.' A pause. 'So where's your real mom now?'

'She died,' Joey said. That's what they told him. He began suddenly to feel anxious. 'I think I'm going to sleep now.'

Next day in the playground Frank and some of the class clustered in a corner, whispering. Joey, kicking a ball around, saw that the others were looking his way. Then Frank called him over.

'You know you told me that stuff about your mom being dead and all . . . '

He could have just said he didn't want to talk about it. But one of the girls told him it was sad, and he began to feel maybe he did want to talk about it. And then one of them said if his real mother came from a foreign place —

'Japan,' Joey said.

— then what was she called?

He should never have told them her name.

'Butterfly? *Butterfly?* What kind of a name is

95

that? Nobody's mom is called *Butterfly*.'

In a moment everything changed: they stared at him, boredom pricked into alertness; indifference sharpened into curiosity.

Often he had dreamed of arousing their interest, finding himself at the centre of the group. Now it had happened and he wished himself elsewhere. He could have simply said his mother was dead, played the orphan. Too late now.

Perhaps if he had looked foreign, if he had exhibited signs of otherness, they would have been prepared, but here he was with the blue eyes, the yellow hair. American. It threw them.

They clustered round him, wanting to know more about this mother, about this woman with a name like no other, but what was there to tell? She was a girl. And then she married his dad.

And then?

The school bell rang, saving him.

She married my dad. And then?

He could have said her name was Cho-Cho, but something told him these kids would find that wasn't even a word, let alone a name. He knew one or two of the others had families who came from faraway places: Germany, Sweden — there was a boy from France called John who had started out spelling his name Jean when he arrived, but at least Jean didn't sound freakish when the teacher read it off the register; there were Americans called Gene. So Joey translated Cho-Cho into Butterfly. But nobody's mom was called Butterfly.

96

* * *

He pressed his hands over his ears now, but through the roaring in his head he could hear Nancy calling from below: 'Joey! Come down now. It's your favourite cornmeal cake.'

He was seven and had disliked cornmeal cake for years.

12

Nancy's father asked Ben, from time to time, how he was doing and he always replied, 'I'm doing okay, Louis.'

He felt he had arrived at a precise and accurate assessment: he was keeping up the payments on the house; the business was building, slowly. Automobiles were the future, so his own future, and Nancy's and the boy's, would be secure. They were doing okay; they should be happy. He wished she smiled more; she used to smile easily and laugh, wrinkling her nose in a way he found sweetly arousing. But life rubs away at a person and after a while it seems harder to laugh. Harder to talk.

'Maybe it's time we had a kid,' he said one day.

They were on the porch, half asleep, while below them Joey squatted with a drawing pad, sketching fat bees homing in on the huckleberry bushes.

'We could do with a little brother. Or sister. For Joey.'

'Why not,' Nancy said, after a pause.

He sensed tension. 'We'll work at it,' he said and brought out a little laugh.

His parents had never laughed much. They plodded along, expressionless. They had cared for their children dutifully, never neglected any aspect of their material needs; but Joe and

Martha Pinkerton went through their days at a steady pace, no spring in their step. As a boy Ben had felt disloyal to have these thoughts but there was no tender place in his heart that the two of them occupied.

One day a lifetime ago they took him to the State Fair. In a daze of pleasure he wandered through the crowd, the music, breathing in the smell of sugar and vanilla. He gazed up at the twirling carousel, but his father declared it to be an unseemly extravagance and walked him towards the cyclorama of the Civil War. Then they went home.

They took his hand when necessary, to guide him safely across city streets. Hugging did not take place. And when Charlie was killed in action, Ben got the feeling that between him and his parents a sheet of glass had grown: they could see one another, but not touch.

Later, when Joey appeared on the scene, they had effectively disowned Ben.

There were moments in his life when he longed for something different: for excess. For freezing cold, driving winds, blinding rain. Fierceness. The sea. Within the house, confined by the yard, he sometimes found difficulty in breathing, needed more air, felt an urge to hit out without having any particular object he wished to punish. Occasionally he snapped at Nancy. He wondered now: were he and Nancy turning into his parents?

As though sensing his thoughts she suddenly stood up and called out,

'Joey? How about some ice cream? I'll fix you

99

a fudge sundae, wouldn't that be fun?'

Sometimes in the early hours, after lying awake for too long, Ben went through the house from room to room, as though checking, like some watchman marking the boundaries of security: doors locked, windows secured. Everything safe. But then again, what did the Good Book say? Forget treasures on earth, store up for yourselves treasures in heaven, where moth and rust do not destroy, where thieves do not break in and steal. For where your treasure is, there your heart will be also.

★ ★ ★

Tonight, hot and sticky, he got out of bed, moving quietly, leaving Nancy sleeping. She lay, as always, on her right side with one knee bent, the fingers of her left arm lightly clenched on her cheek.

Earlier they had spent a while attempting to produce a kid sister or brother for Joey; nice work as Ben said, and he was grateful for the soft, accommodating body lying beneath him. But afterwards they had disengaged quietly, moved apart, seeking cool, uncrumpled sheets.

He went to the window and stared down at the dark street. He had a sense of other streets, those that ran parallel, those that crossed, stretching out, further and further until the tarmac and the houses stopped and the fields took over, roads heading out into a flat landscape; Oregon all around him, land on three sides that led across borders and mountains to more land, and one border that defined itself in cliffs and sandy dunes and a seashore, the curling lip of an ocean stretching out to the horizon, beyond which lay the rest of the world.

They used to have picnics, family gatherings on the beach; Nancy in her bright pink sundress, lying back, eyes closed, face raised to the warmth, while he padded across the sand to the surf frothing between his toes, tiny mouths sucking at his skin, waiting to engulf him.

He recalled the moment: the racing dive into the water, the cool tingle as it washed over him, the salt catching on the fine hairs of his skin. He would head out, a steady crawl, each arm in turn curving in a beckoning movement as though encouraging a swimmer lagging behind, because he was always out front, turning his head every so often to draw breath, then down, knifing through the waves like the prow of a boat . . .

In Nagasaki he had swum in cold green sea, a small figure in a blue and white kimono watching him, seated on the rocks, waving when he looked back, the sun glittering on her silver bracelet.

At the far end of the market, in tiny roadside stalls he passed as he came and went, he had been offered intricate tortoiseshell work and fancy jewellery. In one shop he had noticed a bracelet, the metal surface inlaid with linked silver and gold butterflies and brilliantly coloured enamel. He bought it; he had learned by then that Cho-Cho meant butterfly.

When he got to the house he pulled the bracelet from his pocket and threw it across to her. 'Here you go, Mrs Butterfly. Surprise. A little something for you.'

'Ah! *Cloisonné*,' she exclaimed, which meant nothing to Pinkerton, who thought it was a Japanese word to express thanks. She held out the bracelet and waited for him to fasten it round her small wrist. Then she led him to the futon.

He stared down at the street, at the pools of light, the shadows, the houses opposite, lined up side by side, identical. There were differences, of course. One had a swing-seat on the porch that creaked when it moved in the breeze like the sound of cicadas, another, a tree the neighbours considered too tall, liable to come down one day in a storm. The people next to them kept a dog, that barked; one household kept the dog, Ben commented testily, and everyone shared the barking. A little further down the street, new owners had painted the front door yellow. He couldn't figure out why a man would want a yellow front door. It was an unsettling colour — thunderstorm, headache colour. He could feel a headache coming on now, and headed for the kitchen.

The wooden banister was smooth to his touch. From below, the rugs gave off a smell of warm wool, not unpleasant, though there was something stale about it, something heavy. Light came through the windows, slanting on to the walls. The darkness was soft; he felt it brush his skin and he walked through it almost like moving through water. If he raised his head, he would breathe in air from above the surface, though there was no surface here, the darkness filled the room to the ceiling, and he was a drowned man resting on the bottom.

The image shocked him; he loved water, always had, he was a swimmer, wasn't he? No risk of drowning. He was as safe in water as he was here in his home.

And he was doing okay.

He lit a cigarette and watched the tip glow in the darkness; glow and then, resting between his fingers, dim into something grey as the heat died. When he inhaled, the brightness returned, casting a glow on his hand. That was the trick of it: keep up the heat; keep the brightness.

In the kitchen he filled a glass from the faucet and drank slowly, feeling the liquid slide down his throat. Then he made his way back through the house. Outside Joey's door he paused, turned the handle and stepped into the room. The boy was asleep, bedclothes thrown off, a battered wooden spinning top beside him on the pillow. Hunched into an untidy ball, legs drawn up under him, he looked almost as though crouching, a pale frog ready to leap up and go.

Back in his own room, Pinkerton lowered himself carefully on to the bed and stretched out on the now cool sheet.

Turned away, eyes closed, her cheek deep in the pillow, Nancy listened as his breathing gradually deepened and he drifted into sleep.

13

'My grandpa's family lived in Nantucket and he worked on a whaling ship when he was young, and this is a whale's tooth, a sperm whale's tooth and it's carved with a picture of trees and houses.'

The large, decorated whale-ivory tooth was passed around the class, the children less interested than the teacher, who looked pleased. 'Janet's grandfather was one of many sailors who made beautiful carvings like this. The work is called scrimshaw.' She wrote the word on the blackboard in large letters, the chalk squeaking. 'Scrimshaw. Try and remember the word. And what have we next?'

A red-haired girl had brought along a small bottle of oil. She said the oil was made from little fishes the Cree Indians called ooligan.

'It was a medicine and valuable. My dad says the name Oregon originally came from that word. So that's how our State got its name.'

'That's very interesting, Sandra. Of course there are many different stories about the naming of the State. Travellers told strange stories about us. On old maps Oregon is sometimes called Terra Incognita — unknown land . . . '

The Show and Tell continued. When it came to his turn, Joey had a photograph for the class to see: 'This is a snapshot of my dad when he was in the navy. He can navigate by the stars. Before he was in the navy he won prizes for swimming.'

The teacher's attention sharpened. 'He was a swimmer? Joey, would your father be *Benjamin* Pinkerton?' A nod from the boy. 'But he was a champion! A hero!' She addressed the class: 'Ben Pinkerton won the fifty-yard freestyle in the AAU championship his first year as a contender. He won races in *Europe*; we thought he'd be going for the Olympics!' She looked down at Joey. 'What happened?' She realised the question might sound accusatory. 'I mean what happened to change his mind about a career as a swimmer, Joey?'

The boy shrugged. 'He's never talked about it, I guess.'

'Well. Tell him he has a fan at your school. Next parents' evening I'll be proud to shake his hand. Okay, who do we have next?'

★ ★ ★

'She wants to shake your hand. She said you were a champion.'

'That's all in the past.'

Joey watched his father carve the pot-roast. His movements were careful; he was a man who never hurried. The man in the snapshot had bright hair, his shoulders were broader than his hips and his smile revealed teeth as brilliant as his white uniform. Joey remembered seeing him wear that uniform a long time ago, the white sharp in the shadows of his mind.

105

His father had grown more bulky than he was in the picture, and his hair had darkened into a sort of mustard, a dull colour. His eyes too were dulled. Like the teacher, he wanted to say: Dad, what happened? Because he knew what she was really asking: how come Benjamin Pinkerton stopped being a champ? But Nancy noticed Joey staring at his father and reminded him sharply that he should wash his hands.

The snapshot lay nearby on a side table and glancing over, she recalled the day it was taken. There was another photograph from the same day, of the two of them: Ben in his uniform, and Nancy in a mint-green dress with a heart-shaped neckline and a swirly skirt, laughing up at her fiancé. He was about to embark on another voyage and she was enjoying a secret joke: how amazed he would be when her liner docked in Nagasaki. On the shiny paper of the snapshot, the two of them, laughing, bathed in sunlight, looked young, carefree. And then came the sea journey, and all that followed. It was, she realised, the last time she had been completely happy.

Hands washed, Joey was back at the table.

'Dad . . . '

Pinkerton knew what was coming and forestalled the questions.

'I was good. Very good. Winning races came easy. There was a guy I met called Weissmuller at one of the events, he won everything he went in for, swimmer of the year, a world champ. He's famous now; went to Hollywood. I hear he's making a movie, but I knew him way back, and he told me how day after day he worked till he dropped; he had to swim for hours, the coach was God and took no arguments. I reckoned life was too short for all that. And if I wasn't going to swim *through* the water, I'd sail *over* it!'

Pinkerton knew he was talking too much, saying more than necessary, and also less, with no mention of parents who had regarded swimming as fine for a hobby, but no way for a grown man to earn a living. A bank job had been suggested. Ben's choosing the navy had been their first real disagreement. He pulled back now from awkward places in the past, wrong turnings or turnings not taken. Moreover he had found that life was not too short, life was not short at all, it went on and on and had a way of handing out disappointment.

So Weissmuller had swum his way to Olympic golds, world records. He had done other things. But Ben thought back to how it felt, relived the shining moment, arching upward through the air, slicing into water like a blade, surfacing in a spray of glory. Until one day he had come out of the water and found himself beached, dry.

He studied his heaped plate of meat and potatoes, slick with gravy.

On a low lacquer table delicate fish and vegetables, shaped and razored and layered, one colour set against another, green and dark crimson; amber, pink and white; in porcelain bowls, gleaming like jewels . . .

He picked up his fork and stabbed a potato.

'Why does everything have to be brown?'

Nancy looked up, startled. 'What?'

'Nothing important. Just — nothing important.'

He looked again at his plate: 'This is fine.'

★ ★ ★

For Thanksgiving, they went to Louis and Mary as usual, and Ben watched his mother-in-law carry in the shiny bronze turkey. But she was an accomplished cook and he found himself enjoying the tender bird.

Afterwards there was chocolate meringue and pecan tart and apple pie.

'Like Mom makes,' Joey said, repeating words he had heard from other kids.

'There's too much food here for just five of us,' Louis said comfortably. 'Still, I guess one of these days we'll be sitting down six for Thanksgiving, when Joey gets a little brother.'

'Or sister,' Mary put in mildly.

Ben felt the tightness in his chest, that sense of wanting to hit out at some unspecified target.

'Don't hold your breath.' It came out louder than he intended.

Louis and Mary exchanged a quick glance, and Nancy kept her eyes on her plate, her spoon chasing a crumb of chocolate meringue.

'Well of course, we're all in God's hands in these matters,' Mary said. 'Now: who's for more pie?'

14

The kitchen was filled with a sense of electrical activity: the new coffee percolator bubbling, bread browning in the new toast-maker that scorched both sides at once, eggs frying on a ring, the new refrigerator giving off its high-pitched whine in the corner.

Nancy called up to Joey to tell him breakfast was ready, waiting for the familiar noise as he jumped down the stairs, satchel bumping behind him.

He looked around the appliance-filled room.

'So I'm having an electric breakfast.'

'Be grateful,' Ben remarked. 'Not everyone can afford the latest equipment.'

'Does it make the food taste better?'

Nancy dropped a square of golden toast on his plate.

'Probably not.'

'Then why do we have it?'

'To make life easier.'

'And because,' Ben said, not looking up from his newspaper, 'it's the future. Electricity is the future.'

'Dad, you said the automobile was the future.'

'Well. Maybe both.'

'You should invent an electric automobile.'

'I'll bear it in mind.'

She told herself they were lucky to have this bright, enquiring boy. Had she remained a teacher, she would have prized such a pupil. She touched his hair, lightly, as she passed his chair.

She caught her husband's eye and rewarded him with a smile, nose briefly wrinkling.

When Joey had left for school, running off to join their neighbour, the two boys hopping and skipping, Ben lingered over a second cup of coffee. Nancy reached for the newspaper.

'I'm talking to Daniels at the bank this afternoon. About the loan.'

'You've decided then? You didn't say.'

'I thought about it. Now I'm sure. I need bigger premises, a proper workshop.'

Nancy said, 'Ben? Are we speculating?'

'We're investing. Why do you ask?'

She tapped the paper and read aloud: ''Hoover warns of the dangers of rampant speculation.' I just thought: does the President know something we don't know?'

'Well now, 'rampant'. D'you call a garage expansion rampant? Me neither. The bank's looked at the books; it's a safe bet, pay for itself in five years. Honey, now is the right time to expand.'

Later, recalling that decision, he would bleakly remind Nancy of her father's old joke: 'How do you make God laugh? Tell Him your plans.'

* * *

At first, the problem seemed a faraway affair: something that affected the big boys. The stock market might be rocky for a week or two, but everyday life must go on and small businesses

110

were part of that. The newspapers ran encouraging stories and the local press was quick to offer reassurance to readers. Pinkerton took to reading aloud the optimistic headlines for Nancy's benefit.

'Listen to this, Irving Fisher in the *New York Times*: 'There may be a recession in stock prices, but not anything in the nature of a crash'.'

'The guy's a leading economist, I guess he should know. Here's another.'

But suddenly Wall Street ceased to be some distant place located in the financial pages of the newspaper; it criss-crossed the country on railroad tracks and telegraph wires. Wall Street was right here in the neighbourhood, it was next door, it was tapping on the window at night as Pinkerton drew the blanket close around him, and recalled a time when he had no trouble sleeping.

'Dad? Where's the crash?' Joey asked. 'One of the kids at school's dad says there's been a crash.'

'That's just wild talk. There's no crash.'

And he read out from the newspaper what Arthur Reynolds, Chairman of the Continental Illinois Bank of Chicago was quoted as saying.

'He says it won't have much effect on business.'

That was 24 October. Five days later the Dow Jones Industrial Average lost 11.73 per cent of its value.

'Ben?' Nancy said that evening, 'Is this going to affect us?'

'Stocks and shares? I don't see why. We're not playing the market.'

★   ★   ★

People who knew the family said there had always been something of the golden boy about Ben Pinkerton. At high school and college the star swimmer, glittering like the water that won him prizes. In the navy he shone in white and brass buttons. When he opened the automobile garage — one of the first in town — he glowed with the sheen of steel and spray-paint. Like the business, he expanded. But now he dimmed, the gold dull, like neglected brass.

★   ★   ★

When the bank called him there seemed little sense of urgency. Could Mr Pinkerton drop by at his convenience? Mr Daniels would like to have a chat.

The chat was more formal than he expected. Not at first; Gerry Daniels, who had always been so friendly and helpful was still friendly:

'How's Nancy? And the boy? Good, fine little feller . . . ' But when he moved on, discussing the economic situation, the problems the government was facing, words like contract cancellations, falling values and crisis floated across his desk. He pulled a rueful face.

'Some finance houses have actually collapsed, Ben. Unwise use of investors' funds.'

'Come on, you're not telling me banks are

going bust! Am I supposed to feel sorry for the rich guys?' Ben laughed. Daniels did not.

'It's not just the big boys; we're all in the same boat. Difficult times, money tight all round.'

'What are you saying?'

Daniels shifted his inkwell, blotter and a framed photograph of his wife from one place on his desk to another an inch to left or right. He looked up and smiled, still friendly, but suddenly less helpful.

'The loan, Ben. It's payback time.'

'Hey, we've had ups and downs before this. I can come through, the automobile is the future.'

'Ben, if I had a dollar for every time someone has said the automobile is the future I'd be a rich man today.'

'Actually Gerry, I don't think you would. How many people in this town can have said that to you? Ten? Twenty? A hundred? But it's the truth. The garage was doing fine; it'll recover. Just give me a little time.'

Daniels gave one of his helpless shrugs. 'Well now, that's the problem. Time. I'm sorry, Ben. If it was up to me *personally* . . . '

He, *personally*, would be only too happy, and so forth . . . but the bank required repayment of the loan. Without delay. Ben said he understood, and they shook hands, and Daniels saw him to the door, hand on his shoulder, a reassuring squeeze; give his best to Nancy.

But when, to Ben's dismay, he found himself unable to hand back the money to the bank because his customers were, in turn, unable to come up with the cash they owed him; and when

113

the house payments were overdue and the lenders sent in a repossession notice, he discovered that the Dow Jones and stocks and shares did indeed affect them.

'I'll get a job,' Nancy said. 'With Joey at school now I can manage it.'

'That won't be necessary.'

But quite soon it did become necessary and Nancy took a job. Not one she would have chosen, but choice was no longer an option. The garage had gone, and now it was the turn of the house and the electric kitchen.

★ ★ ★

Nancy kept the focus tight: she concentrated on what to take, not what must be left behind; hold on to the small things — objects of sentimental value, she had heard them called at sales. She was keeping a Mexican plate that had been a wedding present, and a pair of silver-plated grape scissors, to remind her of a way of life that was about to vanish. Ben pocketed Charlie's medal.

She picked out and folded the clothes she habitually wore; in truth, the rest just hung there in the closet for most of the time. Joey trailed behind her, watching. He had never been heavy on toys and she told him he could keep his favourite books.

They packed cardboard boxes and carried them down to the porch. As Nancy reached the entrance two Model T Fords drove slowly past; the cars still looked shiny new but they were

114

loaded with household goods. The remains of their own were neatly laid out in front of the house, marked 'For Sale. No reasonable offer refused.'

What was a reasonable offer? How many dollars could reconcile her to the loss as she watched the pieces she had picked out so lovingly, the maple side table, the standard lamp, the desk with the secret drawer, being loaded on to someone else's pickup?

★　★　★

Nancy said, 'Where's Joey?' but Ben was busy filling boxes, and she went back inside the house, calling his name. By the time she reached the top of the stairs she sounded exasperated: her legs ached and her throat was dry from the dust.

'Joey?' she called again.

★　★　★

Ben heard her calling, repeatedly, her voice growing frantic as she went from room to empty room. Then she was down the stairs and hurrying out on to the porch, running her hand through her hair, looking beyond him to the street.

She said, 'He's gone.'

15

She was out on the sidewalk, looking left and right, calling his name, knowing there would be no response but calling anyway.

'Joey? *Joey!*'

'I've been here the whole time,' Ben said. 'He can't be gone.'

He stood, trying to think himself inside the child's head.

'Did you look in the loft?'

She came running past him, into the house and up the stairs. At the top she paused: only now did she notice the ladder to the loft, the open hatch.

Joey was crouching on the loft floor, in the corner below the tiny roof window, the brown paper bag full of his books clutched to his chest.

Nancy said, her voice calm, 'Joey: we need to start loading — '

He said, 'I'm not going.'

He curled up, hugging the floor, making himself heavy, cumbersome, to discourage any attempt to lift him.

She went back down the stairs and found Ben, but when she tried to explain the situation he became impatient: kid stuff was Nancy's province.

'Just fetch him down. If necessary, give him a whack.'

'A *whack?*'

116

A slow wave of anger built in Nancy, composed of weariness, resentment and a sense of being on her own.

'He's *your* son,' she said. '*You* fetch him down.'

Her legs seemed to give way under her and she collapsed in the porch; slumped, uncaring of dirt and dust on the steps.

'*You* give him a whack. If you think that's what you want to do. I'm not about to start hitting him.'

Ben went up the stairs and climbed the ladder to the loft.

'Hey, kid.'

He peered across at the boy, very small, huddled on the floor, seeming to be hugging the wall. In the corner of the shadowy room he looked less blond, and something about the angle of his head, the way he raised a shoulder as he looked up at Ben, was for a shocking moment a reminder of the past: Ben saw that he was Cho-Cho's child.

Joey began to cry, heavy tears welling and dripping on to his knees.

Ben moved into the room and squatted down, keeping things slow and easy, his back propped against the wall.

'What's going on here?'

Joey said, 'Is Nancy going to die?'

'What?'

'After we leave the house. Will she be dead?'

Nancy was still on the porch steps, hunched, eyes closed, when Ben came back out and sat down next to her.

117

'He's scared to leave.'

Her eyes blinked open. 'What?'

'He said, after he was taken away from home before, he was told his mother was dead and he never saw her again. He's scared the same thing will happen now and he'll get another new mom.'

Appalled, Nancy felt the past rise up and crash down on her, an intolerable weight she must endure.

'Oh God. Oh God.'

'It's okay. I told him that wouldn't happen.'

'Ben. Maybe we were wrong . . . '

Within the house they heard the kitten-soft sound of Joey slowly descending the stairs.

'I told him he could sit on your lap in the truck. You'd be fine as long as he was around.' He added ruefully, 'He doesn't give a shit about me.'

16

When Joey asked where they were going Nancy told him they had a new home. He would have a new school.

'It'll be an adventure. It'll be fun.'

The rented apartment was cramped, though Joey still had a room — of sorts: a curtained closet just big enough to take his bed, with a few toys and books stored in boxes underneath.

Ben looked from the chipped sink to the small table, the light from the overhead bulb showing every scratch on the surface.

'This is no place to be.'

'Maybe we won't have to stay here too long.'

He had managed to hold on to the truck, which he drove back and forth between small-holdings and stores, carrying farm goods, equipment, supplies. Newspaper headlines were no longer optimistic, though Ben tried to keep cheerful when the boy was in earshot.

'We're doing okay,' he said. 'We're doing okay.'

For the first time he gave thanks that there was just Joey to think about. He had expected Nancy to give him a kid well before this, and was increasingly aware of unspoken grandparental speculation. Now — silver lining time — it meant one mouth less to feed.

He could have used a drink now and then but

alcohol, like choice, was not an option: Prohibition had never been a good idea, in his book, but the way the world was now, the ban added just that bit to the load, like the last straw that broke the camel's back. On a bad day, he reflected, he might just break the law. He began to smoke more, but soon stopped: cigarettes didn't grow on trees.

At the local nursery Nancy cared for toddlers whose mothers went out to work. Her hair no longer bounced sleek and shiny to her shoulders; washed less frequently, it hung, lank, tucked carelessly behind her ears. There was packet-mix angel food cake for tea and they became familiar with cheap meat loaf, the breadcrumbs almost outweighing the beef.

★　★　★

Joey had never been a noisy child. He grew quieter.

There were times, lying in the dark of his closet-bedroom, when he thought about his mother. He wondered what kind of a person she had been; all he could recall was a shape, a woman in a kimono who moved silently on the tatami mat floors of a wood and paper house, who stroked his head and soothed him when he cried, and took him walking by the sea. He found it impossible to imagine her face or hear her voice.

He remembers the sound of screaming, he presses his hands to his ears to shut out the

120

sound. But who was screaming? And why? All he knew was that he had been taken away.

In the yard outside the school he waited by the chicken-wire fencing until Nancy collected him after hurrying from her workplace.

One Saturday afternoon, helping her clear away the meal, he looked around the room that served as kitchen and living room.

Above the sink, washing hung suspended from the ceiling, whites that remained grey however hard Nancy scrubbed, shirts that she wrung out and twisted, but that dripped, creating a clammy dankness in the air.

Joey said, mildly, 'It's horrible here.'

'Yes,' Nancy agreed. 'It is.'

She looked at the remains of a corned beef casserole on the table. She made sure he had enough to eat, but he looked thinner.

'Tell you what: why don't I make us a blackberry pie? We'll go blackberry picking, like we used to.'

She made an extravagant decision: they took a bus to their old neighbourhood, then walked, though Nancy made sure they avoided the tree-lined street and the house where they had lived in happier days. Further out, on the edge of town they came to the patch of open land where fat, juicy blackberries had flourished, but found it was transformed: no longer a haven of wild fruit and flowers, it was a place of flimsy shacks and cinders, with torn scraps of paper blowing across the wrecked landscape. The brambles were gone, the trees too, chopped

121

down to be put to use as makeshift walls. Pet dogs had formed themselves into packs, loping the perimeter, seeking out trash cans in the hunt for food.

The boy looked up at Nancy, bewildered. 'What happened?'

'These are people that lost their homes, Joey. This is where they live now.'

They walked on; she led him to the river where, not long before, the family had spent a Sunday afternoon watching kingfishers and dragonflies, with boys seated on the banks fishing alongside fathers. Now the bank was lined with shanties occupied by homeless squatters. Broken-down trucks without their wheels lay alongside the river like ruined barges.

'There are lots of these places,' Nancy said. 'They call them Hooverville, after the President. It's a sort of joke, but it's not funny.'

The two of them looked around silently at the flimsy structures created from rotting planks, cardboard, bits of scrap. There were chimneys made out of tin cans joined together, poking from roofs of tar-paper held down by branches. Nancy saw with a pang that some even had improvised doors that flapped, creaking as the wind hit them.

Women, bodies slack, the hollow of their eyes dark as soot, watched them. She forced herself not to turn quickly aside, to look at these figures, grey as cinders, branded with an invisible scar of shame, and see them as ordinary folk who had once possessed proper homes, where the men had left for work after breakfast, the women had sometimes bought flowers to put in a vase on the window ledge. But they were no longer ordinary; they had slipped through the grid and were drowning in hopelessness. And she became aware that there were no men in sight; an eerie absence at a time when there was really no place else for them to go.

A girl about the same age as Joey squatted to defecate in the scrubland behind a shack. She glanced across at them, her face blank. Nancy took Joey's arm and turned in the opposite direction, talking rapidly to distract his attention.

'Well! No blackberries today. We'll think of something else. One of the mothers at the nursery was telling me she's trying out all kinds of interesting new ideas for food. She made soup out of stinging nettles.'

Joey wrinkled his nose thoughtfully, trying to grasp a fugitive memory.

'Nettles are good. I ate nettles.'

She was surprised. 'When was that?'

'I don't remember.' He began to feel anxious.

Nettles. What next? Nancy wondered. Prices rising, farmers producing less. Perhaps kingfishers and dragonflies would be on the menu; cicadas trapped and broiled. Anything edible.

She recalled a phrase from Ambrose Bierce that she had gleefully committed to memory in college. Bierce said 'edible' meant good to eat and wholesome to digest, as a worm to a toad, a toad to a snake, a snake to a pig, a pig to a man, and a man to a worm. It seemed less amusing today.

★ ★ ★

The toddlers enjoyed singing, and Nancy sang along with them — she loved the high sweet voices wavering through old nursery songs, chubby hands clapping — but there were days when the singing itself became difficult: taking a deep breath she found herself gasping, on the point of sudden tears, lungs swelling, her voice wobbling on the note. It was as though the stream of sound unblocked a cache of sadness she was holding within her. She longed to get it out, wash it away. Instead she gulped, swallowed, beat time and nodded encouragingly at the children.

Unhappiness grew on her, thickening like a second skin, but she did her best to conceal it, and since she was out of practice with smiling these days, concealment was relatively easy. But one day at the nursery, cradling a curly-haired tot who had grazed his knee, she broke down, holding the toddler to her breast and weeping inconsolably into his soft hair, to the alarm of her colleagues.

Brushing away their anxiety she offered explanations. Her time of the month. A few sleepless nights . . . They sent her home: 'You have a good rest now.'

In bed, curled into herself, clutching a pillow, she lay unmoving and sobbed into the empty room. Joey had been a mature three-year-old when she took him on; she had missed the early, milk-sweet moments, the small body expanding from the birth canal to fill a mother's arms; the messy, repetitive demands, the mouth seeking her breast.

Next day she was her usual brisk self, but writing her weekly letter to her mother that night she found tears falling on to the page, smudging the ink.

17

Driving home, Ben worked on a scenario, trying out different words, rehearsing his speech to Nancy, shaping and reshaping it. Should he build slowly to the point, giving her time to take it in, or lay it out up front? They didn't talk much these days. Toss a coin; there was no 'right' way to deal with this one. He became aware that his bones ached.

He had reached the edge of town when he found his view of the road blocked by a thick cloud of dust which resolved itself into a slow-moving cluster of men: husbands, brothers and fathers of the Hooverville women, a grey, shabby column.

He leaned from the window of the truck.

'Anyone need a ride?'

A few men gave him a wave; two on the edge of the crowd climbed aboard, and a couple of women with young children.

'Where to, gentlemen?'

'We're heading for Portland.'

'You can drop us at the turn-off.'

Ben glanced at the men squeezed into the cab of his truck. One of them looked familiar.

'It's . . . Walt, right? You guys setting up something?'

★ ★ ★

126

He rested his buttocks on the kitchen table and sipped from a glass of water.

'So I said, what's going on?'

She continued to get supper ready as he talked, moving from table to gas stove to sink. She did this more and more these days, half listening, half attending to something else. Ben addressed the back of her head.

'You know what he said?'

'Nnh.' She knew he would tell her. As she began to carve slices off a small end piece of ham she paused and looked over her shoulder: 'By the way, I had a letter from my mother today.'

He nodded and drained the glass. 'So anyway, Walt said . . . '

★ ★ ★

The truck rattled and bounced over the rutted road surface and Walter said in his slow way that the plan was for the men to assemble in Portland and head for Washington the following day.

Ben peeled off a strip of gum and added it to the tasteless lump held between his teeth. He chewed for a moment, drawing the cool, peppermint flavour into his mouth.

'Washington county, that's a fair way.'

The two men looked at each other, managing a grin. 'Washington, DC, Ben, the Capitol. The White House.'

'Come on, guys. What, you're crossing the *whole of the United States?*'

Ben overtook the straggling column, inching

his way, slow-paced to keep the dust down, throwing quick looks at the men in the cab. 'Washington DC,' he repeated, in a tone of disbelief. 'Washington, DC? That's what — three thousand miles.'

★ ★ ★

Now Nancy did stop, in mid-slice, and give him her full attention.

'*Washington?* We're talking about the *vets*, right?'

Joey, curled up on the bed in his closet-room, called out, 'Why are old soldiers going to Washington?'

'Not so old,' Nancy said. 'They were in the war. In Europe.'

She was aware that had Ben been a couple of years older he too might be heading for Washington. So would his big brother, only Charlie hadn't come back from France. His was one of the white crosses marking the graves of those fallen in battle.

She moved round the table, concentrating on placing knives and forks and plates. Ben sensed she had withdrawn from the conversation. His glance shifted to Joey. The boy at least was listening.

'Those guys . . . ' Ben shook his head. 'They've got this crazy idea. They've tried petitions, speechifying . . . '

He'd read the stories about rioting; newspapers could take a lofty tone, but he thought about Charlie lying in some French field and he understood the frustration that erupted into the breaking of windows and bones.

★ ★ ★

And today, as the procession wound its way towards town, Ben had seen that these men held within them a slow, determined anger that was building up, and taking them on a long journey.

★ ★ ★

'Crazy,' he said again, 'Some of them are in really bad shape, half crippled.' He sounded tired. 'Washington, DC? They'll never make it.'

Stirring beans, dicing ham, her back to the other two, Nancy listened as Ben talked on.

'See, Joey, they have no work, no homes. This is a chance of grabbing the President's attention. They need their army bonus payments now; they can't hang around another twelve years or whatever, they're pretty much starving.'

Nancy put down the knife and rinsed her hands. She pivoted slowly from the sink, wiping her hands on her apron, smoothing her palms repeatedly over her thighs.

'Ben?'

'I mean they haven't thought it out.'

'You're going to Washington, aren't you.' Not a question.

He stopped. 'What?'

'You're planning on going to Washington.'

'Who said anything about — did *I* say anything — I said they're crazy, you're not listening — '

'I hear you, Ben, even when I don't seem to be listening. Why would you want to join this march? First off, you're not a vet. Second, you have problems of your own. You have responsibilities. Third.' She stopped. 'You want to say something?'

He was slow, digging for the words he needed like a farmer sifting through clogged earth. She cut in:

'You need to be here for us, for Joey and me.'

Washington was about his brother, even if Ben refused to admit it.

'You're worrying about the vets? You should be thinking about us.'

'I think about you all the time. It's what you do when you love someone.'

Nancy noted, distantly, that in his own way he had just told her he loved her; something she hadn't heard for a long time. But they had drifted so far apart that the signal was too weak to reach its destination; she remained untouched.

'The letter from my mother . . . ' She appeared to be changing the subject. 'She thought maybe Joey and I might stay with them for a while. Not a bad idea, seeing that the nursery can't afford to keep me on.'

She knew what she was really saying and she knew that he knew.

He nodded, slowly, as though thinking over a complex problem. But what he was hearing was the solution; problem solved, the words had miraculously found their way to him, the situation that could no longer be concealed.

'Honey, that's great. I'd like to drive you but the thing is, I won't have the truck.'

'It broke down?'

'I had to hand it in. Repo time.'

She gave him a fierce look, aware of the child listening. 'We'll talk later. Let's eat. Joey, wash your hands.' She gave him a bright smile. 'Busy day tomorrow. We need to pack. We're visiting with Granny and Gramps. And your father's going to Washington.'

★ ★ ★

Later, seated on the edge of the bed, whispering, she questioned him, tired, angry.

'What happened?'

'No one needs a truck and driver any more, Nance. The farmers are burning their own corn to keep themselves warm, nobody's buying anything.'

'Why in hell didn't you *tell* me? I could have asked Dad — '

'I can't drag your parents into this; they have problems enough already. I'll find a way. Digging ditches, even.'

'There are no ditches to dig, Ben. If there were, the vets would be digging.'

Without her parents, they would be moving into Hooverville.

In what other country, what other life, had it been that she occupied an electric kitchen? In a house with two whole floors and a staircase that led from one to the other, all air and space and high ceilings? She recalled the soft shag rugs

131

scattered around the house that gave off a comforting smell, like the fleece of a lamb. Through the half-open door she could see into the next room: the stained walls, the chipped, low-grade furniture. The lamplight showed up cracks in the cheap floor covering.

She had hated this apartment, and now it felt precious: a warm place with a proper roof, a chair to read in, a lamp that shone on to the page. She thought of the shacks along the riverbank, the bitter women with their bird's nest hair, the children without shoes, faces marked with grime and hopelessness. She thought of Joey. Ben said,

'I'll find us something better than this. When I get back from Washington. It won't be long.'

He gave her the smile that had once turned her heart. He really meant it. She blinked rapidly, forcing back tears. They were about to pack up their remaining worldly goods; they were losing what they had learned to call home and she was swept with something between sorrow and terror. He reached out and took her hand but it lay limp in his, like a wounded bird.

18

Around three hundred men were gathered at the Portland railroad mustering yard by the time Ben arrived. It was a fine May morning, the heat of the sun tempered by a refreshing breeze. Some wore working clothes, others had put on their old army uniforms — the veterans' Bonus Army, they were calling themselves, not altogether seriously. Quite a few had pinned medals to crumpled jackets.

'Okay: anyone here got cash?' Derisive laughter. Who was planning to buy a ticket?

They reckoned they had $30 between them, but to their surprise, Union Pacific loaded them into empty boxcars and sent them east. The flint-faced rail guards with truncheons and dogs were absent today.

'They want us out, across the state line,' Walt said cheerfully. 'They don't want trouble.'

'We're undesirables,' Ben said.

'Yeah, and that's fine by me. Once we hit Washington we can sit tight till the Bonus Bill gets through.' He called out to the crowd: 'So no panhandling, no illegal drinking. And,' a tired grin, 'no radicalism — they'll have us figured for communists.'

Rocking to the rhythm of the track, packed close, squatting shoulder to shoulder with strangers, breathing in their sweat, bad breath and noxious farts, Ben flexed his stiff limbs and cautiously changed position. As he folded his legs beneath him he relived a moment from a banished past: *sitting cross-legged on a smooth tatami mat, Cho-Cho's cool hands, the small sweetness of her body.*

A world that seemed unimaginably clean and comforting. Through a slit in the side of the boxcar he glimpsed a brilliant, sunlit landscape speeding past, quite close but unreachable. His mouth was dry, his eyes stung. Did cattle feel this way? Was awareness unique to humans? These thoughts had not occurred to him before and seemed unhelpful now. In that other life Cho-Cho had bathed him, first washing off their mingled stickiness then leading him to the bath to steep in the steaming water, holding out fresh clothes.

'Nice?' Her invariable question.

Oh, *how* nice, he now acknowledged ruefully. He saw himself for a moment close-up as if through some telescope of time, swaggering into town, the bright young sailor, buying himself a good time, careless about who or what might be damaged in that fragile world. He saw something ugly — he shook his head as though brushing off flies, to shake away painful thoughts. Instead he brought up a picture of Nancy, whose body too had been sweet and smooth before the bad times, who wrinkled her nose beguilingly when she smiled.

With Nancy there was no 'come here', turn this way or that, lift higher, push harder. Cho-Cho's creamy white flesh had invited violation. Nancy's thighs were suntanned, firm from tennis and swimming; he held back from instructing her how to please him, or experimenting in ways to please her.

From his pocket he pulled a snapshot of Joey. As the intermittent light stabbed into the dark boxcar, he studied the tentative smile, the tilt of the head, the enquiring look. He should have paid more heed to the boy, done more stuff; he barely knew his own son. He'd make sure they spent more time together, when this trip was over.

Closing the door of the apartment had been unexpectedly painful. It was a dump, but it was *their* dump. Or had been. Electric light, a stove. A bed. He was now as homeless as the men around him. Nancy's parents were kind but they too had been hit by events; they'd moved to a smaller house in a neighbourhood with overflowing trash cans and, Mary remarked with a sad shrug, no magnolia tree to shade the yard.

He had to find a job. Words filtered, whispering in his head . . . *If he'd stayed in the navy . . .* He cut them off. He disliked those 'What if?' kind of thoughts. There must be some outfit, somewhere, that needed a man with his skills. Then again: skills. Nancy was the smart one. He would have to read a few books, prepare himself, keep one step ahead, look decent, knock on doors. When he got back from Washington.

Around him the men were singing along sporadically, snatches of half-remembered songs that gradually coalesced into one they all knew, one that brought alive a happier land, the Big Rock Candy mountain, '*where the cops don't snarl and the dogs don't bite'* . . . Someone had brought along a banjo, and above the rattling of the iron wheels Ben could hear the strumming and plunking of the strings, and the voices, some hoarse, some sweet, singing of a place where the brooks were hot as steam, *'full of big stewed oysters lying in a bed of cream'*, where you picked a sandwich from an old ham tree, *'and all the smokes and booze were free'* . . .

The Big Rock Candy Mountain, where coffee grew on white oak trees and the rivers flowed with brandy. A place where a homeless man could sleep easy in a soft bed.

★   ★   ★

Moving from one railroad station to another, begging rides on boxcars and trucks, hitting the road, walking across country, splitting up and rejoining forces, the Portland march slowly progressed. Ben moved among the men, making himself useful, sweet-talking hostile railroad guards with dogs straining to be unleashed.

This was something new for him; his style was to walk away. Mostly, as he admitted to Nancy once, he didn't give a shit. But he was finding out that time can change a man. He must have been around twelve when a teacher at school told the class: 'with age comes wisdom'. He had thought that was crap: with age comes grey hair and weak limbs, a bent back, poor eyesight, was what he had wanted to say, but kids didn't talk back to teachers. In those days kids had been disciplined and protected, treated like pets. Now they lived in the real world.

Wives and a few youngsters had come along for the ride, parents perhaps not fully aware of the journey they would be making. Sometimes, when Ben went ahead into town to organise drinking water, or basic food and sleeping quarters, he made sure a few little ones trailed after him. A tall man with worker's muscles and sun-bleached hair, all smiles and sincere blue eyes, heading up a bunch of kids, this was a reassuring sight for the locals. He could tell they were thinking with some relief that at least this one didn't look like a communist. He felt things were proceeding peacefully.

Ten days and two thousand miles later, in east St Louis, he was proved wrong: the train pulled in and men poured in a shabby stream from the trucks. Beyond the rail stop, exemplars of law-abiding citizenry lined the roadside. Some carried home-made placards: 'No Commies wanted!' 'No Bolshie troublemakers!'

Walt muttered, 'Shit', and trotted around the men like a sheepdog, keeping them in order, telling them to look as unlike troublemakers as possible. Ben kept smiling. He called, reassuringly, 'Okay folks, we're just passing through — ' but got no further. Stepping forward, shoulder to shoulder, a line of cops presented an unambiguous welcome party.

'Back the way you came, guys.' Batons tapping hardened palms.

The uniforms seemed to have won the day as men turned back to the boxcars, but a minute later they were uncoupling the freight cars, filling buckets and grabbing bars of soap: the vets were soaping the tracks. The Governor, watching from an upper window, sent in the National Guard.

Clatter of boots on tarmac, shouts, cries, whistles blowing; trained professional law-enforcers met half-starved rabble, the undernourished bodies easy to knock aside. Ben, swifter, more agile, kept out of the soldiers' way. Around him, batons came down hard; blood flowed.

It was local people who settled the matter; ordinary, law-abiding citizens noisy enough to be heard; women who yelled at the Guard to lay off the vets, and elderly men in suits banging on the Governor's door, so that quite soon he changed his mind, called off the boots and batons and sent in state-owned trucks to pick up the marchers, move them on, 'Outta here. Outta town.' Out of Illinois at least. Let someone else have the problem. The loaded trucks bumped their way to the state line.

★　★　★

As they blazed the wavering trail of the journey Ben gradually became aware that he was with them, but not quite one of them, as Charlie would have been. Divided by a war; not a vet, after all. The men were reverting to a regimental organism, buddies, moving en masse, in accord, seeming to know each other's thoughts. And when they reached Mississippi, the cops wore grins; some of them had served in the army. Vets themselves.

'You guys know how to drive?'

Ben raised his hand. 'That's what I do. I drive a truck.' Other voices joined his: men who could drive, when they had work and wheels.

Not far from the railroad station the road curved to a compound fenced off with chicken wire, the gate padlocked. Behind the wire, a metallic elephants' graveyard, a scene of desolation: huge steel bodies lined up in rows, grand automobiles. Official loot: beautiful cars confiscated from jailed bootleggers.

'Okay, guys; they're all yours as far as the state line.'

The cops swung open the gates, the vets piled into Packards, Buicks, Chryslers, Caddies and set off out of town. Cheering, yelling slogans, drunk on temporary power, at least some of the Bonus Army was running on silk, until the gas ran out. Ben found himself — unimaginable luxury — at the wheel of a Pierce Arrow. He could feel the engine responding to the pressure of his foot; this was class, top racehorse quality, this was Kentucky Derby, Triple Crown stuff, the leather seats soft as a woman's thighs, the suspension smooth. Bootleggers lived in style, smuggling Scotch from London, selling it on, running illegal breweries, rum ships, all to keep their clients happy. By now the owner of this beauty was probably free, sprung on a technicality and driving some other thorough-bred.

Ben shifted the gearstick, released the clutch and leaned into the movement, the ease, the creamy surge forward. He flung back his head and laughed aloud, running his hands over the wheel. The automobile was the future, right? He always knew that. The sleek lines of the car, the deep gleam of the paintwork were visible even through the dust swirling like a storm . . . Crammed in around him, the men cheered, slapped Ben on the back, drew him into their song. The barrier had melted. Washington, here we come. He wished Nance and Joey could see him as he gunned the engine and the car flew.

19

Resting like a convalescent in the shade of her mother's tiny porch, Nancy follows the story in the newspaper; reports of men fighting with rail guards, forcing themselves on to freight trains. Others plodding the tracks on foot. Elsewhere, trucks, jalopies slowly covering ground. She senses a murmuring, a surge, a tracking of the land; the homeless on the move. Not all are bound for Washington: some are just on the road. Men walking, women too, children stumbling alongside, crawling like ants, moving east, moving north, from Reno, New Orleans, Kansas City. These moments, these migrations, recur in history. The land seethes: once it would have been men pushing carts, wagons drawn by oxen, mule trains. Go West; the magical words. Go West. But this *is* the West, and if they keep going there's nothing but water. Next landfall: Japan.

Even here, she can see slow-moving, solitary men passing by on their way to nowhere. At the little general store on the corner one or two stop to buy a can of sardines and salteen crackers, squatting by the roadside to eat them, shaking the last shreds of sardine into wide-open mouths, heads tilted back. After dark, the walkers are intermittently caught in the head-lamps of a passing car, heads drooping, backlit by the flaring lights like figures in a shadow show, their silhouettes racing ahead of them, then as the car passes on, men and shadows fade back into darkness and obscurity.

She imagines them, these sad souls, leaving towns and cities; listless tributaries flowing from state to state, reaching this town, this street, just another stage on a journey. Some of them, at least, have a goal: the White House. Men who fought for their country, now desperate. And among them, Ben, carrying a dead brother on his back, trying to prove something to himself.

What's to become of us all? she wonders.

Once, she might have found comfort in prayer, but though they still attend the local church as a family, Nancy is unable to open herself to the consolation of penitence; she has too long held within herself knowledge of a transgression that sets her apart from the good people around her. They could count on God's mercy, but she continues to live with an old and festering guilt; she finds it impossible to ask for forgiveness of her sins.

She prays aloud, when ordered to do so, but when the prayers move into silent communion her thoughts circle, refusing to rise, heavy as unleavened bread. Her life is divided into Before and After, like a terrain bisected by dark water. On the far side all seemed sunlit, flowers grew, there were family picnics, laughter; a landscape of innocence. On the After bank, an ominous cloud casts shadow on the dry ground; there is a sense of withering away. Between the two lies an ocean, a sea

142

crossed and re-crossed, a moment when innocence was lost for ever and she was expelled from the Garden.

* * *

This week, breathing in the familiar church blend of wax polish and flowers, with her parents on one side and Joey tucked close next to her, for once she was lulled into a sense of peace; the service itself seemed infused with a glow of lost innocence; the preacher evidently perplexed as he spoke of men from Oregon camping out in Washington, making demands. As a law-abiding citizen he recognised they should have obeyed orders, stayed home, trusted in their representatives to speak for them. But as a man who had seen their problems at first hand, their children hungry, he could only pray their voices would be heard.

'Remember: God will comfort, guide and forgive every person, no matter who they are or what they've done.' Amen.

Amen to that, Nancy silently echoed. But could she depend on it?

* * *

May 30th Memorial Day.'*Dear Nance, well, we finally got here . . .* '

Before he left, she had given Ben a notebook with shiny black covers, a batch of stamped envelopes and two sharp pencils.

'Write. Even if you only manage a few lines.

Save them up. Mail them when you can.'
He promised to keep in touch.

'There must be 20,000 of us here, vets, wives, kids, you can hardly move in the streets. The plan is to hand in the petition, get their voices heard . . . '

Once they had been hailed as heroes. Now they saw from the newspapers that the President had given them new labels:

'Hoover's calling us bums, pacifists, radicals. He's locked the White House gates. Some of the guys have moved into downtown blocks about to be demolished, the rest of us are setting up camp on the Anacostia Flats across the river . . . '

The ground was hard, baked by the sun. Ben's shovel hit the dry, cindery earth as though striking steel. Further off, kitchens were being set up, children warned off, as makeshift cooking stoves smoked and crackled. Huts and shanties, put together from junk and cardboard and scrap iron debris, began to spread, confronting the President with the biggest Hooverville in the country.

'Dearest Nance, I'm taking a break from digging latrines. We're putting up a regular home from home here. Great view: I tell you, I'd rather be us looking at Capitol Hill, than those guys looking at us.'

144

Nancy read aloud the scrappy pages that arrived from Washington. Later, in bed, Joey studied the scrawled notes, read and reread the words. In his head he heard the sounds of men at work building the camp, the digging, chopping, clearing; the clash of steel spade on hard ground, the voices calling. It sounded like a distant battlefield.

He began to think about his father in a new way.

20

Ben had helped write out an official statement to the press, but in the end Walter tore it up and walked over to the waiting reporters.

'Gentlemen. Will you take a look at these guys. Most of them married, been out of work two years or more. Offer them a job at a dollar a day, they'd take it. We think they deserve to be heard.'

The reporters wrote their stories, the men waved their banners, and on 15 June Ben wrote jubilantly to Nancy that the veterans' Bonus Bill had scraped through its first reading.

'Hoover threatened a veto but there's dancing in the streets.'

Two days later the Senate defeated the bill.

As the weeks passed, handouts from townsfolk dried up. Food replaced justice in the forefront of men's minds. The camp stank of more than garbage and latrines: it smelled of hunger. Without knowing what it was, Ben inhaled the metallic, acetate tang of malnutrition. He was acquainted with poverty — at a distance: sailing into foreign ports he had seen natives begging. At home, even before his own security began melting like ice in summer, he had been made aware of the homeless and the jobless. Now he was one of them, and it came to him that there was a quality of poverty here which was different from anything he had known before.

Cutting through blackened potatoes and

peeling off rotten outer leaves to make use of a cabbage salvaged from a market trader's refuse, he felt, first shame, then curiously privileged: they were beating the system.

But as the weather grew hotter, tempers too grew heated, and one night the men picketing the Capitol building extended the demonstration by bedding down in the grounds.

Next morning a government minion handed out official bits of paper: the Speaker had invoked a hitherto forgotten regulation that prohibited people from loitering.

'Move along, buddy: no squatting. No sleeping.'

But Ben read the small print and pointed out there was no regulation against *walking* in the grounds.

For the next three blazing days and humid July nights, they shuffled up and down Pennsylvania Avenue in silent protest. There was some stumbling and one or two keeled over, but mostly they kept going. To make sure nobody sneaked in a catnap on the grass, the garden sprinkler system was kept running —

'So we now have regular showers to cool us down . . . God must be on our side.'

In the shanty town a carnival atmosphere began to spread, with children playing on the riverbank and songs round campfires.

On the evening of 27 July Ben began a new letter, the page lit by a lantern hanging from the lintel of the shack. *'It's quiet tonight, Nance. I'm feeling hopeful.'*

He wiped his sweaty hands on a rag, and tried

to put his thoughts down on the crumpled page. There was so much he wanted to tell her, about the men whose stories he was hearing: how they had acquired their wounds, the scars of war, and the invisible wounds that still had them crying aloud and shaking on bad nights . . . and about the sense of discovery he had felt crossing thousands of miles of a country he barely knew. This had been more than one journey: he had made a voyage of his own; found time to look inside his own head; to think, for the first time, about Nancy and Joey, about the way life might be different.

But he wrote down none of those things.

He could feel the heat from the lamp above his head; the wind came over the river like the blast from an oven. The pencil moved across the soggy notebook and spelled out how he missed her. He asked her to hug Joey for him. He would be home soon. He addressed and stamped the envelope and gave it to one of the bigger kids to put in the mailbox.

Next morning the Bonus Bill was defeated.

Optimism began to drain away. Men lost their briskness; sagged. Walter looked suddenly old.

'The President wants us out. He's sending in the army. MacArthur's giving the orders now.'

'The army?' Ben was incredulous. 'Against vets? That has to be a joke.' But no one was laughing.

MacArthur's troops blocked off streets; there were scuffles, some broken bones, and downtown Washington was cleared. A couple of tanks pursued the men to the water's edge. There was a sense of stand-off. Everyone knew the President had ordered the troops to go no further than the river. They were safe, across the water.

Wives prepared food, men discussed the next step as the sun set.

★   ★   ★

Close to midnight, unable to sleep, Ben came out of the hut for some air. He saw what looked like a torchlight procession crossing the bridge, moving fast. There was noise, and the grinding of wheel tracks. Then he saw it for what it was: troops, horses, tanks: an army on the move. He began to shout, pulling on his boots, running between huts to rouse those sleeping, stumbling on the rough ground.

MacArthur had crossed the Anacostia river. Like some invading emperor he set loose his force. Men, women and children fled in panic from the cavalry and the glitter of sabres, bludgeoned by clubs, gashed by bayonets, vomiting from the effects of tear gas. In the confusion shots were fired. People ran as they run from an earthquake, without aim or direction, the crowd scattering as troops moved from shack to shack with kerosene-soaked torches. Flames swept through the camp, leaping high into the darkness and the smoke swirled across the river. As Ben looked back over his shoulder he saw a distant vision: the Capitol in flames.

'Jesus Christ! It's on fire!' he yelled, but what

he saw was a mirror image, the inferno of Hooverville reflected in the Capitol's high windows blazing crimson and gold.

Spread out along the riverbank, the men resisted eviction, fighting back; coughing and half-blinded, women pressed wet rags over children's faces to protect them from the gas. Ben, ducking and wheeling, turned back to give a hand to a weeping woman left behind in the panic, and came face to face with an infantryman. Each hit out wildly, whether in attack or defence, who could tell? Ben was unarmed: the infantryman's rifle struck him hard on the side of the head, spun him around and sent him staggering back towards the bridge. And there a trooper's club, swishing through the dark, caught him off balance and he fell against the parapet and toppled, quite slowly, over the edge and into the river and sank beneath the scum-encrusted waters.

Open-eyed, through the murky liquid Ben could make out above him the flickering surface, the glancing light of the flames. He was comforted; he was a swimmer, wasn't he? This was his element. All he had to do was instruct his limbs to send him upwards. Even as the darkness closed in he knew he was always safe in water.

21

The *New York Times* carried the story.

'Flames rose high over the desolate Anacostia flats at midnight tonight, and a pitiful stream of refugee veterans of the World War left their home of the past two months, going they knew not where.' The biggest Hooverville in the land, sheltering 25,000 people, had been razed to the ground. Nancy read on.

There had been deaths. Officially, the *Times* reported, there were 'two adult fatalities'. Two men were shot, and two infants died, asphyxiated by tear gas. There was a drowning, but that was described as 'incidental'.

Nancy already knew Ben was dead when she read the story in the *New York Times*. She had received the annihilating blow and absorbed it.

One afternoon many years before, home from school, Nancy had been watching her mother refill a tall glass storage jar in the kitchen. As she turned aside, the jar top caught Mary's sleeve and fell to the floor. Surprisingly, the heavy glass stopper survived the fall — it bounced intact, but on the second impact, of just a few inches, it shattered into a thousand fragments. Nancy had never forgotten that moment.

Now here it was again, that second impact. The *New York Times*, arbiter of what mattered, laid it out in black and white: two official fatalities. An 'incidental' drowning. The pathos of that incidental drowning floored her, and her carefully acquired strength cracked like glass. The tears came.

★ ★ ★

The funeral was well attended, the congregation unusual in its shabbiness, locals outnumbered by vets who showed up in force, along with wives and children. Between the hymns there was an old army song.

Ben's parents, surfacing into grief, tried to connect with Nancy's family but seemed unable to find the right words. They stood, grimly accepting condolences, kissed Joey briefly on the cheek and turned away, resentful of their loss. A tall blond boy trailing behind them stepped forward, smiling.

'Nancy? You probably don't remember me. Jack.'

Moving through the day like a sleepwalker, Nancy acknowledged the greeting mechanically:

'Jack . . . ' She paused. 'Ben's cousin. Of course! You were at our wedding. Thank you for coming today.' She turned. 'And here's Joey, you remember him.'

'Hi,' Jack said, not remembering.

By her side, Joey remained silent.

'How you've grown,' Nancy remarked, for something to say.

'Runs in the family, I guess.'

He wanted to say more, tell her that because of Ben he had always known what he wanted to do with his life: join the navy, and as soon as he

152

was old enough, that's what he would be doing. And, he'd like to add, if Ben had stuck with the navy, he wouldn't be lying in a coffin now; he'd be alive, safe at sea, wearing his white uniform. But even at fourteen he knew enough to know you didn't say that to a widow, so he just offered condolences and backed off.

Daniels from the bank was absent, away on a business trip as he explained, when he wrote to commiserate. There were other absences; the better-off, uneasy with the politics of protest. But the marchers were different: they spoke of the dead man with the warmth of comrades.

'We'd see him scribbling away there in his little notepad. Ben was quite a one for poetry.'

Ben? Nancy wondered if she was hearing right. *Poetry?*

Joey recalled that his father had once recited something that could have been poetry, something about a jumping frog . . . he said all a frog wanted was education, and he could do most anything.

Always a quiet child, Joey had been virtually silent since the news came in. So now his father, too, was dead.

He was three when Nancy carried him on to the big ship and showed him the water glowing with green light in the darkness. Later they told him his mother was dead. He wasn't sure what that meant at the time, but he was ten now and he knew about people dying. A man died and was put into a box and buried and everyone said what a good man he was.

His father is a good man. *Was* a good man.

153

Joey found it hard to imagine him not being there. There was a peculiar, heavy feeling somewhere in his body that he couldn't quite locate, the way it was when he tried to find a place that was itching. His nose ached and his throat hurt.

He moved closer to Nancy. The pew felt hard under him, but that just made the empty space on his other side, where his father should have been, even bigger. It felt lopsided and cold, like having the blanket slide off you in bed. When Ben came home from work he smelled of the truck, oily and strong, and sometimes of the farm stuff he had been shifting, but when he laughed his breath reminded Joey of the green beans and mint that Nancy sometimes put on the supper table, and when he remembered to look in on Joey to say goodnight, poking his head round the curtain of the closet bedroom, something of that minty smell lingered.

When the service was over, they moved on into the church hall and the shabby strangers stood about awkwardly. Nancy went round the room and shook hands with each in turn, and thanked them all for coming.

One or two of them told her about the night Ben died, and now she saw it through their eyes, heard it in their bitter words. Then she asked about this other side of Ben she was hearing about.

'He liked poetry?'

'Sort of. There was one guy, Gary, been an actor, before; sometimes he declaimed stuff while he was picketing. Great voice. Ben liked to listen. One day he and Ben and me, we were going past a house in town and Gary was sounding off as usual, and this woman came out and invited us into her kitchen.

'She said she loved to hear poetic language; she handed out coffee, while Gary sat at the table — it had this real pretty cover, shiny, with fruit and flowers — and he spread his hands out on the table and quoted Shakespeare. She loved that, and gave him a cookie, and then he moved on to Walt Whitman, and his voice got stronger and by the time he got on to 'I sing the body electric' he was pretty loud and the woman stood up and said she had to go out now and opened the door, so we left. Gary couldn't understand why Ben and I were cracking up on the sidewalk.'

Joey could picture them outside the woman's house. His father hadn't laughed much since they lost the house with the electric kitchen, but he could recall the way, early on, Ben would fling his head back, laughing, teeth big in his mouth. Joey would find himself joining in, without knowing why: laughing till tears came to his eyes. His eyes prickled now as he blinked back tears, but not of laughter. He swallowed a couple of times and tugged at Nancy's sleeve. He whispered,

'What's funny about Walt Whitman?'

'Nothing. I'll read you some.'

Like pieces of a mosaic dropping into place, these glimpses and snatches gave Nancy an idea of those weeks in Washington, built up a picture of Ben that caught him at another

155

angle, gave a different view of him.

She heard how the Bonus Army was beaten; the terrible final day. And Joel, who had shared Ben's hut on the Anacostia Flats, recalled the government's hostility and contempt.

'They called us drifters, dope fiends, Bolsheviks. Any Jewish name they figured for a communist. We had coloured vets, guys who served in the 93rd. But black and white sharing, that really bugged those Washington guys, so the word 'degenerate' came up. The rest of us, we probably looked pretty crazy by then, we were the dope fiends I guess.' He shook his head, smiling without humour.

'These are dark days for us all,' Nancy said.

Later, alone, she thought about Ben, who had week by week grown closer to her as the distance between them widened. She reread his letters; those crumpled, grubby pages now seemed lit with hope and the possibility of a new beginning. She had closed herself off for so long — an aid to survival — but now, like a thaw after an ice age, she was melting; feeling and pain returned and she wept for the pity of it, the futility, the sad encampment viciously destroyed; the tired, defiant men.

Earlier, Nancy, like others, had blamed the President for losing control: he had given the orders. At the funeral, close beside her, Joey had listened carefully and held on to certain words: some instructions disregarded, others carried out. He knew who to blame: MacArthur had murdered his father.

156

* ★ ★

It was difficult, this emptiness where Ben Pinkerton had been; Joey kept stumbling into it. He would be setting the table for dinner and notice that Nancy had come up behind him and was quietly removing a plate, knife, fork . . . she could not bring herself to remind him they needed one less of everything now.

There were still days when, returning from school, where some faraway unknown country had come up in class, he would automatically think of Ben: his father had travelled, he knew places. And then would come the kick in the head, remembering how things were now, and he would hurriedly get a drink of milk from the fridge, or splash his face with cold water and scrub it dry before greeting his mother, home from work. All this came as a shock: he and his father had never been close; now to his surprise he felt bereft. He and Nancy could have cried together, they could have rocked and grieved. But two quiet people, they found feelings difficult to express.

'How's my boy?' she would ask, and hug him tightly, noting a grubby smear on his cheeks.

'I cut my finger at school.'

'I'll get you a Band-Aid.'

They got on with things.

★ ★ ★

Nancy had never been particularly moved by Whitman, but in her mind she saw Ben and Joel and the ex-actor in the Washington woman's kitchen, and she had a sudden need to look again at some of the poems. She asked Joey to borrow the *Collected Works* from the library.

Elbows on her mother's kitchen table, this one too covered with brightly coloured oilcloth, she opened the book:

'*I sing the body electric . . .* '

She read on through the poem, thinking how that woman in her kitchen might have reacted to some of the more outspoken phrases. She turned the page and came to a line that stopped her, trapped the breath in her lungs till she gasped for air. Slowly she read on:

'*The swimmer naked in the swimming bath, seen as he swims through the transparent green-shine or lies with his face up and rolls silently to and fro and from the heave of the water . . .* '

Did Ben roll silently to and fro in the green-shine, with his face up, in his last moments? Ben the beautiful swimmer, the incidental drowning.

★ ★ ★

In church the following Sunday the thought for the week seemed to offer a practical note of comfort, a message that reached out to an exhausted, apprehensive people. The preacher's voice drifted across her consciousness as he spoke of the heroism of long-dead people, of eighteenth-century Quakers who had set a benchmark for courage:

'Every age has heroes and heroines willing to face formidable challenges, make sacrifices for the common good and speak truth to power. They deserve our gratitude and support.'

At the end of the service the congregation came out into a grey, cold day but Nancy, burning with anger, was unaware of the chill. *Speak truth to power* . . . The President had betrayed them with his power. Across the country people starved, slept rough, were disallowed their dignity as human beings. Schools closed. The sick were dying untended. The land was full of vagrants, travelling to nowhere. Surely it was time for change?

She had taken a job as office cleaner, and sweeping up at the local Democrat headquarters she came upon leaflets asking for volunteers. She looked at the posters, studied the literature. Next day, after work, she was knocking on doors, handing out leaflets.

Not long afterwards, one of the churchgoing ladies approached Nancy, her face contorted into a grimace of commiseration. Voice modulated into appropriate concern she enquired, 'Nancy my dear. What are your *plans*?'

'I'm campaigning for FDR,' she said.

'Let's hope your hero can deliver the goods,' her father remarked, sounding less than hopeful. 'Remember the old fairy tale warning: be careful what you wish for.'

★   ★   ★

When the voters got the president they wished for, Nancy danced round the kitchen table.

'We should be drinking champagne! A toast to Franklin Delano Roosevelt!'

'Well now, we were never a wine-in-the-icebox family,' Louis said. 'Would you settle for cola?'

★ ★ ★

She read the Inaugural Address aloud to Joey from the newspaper:

'So, first of all, let me assert my firm belief that the only thing we have to fear is fear itself — nameless, unreasoning, unjustified terror which paralyses needed efforts to convert retreat into advance.'

There was more: there was comfort, inspiration, when the President told his penniless people that happiness did not lie in the mere possession of money but in the joy of achievement and moral stimulation of work. 'These dark days will be worth all they cost if they teach us that our true destiny is not to be ministered unto but to minister to ourselves and our fellow men.'

On the radio, later, crackling through the ether, he repeated the words that had given her hope: 'I pledge you, I pledge myself, to a new deal for the American people.'

22

Filled with post-election euphoria, as she kissed Joey goodnight, Nancy said, like someone ending a bedtime story with the promise of happy ever after: 'Things will get better, you'll see. Roosevelt will help the homeless.'

As she turned to the door of the attic where his bed was squeezed between storage boxes and empty suitcases, she added, to herself, 'and help us, too, please God.'

'Amen,' came Joey's voice, from beneath the bed cover. Nancy looked startled. Had she spoken aloud? The boy must have sharp ears.

Joey, in the not-quite-darkness of the attic heard her go down the stairs, move around the room below, each sound conjuring up an action: the soft thud of a closing door, the click of a switch, the muffled sound of the radio, a reassuring, unemphatic voice: Nancy was listening to the President.

Once, there would have been a blur of conversation, husband and wife exchanging comments. Once there would have been a father with peppermint breath looking in to say goodnight and ruffle his head. Crying was not something Joey did, but he felt a familiar, lurching emptiness as though a part of him had been wrenched away, leaving a hollow place too raw to touch.

The resonance of the calm, measured tones from the radio filtered through the floorboards, up the metal legs of the bed and through the pillow into his head. Not the words, but a deep, soft buzzing sound that lulled him towards sleep.

He thought of Nancy as his mother, what else could she be? Waiting for her to collect him from school one day years before, he had caught sight of her at the gates across the playground as she spread her arms to attract his attention. Without thinking he had run towards her and leapt into those open arms, leapt up, flinging his own arms around her neck, squeezing tight. He recalled that one of the other parents, passing, had given him an amused look and he had yelled, over Nancy's shoulder, 'This is my *mom*!'

'Well, sure she is,' the woman had replied with a shrug, passing on.

No 'sure she is' about it. Other kids had mothers they didn't need to think about. Joey had felt Nancy's body, warm against his, and her arms tighten, holding him close, and he knew this was different.

'And you're my boy, Joey,' she had said, laughing, though her voice had sounded wobbly. That moment a pact was formed; a corner turned. That was when he stopped calling her Nancy; she became Mom.

His father had been pleased, but Joey thought that to Ben too it had probably seemed something of a 'sure she is' situation: Mom was what kids called their mother, no big deal. And a new order established itself, a family unit. But still Joey had nightmares, he was in a room with a floor made of matting, running towards a woman in white, collapsed on the floor like a crumpled flower, and then running on the spot, like a character in a cartoon movie, getting nowhere. He would wake to find his hands pressed against his ears to try and cut out the sound of someone screaming.

Through his pillow he heard the soft, comforting drone of the President's voice.

★ ★ ★

Not everyone was happy with the election.

A long time afterwards, when she had learned to hate her hero, Nancy could barely recall her shocked reaction, her outrage when she read the newspaper revelations of Fascist conspiracies, secret enclaves of financiers, the machinations of Wall Street elders to bring down the bleeding-heart President. Assassination plots scribbled on boardroom notepads.

★ ★ ★

With no more election leaflets to deliver, no front porch campaigning, her hours at the local Democrat offices moved on from envelope-filling to taking messages; listening to frantic people, hearing how poverty brought despair. There was nothing to be learned from hard times apart from the acceptance of helplessness. Mostly Nancy talked to women desperate for understanding.

'What about the doctor's bill, shoes for the kids?'

But guilt insinuated, and often it was the men who cracked.

'What does a man do?' Nancy asked her father, 'when he's got no work, and can't buy food or pay the rent?'

One man took a belt to his wife, because she was there; another scraped a few cents together to get a rosier view of the world through the bottom of a bottle; one jumped off a bridge, another off a kitchen chair with a rope around his neck. Others just disappeared.

Hard times.

Nancy was an employee now, working at the office full-time; typing up interviews, writing copy for support leaflets, answering telephones, providing information —

'Nancy, Eleanor's discovered infant malnutrition — '

And it emerged that Nancy had studied dietary health care at college.

'Nancy, the local CCC wants a literacy programme for the men. Who do we know — '

Disingenuous: they knew she was a trained teacher. She began setting up local classes, but the city's political leadership was not happy about FDR's initiatives — 'unadulterated communism! Socialist ruination!'

Nancy brought the news home: 'The mayor's rejected what he calls 'federal handouts'. The city council says public housing will depress property values.'

'There goes the neighbourhood,' Louis commented drily.

'What about the work-relief programme?' Mary asked.

'They don't like it. Of course. But we're battling on.'

She got home late, exhausted, and filled the kitchen with an account of her day as Mary reheated her supper and Louis made coffee. Excitement streamed from her; hope was an infection that she caught and passed to others.

'The President's finding work for men all over the country; they're living free in camps, they get their food and a few dollars. It's a miracle!'

'Finish your supper,' Mary said.

By day the men planted trees, cleaned up a slum, painted walls. At night, they took over schoolrooms, big men at little desks, painstakingly mastering the art of the written word, forcing their fists into a new discipline. These were the men — or men like them — Nancy had seen walking, without aim, without hope, as she watched from the porch while Ben was on his way to Washington.

'They're beginning to remember what it's like to feel human — '

'Your coffee's getting cold,' her father said, patting her shoulder.

Later, as he climbed into bed, Louis said, 'She's like a kid, she's like she was at college — remember how she met that missionary and wanted to go out to a leper colony someplace?'

He wanted to say, remember how she was before she married Pinkerton.

Next morning, before breakfast, she was gone: so much to do, people to see, not enough hours in the day, she called out as she left. No time to sit brooding; they were all treading on shifting ground: chaotic but filled with hope; men learning to read and write producing a newspaper for camp inmates, asking for articles, stories, even poems —

'They ran a headline last week: 'Buddy Can you Spare a Rhyme?' Cute.'

'Did you get any?' Mary asked.

'They poured in. Pretty bad, mostly, but that's beside the point.'

Not all the desperate people were illiterate labourers; some had fallen from high places. Nancy heard stories of big-time bankruptcies, yachts repossessed; an entrepreneur husband abandoned: 'She took her diamonds and the kid, and went to Canada.' The servants and the pool man were long gone. He shrugged, managed a smile. 'I had a chauffeur and two European cars.'

'I had an electric kitchen,' Nancy said.

23

The letter from Nagasaki was in excellent English, exquisitely handwritten, bringing Mary information, news. But it was not from her brother.

At the bottom of the page, after a formal farewell message, was a small, square printed seal. Then a signature.

It lay like an unexploded bomb on the table, carrying destruction within its innocuous exterior. Nancy reached out her hand and touched the pale, granular surface.

'So who is it from?' Mary asked, puzzled.

'It's from Joey's mother,' Nancy said, amazed that she could speak the words. 'Her name is Cho-Cho.'

'But she's dead!' Mary exclaimed. 'She's dead!'

Nancy thought back, to that first day in Nagasaki. The disastrous revelation: the not-really wife, the child. And hidden in the undergrowth of the past Nancy discerned a snake hovering between a man and a woman. Across the years she heard the hissing words offering an insidious solution, and the voice was hers. She stood alone, the guilty one.

'But I thought she was dead!' her mother said again, vehemently. 'Didn't you?'

Nancy cast about for a reply — *The woman on the floor; the frightened child* —

Mary reached for the letter and read it aloud: it brought the news that her brother had died. A peaceful death surrounded by his wife and children —

'Wife!' Louis exclaimed. 'Children?'

'Henry had a Buddhist funeral, traditional Japanese, as he had requested, carried out with full ceremony,' Mary read on. 'Crying is felt to be appropriate at our funerals and sometimes people are hired as professional criers. This was not necessary on this occasion as everyone loved Henry and wept because they missed him. In this part of Japan, in Kyushu there is a custom of placing a stone called a pillow-stone on the fresh earth covering the coffin. I placed a stone on your behalf, his surviving sister.'

There was more: an affectionate description of Henry's life as a successful journalist writing about the land he had adopted as his own. His sister, the letter continued, would of course be aware of how much he had done to try to increase understanding between his two countries at a difficult time. She was enclosing a snapshot —

'What snapshot?' Mary exclaimed. 'There's no snapshot.'

'Look in the envelope,' Louis suggested.

Inside the envelope was a small photograph, a family group: Henry Sharpless, his wife and three small, perfect girls.

'The wife's Japanese,' Mary whispered into the room.

'Henry's wearing Japanese clothes!' Louis said. 'If you ask me, he *looks* Japanese.'

'He looks happy,' Nancy said.

Mary studied the square red seal, the signature. 'Cho-Cho.'

She added, 'Joey must be told.'

Must he? Must he really? Nancy imagined an alternative: she would simply tear up the letter, put it in the incinerator. No further action needed. Joey would continue his life, an American boy in America, happy. There were the nightmares; she was aware of the nightmares when he woke screaming, stammering jumbled words. But they were infrequent now, and she soon soothed him back to sleep, stroking the fair curls that reminded her of Ben.

She too had her nightmares, but hers involved water and mud and drowning; and she would wake gasping for breath.

'Who will tell him?' Mary asked.

From the hall, Joey's voice: 'It's okay. I heard it already.'

Nancy spun round.

He stood in the doorway, holding his schoolbooks, nodding slowly, as though listening to unspoken words, his face expressionless. Then he turned away and went up the stairs.

'The house is too small!' Louis groaned. 'No privacy!'

And Mary said, distractedly, 'Oh, that's too bad, the boy should not have heard it unprepared.'

Nancy was already halfway up the stairs. The house was, indeed, too small for three adults and a growing boy, but what alternative did they have, with her at work all day, and Joey to be cared for after school by Mary and Louis? Her own space was as cramped as a closet, but it was somewhere to gather herself together away from the sandwich-like pressures of her parents and her child. And at least here Joey had a room with a real door, not a curtain.

She knocked and waited. After a few moments she knocked again on the attic door.

'Joey?'

The door opened and he stood, holding on to the handle, a questioning expression on his face, as though answering a call from a visiting tradesman. It had not occurred to her, till now, how much he had grown: at fourteen he was as tall as she was. Waiting, he looked her straight in the eyes.

'Can I come in?

'Why? To tell me more lies?'

He released the handle and stepped back with sullen courtesy to allow her to enter. She went in regularly to clean the room and tidy his things, but now she looked at it differently, with the eyes of a stranger. The storage boxes had been moved into the cellar, and Louis had put up bookshelves, and built a makeshift closet on one wall, between the sloping ceiling and the floor.

Beside the dormer window was an old armchair; in the centre of the room, where Joey could stand upright, a small desk and a chair with curved, slatted back. A shag rug. *The floors in the house with the electric kitchen were softened with shag coverings. That warm smell, like sheep in a field . . .*

On one shelf were a number of small objects: a

cylindrical seashell patterned with purple whorls; the tiny skeleton of a fish with every needle-sharp bone intact; a spray of dried seaweed as delicate as carved jade. She had touched these objects, moved them when dusting, without ever really looking at them. She saw now that they were all surviving evidence of past life: a creature had inhabited the shell; a fish had clothed the skeleton; the seaweed had once bloomed in salt water.

There was one last object, man-made, not growing in nature: a wooden spinning top, its paint so worn with time that it had returned to monochrome simplicity, the surface giving no more than a hint here and there of what had once been brilliant red and yellow.

She reached out and touched the battered toy with her fingertip. Her voice thick with tears she said, 'Oh, Joey, the spinning top, you went back for the top. If only you hadn't gone back, if I hadn't gone after you . . . '

And once again she was stabbed by the ugly, racking pain of guilt, of regret — that old lament: Oh, to turn back the clock. But to when? Which moment?

'That day,' she began, 'when I heard you call out . . . '

She had raced back into the paper house and seen the woman crumpled on the matting floor, Joey crouched next to her, his small hand tugging at the white scarf that was slowly dissolving into crimson. A moment of nightmare. Nancy knew what she was looking at: one of the passengers on the ship had explained the

Japanese tradition of suicide. Head whirling, holding back panic, she scooped up the child and the gleaming wooden toy beside him, and fled.

Later she had rationalised her act: the boy's mother had already agreed that Joey was to go to his father. With the woman dead on the floor, what would be the point of subjecting them all to unanswerable questions? An official inquiry could deny them custody, deprive the boy of his one remaining parent, lock him away in an alien institution. But had she been certain that Joey's mother was dead? She could have looked more closely, tried to get help. What kind of a person was she, to have snatched up the child and run from the house? Overtaken by a sort of madness, she had abandoned her humanity.

That day the gates clanged shut. All ease left her. A Catholic could have turned to confession; Nancy had only her silent prayers, asking forgiveness of her sin. Her sins: there was more than one to acknowledge. Abandoning a young woman to die alone was only part of it.

Joey said, 'But if you were unsure, why did you tell me she was dead? You could have checked, found she had survived; you could have told me then.'

And risked losing him. She recalled the day she became a mother, a lifetime ago, collecting Joey from school and he leapt into her arms, clutching her around the neck, almost strangling her. A passing parent glanced, startled, at the child wrapped so tightly round the fair-haired woman. Joey had called out to her, 'This is my mom!' and the woman nodded, moving on, looking away, taken aback by the vehemence of a rather obvious statement.

But Nancy had held the small body close against her shoulder and said, silently, and with amazement, 'This is my son.'

★ ★ ★

She could have made enquiries, discovered that Joey's mother was alive. Yes, she could have. But would it have been better? Might he, perhaps, have said he wanted to go home, to his real mother? 'Perhaps' is a dangerous word; who knows which way things could have gone.

As it was, Nancy took on the thankless role of survivor. Nancy had permitted him to grieve for a perfect, lost mother, a clean grief from which new shoots could grow.

Now, grimly, he confronted a different version of the past. 'So she just gave me away. She didn't want me — '

'She wanted what was best for you, and for your father.'

Well, that was the truth; a version of the truth, not the whole truth.

And what now? she wondered. Would Joey write to Cho-Cho, tell her he wanted to come 'home'? To his real mother, the one who had suffered the agony of birth, had created a child, a pearl from within her own tormented flesh, Nancy merely an arid simulacrum. Nancy cried out, silently, across the vibrating air and ocean, I

173

did my best! I always did my best for him. I loved the child. She looked at him now, frowning, angry, the close-cut golden pelt, the blue eyes, the tall, skinny boy, and felt her heart turn in her breast like a somersaulting swimmer. He saw the involuntary movement she made and said, 'Are you okay?' And when she shook her head, unable to speak, he reached out and enfolded her in an awkward, unexpected hug.

He said, 'She never wrote to ask how I was, never asked for a picture. She has her life, I have mine. Let it rest. It's all in the past.'

★ ★ ★

Later, when the others were busy in the kitchen, he went downstairs, treading carefully. The letter lay on the table, the snapshot next to it. He picked it up and looked closely at the family group: the thin, pale man, the comfortably plump wife and the three small daughters, all dressed formally in kimonos, hands folded, looking into the camera.

These girls were family; cousins, just as Jack, who dreamed of a life in the navy, was his cousin. Caught in the mirror above the fireplace he saw himself: a younger Jack. But within him lay buried seeds that were part of another family tree.

'It's all in the past,' he had told Nancy. But the past is a movable continent.

★ ★ ★

The old town at Portland's North End connected Burnside and the park blocks. Between there and the Willamette river lay territory new to Joey, a foreign country: the neighbourhood known as Japantown — *Nihon-machi* to its own people. Threading his way through its streets, he found it baffling, with its enigmatic street signs, its posters and placards in exotic characters that looked more like angular drawings than writing. Everything was unfamiliar, odd: the grid of streets that stretched to the waterfront, old shops shaded by narrow canopies, tall windows filled with strange goods; unrecognisable food; drifting from doorways, smells that repelled him because they, too, were unrecognisable. And then, on a corner, a surprisingly grand building with rows of arched windows: the Merchant Hotel, looking out of place, like a beached whale.

As he crossed and turned into narrower streets there were old posters for unfathomable events illustrated by bloated wrestlers, masked fencing couples, lantern parades. The streets were filled with figures moving quietly but purposefully. And they too were 'different', small and dark and dressed with unnatural neatness. Swerving, sidestepping, they overtook him as he wandered: these people had work to do.

He had done his best to be ordinary in a new world: troubling threads trailing from a lost life had been severed one by one. Home. Mother. Language . . . Wrenched away, transplanted, he had behaved correctly, kept his thoughts to himself. He had tried to hold on to fragments, moments, but gradually they faded, dimmed. The American flag was big and bright. Slowly he became part of the new landscape. He played baseball, read the funnies on Sunday; went to the movies, learned the words of popular songs on the Hit Parade, thumping along with Fats, using a shoebox for a keyboard. Early on, when Bing crooned his soft, blurry syllables from the radio speaker Ben would sing along, humming, attempting a scat, following the master, *'Where the blue of the night meets the gold of the day . . . b'b'booo . . . '* Joey had learned to do that, copying his dad. Ben was gone but Bing was still around, still warbling.

There had been moments, *the curve of a neck, a pale kimono*, a puzzled question — 'Your mom was called *what?*' — but for years now the situation had not arisen. His mother's name was Nancy, his father was Ben and once upon a time Ben had been a swimming champ and a sailor but then he died. Serious faces. Sympathy. It must be real tough to lose your dad. Safe territory.

He looked around him: the streets seethed like an anthill and he had no part in it. He was an outsider here, an American.

Part Three

24

When Nancy appeared at the consulate, Cho-Cho's child cradled in her arms, his face smeared with tears, Sharpless was disturbed by her appearance: she looked distracted. Speaking too rapidly, like a bad actress delivering lines, she said she had come to say goodbye. An agreement had been reached with the child's mother and she was taking him to America.

'You're *sure* you understood her correctly?'

He was convinced this was an impossible outcome, but it seemed his niece had no time to tell him anything more — the liner was due to sail.

'And Lieutenant Pinkerton — '

'He had to get back to his ship.'

Sharpless leaned towards the child, who looked ready to dissolve into fresh tears. His embroidered kimono was crumpled, grubby.

Sharpless said gently, *'Sachio?'*

'What are you saying?'

'That's his name — '

'His name's Joey, and I need to buy him some clothes. Right now.'

She was stroking the child's head in a repetitive, soothing gesture, holding him close. Sharpless noted how pale she was, almost grey in the face.

'You realise there are formalities,' he began, but Nancy brushed the words aside: the child would go on board as a visitor. She would deal with the paperwork later.

'Please, uncle. Leave this to me.'

He called a servant to show them the nearest clothing shop. He marvelled at how much his niece had altered in the few days since her arrival: the immaculate American girl with her flawless, smiling face was a scruffy mess, her dress dishevelled, stained.

'I hope your frock isn't spoiled.'

She glanced down and for the first time noticed the crimson splotch on the side of her dress, just below her breast. She frowned.

'How did *that* get there? Could it be a fruit stain?'

But as she turned away to the door Sharpless noticed the boy's kimono sleeve, the edge darkened, still wet, and his perplexity shifted into dread.

★ ★ ★

In the heat, the Nagasaki dirt roads were blanketed with a soft layer of dust that rose in a cloud from beneath the wooden wheels and lay thickly on eyelids, clogging nostrils, setting Sharpless coughing as he breathed it in.

He urged the rickshaw driver to go faster, apologising, observing the proper form: even in these circumstances formality must be maintained. He feared that in any case haste was probably not needed; he was almost certainly too late.

He was tempted to get out and run, but he

knew his legs would carry him no faster than the sweating rickshaw man, though run he did, once they reached the steep approach to the house.

His muscles protested, his shoes pinched, he was gasping for breath by the time he reached the doorway, slid open the *shoji* panel and saw the two women: Cho-Cho crumpled on the floor, Suzuki crouched over her mistress, contemplating the crimson scarf that concealed her throat, the blood that had soaked the pale cloth and ran like a wavering banner down the white of the silk kimono and on to the tatami mat.

He dropped to his knees and peered at the darkly welling wound. Beside him lay the knife, small — the blade no more than four inches long. Sharpless recognised it, *kaiken*, traditionally the knife a dishonoured woman would use to kill herself; small enough to conceal in her sash until wanted.

Beneath the thick white make-up Cho-Cho's skin was invisible, her red-rimmed eyes closed. Was there a flutter of a breath? He spoke rapidly to Suzuki, telling her to go for help, but the maid knew this was not what her mistress would want. She remained kneeling, immobile, until Sharpless shouted a savage instruction and swung his arm, striking her hard. Then she sprang to her feet and ran.

★   ★   ★

The doctor looked very young — recently qualified, Sharpless guessed. The surgical gown

181

hung loose on him, too big for his slight body. When he lifted away the bloody garment concealing the dark, clotted wound in Cho-Cho's throat, his face tightened in a momentary flinch. He gestured to a nurse and Sharpless was ushered hastily out of the emergency room.

In the dim hospital corridor he and Suzuki waited, silent; two fearful people presenting an exterior of composure. Figures came by: staff brisk, in a hurry; patients hobbling, occasionally pausing, touching fingertip to wall for support.

Some time passed before the door opened and the doctor emerged, gown smeared with dark patches.

Sharpless got to his feet. He said, in Japanese: 'May I enquire . . . ?'

'She is no longer in danger.'

Then, in American-accented English, 'I guess you know the girl?'

'I am a family friend. Sharpless, Henry.' He bowed. 'And I am addressing . . . ?'

'Dr Sato.'

A long, steady look. Sharpless was aware that awkward questions lay ahead and moved to block them.

'A most unfortunate accident.'

The doctor appeared to be lost in thought, staring at the floor. He looked at Sharpless, at Suzuki by his side He gave a tilt of the head, eyebrows raised.

'An accident.'

A pause. 'We'll need some details . . . '

Sharpless said, 'If you want to reach me, you can find me at the American consulate.'

182

He sensed the hint of a thaw. 'Right.' A nod of acknowledgement. 'I trained in California. UCLA and Irvine med school.'

Sharpless had been surprised by the doctor's reaction when he saw Cho-Cho's injury. Now he made a guess — bright boy, packed off to America, returning home a westernised professional, finds himself in unknown territory, confronted with the messy savagery of a traditional suicide.

Sharpless bowed and embarked on the usual, ritualised form of thanks, but the doctor cut in.

'You can see her later.' A brief bow and he moved on.

Sharpless and Suzuki, alone again, sat, lapped by sounds of pain, cries, moans, groans; the crisply spoken orders of the staff. For them, now, just the waiting.

Hours passed before they were led to Cho-Cho's bedside. She lay, bandaged, washed clean, clad now in the white of a hospital robe, not bloodstained kimono, her skin grey against the bleached linen.

He stared down at the face, immobile as carved ivory; tried to think himself into her mind.

Sharpless had seen Cho-Cho's father's sword once, unthreatening in its ceremonial scabbard with the inscription 'To die with honour, when one can no longer live with honour.' He had used it, when disgrace was the only alternative; had prepared himself for *seppuku*, found the strength to make the appalling cross-cut of ritual disembowellment, 'spilling his guts', as Sharpless had once heard an American describe it, accurately enough.

For a woman, the *kaiken*, delicate and deadly, was the traditional option. For female suicide, *jigai*, the jugular vein, not the abdomen. He pictured Cho-Cho alone in the room. She would bow to her father's sword in its wrapping of dark silk; feel for a certain spot in the neck, almost nerveless, known to all Japanese. Then place the tip of the knife to that spot, and drive the blade inwards . . .

Sharpless was still trying to work out for himself the course of events. Nancy and Pinkerton had presented Cho-Cho with a terrible dilemma. She must weigh up what she wanted most and what was best for the child. Choose. When he last saw her she had been firm in her wish to keep the child, but something had changed her mind. Nancy had told him one thing: the evidence before him told a different story. Where lay the truth?

In Japanese he knew a word for truth: *makoto*. *Ma* meaning perfect, and *koto*, the situation. But how is the perfect situation arrived at? It can be achieved through discussion, analysis, but sometimes there is no time for anything but action.

Cho-Cho could have thought that to kill herself would create *makoto*, the perfect situation, to save the child and give him a new life. But it seemed too simple a conclusion. He recalled a conversation when they had talked about sacrifice. Her father had sacrificed his own life: ruined, his honour was at stake. Sharpless had said forcefully that he thought that was wrong; her father should have stayed to care for her. And now it seemed that she in turn had decided that to remove herself was the best solution. When had she made that decision? And why?

Sharpless's predecessor, handing over the office, had said to him, 'Don't try and argue with the Japanese. They don't argue, they withdraw from the argument. That doesn't mean they agree with you.'

Argument and counter-argument circled inside his head as he sat waiting for some sign of life in the small, pale face, the fragile body. It occurred to him distantly that both ships would by now have sailed, Pinkerton's on to the next port of call, and the liner carrying away his niece with Cho-Cho's child.

Only later did the question surface in his mind: how could blood have found its way on to the child's kimono, and what exactly had Nancy witnessed in the house on the hill?

25

Cho-Cho became aware of pain. A movement of her head sent the pain twisting through her; throat on fire, mouth parched. The pain filled her. She lay flat, eyes closed, feeling her way through blankness as though stepping into night without lamplight.

Why was there pain? Where was she? And then, her heart leaping — where was *Sachio*? He should be by her side as usual, pressed against her hip, asleep, breathing noisily, mouth half open. She listened and could hear no sound of childish breath.

Sharp as a blow, recollection flooded in. The world collapsed, crushing her. She made one frantic movement, and fell back, crying out his name, but managing no more than a rasping croak that tore her throat.

A hand in hers, a voice murmuring.

And now she opened her eyes: blurred, Suzuki's face hung above her like a waning moon, hushing her gently. She was alive, and the child was gone. A tired sadness enveloped her, a slow understanding that emptiness, bitter longing and regret would be with her for always.

As her throat healed, she found herself able to speak — after a fashion — whispering a few words to Sharpless while he leaned closer, at her bedside. The ship had sailed, of course? He nodded.

186

She lay still; only the tears moved, slipping easily from the corners of her eyes, finding a path down her face, into her mouth, salty.

Whispering, she asked to be left alone.

★ ★ ★

In the weeks after the child was taken, Suzuki knelt by Cho-Cho's futon, watching the pale face, fleshless as a skull, her eyes closed against a world she had been prevented from leaving with honour. She refused to speak to Sharpless; he presented himself regularly at her door and was turned away by Suzuki, who whispered an apology.

As a diplomat and an American he had double the opportunity to experience antagonism, and he dealt with its various manifestations — disdain, contempt, resentment — with equanimity. 'If you can't take the heat, stay out of Japan,' he said to one distressed businessman from Texas. 'Why should they like us? We sent in Perry's black ships, we opened up trade — by force. We bring change, when they prefer tradition. We're too loud, too upfront. For good or ill we will transform this country, and neither we nor they know how it will all work out.'

So he was no stranger to hostility. He understood why Cho-Cho, who had been his friend, was now his enemy: he had saved her life, and he could not be forgiven. For the present, at least Cho-Cho was inert. When she was stronger, strong enough to move about the house, that was when he feared she might harm herself; finish what she had already attempted.

Was it the bird that brought about the change?

The bird, a finch, its dark plumage lit by an orange flash at the breast, dropped out of the sky one late autumn day and hopped about the tiny garden searching for seeds or berries, head cocked, alert. Cho-Cho, at the window, looked out listlessly. The bird hopped closer, almost to the entrance, sharp eyes taking in the motionless figure in the window. For a moment or two bird and girl observed each other. Then, with an upward swoop, the bird was gone.

Next day it was back.

Each day Suzuki placed a bowl of miso soup and a small plate of fish and rice beside Cho-Cho, hoping she might be tempted. Usually she removed the plate, untouched. Today, as the bird came up the path in a seemingly random zigzag that brought it closer to the house, Cho-Cho took a few grains of rice from the plate, slid back the *shoji* and sprinkled the rice on the lintel.

The bird watched her. She watched the bird. Suzuki, through an interior doorway, was observing both. Nobody moved. Finally, the finch approached the rice with little running steps and rapidly pecked up the grains. Then it slowly lowered its head as though making a bow, turned its tail towards its benefactor and deposited a spectacular splash of birdshit on the lintel.

★ ★ ★

From the next room Suzuki heard a curious choking sound and came rapidly through the door to investigate. She saw that Cho-Cho, hand to her throat, was laughing.

She turned to Suzuki.

'You see that bird? I've been feeding him. In the old stories he would have had a voice, he would have spoken to me; the bird would probably have turned out to be a prince or a god. Something special. Noble. And look!' She pointed to the greenish-white splodge, smiling wryly.

'Not so noble!'

She laughed gleefully and the childlike giggle reminded Suzuki that Cho-Cho, the younger of the pair, was not yet twenty. In normal circumstances, the maid reflected, a mess of birdshit hardly merited a celebratory response, but circumstances were far from normal, and to see Cho-Cho's face take on a hint of colour, her mouth curve upwards, was an indication of returning life.

'Perhaps,' Suzuki suggested, 'he is offering an opinion on my rice.' She bowed to the bird. 'I'll do better tomorrow, my lord.'

In the following days the bird became a regular visitor, accepting rice, along with seeds and berries procured by Suzuki. While the finch enjoyed its free meals, Cho-Cho absently nibbled her way through the small plates of food placed beside her.

* * *

189

Then came a day when the finch did not appear. The sky was filled with a pattern of migrating birds heading south for the winter and Cho-Cho stared up at the tight flocks wheeling overhead; wondering for a moment whether one bird might detach itself, skim low to flap a quick goodbye at his regular provider, but the flock flew on and disappeared from view.

Suzuki was watchful, fearing the effect of disappointment, another departure disastrously reawakening pain. For a while Cho-Cho continued to gaze out, across the harbour, to the point where sky met sea.

She said, 'The birds must leave us, in order to survive.'

★ ★ ★

Next day she announced she was ready for something a little more substantial to eat.

She was not grateful to Sharpless for saving her life. To be returned to life was the last thing she had desired. She had reached the rational decision — *makoto* — the perfect situation: having arrived there she should remove herself from the scene. Her 'saviour' had spoiled everything. He was granted a brief meeting for her to express — in the politest terms — her feelings.

'Sharpless-san, you knew my father; you are a man of honour. It must be a sadness to you, that you have deprived me of an honourable action.'

190

Sharpless had indeed saved her life, but he knew that it had been possible only because her dagger had missed the jugular vein by a hair's breadth; blood had gushed, but not fatally.

Now he said, respectfully, 'Perhaps the definition of honour needs to be reconsidered. It is possible that over time words can change their meaning.'

'This is not a Japanese view. Tradition is not weakened by the passing of time.'

There had been time, in the hospital and later, for thinking about tradition, and about her life, and those of girls and women who, like her, had no voice, whose lives were spent as receptacles. The words of others, the actions of others, all were to be accepted by these silent figures taught to listen, to smile and laugh appreciatively (fingertips covering mouth). If they had wishes, desires, those inconvenient thoughts were held within them. A woman who spoke up, who stood out, was ugly to behold, so she would become invisible.

'Tradition remains when everything else has fallen away,' she told Sharpless.

But later, alone, she turned the words over in her mind, daring to examine them, question them. Nagasaki was changing, the word 'modern' no longer an insult. And given the dissatisfaction of a reprieve she contemplated the long life stretching ahead of her.

She needed to earn some money, for food, and to repay the obliging neighbour who had loaned her the white kimono to impress the American fiancée. Blood and rough medical hands had wrecked the gown.

Giving occasional lessons in Western deportment and vocabulary to a few tea-house girls was never going to be the answer. Cho-Cho considered her options: what talents did she have, what skills, that she could use?

From the window she looked down at the harbour; as always, it was busy with the movement of goods and people. The waterfront surged: passengers laden with tin chests, boxes, baskets, bundles, waited to go aboard a ship, bound for a new world where they would make a new — a better — life.

But there were old people left behind in Nagasaki whose children had already built new lives in America, whose grandchildren were now Americans, and in that fast-moving, faraway world there was little time for letters — some were no longer able to read or write Japanese. If letters could be written in English, how much more strongly they would link the old and new worlds. The people left behind, Cho-Cho mused, would feel less excluded: their bright young American families would be able to get news from home — in English!

She would offer herself as a scribe; a traditional occupation.

Perhaps she might occasionally write letters of her own, to a lost child, her Joy: '*My Dear Sachio*,' they would begin, but those letters would remain unposted.

★ ★ ★

Mrs Sinclair at the Methodist mission house was an old friend of Henry Sharpless; she knew the whole story. When Cho-Cho arrived at the mission house and asked to see Mrs Sinclair, she hurried out of her office and impulsively took the girl's hand in both her own.

'My dear!'

She looked at the small, pale young woman and wondered what to say next. To enquire after Cho-Cho's health hardly seemed appropriate. She was saved embarrassment: the visitor, though she spoke in a whisper, took charge with a confidence that surprised the older woman.

'Mrs Sinc-u-lair, I have for some time studied Engrish. I can read and write, and have some acquaintance of life in the West. Some Nagasaki families have been making use of my letter-writing s-u-kills, but I have time to spare. Perhaps it is possible for me to give lessons to the mission girls?'

She felt it was unnecessary to mention that she had earlier given lessons to enterprising tea-house girls; the vocabulary and tone of those classes would hardly be appropriate for the God-fearing pupils at the mission house. When the tea-house workers picked their way slowly through their lessons, between the building blocks of nouns and verbs and adjectives, something unspoken also emerged: a search for ways to express secret wishes, to be heard, to have a voice.

To Mrs Sinclair she offered a different, tempting bait: she explained that because of Pinkerton she had set herself to learn about

Methodism, and the Methodist idea: *let your good deeds shine for all the world* . . . Would they accept her lessons as a good deed? And, in return, paying her a little to help her stay alive might also perhaps be considered a good deed?

And so the next step forward was taken.

★   ★   ★

For a while, Cho-Cho's days were filled with English lessons — basic conversation, reading, writing, geography. She had found a suitably indirect way to insist that Suzuki should leave the silk factory:

'The machinery has already scarred your hands. I fear the skin will grow so rough that you may damage the fabric when you wash clothes; as a favour to me, Suzuki, please allow your fingers to regain their former smoothness.'

Suzuki knew what she was really saying, and Cho-Cho knew that Suzuki knew. The maid's hands slowly healed. Meanwhile Cho-Cho's mission house classes grew increasingly tedious, the girls less keen than the tea-house workers, less eager to improve themselves. She fretted, grew bored.

26

Each day, a cycle rickshaw carried Cho-Cho to the mission house and home at the end of lesson time. One morning, as she stepped into the rickshaw, she gave the man directions that surprised him. He turned in the saddle:

'The waterfront?'

It was not an area frequented by respectable young women. He shrugged and moved off, pedalling comfortably.

As they neared the port she asked him to slow down as she peered left and right, studying the sleazy shopfronts and rundown dwellings, the stalls busy with people bargaining, buying, selling. And, threading their way through the crowd, American sailors from a ship newly docked, coming ashore on leave. Young men, looking curiously alike in their white uniforms, pink faces expressing astonishment at this unknown, alien world. Cho-Cho noted one or two of the sailors pausing at shop doorways, hesitant. Lost.

She tapped the rickshaw man on the shoulder. 'Mission house.'

★ ★ ★

Mrs Sinclair was at her desk going through papers. She looked up and saw the girl waiting outside the door. She beckoned her in.

'Cho-Cho?'

'Mrs Sin-cu-lair, I want to learn to cook American food.'

'Why would you want to do that, my dear?'

'Ah, perhaps I could get a job, with an American family. Perhaps you have a book of recipes that I could borrow?'

It sounded a reasonable reply, and Cho-Cho's expression was guileless, but Mrs Sinclair had a feeling she was being fooled. Still, what harm could come of lending the girl a book of recipes?

★ ★ ★

The red and white cookbook was dauntingly thick: too many pages, too many recipes.

Chapters were arranged alphabetically by main ingredients (Beans, Rice & Grains; Meat) or by course (Appetisers & Snacks; Desserts). Cho-Cho studied the headings doubtfully until she came to 'Cooking Basics': this might be the place to start. There were ingredients, methods and something called 'menu plans' which she could ignore. She was looking for some familiar words, and finally she found them: meat loaf, hash brown potato, apple pie. But would it be like Momma makes?

She looked down the page: two pounds of ground beef, two eggs, one yellow onion, one cup breadcrumbs (or three slices stale bread), brown sugar, ketchup, mustard . . .

She handed Suzuki a list of ingredients with a grimace. 'See what you can find in the market; it won't be easy, but the cooking looks simple enough. It just says mix and bake.'

★ ★ ★

Her first attempts were disastrous: the meat loaf crumbled, the potatoes burned and even the birds rejected the apple pie. She persevered, and soon produced results at least recognisably similar to the distressing examples Pinkerton had brought back from the ship. Now she sent for the marriage broker.

He had grown sleeker and less eager to please since their last meeting. Business was good and he had little need for a scrawny woman of twenty with a scar on her neck.

Cho-Cho greeted him briskly and did her best to conceal her dislike of the man. She had a proposition:

'I plan to open an eating house. Small, simple, in the harbour district. I need a loan.'

'Against what security?'

She gestured to the table: wrapped in scarlet silk, her father's sword.

The broker was a realist. He was aware that the sword, however precious, would not cover the expense of opening even a modest establishment.

'What makes you think you can succeed? We have plenty of such places.'

'Not like mine.' She called to Suzuki, and the maid appeared with a tray spread with small dishes.

Cho-Cho handed her visitor a plate containing a selection of unfamiliar items. Intrigued, he

197

picked up a morsel with chopsticks, and tasted it. His eyes bulged; he rubbed his head, went through an elaborate pantomime of shock, dismay and disgust. He disposed of the mouthful.

'This is filth.'

'Yes!'

She had a memory flash of Pinkerton one morning trying a mouthful of fermented bean paste, spitting it out and asking, incredulously, 'What is this filth?'

'It is *natto*,' she told him. 'Traditional breakfast food.'

'It stinks,' Pinkerton had replied, 'and I never want to taste it again.'

'This is meat loaf. Traditional American food,' she told the marriage broker. 'My customers will be Americans. Homesick sailors.'

The marriage broker considered her words, put a question. Listened. He looked at the dish of food, then at her, with new respect.

'This place you want to open . . . '

* * *

It began as a slot between two buildings, barely larger than a shed; a counter and some stools. Cho-Cho was at the stove, Suzuki serving. Outside, a large board, boldly lettered in English.

Nagasaki American Kitchen
MEAT LOAF HOME STYLE
APPLE PIE LIKE MOMMA MAKES

The first sailors treated it as a joke; they ventured in, expecting some crazy Jap version of real food. Soon they were lining up at the door. The crowd became an embarrassment; Cho-Cho hired a waitress. They moved to bigger premises, brought in tables, expanded the menu. Beer was served.

Cho-Cho was up before dawn, off to buy vegetables at the riverside market, fish on the quayside. She had business cards printed for the Nagasaki American kitchen. Tucked into the obi of every tea-house worker, they earned the girls a small commission from Cho-Cho for each customer they sent her, customers that now included officers.

She was dishing up a New England chowder when she saw him pause in the entrance; the white uniform, the golden hair, cap tucked under his arm. She made a small, involuntary sound, then he came out of the shadowy doorway into the light, a fresh-faced stranger asking if he could make a reservation for later.

'Of course,' she said. 'To avoid disappointment.'

★   ★   ★

After she had engaged, and trained, a cook and a second waitress, Cho-Cho sent a message to Sharpless requesting a meeting.

The consul found himself in the unusual position of being inarticulate, for once incapable of reaching for the emollient bridging phrase, the convenient comment — the usual stuff of

199

diplomatic social intercourse. He knew she was no longer giving lessons to the mission girls — the restaurant kept her too busy — but he hesitated to offer the normal congratulatory noises. Had she forgiven him?

For a while the two remained in silence; Cho-Cho looking down at the matting by her feet; Sharpless allowing himself an occasional glance at her face, remembering the hours he had spent by her side, watching over her, waiting for signs of returning life. She looked well, but there was an intentness in her face that was new.

He coughed nervously. Cho-Cho touched the pale scar at her throat, a gesture that had become a habit. When she spoke, her voice was barely audible.

'Have you news from America?'

'A letter from my sister. She says . . . everyone is well.'

She had said considerably more; Mary had written an intemperate screed, furious with Henry, who had clearly been aware of the disgraceful affair going on in Nagasaki. Was this, she asked, what the government paid him for, to supervise illicit unions between decent American boys, lost and confused in foreign lands, and local women of ill repute? Nancy, she added, had borne up bravely, but her life was ruined.

He had attempted to respond, filled page after page with calmly reasoned explanation, and then with equal calm had torn up the pages. Finally, he decided too much time had passed, and he placed her letter in a drawer and turned the key.

'And have you replied?'

A shake of the head.

'I think you should.'

The words surprised him, and she noticed.

'Sharpless-san, I have lost my child. What will help me to live is to know something of his life; to know that he is growing, is in good health. Is happy. It would help.' A pause. She touched her throat. 'It would help me if you were to write to your sister. Ask for news of.' Another pause. 'The child. Will you do that?'

And so it began, Henry becoming, to his sister's surprise, more of a family man, requesting news of Mary herself, and Louis; enquiring after the well-being of his niece and her child. At appropriate times of the year he requested a snapshot of Joey: 'they grow so fast. I still think of Nancy as a toddler.' To Nancy herself he was incapable of writing: the mystery of the day of her departure; her failure to tell him Cho-Cho was bleeding to death on the floor, though she must have known, all this created a barrier as solid as stone.

★ ★ ★

But for Cho-Cho's sake he wrote regularly to his sister and she wrote back, and in Nagasaki an album was slowly created, formed of tiny black and white snapshots with dates — Joey's first bike — Joey playing the flute in a school concert . . . winning a geography prize . . .

Cho-Cho's relationship with a lost boy, regained, at one remove, on paper.

Mary and Louis discussed the change in

Henry, and agreed that it was probably due to his status as an ageing bachelor far from home and family. His sister softened: poor Henry, of course he missed them. In her next letter she told him she prayed to God to bring him some measure of joy in that strange, unchristian land where he must be lonely.

So when Henry asked Suzuki to be his wife and she agreed, he made no mention of the fact in letters home.

27

Suzuki was hesitant about accepting Henry's proposal. She had adored him for years, in the way she would revere a distant god. For a servant girl to be noticed at all by such a figure seemed beyond expectation. But from the beginning Henry had talked to her as an equal; they understood one another. He had known Cho-Cho's father and he had feared for the future of the orphaned girl. He told Suzuki once that if he could have adopted Cho-Cho when her father died, he would have been a second father to her. With time, Suzuki saw, his feelings had changed. Perhaps before he knew it himself she was aware that Henry was besotted with her mistress.

From the day when he arrived with Pinkerton at the little house overlooking the harbour, through the years that followed, Suzuki watched that devotion grow. But Cho-Cho was always tantalisingly beyond Henry's reach, and Suzuki saw the three of them moving in a sad, circular dance like figures on an Imari vase, linked but held apart: Suzuki loved Henry, who loved Cho-Cho, who loved Pinkerton, and so it would continue.

Suzuki accepted him because she was Japanese and, like Henry himself, a realist: she accepted the possible. And she felt guilt because incomplete though it was, her life would be richer by far than Cho-Cho's.

Suzuki's family, at first mistrustful, met the consul and discovered that he spoke their language fluently, that he was at ease with their culture and — for a foreigner — had a reasonably pleasing appearance: small, pale, black-haired, with sharp cheekbones and narrow eyes. He was considerably older than Suzuki, therefore experienced in the ways of the world; a good thing. He was also, being American, wealthy, while their own poverty was showing ever-sharper teeth. He was made welcome.

'Your daughter will have a traditional wedding,' Cho-Cho reassured Suzuki's parents. 'Sharpless-san would want that.' Faced with this unexpectedly forceful young woman, the parents, to their own surprise, allowed her to take charge of arrangements.

★　★　★

Cho-Cho ticked off items on her list: comb, sandals, sash . . . she recalled that once before, long ago, she had rehearsed these details, but this time the paraphernalia would be real, not the furnishings of a hopeless dream. The bridegroom would provide.

She concentrated on each item: Suzuki's wedding kimono would be of heavy silk, *shiromuku*, the whiteness denoting purity. The white headdress would be placed over a gleaming ceremonial wig. She assembled the little purse, the mirror, the fan and the *kaiken* — there was a momentary faltering when she came to the traditional bridal knife in its silken sheath. She touched her throat, paused. She sensed Suzuki watching her with an anguish that was not wholly concealed.

She wanted to reassure her old servant and friend but troublesome emotions were better left unexpressed. And besides — a fingertip to her throat — she suspected she would be unable to speak the words.

★ ★ ★

The Shinto ceremony moved at the traditional, stately pace with an exchange of rings and nuptial cups. The priest led the service, the bridal couple recited oaths of obedience and faith and at the sanctuary they offered twigs of the sacred Sakaki tree. Henry wore the appropriate kimono, the *haori-hakama* and — unusually for him — looked cheerful. Cho-Cho saw with surprise that his features had acquired a nobility, even if only temporarily.

And she saw, too, that happiness really did lend beauty to the plainest face. Suzuki's eyes shone and her skin glowed in the reflected light of the pearls she wore — her husband's wedding gift.

★ ★ ★

When Suzuki had her first child, a difficult birth that left her weak and exhausted, Henry was apprehensive not only for his wife's welfare, but for Cho-Cho's state of mind: how would she respond to the new arrival? As always, she surprised him, briskly offering help.

'The restaurant is running itself; I don't always have to be there.'

This time it was her turn to care for a fragile woman, coax her to eat, to return to life. Once, her servant had helped her to live; now their roles were reversed.

She knelt beside Suzuki, bowl and spoon in hand. 'Remember the bird? How hungrily he gobbled up your rice?' She rested the spoon gently against Suzuki's lips, 'The way he peck-peck-pecked at the seeds?' A little *natto* in miso soup found its way into Suzuki's mouth. 'And then — shitting all over the doorstep!' Surprised by the bold language, Suzuki opened her mouth, involuntarily took in more soup, joined Cho-Cho in nostalgic laughter. The corner was turned.

The second birth was easier. The third, routine. Cho-Cho became as skilled as Suzuki herself in caring for the infants. As the two women together fed and cleaned the young ones, working with the familiar harmony of a team, Cho-Cho remarked that she was enjoying the advantages of motherhood without the pain of responsibility. 'I shall watch them grow, worry over them as you do, but without the fear that I should have done things differently.' She added, with a note of determination, 'I shall love them.' Silently, she vowed that she would also teach the girls about life and how to deal with it.

★ ★ ★

Nagasaki was burgeoning: silk was in demand and the Mitsubishi steelworks had expanded, was modernising. Western visitors multiplied: businessmen, buyers, importers, exporters, arrived and found their way from dock to town, factory floor to boardroom.

The wives had different needs. With a diplomatic nudge or two from Henry, Cho-Cho was invited to give professional guidance. A successful restaurant owner, she could be accepted socially, her past conveniently forgotten; the world was changing, modern ways were superseding tradition, at least on the surface.

Here was someone these men of the world could trust to escort the ladies from the safety of their hotel, to show them where to acquire the most delicate fabric, the finest lacquer bowl. Someone to show them the local tourist sights — the Glover Garden, for example.

She led them round the curving paths, past the glowing flower beds, then paused at a small statue:

'Mr Glover's wife.'

Whispers among the ladies, expressing astonishment. They stared at the statue, glancing surreptitiously at the living woman who was their guide — Mr Glover had married a Japanese woman! Cho-Cho's expression remained impassive.

'And now we will visit a craftsman who does very fine *cloisonné* work, silver and gold.'

★   ★   ★

207

She thanked Henry for the introduction. 'It was kind of you.'

He shook his head. 'I was simply being devious — in the Western, not the Japanese way.'

She looked puzzled.

'It's a way of altering your perception of me. So that you will perhaps not hate me.'

'I don't hate you, Sharpless-san. You are a part of life's pattern, and I have learned to accept my part in it.'

'I had hoped I was a friend.'

She smiled and offered no contradiction.

It was then that he suggested, diffidently, that she might address him by his Christian name.

She tried it out, cautiously: 'Henn-u-lee.' She frowned. 'Not an easy name to say.' She gave a nod. 'But I will persevere.'

Later, Henry reflected on the law of unintended consequences: if he had not given Cho-Cho the parcel . . . if she had not read the contents . . . but he had and she did and a shift occurred.

She took the neatly wrapped parcel with a bow of thanks.

'Just some journals, and a book you might find of interest,' Henry murmured.

She turned a few pages. 'Ah: the outside world! To take my mind off my empty life?'

She was mocking him, but she accepted the gift, and the next time Henry saw her, the outside world had elbowed its way into her secluded existence.

She greeted him, eager with questions:

'Have you heard of someone called Ichikawa Fusae?'

'Yes.'

'Why have you never told me about her, about what has been happening?'

'My apologies. I didn't realise you were interested in the Women's Suffrage League.'

'I am a woman.' A sad shake of the head. 'Do you know what that means? What it *really* means?'

Henry felt a sense of unease. 'Those women are courageous, but possibly foolhardy.' Unspoken: their actions could prove dangerous — for themselves and for anyone else involved. 'An inexperienced swimmer should approach the ocean with care. Turbulent waves, strong currents — '

She broke in. 'Do you recall that day you brought Pinkerton to the house? You were there to witness the transfer of an object, a commodity from one man to another. Women had no voice, we *have* no voice. Now, I am reading about a woman — about women — who are trying to do something about that.

'I feel shame, that until Suzuki went into the factory I knew nothing about the horrible conditions, the hours they work, the crowded dormitories. Those women are prisoners.

'If they are not workers, they are prisoners in their homes, as they always have been. Do you know why women are not allowed to vote? Because that is the way it has always been.' Her voice was bitter. 'Tradition!'

She picked up a newspaper and held it open like a precious scroll. 'Thank you for sending me this.' She read aloud: ' . . . 'We maltreat and

209

insult our women to a graver extent than any other country on the globe.' At least here's one man who has the courage to speak the truth.'

It was the beginning of Cho-Cho's acquaintance with 'those women', as Henry continued to call the campaigners. When they won the right to attend political meetings, Cho-Cho hovered across the street, outside the lecture hall. The following week she slipped in timidly at the last minute. The next time she was bolder.

Henry, increasingly anxious, noted the change.

'We have a voice!' She was excited. 'Women are being heard!'

★   ★   ★

Usually Henry responded humorously, with the reactions expected of him, grumbling about the rising power of 'those women', but today he was subdued. She noticed immediately.

'What is it? Do you have bad news from America?'

She had been following events since the Wall Street crash, though when Mary sent him gloomy letters he had softened the family situation somewhat.

'Yes.'

'Is it about *Sachio*?'

'No.' He paused. 'Well, in a way . . . No, no, it's not about Joey.' He sounded reassuring, though his expression remained grim. 'It's about Pinkerton.'

He had never been entirely certain how Cho-Cho now felt about Ben Pinkerton. She maintained a coolness, a distance, if his name entered the conversation, restricting herself to questions about the child. But, as he well knew, that was the Japanese way. Now her composure was to be tested.

'He went on a march, with some war veterans — homeless ex-servicemen.'

She waited.

'It was to make a protest. Like your women.'

She waited.

'They gathered in Washington and the President brought in the army to clear them out.' There was no easy way to say this.

'He's dead.'

So total was her lack of reaction that for a moment he thought she had not heard.

Then she asked, 'How? How did he die?'

'He drowned. In the river.'

'But that's *impossible*! He loved to swim, he used to go down to the sea and swim for hours, far out from shore, diving like a dolphin, he would float on his back and wave, his arms gleamed in the sun when he waved — ' She stopped, lips pressed together.

'What happened?'

Henry said, 'The soldiers were driving them off their campsite. I think he was struck on the head by a rifle. He fell into the river . . . '

She seemed to shrink, crumpling into herself. She said, 'Please go now.'

He turned at once to leave. As he reached the door he glanced back and saw her collapse slowly on to the ground, bent over, forehead resting on the floor, and he blundered from the room, recalling the last time he had seen her destroyed. As he left he caught the trace of a sound, a low moaning, a lament of inconsolable sorrow.

★   ★   ★

After Henry had gone she remained in the room without moving. All sensation seemed to have drained from her body and only her mind was alive. How long had she been here, lying, crumpled, breathing the grassy smell of the tatami mat? She became aware that the woven strands had pressed deeply into her cheek. The sun had dipped below the hillside. She sat up, smoothed her hair. She allowed herself very tentatively, as though touching a wounded place, to examine how she felt, and she realised that she was facing her real farewell to Pinkerton. Since she had returned to painful life in the hospital bed she had dwelt often on that last sight of him leaving the house with the American woman; she had begun to nurse the secret fantasy that one day he would reappear, holding Sachio's hand, and that happiness would return.

She knew now that it could never be.

She forced herself to explore the area of pain; to think of him as he was: beautiful, golden, lazy. In the bath, his body contained by the watery tank like some pale creature from the deep, he wallowed, submerging himself, then surfacing, shaking water from the wet-darkened curls. His growing tenderness — with time he learned to undress her more gently, she learned how to

212

respond. Small moments of sweetness — 'Here you go, Mrs Butterfly, surprise for you,' — Portuguese castella cakes from the market, a piece of fine silk, the *cloisonné* bracelet she had not worn since he left her . . . at those moments she had permitted herself to dream, to believe that one day he would return.

Now he had really left her, sinking, choking, lungs filled with green slime, and she too was choking, throat clotted with tears, lungs heaving, and though she knew that one day life would return to her limbs, she would walk and talk quite normally, still she sensed a withering. A part of her had died.

★ ★ ★

Some time later, when she could safely speak his name, she talked to Henry about Pinkerton, and wondered which of them could say they knew him. 'What was he like, really?' And Henry debated what to say: could he tell her Pinkerton was a selfish bastard without a sensitive bone in his body — but what did he know, in fact, about the man who died that night, fished out of the Anacostia river, his body laid on the earth alongside an ex-serviceman shot by a trigger-happy trooper?

Mary had written, 'Nancy is devastated. There's a rumor President Hoover never meant the operation to get out of hand to that extent but who can ever know the truth of these matters?

'You should know, Henry,' his sister wrote, 'I

213

was not happy about Nancy marrying Ben in the first place. What happened in Nagasaki, the child, it was not what I had hoped for my daughter. And this proves I was right to be anxious. Ben seems to have been of help to the men on that sad march, but he did not have to go, he had a family to consider. I do think he was a good father, in his way, but now Nancy is left alone to care for the child. We must all pray for him. God welcomes a repentant sinner.'

So what should he say to Cho-Cho, waiting now?

'What was he really like? Well now, which of us ever knows the full picture? I can say one thing. He was a good father.'

He threw her a quick glance but her face was expressionless. He had no idea what she was thinking.

PART FOUR

28

'Anthropology? Where will that take you? Louis asked. 'Will anthropology give you a foot on the corporation ladder?'

Joey shrugged. 'Probably not. But I don't want to work for a corporation.'

'Young people today, they think college is a game. Jobs don't grow on trees, Joey.'

'Well they do if it's a mulberry tree and you're into silk.'

'Don't get cute with me, kid!'

'Okay. You're asking why anthropology. Well, Margaret Mead said — '

'And don't give me what the smart-asses say. That's how they earn their bucks and their Pulitzers.'

Joey found it difficult to explain to Louis why the study of difference and similarity, social systems, alien cultures and faraway countries held a certain appeal. And in any case that was not the whole of it

'Gramps, anthropology tries to show us what makes us human; the world's full of people killing each other . . . Maybe that would be just a bit more difficult if we didn't think of it as Us and Them all the time. If there could be another word, a word for the whole mix. What we have in common.'

He stopped. Inside his head, there was nuance and complexity. He was aware that what emerged was too simple, naïve.

Long ago, when he was a kid, Nancy had read aloud to him a story about a girl who fell down a rabbit hole and had adventures. But she fell very slowly, so that she could take a look at what she was passing. Anthropology was a bit like that: falling into the past, but slowly, so that you could reach out and pluck things off the shelf of time and study them as you progressed. You immersed yourself in a strange world; you couldn't change what you saw, but you could learn from it.

He shrugged helplessly.

'You know: if you prick us do we not bleed? If you poison us do we not die — '

'Oh, right,' Louis said. 'If we're getting into that, I'll tell you what I think of anthropology: Much Ado About Nothing!'

He punched his grandson affectionately on the shoulder. 'Just kidding.'

From her rocker by the window, engaged on a seemingly endless piece of patchwork, Mary said mildly to Joey. 'I remember, at the beginning, you didn't know what it meant to squeeze a lemon. What a baseball mitt was. What I find fascinating is the way people can change.' She glanced at Joey over her glasses. 'But I'm not an anthropologist.'

Despite the growls and cartoon harrumphing, Louis was enormously proud of the boy, secretly supposing him the brightest kid at Oregon State — even if he *was* studying a load of hooey.

'What I'm thinking about,' he remarked when Joey had left the room, 'is the war. I know the

218

action's a long way off, and there's an ocean between us, but FDR's cosying up to Winston Churchill like a long-lost cousin, which I personally find worrying.'

'Nancy's working for the Democrats and she thinks he's the greatest thing since sliced bread — '

'And *that* may yet turn out to be a flash in the pan. Well I don't trust Roosevelt, the mealy-mouthed bastard, and I certainly don't trust Churchill: it's not enough to have an American mother.'

Mary picked up a new hexagonal patch and slipped a template into position.

'If we're drawn into this war,' she murmured, 'Joey could be drafted.'

'You think I don't know that? You think I want to see our boy brought home in a coffin?'

'Don't worry,' she said. 'Roosevelt's a smart guy.'

'That's what worries me.'

29

Cho-Cho had retained her slenderness. The body once childlike and weightless, later bony and undernourished, now flowed gracefully from nape to ankle, though her skin had lost its milk-white gleam and was shadowed with an ivory pallor. She was in her mid-thirties, but the ironic half-smile, the knowing look and fine lines around the eyes, gave an impression of someone older. Experience is an ageing process.

Today she was engaged in an argument with Henry. They argued frequently and amicably; it was a conversation that had been going on for years, sometimes with fierce disagreement, usually breaking up in shared laughter.

Cho-Cho no longer covered her mouth with her hand when she laughed. As Henry said, 'Those women have ruined your traditional charms.'

'My dear, you are so *nihonjin desu-ne.*' She shifted into Japanese.

'"Traditional" is simply another way of saying 'handed down'. And who does the handing down? The men. Confucianism told us a woman should obey her father as a good daughter, her husband as a good wife, his parents as a good daughter-in-law and her son as a good mother. Why should women be controlled by something so obviously against their interests?' She added, in English, 'Give me one reason!'

He threw up his hands in a comical gesture of self-defence.

Kneeling nearby, Suzuki listened as the other two talked on in their mingled stream of English and Japanese. Never beautiful, with the years Suzuki had acquired a maternal serenity, her face unlined, her small eyes bright. She could understand most of what was said, and she enjoyed the verbal fencing from the sidelines. She provided Henry with the traditional marriage they were both comfortable with: her voice was not often heard, at least when others were present. She smiled indulgently now as her husband accused Cho-Cho of becoming increasingly westernised:

'You'll be cutting your hair next.'

'You men are so unobservant: I cut it months ago — discreetly!'

'And you spend too much time with Americans — '

'I spend time with customers who come to my restaurant.'

'To eat pot-roast and apple pie!' He shook his head. 'They should be trying eel and vinegar rice. You're betraying your culture.'

'Poor lonely *gaijin*, missing their home town; the last thing they need is peculiar foreign food!' She mocked him: 'You're so naïve, *oniichan*! My restaurant is successful *because* I don't serve eel and rice. They regard me as a mixture of an American momma and a geisha too mature to be dangerous. I provide them with stories to take home; I am exotic but safe!'

'But how can you pass your time with these limited people?'

'Because they amuse me. I don't need your seriousness all the time. With you it's all *wabi-sabi*, beauty in the sadness of things, the imperfect . . . ' She shifted into English for the wordplay she had learned from him, and he had learned from the Japanese: 'I like to find the *fun* in profundity.'

She relapsed into Japanese: 'It was once traditional for women to wear leather socks in bed — though I can't remember why, perhaps it was to rub their feet smooth. Or perhaps to punish their husbands. Would you like Suzuki to be traditional with her nocturnal footwear?'

Henry said mildly, 'What you're really doing is proving the truth of the old Japanese view of male and female, that a man is a child in a suit of armour, a woman is a velvet glove over a hand of steel. The gods protect me from steely women!'

Cho-Cho exclaimed in mock-despair, 'Suzuki, how do you put up with him?'

'Because he is the perfect husband.' Suzuki, too, could engage in straight-faced response. 'The Samurai believed a woman should look upon her husband as if he were heaven itself. Who could find fault with heaven?'

She rose to her feet. 'Now, we will eat.'

Cho-Cho shook her head. 'I must go in two minutes: I have a new man in the kitchen — he might poison the customers.'

Suzuki left the room, her plump body lent grace by her dark kimono, appropriate clothing for a married woman.

222

Henry had abandoned the Western uniform of suit and tie: no longer an American official, he had taken to wearing a Japanese robe. He displayed, as Cho-Cho teasingly put it, a chameleon quality. In the street he blended with the locals: a husband, a father.

'Just another Nagasaki resident. What would your sister say!'

She glanced round the room but decided not to provoke Henry today by mockingly noting how traditional it was. This was where he spent quiet hours writing articles to explain the country he loved to the outside world; explanations that became increasingly difficult when the long, draining war with China flared into what the Japanese called incidents and the West condemned as massacres, war crimes, inhuman brutality. That, too, was part of tradition; the iron grip that held them prisoner.

He saw her to the door now and together they looked out at the view. The Sharpless residence was tucked into the hillside not far from the Glover House, visible over treetops.

'Remember, so long ago, when you brought me up here to show me the Glover estate? How silly I was . . . '

'Why silly?'

'For wanting an American garden, for one thing.' She looked out at the green landscape Henry and Suzuki had created; the rocks and moss. 'This is perfect. Youthful wishes can be silly; part of being young, I suppose.'

Unspoken: she had wanted an American garden to go with her American husband, and her American son. She had had them all — for a while.

In the room behind them there was the sound of children's voices; the girls coming to the door to say goodbye to their favourite visitor. Cho-Cho embraced them in turn. She lingered for a moment with the tallest.

'How is my clever Mayu? What are you reading?'

The girl had inherited Henry's fine bones and Suzuki's calm, slow smile.

'The book you brought me, about the girl from the sea.'

'Ah! The Little Mermaid. Well, she made a bad choice, poor girl. We'll talk about that next time.'

30

Shortages were announced almost daily, patriotic sacrifices demanded. Now Cho-Cho was presented with a batch of government leaflets to hand out to her customers, encouraging austerity: '*Luxury is antipatriotic*'.

For someone trying to run a restaurant, this was not an attractive idea.

'They might as well tell me to send the customers home,' she complained to Henry. He shrugged.

'The national love affair with America has gone sour. Germany seems seductively *disciplined*.'

Worse was to come. When Henry called in for his daily coffee, he found Cho-Cho distraught.

'They've banned political meetings. Provocative assemblies, they call them — and of course women's gatherings are provocative, unlawful.'

Henry began to sympathise, but she waved a dismissive hand at him. The law was unjust; so they had decided to ignore it.

'I'm leaving the waitresses to take care of the restaurant this afternoon. I'm going to a meeting.'

★ ★ ★

When the troops arrived at the doors of the lecture hall the women envisaged a confrontation; perhaps some noisy intimidation — enough to discourage a normal female congregation. But the army had more specific instructions: arrest the speaker, drag her out, throw her in a wagon. When the audience protested, the soldiers moved in to break up the meeting by force.

Driven out of the hall like cattle, the women poured into the street. Their cries mingled with the shouts of soldiers who were thrown off balance by this unruly throng — some women in flapping kimonos, others in Western dress displaying arms and legs to an alarming degree. The men bawled abuse at the unnatural creatures, penning them in, the bright colours slowly crushed within the tightening barricade of khaki uniform.

Pinned against the wall, arms flung up to protect her face, Cho-Cho fought fiercely, defending herself, sensing a giddy moment of reunion: she too might be struck by a baton or a truncheon, be thrown into the river. The Urakami flowed past, just the other side of the street. She would sink through the green water, weighed down by her clothes; the swirling river uniting her with Pinkerton.

The crowd surged, there were shrieks; wet blood in the street fed the panic of the mass. Dimly she thought, can a crowd make decisions? Who will take control here?

Then she was knocked aside, fell to the ground and the pullulating organism flowed on. Hours later she stumbled into Henry's house and Suzuki's soft arms. How foolish to imagine she could mingle, one river with another, one

226

soul with another. This time she wept for herself.

When the bruises healed, she got back to work: there were new instructions for the cook.

Political friction and sabre-rattling had segued into untidy conflict; the long, stumbling war with China dragged on, and the Americans tightened sanctions. Cho-Cho adjusted her position: the menu was global now, with a hint of northern Europe, as Henry noted.

'No more apple pie, I see. Well, it makes a change from wasting Kobe beef on hamburger addicts.'

As always, the conversation continued with Henry provoking her and Cho-Cho demolishing his arguments with the affectionate ease of years: parry and thrust, sharp words that never cut too deep, though to a silent listener they could cause unintended pain. Occasionally Suzuki wept. No one witnessed these moments of weakness and she was firm with herself, making sure she displayed no outward signs of sadness. Why should she? She had no cause to be unhappy: Henry loved her as much as any wife could reasonably expect. She had her daughters. At a time when she could have been sharing the harsh and growing poverty of the people, she had servants. She was privileged, protected. It would be ungrateful to indulge in unhappiness; to want more.

Just once did Henry catch her crying, but she found reassuring words: it was, she reminded him, traditional for women to weep. The old expression *tsuyu* meant not only

227

'women's tears' but also 'dew' — a naturally occurring event. Did he believe her? Certainly he wanted to: Suzuki was an essential part of his own happiness; it would be unthinkable for her to be unhappy.

31

As a child Nancy had waited impatiently for the Advent calendar to be placed on the mantel; it was her privilege to lift the covering cards and reveal the picture beneath, each one leading her closer to the final, glowing Nativity. She had been surprised to learn that some children in her class got chocolates and candy on Advent Sundays; Nancy's Methodist family had never been party to such self-indulgence.

In the school Nativity play she usually played an angel, a benign bit-player, except for one thrilling year when she was chosen to play Joseph, with a grey wig and beard. Christmas was important to her and she wanted it to be special for Joey: carol services, the crib glowing with light . . . even in the worst days she had managed an Advent calendar, a small tree and some lights. Presents, however modest, were wrapped in thrillingly shiny paper.

Busy in the kitchen on a chill December day, she had forgotten this was the second Sunday of Advent. She had a number of things on her mind: her mother's failing health; Joey at college, another letter from Nagasaki, with a photograph, about which a decision had to be made. She was living simultaneously in the past and the future, bypassing the present.

This was not her usual way of dealing with an imperfect life: usually she got on with things, that was her style. But just occasionally, as when she studied an envelope bright with foreign stamps, tapping it on the table, putting it away in a drawer, she thought of how things might be different, if . . .

She could see her father by the radio, sitting close, doing his usual thing, harrumphing when he disagreed with the announcer, humming along to the tunes he approved of. When the music stopped in mid-phrase he tapped the veneer radio casing, irritably. 'Darn' thing.'

But the radio was functioning perfectly. A moment later the silence was broken by the announcer's voice — a news bulletin: Japanese planes had bombed Honolulu.

★   ★   ★

Afterwards, when Lois thought about that December Sunday morning, retelling it, reliving it, the scene came up like something out of a movie: a series of dreamy dissolves, houses with curtains drawn, a calm day waiting to unfold, untroubled folk drifting in their dreams. Pearl City jutted out into the harbour parallel to the naval base of Ford Island. Navy ships were tied up to piers on the east and west side of the island, and the south end of the peninsula. The sea placid, the ships, too, seemed to be sleeping, like gulls at rest, like Lois and Jack, deep in the untroubled slumber of the young and blameless.

When Jack Pinkerton married Lois, he decided against sending an invitation to Nancy. He thought it might remind her of another wedding: her own; of another groom, young and bright-faced in white naval uniform. He sent her a letter with a snapshot.

Before marrying Jack, Lois had been a very small cog in the burgeoning movie industry, working in downtown Hollywood and living in the valley. It seemed to her at the time that California was full of Germans, some of them unable to write in English, which struck her as a drawback for people creating scripts. Later she found they were Jews, refugees from Nazi persecution. She was assigned to one of these, a lowly member of the studio chain gang. According to Personnel she was his secretary; she considered herself rather more: she corrected his English before she typed his letters, and learned to live with the smell of garlic sausage emanating almost visibly from his filing cabinet drawer.

Marriage took her away from all that, and sometimes she missed the exotic underpinning to her office surroundings — the men who came and went carrying manuscripts and groceries in string bags, the chessboard and piles of old books; tea with lemon, drunk from tall glasses. Very different from the all-American offices of those they called *goyim*, the clean-cut young men with their Ivy League shirts, fresh from Berkeley and UCLA. Very different from her husband.

With marriage to Jack came life as a naval wife and anxiety about the spreading war in Europe. Jack's father had a cousin Charlie who had fought in World War One and never came back

231

from France. The move to Hawaii reassured her: the naval base with its palm trees and beaches seemed a safe backwater to the main flow of action. Hawaii was a good place for a Californian newly-wed couple.

They were jolted awake when the first explosion rocked the harbour, rattling windows and sending roof tiles crashing to the ground, the dreamy montage savaged by planes diving out of a cloud-filled sky to the roar of engines, the boom of deafening explosions. Then the shock editing:

Planes fall like birds of prey on to the ships. *Cut!* Bombs! *Cut!* Sailors racing to man anti-aircraft guns, *Cut!* Civilians running scared. *Cut!* A ship explodes in flames. Another. And another.

Through the window Jack saw a line of planes approaching in tight formation, moving in and out of the thick cloud hanging low in the sky. Then planes were roaring overhead at treetop level. He glimpsed an emblem painted on the side of one fuselage: a Rising Sun. The Japanese were attacking Pearl Harbor.

Above the sound of shrieking ships' sirens he yelled at Lois.

'Get the hell out of here, *now!*'

Minutes later he was on his way to Ford Island, pulling on his uniform as he ran, and she was in the car, heading for the hills.

The road was choked with cars, women and children fleeing the waterfront. As she swung uphill Lois heard the drone of the planes behind her, the thud of explosions, the quick coughs of gunfire. Women leaned on their horns as though the concerted sound would somehow get the cars ahead to move. Behind Lois, a woman with a child clutched to her breast leapt from her vehicle and began to run, leaving the door hanging open behind her. Over her shoulder, as she passed Lois, she screamed:

'Machine guns! Get off the road!'

Lois felt panic break out like prickly heat over her body; she fought the handle, flung open the door and sprinted for the side of the road as the planes roared louder, the gunfire chasing her.

The pain seared her legs, agony shot up her body. She thought: *I've been hit, Jesus, I've been hit*, expecting to fall, crippled. Then she saw that she was running through pineapple fields, the razor-edged leaves lacerating her legs and thighs, shredding her skin. Blood drenched her cotton dress. She stopped, crouched low between plants and looked up at the sky. The planes passed overhead, their bullets raking the road, piercing the metal of the cars. They banked, turned and headed back towards the harbour.

★   ★   ★

Caught unprepared, the fleet lay helpless as planes dropped their load, swung round and came in for another strike, bombing and strafing the airfield and the vessels lying at anchor. From one — the battleship *Arizona* — a column of dark red smoke rose high into the sky, then there was a blast and a column of fiery black as the powder magazine exploded. Ships canted at alarming angles began to settle in the water as they burned, white-hot steam scalding the men desperately swimming away from the flames.

Jack, aboard a small motorboat, criss-crossed the turbulent water, searching among the burnt and the drowned for men still alive. The frail craft rose and fell, flung violently into the high waves by the force of explosions as Jack tried to keep out of the path of bullets sprayed by the planes, strafing the bay.

Then, quite suddenly, it was over. The Japanese squadron made one last circuit, banked, and flew, glittering, high into the sun above the clouds, leaving the American fleet — five battleships, three destroyers, three cruisers and almost two hundred planes — destroyed. Over two thousand men dead.

And everything was changed. The calendar twisted out of shape; the day lost its anonymity: 7 December became Pearl Harbor.

★ ★ ★

Interrupted by crackling, the announcer stated the facts. Something between fifty to a hundred planes from a Japanese aircraft carrier . . . bombs . . . ships sunk . . . civilians machine-gunned from the air . . .

And after the news bulletin, clutching on to normality, back to the programme: Hoagy Carmichael's 'Stardust' filtering through the speaker.

Louis stood up. 'I'll just tell your mother. She feels left out, up there.'

'Dad?'

He turned back. Nancy gestured towards the radio.

'I guess this is it.'

He looked suddenly tired. 'Oh yes, I guess so.'

★　★　★

Through the day news bulletins interrupted the programmes: we bring you the latest from Pearl Harbor . . . And now back to 'Paradise in Waltz time' . . . heavy damage and loss of life in Hawaii . . . And next, an André Kostelanetz selection . . . three ships sunk including the USS *Arizona* . . . a medley of Southern airs on the banjo . . . When the music faded, normality ceased to exist: *Japan announces she has entered a state of war with Britain and the United States from dawn today . . . President Roosevelt is dictating a message to Congress.*

★　★　★

A vast swathe of smoke hung over the harbour. There was a smell of burning wood and something metallic, stinging. Rescue teams moved charred bodies from water to land, carrying them ashore, laying them carefully in long lines by the side of the bay, to be identified by colleagues or relatives. Lois, frantic, searched for Jack. His boat had been washed ashore, empty.

Years later, when war gave way to peace and the nation went wild with celebrations for the safe return of its boys, Lois waited to welcome Jack home, with the flags and ticker-tape and the bands playing, and remembered that other day, as she ran between the lines of bodies in a hangar, racked with the terror of loss, searching the faces so similar in death, smoke-blackened, drenched. Jack's mother had told her family stories about ill-fated Pinkerton men, one drowning in the liquid mud of a Flanders trench, another sinking to the bottom of the Anacostia river in a Washington riot, and she had prayed, her heart squeezed in dread, that the waters of the blazing harbour had not claimed her man.

And then the shock, the leaping relief as she caught sight of Jack, not among the bodies but walking towards her, and she ran headlong into him and held him so tightly that he laughingly cried out, warning her he had bruises and some burns, as he wiped away her tears.

★　★　★

Monday morning, and Nancy at her desk confronted a pile of letters and paperwork that had overnight become irrelevant. Newspapers carried the unforgettable images of the day: bombers snapped by amateur photographers, ships smashed and burning, columns of smoke, flames. The headlines were a Greek chorus of lamentation: the attack was a violation that left a nation in shock.

Down the corridor she heard raised voices, the ringing of telephones and the sound of hurrying footsteps. A girl from the typing pool called through the door as she passed, 'The President's on the radio!'

This was 8 December 1941 and the President was speaking to the nation to tell them America was at war with Japan. And beneath the sound of his voice, those patrician Roosevelt syllables, Nancy detected another sound, something resembling a train just beginning to move out of a station, getting up speed — a thousand trains, a million; a slowly building cacophony of assembly lines, machines whirring in workshops turning out uniforms, the roar of munitions factories, transports, the movement of men, the packaging of provisions, the grinding of tank tracks, the whir of propellers, the sound of a country preparing for war. The Depression was well and truly over.

32

Nancy had taken to an occasional bourbon — 'I'm not *drinking*,' she told Louis, 'it's medicinal.' A Lucky Strike after work also helped calm her nerves.

In her bureau drawer lay a letter stamped Nagasaki, but America was at war with Japan. There would be no further clandestine correspondence between two mothers. With war, life was put on hold.

As for Joey, he had wiped Cho-Cho, his uncaring, unnatural natural mother from his mind after the first letter arrived. Or so he told Nancy.

In her accustomed chair beneath the reading light she took a sip of bourbon and thought about the page she had just read: a long-dead French aristocrat suggesting that fear does strange things to a man. Sometimes, he said, it gives wings to his heels, sometimes it nails them to the ground. And — she would have underlined the words but for the respect she had for the printed page — there is no other passion which sooner carries away our judgement. Nancy took another sip. Well Pearl Harbor had certainly proved his point.

First came the reality: America was at war. Next the panic, the questions: would cities be blitzed? Would firebombs rain from the skies, shells be launched from the surrounding seas?

Fire drills were practised, gas masks demonstrated, though not distributed, barrage balloons assembled, blackouts proposed, rationing discussed. She had seen the newspaper pictures, the wrecked ships that sat in the foreground of the nation's vision, evidence of an unimaginable vulnerability. Paranoia whispered that the enemy was everywhere.

Nine years earlier, when Nancy's hero was sworn in as President of the United States, in her careful copperplate she wrote out the words of his inaugural address and pinned it to the kitchen wall. Like most people she was unaware at the time that Roosevelt, a great borrower, was paraphrasing Thoreau. She knew now, from the page before her, that Montaigne had said it first: *The thing I fear most is fear.*

★　★　★

The knock came as Nancy was about to carry her mother's breakfast tray up the stairs.

She opened the front door, balancing the tray precariously on her arm. A man in a dark suit, carrying a sheaf of papers, raised his hat.

'Ma'am? I'm looking for someone in the name of Pinkerton.'

'I'm Mrs Pinkerton.'

'Ma'am, we understand you have an alien resident as part of your household.'

Nancy stared at the man in puzzlement. She had no idea what he was talking about. Alien resident? Did he mean a foreign visitor? They had no foreign visitor. She shook her head.

'You must have the wrong house.' Holding the tray, she was closing the door with her knee.

'Ma'am, we have the documentation — '

'Well then, there must be some mistake. This is my parents' home. There's just the two of them, and me and my son.'

'Your son.' His pen hovered. 'Would that be a Joseph Theodore Pinkerton?'

'That's right.'

'Ma'am, our records show that Joseph Pinkerton was born in the town of Nagasaki, Japan, maternal parent Japanese. That makes him a resident alien — '

She stopped him. 'Wait here, please. My mother needs her breakfast.'

She left the door open, and went cautiously up the narrow stairs, taking care not to knock the tray against the wall. Two minutes later she was back in the hall, confronting the dark-suited man with his weasel features, his sharp eyes, his clawlike hands . . . She realised she was demonizing an innocent messenger.

'You were saying?'

He talked on, in a flat, expressionless voice, his words blanked out by the noise invading Nancy's head; a roaring that came like a pain.

She broke in. 'I'm sorry, I didn't quite get that. Could you say it again?'

He seemed to be repeating everything word for word, like a record when the needle jumps, steel skidding on shellac, and this time she held on to the sense of it, the almost incomprehensible fact that because her son had a Japanese maternal parent he was required to register at a

240

neighbourhood civil control station —

'He should have registered already, like the others. West Coast Defense Command notices are up all over town.'

Nancy said, 'Notices? I'm not aware of any notices. And why does he have to register?'

'So that he can be allocated a number, ma'am.'

Once again she was losing the sense of it.

'A number for what?'

'For transportation. When he reports, he'll be registered, numbered and tagged — '

'Tagged?'

'He'll need a shipping label.'

'What is he — a parcel? What d'you mean, shipping label? Where's he supposed to be going?'

'Ma'am, he'll be put on board the bus or train to one of the temporary detention stations . . . ' He paused, adjusting his words. 'To a residential centre, I should say.'

Nancy felt a freezing in her blood; her brain seemed out of reach, she found it impossible to bring appropriate logic to bear on the situation.

She stammered, 'Joey can't go, he has a college field trip coming up.'

The man handed her a flimsy leaflet. 'Not any more, he don't. Here's where he has to go. Like the rest of the Japs.'

He added, 'You could say he's already broken the law, not registering like he should.'

Nancy, puzzled, said, 'So you don't go knocking on everyone's door, to check. How did you know there was a — resident alien here?'

241

'A neighbour gave us the information.'

He looked up and saw her face. 'I'm sorry, ma'am.'

She closed the door and went slowly back into the sitting room, holding the leaflet, carefully, as if it were a dangerous object, which of course she realised it was.

Her father was in his chair at the kitchen table. He had an open atlas before him while he waited for his breakfast, though his eyesight prevented him from doing much more than poring over the pages with a magnifying glass, searching for a crescent-shaped scattering of islands in the Pacific Ocean.

'Nancy? Was that someone at the door?'

She saw how frail he looked. She and her parents had swapped roles in this bitter comedy they were living through: it seemed she was now the guardian and source of reassurance.

She said briskly, 'There's obviously been some administrative mistake. It seems Joey is expected to register as a — ' Pause. 'A resident alien.'

She made no mention of transportation or detention camps. Still, he looked concerned.

'I could make some calls for you, try and find out more.'

'It's okay, dad, I'll talk to Harry in the office; we'll sort it out.'

She tapped the leaflet with her unpainted nails. 'This can't be right.'

In the office she debated how to handle the subject. She had never deliberately concealed Joey's background; it had simply not come up. So now she kept things impersonal; took

242

soundings. They were all good, hard-working Democrats, concerned with liberty and justice, surely this went against all they stood for? Where did this idea come from anyway? Finally she raised it with her boss.

'Harry? This . . . Executive Order — 9066. It can't be legal, surely?'

He was brisk. 'Entirely. What it really means is that anyone considered to constitute a danger must vacate their home — '

'So — what, some kid with maybe a Japanese mother is *dangerous*?'

'After Pearl Harbor anyone with Japanese connections is considered a threat — a possible spy. I was talking to a guy in the San Francisco office yesterday; he's on the board of governors of a Catholic orphanage. The Father who runs the place called up the State Department, got through to some guy in Relocation and told him they have children of Japanese ancestry, some half Japanese, others one-fourth or less. So he says to this Major Bendetsen, sarcastically, 'which children should I send?' And the guy says 'Any that have one drop of Japanese blood in 'em.' I guess this will affect around a hundred thousand people.'

Nancy stared at him. 'Who signed this thing, this order? Who the hell approved this document that's putting innocent people in prison?'

'Well, the President, of course.'

'*Roosevelt*?'

'Strictly between you and me,' he said, 'I hear the White House is panic-stricken, Eleanor's in a rage about the whole thing but they're stuck with

243

it. Security. Safety of the Nation.'

He became aware of her distress. 'Nancy? What is it?'

'My son — ' Her voice had gone dangerously high. She stopped. For the first time she was not at ease here, not safe; a line had been drawn and she was on the wrong side. Even among friends.

'My son has a friend whose mother was Japanese . . . Could this affect the family?'

'I hope not, but I have to tell you it doesn't look good; they're running around like headless chickens in Washington spouting stuff about the enemy within and alien spawn of a fiendish empire.' He shook his head. 'It's fear.'

She went back to her office and closed the door.

Later, she called Joey.

'Can you get home for a few days? Something's come up.'

The line crackled but his voice was clear. 'Ma? Is this about Order 9066?'

'How d'you know about that?'

'Are you kidding? They've been all over the campus, picking up people. They took someone out of the dorm yesterday.'

'Come home, Joey. Right now. We'll go down to the registration place together and clear this up.'

★　★　★

He was home by nightfall, and went straight up to Mary's room. He bent down and hugged her gently, feeling the weightlessness, the twig-like

244

bones beneath her knitted bed-jacket, breathing in the familiar lavender and talc smell of her.

'Joey dear . . . '

'How's my best grandma?'

My only grandma, he added silently. How grateful the Pinkertons must be that they had rejected this alien child right from the start. No chance they might find themselves tarnished by association, now.

After Louis had said goodnight Nancy and Joey stayed up, talking quietly. There were ways of getting round the exclusion order: people who could find a sponsor were allowed to move out of the area, to the east. She knew someone who knew someone —

He reached over and took her hand. 'Have you read the newspapers? The Fifth Column traitors? The Yellow Peril. Walter Lippmann in the *New York Herald Trib* said a million Japs are poised ready to take over the whole Pacific coast.'

'Where is this million-strong Japanese horde?'

'Search me. But apparently I could be one of them.'

'Anyway,' she said dismissively. '*Lippmann*? A man who's warning us sabotage is about to explode *because* there's no sign of it? Please.'

Joey said, gently, 'A couple of department heads at college did some calling around last week, to see if they could fix relocating their students outside the zone. They got some interesting reactions: nothing personal, but the message was, if these people are too dangerous for the West Coast, we don't want them moving in on us.' He shrugged. 'And you want to go

245

down there and tell them your son is different. The problem is he's not actually your son, is he? His mother's a Jap.'

She was crying now, filled with a guilt he would never understand. How could she have failed to see where things were going? She could have quit her job, moved east, out of reach of West Coast panic. And now it was too late; her mother bedridden, her father frail. She was stuck.

'I'll come to the interview with you,' she repeated. 'I can talk tough. They'll listen.'

He grinned. 'You're about as tough as baked custard. I'm a big boy, I'll go alone. Anyway, they'll probably take one look at me and decide somebody's pen slipped.'

She rubbed her cheeks with the back of her hand. 'Exactly. Who ever heard of a blue-eyed, blond enemy alien?'

'Unless you're talking Germans, of course.'

At least he could still make her smile. But they weren't rounding up Germans.

* * *

Next day, trying to get his bearings in this subtly changed world where the ground was shaky underfoot, he went back to the old town, hoping to learn how others were dealing with the situation.

The whole neighbourhood had become a ghost town; shops shuttered and locked, blinds drawn, some with signs in English: 'Evacuation Sale'.

The streets were empty; a few elderly locals hurried past with bowed heads, stepping out of his way. As before, he was a foreigner here, but a word on a piece of paper had locked him into confraternity with these outsiders.

He returned home in a dark mood, long-forgotten images clouding his mind, an echo of distant voices inside his head, words whose meaning he no longer understood. In the mirror an all-American face looked back at him, but it belonged to a stranger.

★   ★   ★

Nancy had a school friend who had married her childhood sweetheart and moved to Wyoming. The two had kept in touch — birthday and Christmas cards, an occasional letter. Hilary had often added a line to her cards: 'Why don't you and your boy come visit?'

Wyoming was outside the exclusion zone. Nancy made a call.

Hilary's voice was bright with pleasure and the usual questions followed: how was Nancy? And her parents? And Joey?

And here the conversation left the tracks as Nancy for the first time gave her old friend the facts about her son. And then. 'There's a loophole. If he can find someone to take him, outside the military area, he'll be allowed to go.' She took a breath: 'Hilary? Will you take him in?'

Afterwards Nancy wondered who was more wretched: she, with dashed hopes, or her old friend who closed the loophole; who explained that if it was up to her, of course . . . but local feeling was so strong the Governor (with re-election in mind) had announced that if any Japs were found wandering free in his territory they'd be hanging from a tree next day.

33

Only the twitchy speed of her movements showed that Nancy was frantic. Most of the time she managed to keep up her usual front of brisk efficiency. Now and then she dropped her guard, imploring Joey one more time to let her come with him to the station. Even now, though he was registered, she held on to the notion that if she could just get to speak to the right people they would realise that he should not be here; they would remove him from the list.

He rubbed his shoulder reassuringly against hers, like a cat, an old gesture from his childhood.

'Thanks, Nancy, but I think I'll stick with my people.' Heavy irony on the last two words.

She noted with a pang that she was Nancy. No longer Mom. Understandable, since the Japanese mother was defining him now.

She packed the bag with quick, efficient movements. They read the instructions together: he was allowed to take only what he could carry 'in his hands', as the form put it.

How else would you carry something? he wondered. On your head, like an Indian porter, or on your back, mountaineer-style? (But of course the instructions were aimed at not-quite-civilised people, weren't they; who could tell how resident aliens might carry things?) And what did a person take with him, when the duration of

249

the trip was uncertain? On that at least the instructions were clear.

Evacuees must carry with them on departure for the Assembly Center, the following property:

a) *Bedding and linens (no mattress) for each member of the family.*
b) *Toilet articles for each member of the family.*
c) *Extra clothing for each member of the family.*
d) *Sufficient knives, forks, spoons, plates, bowls and cups for each member of the family.*
e) *Essential personal effects for each member of the family.*
NO PETS.

Two words to sum up a thousand moments of heartbreak: cats, dogs, canaries, white rabbits ... to be given away or put down before departure.

★   ★   ★

'Okay,' Nancy said. 'Clothes, spare shoes, soap, toothbrush, toothpaste.' She picked out cutlery and found enamel plates — lightweight, unbreakable.

'Books,' he said. 'I guess they'll allow books — unless they think they're in code and confiscate them.' A few weeks later he found one of his textbooks being studied suspiciously, the camp bureaucrat puzzled by mysterious digits — 'What are these here little numbers next to the words?'

'Those are footnotes,' he explained.

He had decided to take some coursework. Nancy approved: 'That way, when you get back to college, you won't have fallen behind.' He doubted that he would be back in college before the course was finished, but he packed the books anyway. Also pens, ink, pencils, notebooks. A photo of Nancy and his father, the picture faded to sepia, the corners crumpled. What else? Nothing fragile, nothing precious — apart from a battered wooden toy, an old spinning top, tucked into a corner of the bag, alongside a pair of socks.

He was about to close the bag when Nancy handed him an envelope, the postage stamps oddly coloured, the ivory paper grainy and rough-textured like some rare old book.

Inside was a photograph of a woman, pale-skinned, black hair cut short and severe. She wore a flowing dark dress, her hands resting in her lap, white as marble. Bleached out in the printing, her features were barely visible, but above the unsmiling mouth Joey saw that her eyes were almond-shaped.

'It's Cho-Cho,' Nancy said. 'It's your mother.'

★ ★ ★

After the arrival of that first letter from Nagasaki, addressed to Mary, there had been furtive family conferences when Joey was out of

251

the house. Mary felt betrayed:

'To conceal his marriage, his family! Henry was not honest with us; we deserved better. And now this.'

Nancy thought the letter should be acknowledged, though it was clear Joey did not wish to revive the past: it seemed that Cho-Cho was indeed dead — to him. Louis felt unqualified to pronounce — this was women's business.

Time passed. Then Nancy wrote back — briefly, ambiguously. Just how should a wicked stepmother pitch a description of a stolen boy's condition? To say he was happy and settled might well seem callous, emphasising Cho-Cho's lack of importance to him. In the end she simply said the boy was fine, and doing well at school. She sent a snap of him at the beach, sunlit and gleaming from the sea, a thinner, younger Ben. She added that he now knew his mother was alive; a shock for the boy, and one he would need time to get used to, but — a tentative suggestion — perhaps Cho-Cho would like to send a photograph for Nancy to pass on to him?

There was no response, and she regretted writing, but much later, a second letter had arrived, containing a photograph, and a brief note: 'I do not want to intrude into your lives. The past was a bad place, not to be revisited. The good that has come out of it is that my Joy — your Joey — is happy.'

★ ★ ★

Joey stared at the photograph now. He felt confused, betrayed. Where was the figure in the kimono he recalled, glancing over her shoulder, hair piled high, the graceful curve of neck and cheek? The woman he had tried to hold on to by covering sheets of paper with scribbled sketches, laborious drawings. Sometimes he had pressed the paper to his face, breathing in deeply, trying to retrieve her elusive fragrance through her image, trying to keep her fresh in his mind; the woman he had walked beside on the seashore, who had run out into the spring rain with him, face tilted up at the sky, laughing . . . This woman was a stranger.

'She looks different,' he said.

'Different from what?'

'From the way I remembered her.'

He replaced the photograph in the envelope and slipped it into his pocket.

He checked the bag one last time and his fingers touched the old spinning top. He pulled it out, balancing the battered sphere in the palm of his hand.

'She gave it to me.'

Nancy, unaware that it was Ben who gave him the toy, that it was Suzuki who bought it, did not contradict his unreliable memory. Only Cho-Cho could have described the true scene.

He closed the bag. 'I'll say goodbye to Gran.'

In the wide bed Mary seemed insubstantial, barely disturbing the blanket.

She peered up at Joey. 'You've grown so tall . . . '

She was plucking fretfully at the patchwork

253

covering, angry with herself for being unable to 'get down there' and harangue the men in charge. This whole internment business was being mismanaged, in her view: why hadn't the Church done something? The Quakers had protested, why had the Methodists not raised objections? She felt mortified. Raising herself from the pillows, she gripped Joey's arms and kissed him fiercely.

'We'll pray for you.' Adding hastily, 'Not that there's anything to worry about, of course.'

He touched her soft, papery cheek and ran down the stairs, swallowing to hold back tears. When Nancy was at work it was Mary who had collected him from school. She would hug him, before he grew too old for such things, her face smooth against his, and step out smartly to keep up with his skipping, jumping pace. Now, the outside world was contained in the view from her bedroom window. Only her mind still moved, restlessly.

'Listen, kid,' Louis said, and then seemed to have no further words available. He cleared his throat, squeezed Joey's shoulder, hugged him, punched his arm, gestures standing in for language that escaped him.

Nancy straightened his jacket and slipped a scarf round his neck.

Joey said, protesting, 'Hey, I'll boil!'

'It might get cooler.'

She held him tightly, her face buried in his jacket, dry-eyed.

'I'll write every day. You write when you can.' She shook her head. 'What am I saying? You'll be home before the mail gets delivered. Once they realise.'

Once they realise what? The sentence was never finished. Once they realise he's not 'really' Japanese?

Walking down the street he felt Nancy watching him from the porch, arms crossed, clutching herself, holding on. At the corner he turned and waved and saw her step back into the house, closing the door quickly behind her.

He hefted Louis's travel bag, shifting it from left to right hand. It was a strong bag, serviceable, but heavy even when empty. Joey could have taken something lighter, but to reject the bag would have hurt Louis's feelings and today was hard enough already. Not for him to twist the knife.

The first time he had presented his papers, the official at the desk checked the details against a list before him.

'Joseph T. Pinkerton, right?' A routine glance up, down to the papers, up again. A double take.

'So . . . Okaaay. Let's check this out . . . '

How many lines had he waited in, since then? How many blurred-ink imprimaturs had been stamped on how many forms, how much checking of documents, instructions and counter-instructions followed . . . how many moments of perplexity?

Here lay confusion: all-American Joe Pinkerton, *but* born in Nagasaki. Son of an Oregon hero, a gold-medal swimmer, *but* maternal parent Japanese — and what was her name

255

again, the mother? What kind of a name was *that*?

Joey grew accustomed to the discomfiture, the mistrust and the hostility engendered by the mismatch of his identity and appearance.

He was aware that he stood out as disconcertingly as if a wolf had been rounded up with the sheep. They were a herd, docile; they were slight, he was big-boned. They were dark, he was fair. Their murmured exchanges lapped around him in a language he had no knowledge of. They glanced up at him, anxious, puzzled. He looked them over with a dispassionate, assessing glance, this tired, huddled, relatively small mass. He had learned the categories: the Issei, who came over early and were never permitted citizenship; the Nisei, the second generation, born and raised American. Citizens. How fragile the word now seemed. And where did he fit into this categorisation?

There was an odd smell in these stark rooms, acrid, almost chemical. This too Joey learned to categorise: he came to recognise it as the smell of the sweat that breaks out on the skin of frightened people.

* * *

Registration had been the first shock, his realisation that here the human element did not exist; documentation ruled. There were no discussions, no nuances. A piece of paper, a signature, a stamp. Sheep and goats. Blessed are the pure in blood for they shall inherit the earth.

The Japanese mother, the birthplace, these were the facts that categorised him. Duly identified, registered and above all documented, Joseph Theodore Pinkerton was set on a path without deviation. All that remained was to pack his bag and report back: a number, a cypher, tagged with a shipping label and dumped in a room to await transportation. Around him, other numbers, registered and tagged, waited in lines — men, women, children; ignorant of what was in store for them, gradually filling a vast hangar which had once been something else — possibly a postal depot or a storehouse, but was now the Portland Civil Control Station.

★ ★ ★

Walking into the control station he experienced his first encounter with the new order; a moment that somehow encapsulated all that was to follow.

As he made his way into the reception area, a guard lounging by the doorway caught his eye and beckoned him over amiably.

'Sir? May I help you?'

Joe held up his bag, tagged and numbered. 'Well now, you tell me . . .'

He watched the guard's face switch expressions with the speed of a kid's flicker-page booklet — from benevolence to astonishment to something approaching rage.

'Okay, buster. Get back in line with the rest.'

He got back in line, looming over the heads of those around him, blue-eyed and six feet tall. No wonder the guard had mistaken him for a person.

★ ★ ★

The Portland Assembly Center — previously the Livestock Exhibition pavilion — had been hastily converted to its new role, that of way station, a halfway house while the detention centre proper was set up elsewhere.

Climbing from coaches and buses the 'evacuees', as they now were, milled about, uncertain where to go next. An elderly couple came towards Joey; then bowed and instinctively sidestepped, murmuring an apology. He wanted to grab them, shake them, spell it out: they didn't need to get out of his way or apologise. He, too, was just a number.

Waiting in yet another line, leafing through a discarded newspaper, Joey paused at the obit page, glancing over a montage of faces: the famous recently deceased. Lives of achievement or notoriety reduced to a block of newsprint. His eyes slid down the names: *Bronislaw Malinowski, born Krakow, Poland 1884 . . . influential British anthropologist and the founder of Functionalism.*

He patted his bag, tracing the pack of books inside, among them his copy of Malinowski's *Argonauts of the Western Pacific*, the pages dog-eared and marked with coffee stains. All that travelling — Papua New Guinea, the Trobriand islands, the Solomon Sea — and then the great man shuffled off his mortal coil in Connecticut, on a stint as Visiting Professor at Yale. We're all connected, Malinowski said. Joey Pinkerton, resident alien, was also American.

A guard tapped him sharply on the arm with his baton: 'Keep up with the line, feller.'

So: not American, not any more, his old identity consumed in the flames of Pearl Harbor, the waves that closed over the sinking ships washing away the last traces. Now, magically transformed, he had been reborn Japanese. The enemy.

He stood for a moment, swept by a sense of unbelonging, out of reach of earth and sky and air around him, like a fish floundering out of water. Silence rang in his ears.

Gradually, as though reaching him from a long way off, a susurration of meaningless words filled the air. He became conscious of grit in his shoe, an itching between his shoulder blades, thirst. He became aware of his surroundings.

In the distance an ugly, apparently derelict building sprawled, bulky against the sunlight. Next to him, a boy's voice:

'I guess that shit-hole has to be it. Home from home.'

Bawled instructions and counter-instructions; shouts, whistles . . . a wall of amplified noise falling on the bewildered crowd. A few boys of Joey's age found themselves taking charge of what was becoming an unmanageable flock. Like a docent on a school outing Joey guided lost children back to their parents, took a pregnant woman's bag, motioned others on ahead of him. Most were dressed with formality, as though

259

bound for a family outing; the women in hats and gloves, the children unnaturally neat. But the faces were anxious, bemused. Old ladies wept quietly, trying to remain invisible.

When they reached the vast barn, it engulfed them, a labyrinth of empty spaces, like an unfinished theatre awaiting set-dressers and cast. Brusquely moved on by armed soldiers, the evacuees trailed through the corridors: elderly men and women, young mothers, grim youths, children, looking about them apprehensively. Part of some predetermined pattern, they waited. A strong smell of animal dung hung in the air.

★　★　★

Flimsy boarding divided the building into cramped temporary 'apartments'. As Joey paused at a doorway a thin, dark boy with a scar on his cheek edged in behind him.

'Jesus. They told us not to bring mattresses, but have you checked out these babies?'

On each iron bedstead an envelope of mattress ticking was filled with prickly hay.

Wordlessly the pair stepped into the cubicle and threw their bags on two of the beds.

'Joey Pinkerton.'

'Satō Ichirō. Since we're all Japs here.'

'So what do I call you — Satō?''

'That's my family name. You call me Ichirō.' He regarded Joey, head cocked. 'There's an old Japanese joke. I'll cut to the punch-line: 'funny, you don't *look* Japanese' . . . '

'My mother,' Joey said. 'I was born in Nagasaki.'

'Holy shit, you're worse off than me. At least I was born in Benton County. You were spawned in the devil's empire.'

'Think they'll shoot me?'

'Only if you run,' he said. 'This is America. Home of the free, remember?'

The scar on his cheek was fresh, the jagged line dark with dried blood. He touched it with a fingertip.

'In case you're wondering; neighbourly gesture of farewell. Something to remember them by.'

'What happened to your parents?'

'They went home on a visit, the annual pilgrimage to the old folks. Planned to be back for *shōgatsu*.' He saw Joey's expression. 'New Year's? They always come back loaded with the full traditional shopping basket and we spend the whole holiday stuffing ourselves with *osechi-ryori* and all that jazz. Why not? It makes the grandparents happy.'

He had been going through his pockets absent-mindedly and now produced a couple of cellophane — wrapped candies. He offered one to Joey, unwrapping the other slowly, following an unspoken trail of thought.

'Well there won't have been many pretty postcards sent this year, not really a time for *nengajō*.'

Joe wanted to ask: what city were they in, Ichirō's parents? How traditional was the family? What was *nengajō*? For the first time he became aware of the extent of his ignorance: the order of

261

names, the celebration of festivals, the food, the customs — all a blank page. There must have been a time, between learning to talk and being carried off to America, when he would have been familiar with these things, would have recognised the New Year dishes, played the traditional games. Now, he stood, stupid as a tourist, lost in a foreign, exotic world.

He unzipped his bag and looked around for shelves, but the walls were bare. The Portland Assembly Center was temporary; till the real camp was ready. But what did temporary mean? A week? A month?

For twenty-four hours they were stunned into shock, paralysis. Then, like a collective mechanism clicking into gear, everything changed. Men drew up duty rosters; everyone got busy: women in the communal laundry, scrubbing, wringing out, hanging up clothes; young men setting up lessons for children, others checking out the kitchens, organising communal latrines. Girls draped stark cubicles with colourful scarves, teams of volunteers washed down walls and floors to try and eradicate the lingering reminder of dung.

Joey offered his services in the clean-up operation and was met by exquisitely polite refusals. Smiling, bowing, one after another they explained they had enough help already . . . so kind, maybe another day, or when they changed shifts perhaps . . .

They didn't trust him.

'Do you blame them?' Ichirō said. 'The way you look? You could be a government spy.'

262

There came a day some ten weeks later when everything shone clean; when disinfected live-stock stalls had been painted in harmonious colours, children placed in improvised school-rooms and a handwritten daily news-sheet produced — even though there was, of course, no news in the usual sense.

The inmates had, by a communal act of will, created a village within a steel cavern.

Next morning came the announcement: the relocation camp was now ready; it was deporta-tion time.

34

When no more bodies could be fitted into the train, when even the corridors were packed solid, the guards opened up a baggage car for the remaining 'passengers'. Joey climbed in with the others and moved up to make room for Ichirō and his bag.

He thought about cattle travelling like this. At the end of the ride the cattle faced slaughter; for this motley freight-load and others like them, there was a blank. Nobody had felt the need to explain what lay ahead, other than to repeat the now familiar word: detention.

*   *   *

Thinking these thoughts was no way to make the best of a bad journey. And to be locked inside a windowless space was no way to travel.

Back braced against the wall, sitting cross-legged on the floor, swaying shoulder to shoulder with his neighbours, Joey breathed in stale air that grew thicker as the hours passed. The others occupied the body of the train, in compartments whose windows had been blacked out, for fear the occupants might signal to hidden enemy agents or draw dangerous information from the passing scenery.

The wheels turned and from the south-western seaboard a hundred thousand people

264

rattled across an unseen landscape in ramshackle rolling stock brought out of retirement, heading for hastily constructed camps in desolate corners of the land. The sound of this particular train's metallic rhythm pounded in Joey's head. Next to him, Ichirō picked up the beat and improvised his own version of 'Chattanooga Choo Choo':

'Pardon me, boy, is this the train for Chattanooga now?
No, no siree, not this train, no how!
This train's for Utah, Wyoming, or somewhere not so near:
Idaho, Nevada. Or could be California out
there, Arizona. Colorado, Arkansas, some
hot dam' camp somewhere!'

Through a crack in the wall tantalising glimpses of landscape flitted past, flashes of blinding white intermittently cut through the darkness. Hours passed. The train clattered on.

★ ★ ★

This was how his father had travelled when he made the journey to Washington, DC with the vets ten years before. But mood can transform an experience: Joey remembered Ben's letters to Nancy, the picture they gave of the men; their buoyant spirits, their hopes on that outward journey, rocked by the train, retelling old army jokes, occasionally enjoying a shared slug of whiskey — an illegal activity under Prohibition — singing old songs. There had been army

265

ditties, but also a song that Joey remembered hearing hobos singing as they tramped past his grandparents' house years before, a song that at the time he thought was funny, with its chorus of sandwiches that grew on trees and streams of lemonade, but which he now saw differently, heartbreakingly, as a bum's picture of a place of plenty. 'The Big Rock Candy Mountain' was just another way of describing a land of dreams, Cockaigne.

The men Ben rode with then were noisy, shaggy, shabbily dressed and confident; en route to confront the government, demand their rights.

Around Joey, barely visible in the boxcar gloom, his fellow passengers swayed with the train. At the assembly Center they had been euphemistic evacuees. Now, bound for the camp, they would be prisoners.They crouched, sat or squatted neatly, elbows tucked close, trying not to embarrass their neighbours with bodily contact. Nobody lolled or sprawled; the older men attempted to protect their clothing from the filthy boxcar floor by placing scraps of paper precisely beneath buttocks, like doilies under cakes. They made no noise, and certainly no one would have thought of consuming alcohol. The mood was quiet, crushed. Not far from Joey an old man wept quietly; shamed, mortified: he had wet his pants. They had committed no crime but they were on their way to prison and they knew that none of them had any rights.

In Joey's pocket, the cream-coloured envelope plastered with stamps had grown grubby. He drew it out now, and squinted inside, at the photograph. Cho-Cho looked grim, admonitory. Half closing his eyes, he attempted to superimpose a younger, softer image on this angular woman. In the dimness he tried to imagine his mother's mouth curving in a smile.

✳ ✳ ✳

The sun from an early morning slant had moved high overhead, later sinking low in the sky. From time to time the train stopped, its engine dying into silence. Peering out, Joey would find they were stranded on a stretch of track in the middle of nowhere, shrivelled bushes casting no shade. Then, with a jerk and a laboured clanking, the train moved on, rocking, wheezing, sighing steam.

This time, when the train came to a halt, instead of silence they heard a clamour of voices, the barking of dogs. They had arrived at Tule Lake.

When they first heard the name, learned to pronounce it correctly: *Tulee* Lake, there had been conjecture. A lake. Would there be trees, the sound of birds, fish beneath the surface? Or would it be an urban lake, an unknown Chicago, set about with modern blocks, noisy with streetcars?

Stiff from the journey, they climbed awkwardly from the baggage car, urged on by soldiers with rifles and bayonets. The rest emerged from the train, blinking in the sunlight. The corridors were awash with fluid and there was a stench of urine; toilets had overflowed, soaking shoes and baggage stacked in the corridors. Mothers held babies clasped in their arms. A group of unaccompanied children, dressed alike, faces blank, small hands linked, moved as one, bunched tightly together. All around, dry flatness encircled them; there was no lake to be seen. Far off, dull green patches indicated some sort of cultivation, but the green was thick with dust. They were in a place of dust; dust baked into a substance as hard as rock beneath their feet, the only landmark a low hill rising in the distance.

No streets. No streetcars, just a line of coaches waiting to suck in unwilling passengers and spew them out a few miles further away, at their desert destination.

★　★　★

Set in a shallow dust-bowl like a scattered house of cards stood row upon row of huts. Raw timber, tar-paper, crudely constructed, flimsy shacks. Joey recalled a long-ago walk with Nancy, looking for wild blackberries. They had come upon a cluster of huts thrown up by desperate and homeless men using whatever they could cull from the waste ground around them. The inmates had called such places Hooverville — a bitter joke at the expense of a president they held responsible for their plight. The huts before him now, geometrically placed in a grimly functional grid, formed the official equivalent of a Hooverville; a government-commissioned shanty town. But there was a fundamental difference: when the homeless had put up their scattered, patched and tattered dwellings they were free to come and go as they wished. Here, stumbling from the coaches, the new arrivals could see the campsite was ringed by barbed wire with watchtowers at the corners. In the watch-towers were guards, with machine guns. The guns were trained on the camp itself, for the enemy lay within.

* * *

No one expected trouble on day one. The buses had disgorged them, shaky and exhausted, the walk to the distant gates was daunting. Children dragged their feet and soldiers called out mechanically, telling them to keep moving, khaki-clad sheepdogs rallying a tired flock.

Mr Takahashi felt more than tired; he felt unwell, and he stumbled, tripping on loose stones.

The day before, with his home clean and tidied, stacking dishes on shelves as though he were simply leaving on a short vacation, he had been approached by a neighbour, who had offered to buy his car.

'I guess you won't be needing it, where you're going.'

The tone was amiable and Mr Takahashi was not offended by the insensitivity. After all, the statement was true. He pondered what the car might be worth; he had looked after it carefully, maintained it in immaculate condition.

His neighbour tapped a wheel thoughtfully

with the toe of his shoe. 'Tell you what: give you a dollar for it.'

For a moment Mr Takahashi thought it was a little joke; the American sense of humour. Then he saw the man was serious. A sourness rose up in his throat, a nausea. He said levelly, 'The car is not for sale.'

'No? Suit yourself. Be a heap of rust before you see it again.'

Long before, when Mrs Takahashi was still alive, the couple would drive out on a Sunday, heading east on the highway, then taking the back roads to a quiet fishing spot for Mr Takahashi. Though neither of them ever spoke of this, the setting was one that brought back their Tokyo childhood. In the distance Mount Hood loomed, its volcanic peak catching the sunlight. Below its slope the woods spread out, and curving below them was the river. Changing colour with the seasons, the scene unrolled before them like a Japanese woodcut.

Now Mr Takahashi locked the door of the house and got into his car. Unhurriedly he followed the old route until he came, not to the fishing spot but to a place where the road ran alongside a high cliff overhanging the river. He got out of the car, released the brake and pushed hard — a small man, he needed all his force to get the vehicle moving. At last it inched forward, gained momentum and sped towards the edge. He watched as it flew on, beyond the rim. It seemed to hover for a moment, as though airborne, then dropped. There was a splash, a gurgling, and the car vanished beneath the dark

270

blue water. He turned and walked back towards the road. He knew there was a filling station not far away. Somehow he would get a ride back to town.

★ ★ ★

Mr Takahashi stumbled on towards the camp gates. His abdomen throbbed, sending flashes of pain to his groin. A young man with a scarred cheek offered a helping arm and he accepted, nodding politely. They walked on in silence, slower than the rest, so that gradually they fell behind, overtaken even by a tiny, white-haired old woman holding a toddler by the hand. One of the soldiers barked an order to 'keep going!' Neither of the men looked up or replied, the younger simply increasing his support so that he was half carrying his companion.

They arrived at the gates and moved on through to the compound where Mr Takahashi disengaged himself and bowed briefly to his helper.

Ichirō bowed in return, carefully handing over the bag he had carried from the station.

'You need a doctor, *senpai*.'

Mr Takahashi wandered away clutching his bag, his free hand pressed unobtrusively to his side. All around him voices filled the air — frightened children crying, parents calling out anxiously, soldiers shouting orders. Bemused by the noise and uncertain where to go, his glasses thick with dust, Mr Takahashi had unknowingly circled back towards the barbed-wire fence and the gate. Startled by a shout, he quickened pace.

From the other side of the compound Joey heard a soldier bellowing, one among many that made up the general pandemonium. When the shouts were repeated, louder and with increasing stridency, he glanced about to locate the source.

More yells. A gunshot. A cry. Two shots in quick succession, a metallic counterpoint to the hubbub. Mr Takahashi staggered and turned. As he collapsed into the mud his face expressed bewilderment.

People came running, shouting accusations. It was a misunderstanding, the soldier yelled, almost tearfully. He thought the prisoner was trying to escape.

'He was heading for the wire, for the gate!'

He had ordered the prisoner to stop. The man carried on walking towards the fence.

'He shoulda stopped! I hollered loud enough!'

He stared around at the now silent crowd.

'He coulda been trying to escape!'

A voice from the crowd: 'He was sick! He barely made it from the station.'

Sweating and scared, the soldier called for backup: these people had landed him in trouble.

He was reprimanded. A senior officer pointed out that the men should remember not all prisoners understood English. ('Well they friggin' should,' one guard muttered. 'Bin here long enough.')

Mr Takahashi was carried to the hospital block. His registration details were noted; a number had become a statistic: the first camp 'incident'.

35

Joey surveyed the barracks: absurdly insubstantial, set in straight lines like children's building-block dwellings. No big bad wolf would have a problem here: a huff and a puff would blow them all down without difficulty.

The huts were pitifully empty, all home comforts left behind. Theoretically, significant household goods — iceboxes, washing machines, valued furniture — were accepted for storage at the assembly centers 'if crated and plainly marked with the name and address of the owner'. Much later Joey caught up with the reality: pianos, family heirlooms, lamps, crystal glasses, all carefully packed, crated and marked — and never seen again.

Thin sheets of plywood divided each flimsy structure into half a dozen 'apartments' for four, six, eight or ten occupants, defined by the number of beds they could hold. Many of the plywood walls extended only part of the way to the ceiling, lit by a single, bare light bulb hanging above the rooms.

A couple in front of Joey paused, hugging their possessions, to peer aghast through one of the doorways.

The young wife whispered a word or two, turning to her husband, appalled. Pressing fingertips to her lips in distress, she lifted a hand in a nervous movement to smooth her hair.

Joey caught the gesture, the curve of her cheek, and something fluttered at the edge of his mental vision: a woman, her head half turned, her rounded cheek, the collar of her kimono falling away from the nape of her neck, hair piled high. Fugitive, she was gone before he could study her. In his pocket a photograph of the same woman in a dark frock, gazing directly at the camera, hands firmly in her lap.

★ ★ ★

A brief tour of inspection told Joey that one Tule Lake hut was much like another; the difference lay in the occupants. When Malinowski stepped ashore on his first Trobriand island and walked up the beach, he may not have been thinking of where he would sleep that night, but soon enough the decision would need to be made. Joey had assumed the great man occupied a wood and thatch hut, one of the village structures that encircled the yam store, the spiritual centre of the community. Until he saw a photograph of Malinowski sitting outside a tent, and readjusted his mental picture: of course the professional observer needed a tent set apart; it provided him with privacy and a chance to write up his day's work. Joey, surrounded by strangers as foreign to him as the islanders to the anthropologist, possessed no tent; he would have no privacy here, in this 'village' of shoddy boxes.

The huts were built of cheap raw pine. As the wood dried, the planks had cracked and warped, pulling free of nails, the wood shrinking so that the dark knots contracted. When Joey touched one, the neat circle dropped out, leaving a hole.

Behind him a voice: 'This could be a Peeping Tom paradise.'

Ichirō had decided Joey would make a congenial room-mate. He plucked two strangers from the crowd and manoeuvred them through the door: Kazuo. Taro. Now room-mates.

One by one, huts were filled. No squabbling, no pushing; tradition dictated that young deferred to old. Larger families took the bigger rooms, six or eight squeezed into a cramped living space, possessions piled against walls or stored under narrow army cots. No running water. In each room a pot bellied, wood-burning stove stood centre floor, steel stovepipe piercing the roof. No one was deceived into thinking this was a temporary holding place: a shoddy box without curtains, rugs or furniture was now home.

On the first day Joey carried his tin plate to the mess hall and lined up with the rest at the counter. An elderly couple ahead of him stared with dismay at grey American meat and potatoes. They moved on, to the next dish.

'What is this?'

'Spam sushi.'

'Ah!'

'It's a Hawaiian specialty.'

'Ah!'

They examined a dish of overcooked and pallid vegetables. Moved on.

They accepted a spoonful of rice and found somewhere to sit. Tasted. Exchanged glances.

'Undercooked,' she whispered. 'Burnt,' he said. They nibbled the bread.

The young ones in the line were equally unhappy. 'What happened to the burgers?'

'The hot dogs?'

The mess hall guards watched, baffled: what was the problem with these people? Some of the best Japanese cooks in Portland had volunteered for the kitchen. What more did they want?

The army delivered B-rations, cans by the crateload, blocks of cured meat, sacks of beans, rice, flour, sugar. The internees lined up. The garbage bins overflowed.

★ ★ ★

Waiting in line became a part of daily life. Joey fell into line for the mess hall, the post room, the wash house and the toilet.

Stepping out of the hut door after lights out, heading for the latrine block, he was picked up by a blinding beam: the searchlight from one of the watchtowers. It followed him to the latrines, and back to his hut, like a stage spotlight following the star. Without doors, or division stalls, there could be no privacy beyond the basic male and female separation.

Dear Nancy, he began — a letter that, like many others, remained in his head, unwritten — *I'm in limbo, surrounded by people I wouldn't spend time with and whose state of mind I can't understand, I hate the way they look — I mean the way they look at the guards: their smiling, bowing eagerness to be agreeable. Why should anyone be agreeable here? This is a place of wickedness and we should bang our tin plates on the table, rattle our cutlery, hurl rocks. I'm surprised they allow us knives to cut up our food, dangerous enemy aliens that we are. I'm thinking: I should organise a protest march, but who would take part? To the guards I'm one of the enemy shiftily disguised to look like an American. To the inmates I'm a puzzle, probably a spy . . .*

Writing letters in his head helped, to a point. Real letters were more difficult. Long ago, Joey had read and reread his father's letters from Washington, those scraps scribbled in odd moments from the vets' encampment on the bank of the Anacostia. The determined cheerfulness and circumscribed subject matter had rung false to him. But now he understood and saw those letters differently, he could decode them, now that he found himself faced with writing home.

He skimmed over everyday matters: the weather, 'changeable'; the way people were settling in, 'surprisingly well'; the food, 'home-cooking it ain't'. None of this bore much resemblance to the truth. The weather was enervating, the food disgusting, the old people dazed and helpless, the young angry. He made no mention of the sirens that blasted them awake in the morning; of quiet, hopeless weeping, of snores or squabbles from the adjoining rooms.

277

Nothing about sickness or death, nor of the ever-watchful eye of the searchlight. He saw that there was a convention to the writing of letters home: you did not moan on the page and you tried to find ways to cheer up the reader. When Nancy's letters arrived, strewn with little jokes, drawings, and a line or two from a favourite poem, he became aware that she too was obeying the rules. 'Well, we had the rose festival, as usual . . . ' She described the patriotic floral banners carried through the streets. 'But no parade of automobiles smothered in blooms this year.' She did not mention the shortage of gas, so the letter reached him uncensored.

Others were less adept at navigating the rules: sometimes letters were delivered with lines blacked out, or scissored from the page. Parcels were searched insensitively.

Ahead of Joe, collecting her mail, a woman asked, politely, 'Why have you slashed this garment please?'

'Checking for contraband, smuggled items.'

'What can be smuggled in the hem of a skirt?'

'Who's to know? That's the point, lady.'

One day Mrs Yamada, the young wife from the next room asked Joey, diffidently, 'For what reason are you here?'

'My mother comes from Nagasaki.' *Comes, not came: she's still there. Isn't she?*

Mrs Yamada studies him closely, trying to find some visible confirmation of his words.

'Her name is Cho-Cho.'

'Ah. A beautiful name. How does she write it?'

278

How does she write it? The question is incomprehensible.

'I'm sorry . . . '

She smiles again. 'There are different ways of writing names. The characters — ' She sees his confusion and moves on, tactfully.

'So. Beautiful name, symbolic of transformation. Caterpillar, cocoon, butterfly. There are many stories about butterflies. Mostly sad.'

He recalls his childhood name, the word his mother sometimes used when she called to him. He speaks it aloud — '*Kanashimi*' — and Mrs Yamada repeats the word and nods, smiling: 'Ah. It means 'sorrow'. Also 'trouble'.'

He had been well named, then.

Later, she confides that her marriage to Mr Yamada had taken place two days before they had to leave their home for internment.

'This is our honeymoon.'

★ ★ ★

Ichirō became exasperated by Joey's refusal to join in, be part of the group.

'Lighten up, man, or you'll go crazy in here. You laugh or you lose it.'

He helped set up a loudspeaker system in the canteen. Someone magicked in a jukebox. The young crowded in, clustered, relaxing to the familiar beat: Glenn Miller, Benny Goodman, Harry James and his new singer, Frankie Sinatra.

But Joey obstinately remained outside the stream of camp life. Stranded in an interior exile he used observation as a tool: for him this was

279

not imprisonment, it was extreme fieldwork. Malinowski urged the study of primitive institutions as living, functioning realities; he had looked at sea-washed shores, yam gardens and complex kinship laws; here the exotic was set in a mundane bleakness. Inside the bare huts Joey noted colourful posters and hand-painted pictures being pinned to walls.

A truck pulled in at the gate loaded with scrap timber which vanished before nightfall. In the next few days, glancing through windows as he passed, he saw the rough planks reinvented as bookshelves, dressers, frames to be draped with cloth as room dividers. Curtains were soon improvised to prevent guards or curious outsiders like Joey from looking in.

From the sidelines he saw how a social order was established — committees, hierarchies. The helpers and the helped. Where there were children, there was a schoolroom and teachers, albeit without desks or chairs. Where there were sickbeds, nurses. Project farm workers needed? Four hundred volunteered. Maintenance men? Another four hundred. Construction workers, garbage disposers, janitors, firemen, transport drivers. Round the barracks optimistic women planted shrubs, hedges, and flower beds to soften the stark environment. Old men slowly created a Japanese garden in a shadowy corner, carrying rocks, gravel, a stunted tree, watering obsessively to encourage moss.

Fifteen thousand people, bobbing rudderless on a sea of anxiety and fear determined to build a viable social structure by recreating within the confines of the barbed-wire fences a simulacrum of a normal world.

* * *

As the others organised their days, improved their surroundings, watered flowers, grew herbs Joey found himself maddened by their docility, their acceptance of injustice, the way they bowed and smiled; the way they listened, dark eyes intent behind their heavy glasses. He was not one of them, not part of this keep busy, keep despair at bay movement. Perversely, he was irritated by their skill and speed and ingenuity; he did not accept the nothing-to-be-done-about-it fatalism of *Shikata ga na* — one of the few phrases he had learned to translate.

But inside the cramped, comfortless hut, barriers slowly dissolved. Kazuo was training to be an accountant and had been preparing for an exam when the Defense Command Order was pinned to the wall in his office; Taro's family had arranged for him to marry a rich girl in Tokyo, when Pearl Harbor changed their plans; now parents and younger siblings occupied a hut further down the row.

'They're not happy; they wanted me to squeeze in there with them, where they could keep an eye on me.'

Kazuo punched the air. 'Man, this is your break for independence! Freedom!'

Combing his hair in the hut mirror, Ichirō paused to admire his reflection: an all-American dude, cool and sardonic — perfect. Ruefully he

281

confessed his love of things American: the language, music, clothes, movies and, closest to his heart, the classic comics — 'Batman! Superman! Captain America! I love those guys. I was planning to suggest a Japanese superhero for Marvel. Not any more, I guess.'

Conversations as closely harmonised as a barbershop quartet swung the four through personal biography, thwarted aspirations and shared anxieties. Gradually reticence slipped away and Joey could speak of his mother without embarrassment, could allow himself to wonder aloud what might be happening in Nagasaki: the town had docks and factories, inviting bombs. At night, after lights out, the murmured voices hung in the air, helping him into sleep.

Though even here he had spasms of uncertainty, wondering if the others, when he was absent, shifted into a different key, to a place where he could not follow them.

Deracinated, he felt at home nowhere — and certainly not in a tar-paper hut in a dust bowl. Most evenings he lay on the narrow bed, reading, tilting the book to catch the weak light of the overhead bulb, dwelling on exchange systems, solicitary gifts, wave-pattern navigation, magic necklaces, the sexual mores of remote peoples; the role of a father. It was difficult for tribal reasons for a father to give a gift to his son; what he passed on were intangibles: magic and dance. Assets that no one could take away. What would Ben have passed on to him, Joey pondered, had he survived? What precious, intangible paternal gifts would he now be cherishing?

What would those ethnographers have made of this community, this closed society? Almost certainly they would have integrated, tried to learn the language, investigated ceremonials and social customs. Joey could not do the same — or rather, he chose not to. He gazed into the darkness that lay behind his eyelids, and absented himself. The people he observed were no more than figures in a landscape. He himself, sealed in his bell jar, could not have been heard even had he called for help. And again that emptiness loomed, a chill place where warmth and comfort should have been. A shoulder to cry on, though Joey never cried.

He spent daylight hours in the open air, pacing the camp perimeter, gazing out over the flat land to the turtle-shaped hump of hill on the horizon. He was edgily aware of the watchtower looming above the barbed wire, the machine gun swinging lazily as the guard moved — but there was little personal risk that he'd get shot: blond haired, in his open-neck shirt he could have been an off-duty guard. Between pacing he made drawings: birds in flight or feeding; insects creating supply routes . . . When some of the women constructed a chicken-run in the compound, he sketched the strutting fowls, colouring his drawings with paint from the camp schoolroom.

Ichirō studied Joey's rough drawing of an aggressive rooster, nodding approvingly: 'Hey man, you're an artist.'

'No. I lack originality.'

'That's Yankee thinking. The old Japanese artists were never expected to be original; they'd have got some funny looks if they tried originality. Follow the masters, was the rule. That's why I'd be good at the superheroes. Keep faith with the masters!'

★ ★ ★

'You need to come out of your shell,' Taro said as they lined up for a shower. 'This not talking to people, it's no help.'

'I'm not *asking* for help, I just want to be left alone.'

'There's a dance tonight,' Ichirō called from the open concrete shower stall. 'You should come.'

'I don't think so.'

'You'll be sorry.' He towelled himself dry and slipped on his shirt. 'You wouldn't want to miss the Café International Cabaret, featuring . . . ' He reached into a pocket, read aloud from a flimsy leaflet, 'gaily attired Tri-State girls'. Who could ask for anything more? *Tanoshimi yo!* Let's party!'

Taro called over: 'Ever dated a Japanese girl, Joey?'

'Never met one.'

Kazuo said thoughtfully, 'I always meant to cross that fence, the word was, American girls are easy — '

'Easy like a porcupine!' Ichirō laughed ruefully.

' — but I never dated an American girl. I never knew how to get through to them. I guess I just don't understand them.'

Joey said. 'It's not easy.'

Girls were a foreign country with their own customs and prohibitions. There were girls in that now remote outside world who gave signals Joey thought he understood, that encouraged border-crossing and exploration. Then, at a certain point, they threw up barriers, became as protective as aboriginal natives fending off unwelcome visitors to sacred sites.

American girls, blondes with June Allyson hairbands or Betty Grable sweaters, college classmates from homes no different from his own, were tricky enough. These Nisei, born in the USA, inhabited a terra incognita criss-crossed with cultural fault lines that could crack open beneath his feet. The old people believed in the old ways, but what of the young females? What did the books say about that? Check the footnotes, look in the index for culture, society and human behaviour. See under: Virgins.

★   ★   ★

By the time Joey arrived at the dance, Woody Ichihashi's Downbeats were well into their repertoire of Glenn Miller and Woody Herman. The dance floor was crowded, the music soared, coloured lights hung from the ceiling. As Woody put it: with the Downbeats on board, the mood was upbeat.

Joey wove through the crowd, keeping away

285

from the dancers. Two circuits of the room confirmed what he had suspected: this place was not for him. Points of light glittered off shiny black hair and spectacles; mouths wide in laughter revealed teeth so even and so white his own seemed dull as old tombstones. He was caught in a crossfire of voices, none individually loud, built into a bombardment that almost drowned out the music.

A plump, jolly girl beckoned to him from behind a white-clothed trestle table.

'Hi, welcome, *irrasshaimase*! I'm Amy.'

He nodded. Offered a half-hearted response.

'Joey.'

She waved at the table.

'So, Joey, help yourself: lemonade, cola — we even have ocean cocktail — *sort of*. I used tomato water, soy sauce and a drop of rice vinegar. It's okay, maybe needs more salt.'

He looked doubtfully at the jug of liquid. 'What's that floating on top?'

'Seaweed. Dehydrated. Not as good as fresh, obviously, but it's not bad.'

'Thanks.' He took a glass of lemonade.

'Where you from, Joey?'

'Portland.'

'My folks are from Washington county.'

'Ah.'

He moved off, skirting the dance floor, aware of her disappointment, feeling bad but not so bad that he was prepared to extend the conversation. One slow circuit of the room and the lemonade was finished. He placed the glass carefully on a side table and headed for the door.

'You don't like the music.'

She wore a pale green dress printed with red flowers and in her hair a barrette on to which she had threaded an artificial crimson flower. Small, delicately built, she looked closely at Joey, her face tilted upwards.

'My name's Lily.'

'Joey.'

'Hi. So you don't like the band.'

'No, I mean yes. I like the music . . . Actually, I can't really hear it. Too much noise, I guess.'

'And you don't like the people.'

'Why do you say that?'

'I can tell.'

He shrugged. 'I only got here a few minutes ago; that's pretty quick to draw conclusions.'

'Not really. You walk around the camp, always alone. You don't come to the social evenings in the canteen.'

To be made conscious that he had been watched gave Joey a sense of wariness. In the future he would no longer be able to lose himself in solitude; she had taken away his greatest freedom: the ability to act unselfconsciously, and he felt a spurt of anger.

'I certainly don't like the idea of being watched — more than we already are, here.'

'But *you* watch everyone. All the time. That's okay?'

Suddenly he was part of someone else's field trip.

'Leave me out of this, okay? Get yourself another hobby.'

He stepped out into the warm night. Glancing

back just before the door clicked shut he saw her face, a flinching whiteness, a recoil as though she had been slapped.

He should go straight back and apologise; he had been needlessly rude. He should go in and say sorry; she was standing right by the door. But as he stood debating with himself, a couple moved past him, murmuring polite phrases, blocking the doorway. A boy was approaching the girl in the green dress; he touched her arm and led her on to the dance floor. The door closed.

Backing away, Joey came in line with the window: the bright room was framed in the darkness like a movie screen — the naked light bulbs, touchingly transformed into glowing orbs with cheap coloured paper; the packed dance floor, bodies moving to a jumping beat. He picked out the girl in the red and green dress, the flower in her hair, smiling at her partner, looking straight into his eyes, no upward tilt.

He stood for a while, then walked on towards his hut, the music still loud in the night air, coming through the thin wood of the dance hall walls. He threaded his way through the barracks, glimpsing in the gaps of half-drawn curtains parents and grandparents sitting on upright chairs in their bleak huts, reading, or staring at the wood-fire while their offspring sang along with 'a Gal in Kalamazoo,' and jived away 'Deep in the Heart of Texas . . . ' The music streamed through his body, gradually rinsing him clean of gloom and resentment. He reached the hut and stood for a moment, feeling the throb, receiving it through the soles of his feet. He began to sway, to move, then to dance, singing aloud, spinning in the tiny space, swerving to avoid wood-stove, beds, and home-made dresser. Arms flung wide, stomping on the beat, he swung round to find Ichirō standing in the doorway, head cocked, observing him.

'There's actually a dance floor just down the way. You'd have more space.'

'I don't dance.'

'So I see.'

Ichirō crossed to his bed, combed his hair and stared at himself critically in the small mirror hanging on the wall. 'I'll be back late. Got a date.'

'A *date*?' Joey looked sceptical. 'What? Cocktails? A piano bar? Gourmet dinner — '

'A date, Joey, does not require that stuff. Just the night sky and a little privacy.'

He was gone, and though the bouncy music still drifted through the darkness, for Joey the beat of life had gone out of it. He dropped on to the narrow cot and sat reviewing the brief, unsatisfactory evening. He found himself, like the old people he had glimpsed, staring blankly at the wood-stove. *Blues, in the Night*.

A green dress printed with pinky-red blossoms. A crimson flower in her hair. A flower name. Lily. She had smiled, touched his arm, tentatively. He had behaved like an asshole.

He re-ran the scene in his head, changing the dialogue, reaching for a line to make her smile. She was about to laugh: would she throw back her head, American style, wide-mouthed, showing even white teeth, or would she stifle the impulse, cover her mouth with her hand in the traditional way of the old country?

Next time they met he would apologise; tell her he'd been in a lousy mood. She would forgive him, and they would linger over a canteen meal, cutting the overcooked fish into ever-smaller pieces, no longer aware of taste or texture. In the movie-house of his mind they were dancing; he touched her cheek.

Next day he looked for Lily but it seemed she and her parents had left Tule a couple of hours earlier: the Quakers had found a family to sponsor them in Boston.

★   ★   ★

That evening in the hut he noticed lying on the table by Ichirō's bed, next to his watch and some candies wrapped in cellophane, a crumpled red flower. He picked it up.

'Where did this come from?'

Glancing up from his book Ichirō reached for one of the candies.

'I told you I had a date.'

Was her name Lily? Joey wanted to ask. *Did she — Did you —*

He dropped the flower back on the table, picked up his towel and headed for the shower block.

On the next social evening Joey was approached by one of the 'gaily attired girls', one with fashionable, unnaturally curly hair. She tapped him playfully on the arm and asked him to dance.

'My name's Iris.'

'Really?'

'No, not really. It's really Ayame, but that means iris. Well, *really* it means moonflower, but that's way too Japanese!' She laughed, showing her teeth.

As the music died away while Joey's arms still encircled her, she tilted up her head and allowed her body to sag against his. She smelled of flowers and face powder.

'Would you like to go on a date?'

'Yes,' he said fervently.

'I have a rubber,' she whispered. 'Mail order.'

36

The presidential cavalcade moved slowly through the streets, Roosevelt waving, smiling his bright, paternal smile, cheered by his loyal subjects. As a morale-boosting exercise, FDR was visiting the shipyards and war industries in Oregon.

Nancy, part of the Democrat support team, moved with the parade, saw the President smile and wave from his open-topped limousine, cloak flung back from his shoulders. The sun glittered on his spectacles, masking his eyes. What was he thinking? He was a world figure now, meeting other world figures at summit conferences. They inhabited an exclusive universe, these people, the air around them filtered, their bodies guarded, protected from the tribulations of unimportant individuals; monarchs in all but name.

'We have nothing to fear but fear itself!' he had declared once, giving new hope, a new deal to desperate people, Nancy among them.

Great days. A great man. But times change and men with them, and she was less easily persuaded by politicians today. He had earned their trust, then. Now he smiled and waved but not all of his loyal subjects were sheltered by his paternal wing: some were rounded up and shipped out to bleak corners of the land to languish behind barbed wire.

This grim Oregon neighbourhood was no jewelled route to glory, no road to Samarkand, but a glow of satisfaction came off the President's countenance that she had observed on other politicians. It came with power, perhaps.

She had thought of FDR in earlier days as the true Democrat, a calm, philosophic prince, a Solomon dispensing wisdom, a good man; but 'good' could depend on where you stood, and why.

With the cheers of the crowd in her ears, for a dizzy moment it seemed to Nancy that Roosevelt had metamorphosed into a modern Tamburlaine, riding in triumph through the city.

Around her, arms and flags waved. The President smiled, raised his hand, a patrician salute acknowledging the populace. Nancy's arms hung rigid by her side.

37

The names tantalised: Tule Lake, Klamath Falls and Link River . . . In strong winds the flow had been known to blow backwards, north into the lake, leaving the riverbed dry, the clay swirling, following the pattern of the vanished stream. The names tantalised, conjured up moisture, but all around was dust.

Guards checked the perimeter, bored, firearms loosely swinging. With dust coating their uniforms, pink flesh obscured by a sandy veil, they looked like figures of straw and clay, clumsily executed. High above the barbed wire the watch-towers loomed, machine guns turned inwards.

The soldiers disliked this term of duty; they disliked the enemy aliens, pale, fragile women, quiet children, sullen youths and small men whose lowered eyelids concealed their thoughts. The soldiers wished themselves elsewhere — in the real America, the land of the free and the home of the brave. Or on the battlefield, where they could be shooting the bastards instead of checking them in and out for work projects or farm duty; counting numbers for sickbeds. Individually these people were weak as kittens, but among the guards it was a known fact that Japs could operate with the awe-inspiring team spirit of termites destroying a building. In that solidarity lay their strength. They needed watching.

* * *

The watchful eyes, the mistrust, fed a determination to simulate 'real life' to fight off despair. So there were baseball games, judo classes, basketball, chess, badminton, music — 'Don't miss the symphony concert, Tuesday!' Joey learned to recognise the traditional festivals — cherry trees improvised from rags and twigs, lanterns from scrap metal, giant chrysanthemums out of wrapping paper. Older internees recited haikus by Basho. The young, defiantly modern, dressed up for Hallowe'en.

Joey continued to slip through the social net: he volunteered for necessary maintenance work, chatted to those who ate at the same table; listened to recitals, dropped in briefly at dances and went on an occasional date; but he was never part of a group.

Was it his imagination or did the conversation flower into vivacity when he left the table? He was not the only product of a mixed marriage — what Ichirō called 'half-breed kids'. But the others, less physically different, had assimilated painlessly, had been drawn into the community. Was it his fault or theirs? Nurture or the legacy of Pinkerton genes that kept him apart?

He read Nancy's latest letter with its snippets of anodyne news, mention of a book she had read. His grandparents sent love; Mary increasingly frail but bearing up bravely.

'And how goes it, Joey dear?'

Rain, seeping from the roof trickled down the tin chimney of the wood-stove, hissing into

295

steam. The room felt humid, tropical. His inner South Sea island.

In that faraway country, the outside world, the war went on. Sequestered and alienated, the young ones blotted out the fact of the conflict with music and gossip and sometimes feverish laughter, furtive sex; older internees took it silently, in the spirit of *gaman*, clustering round radios and listening anxiously to the ebb and flow of events from the impossible position of limbo.

Limbo was an undiscovered country that Joe was becoming familiar with: which side should he cheer on? The army defending families in Japan, or the army fighting the enemies of America? Those who had bombed the ships on Honolulu, or those who were now his jailers? After Pearl Harbor came the battle of Midway — each a disaster or triumph, depending on where you stood.

'The Japs are finished,' one guard called to another, pitching his voice louder than necessary. 'Finished!'

Wrapped in barbed wire, powerless and voiceless, the internees hung in the balance, losers whatever happened.

Shikata ga na. Nothing to be done about it.

38

Nancy celebrated her birthday by packing bandages. At forty-one she felt too old for a party. And who would she invite? From office desk to Red Cross station to volunteer counter at the military coffee shop, she was running as hard as she could, getting nowhere, but there was nowhere she wanted to be. She felt useful. She was exhausted, but that had its advantages: a tired mind in a tired body; a way to keep thought at bay.

War brought gloom and fear. Uncertainty. She became adept at deciphering the news. From what the government allowed its people to hear she could infer considerably more; it was not always encouraging.

Closer to home, reading between the lines in his letters, she feared for Joey: withdrawing from all he had considered himself a part of, he seemed at the same time to be rejecting a past that was not his, but might have been. Had she been wrong to bring him up the American way? Maybe she should have shown him more of that other world, introduced him to what was, after all, a part of his past, a culture that had survived a sea-crossing and flourished here in its own quiet way. But she had been afraid. Ah, there it was again, lurking; that weasel word. Fear.

Increasingly, she felt an unfocused sense of dissatisfaction. She could recall how, long ago, she had looked forward to being 'grown up', mature; to resembling the older women with their style and confidence. Now she was an older woman and it was the young who called the tune. Surely there should have been a point when she was grown up and confident, before the downward spiral, the sense of defeat? She must have been too busy to notice.

Filling the hours seemed the easiest way to fill the days, the weeks, months. Life became a jigsaw, one piece of her schedule slotting into the next, leaving her no time for anxiety, and not much time to dwell on thoughts of other possibilities. Had Ben lived . . . Had the Japanese not bombed Pearl Harbor . . . Had she met and married someone else, would she once more be alone, the imagined man whose body had warmed hers now swept into the conflict?

She was busy stacking dishes in the coffee shop when a man on the other side of the counter said ruefully, 'You don't recognise me.'

She glanced at him: tall, thin, a touch of grey in the dark hair, face an anonymous oval, like a cartoon character with sketched-in features — two dots for eyes, a vertical stroke, a horizontal dash.

'Should I?'

'Well. We had a rather jolly conversation last week while you made me a cup of something you described as tea.'

'Oh, right. The Englishman.'

'Defined by my accent. Rather depressing, that.'

'Not your accent. Your perfect manners,'

Nancy said, stating a fact, unflirtatious.

'Ah!'

She glanced at the sky as a grumble of thunder came and went. A sudden sweep of rain hit the windows.

'You've brought us English weather; I'm sure our climate used to be better behaved.'

'You could be right. But I'm not sure the meteorology of nostalgia can be trusted: those endless golden summers, snowball fights at Christmas — was it really like that?'

For a moment she was disconcerted: surely her memories of lost innocence must be true? Sun on the seashore, beach parties with toasted marshmallows, a swimmer waving from beyond the surf . . .

* * *

Charles considered the woman at the coffee dispenser. Dark blonde hair, cut unflatteringly short. Dress a practical brown, its shape unbecoming. Make-up confined to a dash of lipstick. This was a woman who gave no thought to her appearance.

He noted the downward droop of her mouth, the shadowed eyes. The wedding ring. Charles was not given to small talk, but this woman with her abstracted air, her neglected hands, her stillness, drew him. To hold her attention he asked her, conversationally, if her husband was with the American forces in Europe.

She stared at him, shocked by the unexpectedness of the question.

'My husband has been dead for ten years.'

He groaned, 'Oh God. I'm sorry.'

'Why? How were you to know?'

About to move off, back to clearing cups and plates, she gave him a quick, forgiving smile. For a moment her drooping mouth curved upwards, other muscles lifted; her nose wrinkled sweetly. Fleetingly, her face was transformed.

Charles had the strongest sensation that if she took even one step away from him he would lose her for ever, and he could not allow that to happen. He must keep her talking, however creakily he engineered it.

'Look. My name is Charles. Charles Bowman, I'm over here working with your people for a while.'

'Uh-huh. Is that Bowman as in bows and arrows? Were your ancestors archers, fighting for Henry the Fifth at the battle of Agincourt?'

'Actually,' Charles said, 'they were in the wool trade. In a particularly flat bit of south-east England.'

He saw her pause, watched the muscles in her face relax; she was almost smiling. He considered his options and dived. 'The name was given to the man who untangled the wool. He used a bow — seriously, he did. It was the Italians who thought up the process but then we pinched the idea.'

'When did all this go on?'

'Oh, quite late . . . thirteenth century?'

And at that she laughed out loud. 'Right. Really late.'

He added, encouragingly, 'I could tell you all

sorts of exciting stuff, about my good old ancestors vibrating the string of the bow in a pile of tangled wool to separate the fibres — '

'You're putting me on.'

'I'm deadly serious. It got us the finest, softest thread you can imagine.'

She was stacking plates again; he was losing her. He began to gabble.

'The old methods produced yarn that was so resilient it could be bent thirty thousand times without breaking or fraying.' Desperation dried his mouth. Words, words, words; he was on a slippery slope to oblivion — what woman would want to talk to a one-track wool-twit? He felt like an old buffer addressing a Women's Institute knitting circle.

'We exported the stuff. Look what wool did for Florence, the most beautiful city in the world, the art, the treasures, but then the Black Death . . .'

He took a deep breath and risked a change of tack: on his last visit he had noticed her, off duty, absorbed in an old, fragile book. 'Dante said a few things about the city.' She glanced up. 'Would you like to know more?' he asked. 'Over dinner?' he added. 'I promise not to say another word about wool.' Cautiously, 'How do you feel about poetry?'

★ ★ ★

When Nancy next wrote to Joey she mentioned she had met an Englishman, doing some kind of liaison work in the US.

'He's *funny*,' she wrote: '*funny ha-ha, not funny peculiar. It's a while since I laughed.*' She needed cheering up, with Mary gone. All that time never moving out of her bedroom. Yet, since her mother's death the house seemed empty; Louis was shrinking, growing ever more silent.

She asked about Joey's health, and the food, on which subject she was sending him another parcel; she had baked him a cake . . . As always, the letter was firmly optimistic. Dark thoughts were excised, and in any case she often wondered whether anything controversial would get past the censors. What was the reality of their communication? Of his state of mind?

No more was said about her own activities, but in her next letter she sent him a new poem. She said she had 'come upon it'. No mention of the Englishman who made her laugh.

Joey put her letter with the others, in the bag beneath his bed, tucked between the pages of Boas's *History of the American Race*. He put the poem aside, to look at later.

39

He had given up making drawings. He had given up reading. Anthropologists who travelled to faraway places for their encounters with strangeness offered no insights on internal exile. He avoided participant observation; shunned the festivals and took no part in the communal gardening, all the complex patterns of giving and receiving that the South Sea villagers would have recognised and approved of. Between voluntary work shifts he lay on the narrow iron bed and stared at the wall. He watched a fly, or studied a shaft of sunlight as it moved across the wall and floor of the hut, saw how its heat had bleached the raw wood, day after day, into a sunbeam pattern, the fibres of the planks drying into something resembling crushed straw.

He had arrived at a point of suspended animation that got him through the day. Curb your imagination, he had decided. Far away the war went on; battles were won or lost, people killed and got killed. *Among those who got killed — bombed or blasted — was there a woman in a wood and paper room who wore a kimono, who fed chickens and ran laughing into rainstorms?*

Immobilised and powerless, he had no part in life as it now was. Learn to love your blinkers. Sufficient unto the day.

★ ★ ★

Every morning, early, the trucks arrived to take workers to the beet fields, dropping them back at the gates at the end of the day. Joey was aware he would have made a poor beet-farmer: soft hands, a spine inconveniently long for crouching over low-growing plants, untutored in the ways of this curious and valuable crop. Ichirō, Taro and Kazuo, urban boys without farming experience, quickly demonstrated an acceptable level of dexterity, moving along the lines of bunched green leaves, weeding, checking for disease; thinning the tightly packed rows, plucking out young plants to leave room for the rest to grow. The skill, speed and energy of the internees were saving the harvest.

Ichirō was realistic about the exercise — 'The farm boys are all GIs now, serving overseas. They'll take anyone with the usual number of arms and legs; they'd even use you, Joey. You could earn a dollar or two. Why not come along for the ride?'

Through the window Joey watched them assembling by the trucks as the early sun cast long, attenuated shadows on to the dusty compound. They climbed aboard, voices and laughter drifting back to the hut. Engines coughed into life, grumbled, dissolved into distance and silence. He lay curled, too big for the undersized bed. Inert. He had become a rare breed of sloth, with a slowed rate of metabolism thwarting movement. Unlike the sloth, he could not rely on camouflage to protect him; no algae grew on his body, no protective disguise; he still stood out in the crowd, sore thumb, square peg, all that jazz. Everyone knows what a sloth is, what it looks like. But how does it feel? That almost immobile existence, that upside-down view of the world, how was the sloth *feeling*? Did it feel stranded, cut off from everything moving so fast around it, the rustling leaves, the spinning globe, the speeding birds, the racing ants, the wind that shakes the branches. Did a sloth, lost and alone, howl silently? Feel pain?

An hour passed. The sun moved across the floor. He began to re-count nails in planks.

When Mrs Tanaka knocked at the half-open door he offered a listless invitation to enter and regarded her without interest as she bowed and stood calmly waiting. After a few moments Joey cracked: he slowly got off the bed and managed a vestigial bow to the elderly woman. Through observation he was aware that this was the correct thing to do.

He took her in, the body taut as wire, the steel-grey hair, the face ageless as an ivory carving.

'Did you want to speak to one of the boys?'

'I wanted to speak to you, Mr Pinkerton.'

'You can call me Joey.'

'But we are not friends.'

'We're fellow internees. Isn't that enough?'

'Enough for propinquity. Not for intimacy.'

Quiet, unnervingly confident, a trace of East Coast vowels in the wholly American delivery. Central Casting would have her down for an Ivy League academic. Or possibly a scary grandma.

Clearly she had something she wanted from him now. Tiny, she seemed to grow taller as she returned his gaze.

'Mr Pinkerton. I have observed you.'

Again a woman watching him. Again he felt irritated.

'I have observed you observing others.'

'It passes the time.'

'There are perhaps better ways of passing the time. You could become involved — '

He broke in. 'I have no wish to become involved. I am here because of a bureaucratic detail. I have nothing in common with these people, I feel nothing — '

'You *know* nothing. Why should you feel? You need to learn a little about . . . ' Pause. '*These people.*'

Her tone, her expression, were benign. The eyes behind their small glass shields were not.

He felt increasingly provoked. What did this woman want from him? Was she simply here to lecture him, to tell him to pull himself together? Acting the mother? Well he had two of those already, more than enough.

She said, 'We have many children in Tule Lake and it is essential to keep them occupied. Also to extend their education.'

'There are teachers.'

'I was not thinking of formal lessons. There are children here who are falling between two languages. Lost between tongues, they grow mute. The right person could reach them, give them back a voice.'

'I don't speak much Japanese.'

'Precisely.'

'I don't see it.'

'You will.'

There were ways to deal with pushy old ladies: he could say, politely but firmly, that he was not interested; he could give her the silent treatment and then forget the whole thing. He could be actively rude and tell her to get lost.

She said, 'It must be a consolation, Mr Pinkerton, to know you are superior to your fellow internees.'

'I don't regard myself as superior.'

'But different?'

He waited.

'And that gives you the freedom to behave impolitely.'

'I can't begin to fathom,' Joey said savagely, 'what the Japanese would regard as impolite.'

'I think the way I am behaving now would be considered extremely impolite, Mr Pinkerton. I think I am behaving with quite American manners. That should make you feel at home. But whether or not you feel anything is of no interest to me. I want to do something about these children.'

Joey had heard of Chinese water torture. He thought this could be a matronly Japanese version.

'Mrs Tanaka, you're bullying me,' he said.

They regarded one another for a moment.

'If so, I must apologise; it would mean I was behaving very badly. But there are more ways than one of doing that.'

Joey decided that her eyes were indeed sharp, but not as sharp as her tongue.

She raised her eyebrows enquiringly. 'Shall we talk?'

40

He walked into the classroom expecting trouble: inattention, a degree of fidgeting, possibly some impudence; the sort of brawling misbehaviour he recalled from his own schooldays. Instead he faced silence. Seated cross-legged on the floor — no chairs or desks were available — children of varying ages stared up at him impassively. He felt a flutter of panic in his guts: this could be even worse than he had thought.

Greeting them, to his own ears he sounded hearty, phoney. In their place he would mistrust a pink-faced jerk who spoke no Japanese, who didn't even wear glasses: how clever could *he* be?

He decided to dip a toe, go slowly, work the room. There were kids here who, like him, spoke virtually no Japanese, alongside others for whom English was a second language. He would approach this thing from the other angle.

'*Ohayō gozaimasu!*' he called out, cheerfully, using one of the phrases he knew.

They erupted in giggles, rocking in delight. His attempt to greet them in Japanese may not have been accurately pitched but it had certainly broken the ice.

He held up a hand. Instant silence.

'You will now show me how it *should* be said. I want to hear from each of you, right?'

He stood over them, encouraging, and in turn they repeated the phrase, some fluently, others as haltingly as Joey. When everyone had spoken, he repeated it. This time no one laughed.

Joey set a lazy pace. How many spoke English? Hands up. And how many spoke Japanese as well? And who spoke no Japanese? Okay. He picked a noun, an absurd adjective, an unlikely verb, and asked for Japanese equivalents. At first they remained silent, unwilling to expose themselves to this childish game. Slowly he drew them in, easing his way to Japanese phrases where he was the useless one, where they could help him out.

He moved them around, pairing up the English-speakers with the Japanese-only. Varying the pattern. He began to ask questions, keeping it simple, repetitious. Did they notice that he too was repeating the Japanese, noting down each word? This was indeed learning by heart. A syllable, a sound, a gradual understanding; ritualistic, the naming of parts.

They listened, repeated. Began to ask questions. He had them locate and name objects in the classroom. Sometimes he made them laugh.

By the end of the lesson Joey was exhausted; the children bubbling.

Each day he moved them on a little. From nursery rhymes for the youngest, he took them to a verse or two of 'Paul Revere's Ride'; he even risked 'archy & mehitabel' — 'Okay, there's this cat, this *neko*, and this cockroach — cockroach? *Gokiburi?* Right. And they're buddies . . . '

Meanwhile, he did his homework: in his hut

he copied out words, marked vocal inflexions, checked nuances.

One day he introduced a new ingredient: personal possessions. He explained the concept of Show and Tell. Next lesson, one child brought a signed picture of Bing Crosby, another unrolled a piece of embroidered green silk that belonged to her grandmother. A harmonica sat beside an object resembling a small piece of candy which turned out to be a seal: 'hanko — for stamping your name, like a signature.'

A small, square printed seal at the end of a letter from Nagasaki; Nancy's voice, 'It's from Joey's mother. Her name is Cho-Cho.'

One girl brought a new basket, smoothly and intricately woven.

'My mother made it, from tule reed, sort of bulrush that grows here. It's bound with string she unravelled from an onion sack in the garbage from the kitchen.'

A boy held up a tiny carved monkey made of jade.

'Netsuke.'

'Pretty.'

'Useful,' the boy said.

And Joey realised it was not enough to know the word. The *use* of this object required an explanation. The naming of parts should include the knowledge of its function, as in the poem Nancy had sent him, passed on from her British friend.

That lesson the class discussed *netsuke*, miniature sculptures, the word of two characters that meant 'root' and 'to suspend'; the tiny object that long ago solved the problem of how to keep safe personal belongings in robes that had no pockets.

One of the older boys stepped in.

'Small objects, such as coins, were placed in cloth containers and hung by a cord from a sash round the waist. The sash, *obi*, is — '

'I know what an *obi* is.'

He picked it up, feeling the netsuke's smoothness against his fingertips, returning the dark gaze of the monkey's eyes.

Next day an elderly, silver-haired man appeared in the classroom door. Mr Murakami apologised for interrupting the lesson, but he had something to show Joey that might be of interest: a wooden carving, so small it fitted easily into his closed fist.

'See no evil, hear no evil, ah, speak no evil — *mizaru, kikazaru, iwazaru*.' He held out an exquisite carved trinity. Someone must have reported back that Joey liked monkeys.

'Perhaps a play on words, our word for monkey is *saru*. This is a poor copy I have attempted of a seventeenth-century temple carving, in Nikko Toshogo shrine.' He glanced round the room and said a few words rapidly, in Japanese. A ripple of laughter from the children.

Mr Murakami gave the slightest movement, a hint of a bow. 'I have explained to them that I am too old to share their class. I must not interrupt you, *sensei*.'

The word, delivered with gentle humour, meant nothing to Joey until much later, when he was able to appreciate the nuances implicit in

311

sensei, for which no English equivalent exists — he guessed the French *maître* came nearest. When he had moved from ignorance to a tentative, fumbling understanding of the cat's-cradle complexity of Japanese semantics, Joey thought back to that moment and came close to tears.

★   ★   ★

He had not intended to contribute to the Show and Tell but after the lesson he found himself pulling out the bag from under his bed, rummaging around. Next day he reached into his pocket and placed a grimy wooden object on the classroom table.

Where Joey's American classmates had been baffled by his possession of this unprepossessing article, there was no such puzzlement here, only shouts of recognition:

'*Komo!*'

'Hey, you got a spinner!'

For many of his class, as he now thought of them, the spinning top was a part of family childhood. Clustering round the table they clamoured to speak. One talked of *tsukurigomai* — tops with a hole, which made a humming sound, another of *togoma* made from bamboo. They touched his battered example, smiling.

A small girl picked it up and handed it to him, silently requesting a demonstration.

'Once it was bright yellow and red,' Joey said as he set it spinning. 'The paint was shiny.'

The words were passed around. Heads nodded.

'It came from Nagasaki. Where I was born.' Then, 'My mother is Japanese.'

Is Japanese. My mother. A woman in a dark dress. Seated, pale hands in her lap. Or maybe lying under rubble, crushed. Dead for real this time.

There was the usual murmur, the grandmother's footsteps of phrases, words, information jumping from one to another. Heads nodding.

He saw they were all looking at him, but differently now, studying him doubtfully. He thought of Ichirō's old joke: funny you don't *look* . . .

* * *

He knocked on the door of Mr Murakami's room.

'Ah, *sensei* . . . '

'Your carving,' Joey said, 'the monkeys.'

'Ah. Useful exercise, I found a fragment, some wood by the perimeter fence. Hard. Good for carving, even with improvised tools.'

He waited, smiling at his visitor. The boy had not come to talk about monkeys.

'The class is going well?'

'Yeah. I was expecting trouble, but they're . . . quiet.'

'Ah. You are enjoying the benefits of *giri*.'

'Which is . . . ?'

'Difficult to translate . . . A mode of behaviour, an ethical code instilled into us, a mix

313

of duty, obligation, a sense of justice and morality. We are bound by *giri* towards our parents but also . . . ' a smile 'towards our teachers.'

'So that's why I'm having such an easy ride. Tough for the kids.'

'They would not think so. *Giri* is so important that Japanese have been known to commit suicide rather than break it.'

It was not easy for Joey to explain why he was there. He wanted information, he needed answers, but the field of his ignorance was so vast that he was unable even to formulate the questions.

'It's hopeless. I'm bogged down in the detail before I even get to the big issues. Where should I begin?'

A long, doubtful intake of breath. Mr Murakami seemed to be overcome by an attack of tics and twitches: he shook his head repeatedly, clicked his tongue, rubbed the back of his neck, apparently lost in thought. In time Joey would become familiar with a traditional Japanese reaction to a tricky question. This first time he anxiously watched the small elderly man going through what appeared to be a painful process.

After a lengthy silence, Mr Murakami spoke. He offered the view that the Japanese were good at small things, their skill less suited to the grand gesture. Joey was relieved.

'Small I can handle.'

If truth be told, he was unsure what the big gesture was.

'This word I've heard . . . *wabi-sabi*? I can't

314

seem to work out the meaning.'

'Ah. Not a word but a phrase; not one meaning, but many . . . *wabi-sabi* is to do with Tao and Zen, which are universes in themselves. All things are impermanent. All things are imperfect. All things are incomplete. Let us say *wabi-sabi* involves the — ah — transience of life, the pleasures of impermanence, the beauty of imperfection. A cracked vase has its own beauty.'

He registered Joey's growing consternation: 'One is entering a maze. Easy to get lost!'

But a draughty hut in a tar-paper barracks in an unforgiving landscape was as good a place as any to take the first step.

'We cannot hurry; you may find pu-ro-gress somewhat slow.'

But with time, Mr Murakami said reassuringly, they would advance. He added, less reassuringly, that progress involved *kokoro* which meant 'the heart of things' or 'feeling' and this too would need exploring, though one could never be confident of having indeed reached the heart of things.

'I'm wondering,' Joey said, 'if a foreigner can ever understand Japan. It's looking-glass country: the closer you get to it, the further off it is.'

Mr Murakami brought out a Japanese word — *kaizen* — which might be translated as 'continuous improvement', though he feared — a small smile — that there was no precise American equivalent. However, they would press on.

★ ★ ★

As they explore together that faraway country of Joey's birth, its history, the reasons for one thing and another, the beginning of this or that, Joey feels himself slowly spinning. Between waking and dreaming he touches fugitive moments, fragments of long-forgotten experience. He has more than one past to remember.

Unwinding, he hangs suspended in a state of non-existence. He had thought he was examining a matter of identity, the old question: who am I? Travelling deeper into the maze he finds the question is more: what is an I?

★ ★ ★

'There are many words for I and for You, each with its own meaning, its own restrictions. There are also echo-words, words that . . . simulate the sound or the feeling of a word. This is important . . .

'Take the word: 'flows'. A clear stream flows *sara-sara*, which gives the sense of the water. A fine lady walks *saya-saya* with the sound of the movement of her clothes . . . '

'Yes!'

Joey's exclamation was jubilant. Nancy read him a poem once, where a poet watches his lady walk towards him, and it taught the boy a new word, which now bore fruit in *saya-saya*.

'There's an English poem. 'Whenas in silks my Julia goes, then, then methinks how sweetly flows that liquefaction of her clothes' . . . '

And Mr Murakami nodded. *Liquefaction.* 'Ah, yes.' He reflected aloud that after all,

316

English had more in common with Japanese than he had thought, and they were making progress.

'Next we might look at puns, pivot words — *kakekotoba* — wordplay, you would call it. This will be amusing.'

But *kokoro* lay far ahead.

Meanwhile, Mr Murakami suggested a cup of tea; on the wood-burning stove he had improvised a means of heating water.

On one wall of the hut, a scroll was suspended from a rusty nail; a scribble of lines, mostly grey or black, not an object Joey would expect to be hung on the wall like a Georgia O'Keeffe poppy or a Wyeth landscape.

Without giving any sign that he had noticed Joey's observation of the scroll, Mr Murakami raised the subject of Joey's drawings: he would consider it an honour to look at one or two, some time. Once again Joey became aware that he had been an object of interest. Mr Murakami handed him a small, porcelain cup of greenish liquid. Sipping it, Joey wondered what the Japanese for 'vile flavour' might be.

'Do you consider yourself an artist?'

'No. I consider myself at best a craftsman.'

'Ah.'

Mr Murakami then remarked on the curious fact that until quite recently there had been no word for 'art' in Japanese.

'The word that comes closest is *geijutsu*, which you could translate as 'form and design'. You might say that for us, art is the same as living, both should include functional purpose,

317

and spiritual simplicity.'

He took down a book of woodcuts from a shelf built of scavenged planks and began, slowly, to turn the pages.

'The Japanese artist is a *poet* rather than a painter. He disregards the laws of perspective and of light and shade. He is attempting to capture the feelings evoked by the *memory* of a scene, the feelings that he experiences between waking and dreaming.'

Joey took the book in his hands, while Mr Murakami talked of calligraphic quality, strength of line — 'perhaps due to the Japanese way of drawing from the elbow, not the wrist, as is the case in Western art.'

The memory of a scene . . . the feeling between waking and dreaming . . .

Somewhere a wheel is turned and with infinite slowness he is flayed, the flesh gradually stripped from his body leaving him peeled of his American sense of self. But what will take its place?

41

As summer slipped away the sky took on a dirty yellow tinge, the sickly trees around the perimeter lost their foliage and withered leaves dropped slowly, like stained snowflakes, lying in drifts on the hard ground. In the camp a division could be seen as clear-cut as the red, white and blue layered angel-food cake served up on the Fourth of July. The split was generational: the children had classes and team games. The young men clustered, buzzing like wasps, radiating resentment. The older internees watched and waited, with the patience a lifetime of experience had taught them.

As the temperature dipped, the barracks simmered. Labour disputes, hostility, long-drawn-out pain of one sort and another merged and flared into riots. There was an accidental shooting: a man shot allegedly trying to escape. The soldier was punished: for 'misuse of official property' — a bullet — and fined one dollar.

For Joey, increasingly sunk in the past, when the present intruded as it did now, it collided bruisingly with a lost world described by those who were still able to revive its essence. Real life jolted him out of the seductive tranquillity of contemplation where he was living a dream; guided by old hands his telescope moved across the landscape of the past to show him ancient courts and emperors, warriors, ceremonies, the forming and refining of a closed realm.

And there was the more recent past, Perry's five black-hulled American frigates that steamed into Edo harbour in 1853, and what followed, as one century gave way to the next. Within the cramped horizon of the camp he explored unknown worlds, absorbed the small tragedies and triumphs of ordinary people; their hopes and disillusion.

He moved through the barracks, passed from one bleak room to the next, sitting cross-legged, listening to these quiet people, some fluent, others faltering, as their voices drew him into their past.

... 'My grandmother was a picture-bride ... she saw my father first time on Ellis Island. Before that, just photos; he proposed by letter. She was wearing a hat with flowers. She pulled out a flower and gave it him ... '

... 'My grandfather came from Osaka to Oregon. A farmer. He grew cabbage and squash. Never a day off in forty years ... '

... 'My father went to college. He studied science, mathematics. Masters, Ph.D ... My mother gave thanks he died before Pearl Harbor.'

... 'My family has a shop — *had* a shop — we sold shoes. American shoes are too big for Japanese feet, we imported small sizes ... '

... 'We have fishing boat ... No time to sell when internment came; we tie up boat in harbour ... '

... 'Before she came to America, my mother arranged the flowers every week in the Baptist church in Nagasaki — '

320

Nagasaki? Would she have known a girl called Cho-Cho who married an American sailor?

But the flower-arranger, Mrs Shioya's mother, was part of a vanished past where everyone was long dead. Unlike Cho-Cho who lived on, unreachable. Unless she, too, was now a statistic.

42

Nancy had found a college in Massachusetts that would accept Joey; where he could continue his studies. She wrote to give him the news, ending with a happy flourish: 'So as of now, you're out of there!!'

Afterwards she realised she should have picked up from his letters the way he was thinking. His reply came as a shock.

'Dear Nancy, it's good of you to go to all that trouble, but I want to stick around and see what happens here. I guess camp is the place for us enemy aliens. I have to keep this short — there's a concert tonight and we need to rehearse. Who'd have thought school flute lessons would pay off! Not that I have more than a few bars to play, but it's tricky stuff: would you believe Charles Ives?'

Joey and the band came out of the canteen hut into a riot: internee coal workers demanding better wages had been fired. Docility exploded into rage, the air filled with flying bricks and insults. Mortified, Joey realised that while he and the band had been rehearsing a concert of American music inside the hut, men had been marching to a different beat outside.

Autumn ushered in a bitter season: dishes of Thanksgiving dinner lying untouched —

322

'Thanksgiving? For what?' Japanese festivals were celebrated without joy; Christmas an uneasy mixture of coloured lanterns and carol-singing. Santa Claus figures made of cheese and sticky rice, and decorated trees that looked neither Japanese nor altogether American. A bleak New Year.

★ ★ ★

Joey was on his bed, eyes closed, open book on his chest, when Ichirō threw open the door.

'Are you asleep?'

'I'm deep in the Mexican pueblo with Ruth Benedict.'

'Tell her to get screwed.'

'Ichi, they're so *Japanese*. The culture of restraint — '

'The whole camp's buzzing.' A baffled shake of the head.

'There's a loyalty questionnaire. I just read it. It's garbage. Joey, these guys are nuts. They want us to swear *loyalty*? To a country that's put us behind barbed wire. Does that make sense?'

'They're always paranoid — '

'There are two special questions that need a yes to get you through. They want everyone to renounce Japanese citizenship. Who do they think they're kidding? Some of the old people, that's the *only* citizenship they have, the government never would allow them to become US citizens. It's lose-lose: if they sign they'll be stateless.

'And they have to agree to renounce allegiance

323

to the Emperor. People are totally bewildered, scared: it's like they've been supporting the Emperor till now. Like when did you stop beating your wife. The old ones are in tears. All over camp, you can hear them crying. They're lost, Joey, we're all lost. What the fuck is going to become of us?'

Without waiting for an answer he slammed out of the hut. Joey got up and watched him walking away fast, shoulders hunched, rubbing his eyes and shaking his head from side to side, like a dog shaking off water.

Joey suspected this would turn out to be one of those camp myths, but it was genuine: 'The loyalty questionnaire must be completed by all internees over 17 years of age.' Men and women ranging from the resentful to the bewildered, some not even able to read English, were confronted by a long list of questions that must be answered, signed and witnessed without delay.

★ ★ ★

The admin office door was open but Joey waited outside, watching the slightly overweight lieutenant studying papers. Finally he looked up and indicated with a slow blink that he was available. He waited, jaws moving, gum shifting from side to side. Silently Joey dropped his documents on the desk. The lieutenant squinted at the papers, drew them towards him with the flat of his hand and glanced at them with a glazed, almost exhausted look. He glanced up, then back at the papers.

'Okaay . . . '

Joey recognised the tone, a familiar symptom of suspicion. At the filing cabinet the lieutenant checked the papers against documents in a folder. The sight of an apparently all-American internee threw him. The officer found himself on the back foot and didn't like the position.

He sat down across the desk, the swivel chair squeaking under heavy buttocks, and handed Joey a questionnaire, one of a pile stacked in a wire tray. Taking his time Joey studied each page carefully. He sensed the lieutenant's growing impatience, the chair squeaking as he moved, his leg jiggling, fingers tapping the desktop as Joey read his way to the last page.

'How d'you respond?'

'For a start the questionnaire is crap. Would you expect anyone here in their right mind to say yes to this garbage?'

The lieutenant's pudgy face slowly progressed from pink to a darkening crimson.

'Watch your mouth, bud.'

'Why?' Joey asked pleasantly. 'Is it because if I give the wrong responses you'll lock me up in a stinking dump, lieutenant, with armed guards and maybe barbed wire to stop me breaking out?'

The officer's voice was thick with held-in loathing.

'A troublemaker like your fucking commie father. We know about Benjamin Franklin Pinkerton. Pinko Pinkerton. The Washington riots. It's all in the file.'

The unexpectedness of it rocked him. Dirt in

325

the files about Ben? Ben the champ, the local hero, the patriotic sailor. But of course Ben had also marched on the Capitol. With bums and degenerates.

'Yeah. Right.'

Joey kept it carefully conversational. 'You've got in the file that he served in the navy? And went to Washington with the vets, right, lieutenant? Vets who fought to save people like you, lieutenant, and then found themselves homeless? My old man was in Washington because of his brother. My uncle Charlie would have marched, but his bones were buried someplace in France. He was killed, but at least he was shot by the enemy. The vets who won the war, who went to Washington because they were starving, they were shot by you guys. Orders of General MacArthur. That's what they call irony, lieutenant.'

Voice strangled with rage, the man said, 'I'm putting you down as double-no.'

Joey said with quiet savagery, 'You don't put me down as anything. I haven't signed yet. I asked you a question. You haven't answered it. You can put down I'm thinking about it.'

'You gotta respond!'

'Fine. You have a deadline? Is there a closing date for this? Show me where it says I don't get to think about it first if I want. In this great country of ours am I still allowed to do that?'

At the door, he paused, 'I'll let you know.'

Joey would sign the document, in due course. But pushing the lieutenant into apoplexy brought him a deep satisfaction.

Tule had become a dumping ground for dissident internees from other camps; a segregation centre. Each day brought new ways to show anger: the morning salute to the flag — 'My Country 'tis of Thee' — once sincere, now sung with bitterly ironic fervour. Anger lay like a minefield in the barracks, erupting in explosions of violence: Kazuo had seen one inmate, suspected of being an informer, beaten by his hut-mates; there were clashes with guards. And always, stories circulating.

'Roosevelt's reversed the policy.'

Joey looked up from his book.

'What?'

'Military service. We can volunteer.'

'This is another rumour — '

'No, it's true.'

'We're not 4C enemy aliens any more? This has to be good news.'

'You think?'

In the hut, late into the night, the others exchanged anxieties:

'The whole thing could be a ploy.'

'How, a ploy?'

'To confuse us, set up guilt, fear, you name it.'

Joey lay, breathing evenly, sleep out of reach.

The trouble took various forms: meetings, disagreements of opinion, angry exchanges, unrest. A difference of opinion at a baseball game exploded into a riot, at first aimless, then vicious, as the soldiers intervened. The guards made creative use of baseball bats — 'Hey, a ball game, and no balls needed!'. The crack of wood on skull lent a new dimension to the rules. Two strikes here and the player was not only out, but out for the count. In the mess hall there were overturned tables, smashed chairs and dishes; defiant slogans daubed on walls. An elderly man hurled himself at the barbed-wire fence in a silent declaration of despair. Ungentle guards pulled him free, tearing his clothing and flesh. Protest gatherings created mobs which spread into mass demonstrations. A fog of sour disaffection hung over the camp.

Then, weirdly, a counterpoint to the hostility, young men slowly began to come forward to sign up; some cynically, others in despair, volunteering for service to their country.

Ichirō said wearily, 'They want to prove they're true Americans. For 'they' read 'we'.'

43

The barber's hut appeared to be empty. Joey paused in the doorway, and from behind the open doors of a cupboard, a voice called out questioningly.

'Yes?'

'I wanted a haircut, but I guess Shiro's not around — '

'I'll do it.'

She came round the cupboard. Tiny, her black hair cut sharp and glossy as lacquer. Cool, unsmiling, she gestured Joey to a chair, swiftly tucked a towel around his shoulders, picked up comb and scissors and began snipping fast.

Joey was disconcerted: she could at least have asked him what sort of cut he wanted. He listened to the scissors snapping at his hair like the jaws of a hungry predator. Perhaps she was shy; perhaps he should take the initiative.

'So, were you a hairdresser, before?'

She paused, regarding him in the mirror.

'Do you always categorise people in this way?'

A voice as cool as her gaze. The delivery north California. Good at giving orders, he guessed.

'Listen, I was just making conversation . . . ' Joey felt guilty. She had a right to be irritated, to resent him pushing her into the wrong pigeonhole. To keep things more general he wondered aloud if she had been at the movie show the night before.

She said, sharply, 'I don't like black and white movies.' Snip.

Joey said, incredulous, 'You mean you don't like *any* black and white movies? But that's most movies.'

'Black and white movies are slow.'

'*Slow?*'

'Colour is more interesting.' Snip.

He twisted round to confront her: 'You don't think *Citizen Kane* is interesting?'

She had not seen *Citizen Kane*. Snip, snip.

Her skin was milk-white, eyes dark as prunes. He wondered why he was thinking of her like some kind of food display. Watching her pale hands hover around his head, steel blades flashing, he was about to ask if she had seen *Snow White and the Seven Dwarfs*, at least it was in colour, but she might think he was treating her as a kid. Fatal error. Hard to assess her shape beneath the dark shirtwaister, but he saw she was slender, with narrow hips and long, graceful arms.

'Okay,' Joey said cautiously. 'What about *The Maltese Falcon*? It's black and white but it's also a fantastic movie.'

She suddenly became furious: it was a *ridiculous* movie; the plot didn't make sense and she couldn't understand the ending.

'True,' Joey said, 'the ending is a problem, but on the other hand it does have the greatest last line of any movie I've ever seen.'

Snip! She whipped the towel off his shoulders. 'You're done.'

Caught up in his defence of favourite movies

330

Joey had neglected to check progress in the mirror. Only now did he register the full extent of the cut: his head shorn almost to the scalp.

'Wow. That. Is. short.'

'Yeah.'

She added crisply, 'Actually, I preferred it longer.'

'So why?'

'Well if you decide to volunteer, you won't be given such a hard time, without those cute curls.'

'Only a mug would volunteer. Why would I do that?'

'Sure. Smart-ass like you, why would you?'

Joey stared at her, baffled: why was he arousing this hostility? He stood up and asked what he owed her.

'It's on the house.'

'Why?'

'Because I feel like it. By the way, that's where Shiro is. He volunteered. A mug, right?'

She began sweeping up the floorboards. As he reached the door she said, without looking up, 'You have perfect hair.'

'What, the cute blond curls you're sweeping up?'

'Hair grows back.'

Joey said, struggling against a wave of irritability, 'I don't know your name.'

'I know yours.' She closed the door.

44

That first evening in the army canteen, Charles had talked on, whipping up a blizzard of words just to hold Nancy's attention. If she moved on, he was lost; he knew that, so he kept the phrases spinning. Until the patter ran out and he found himself left with the only words he actually needed — 'Have dinner with me?'

She took a closer look at him: the oval face no longer anonymous, the brown eyes bright with amusement, the long mouth unexpectedly sensuous.

He was older than her, late forties probably, and she thought of him as old England; relaxed charm, old-fashioned manners. It was with considerable surprise that she found herself in bed with him.

Before Ben and Nancy were married she had expected Happy Ever After to follow the ceremony, which would be a fairy-tale affair: a white satin gown, the bouquet thrown to eager, giggling bridesmaids; speeches, her mother in tears, a honeymoon in San Francisco or Hawaii. Joey, and all that went with him, changed things: the wedding was less grand and more subdued than she had anticipated. As was the consummation.

Nancy was not a prude, but saving herself for marriage had always been the plan. That Ben had not similarly saved himself came first as a shock and then as a lingering disappointment. He was careful, even deferential when he approached her; she sensed no pulsing flare of arousal, an absence of passion. Their couplings were restrained, without wildness, never soaring free of bedroom respectability. And she was unable to fend off thoughts that Ben had obviously done this before. Perhaps the Nagasaki woman had even taught him a trick or two.

Charles was gentle where it mattered, but he could be masterful, and she was grateful to be shown ways to please and be pleased.

Evenings usually began with a drink at the bar of the Benson Hotel — Nancy drinking cocktails! — another new experience that took her by surprise. She had hesitated the first time Charles enquired 'What will it be?' Her occasional, 'medicinal' thimble of bourbon was all she knew. Now she found she liked a Manhattan, just the one, enjoyed in comfort and the flattering glow of softly shaded lamps. She sipped, they talked, laughed. Later they moved to his neat rented apartment and made love for a leisurely hour, not always in the bedroom. Then perhaps a restaurant, though Charles liked to cook, transforming red snapper into British fish and chips, learning the American way with steak.

They both knew that he was only visiting, that one day he would get on a ship and go back to England, where life, he had murmured one day, was complicated. But words like 'leaving' or 'going home' never figured in their conversations, though there were times when he pulled her close to him and groaned with a sort of regret or when, close to sleep, he kissed and stroked her throat — a throat no longer as smooth and taut as it had once been. At those moments Nancy allowed herself to think that perhaps there might come a day when he would ask her how she felt about seeing England. But he never did. He told her about Italy, the curious Florentine mix of wool and art and history, showed her the correct way to season a *ragù*. His own country remained unexplored, though he introduced her to English poetry. In return she gave him Robert Frost and Wallace Stevens. Not Whitman.

★   ★   ★

From the bed Nancy could see the street beyond the window, partially obscured by Charles's naked shoulder. The evening had gone well: the drink at the bar, the stroll to his apartment. The easy move to the bedroom, it was usually the bedroom now. They had made love, and soon it would be time to eat. She realised they had fallen into a pattern, and the thought gave her pleasure, lent a spurious permanence to their arrangement.

He lifted her hair away from her neck and breathed in the warmth of her flesh.

'Thank you for the book. I liked the one about the blackbird.'

She said, sleepily, 'Thirteen Ways of Looking . . . '

The poem, he said, reminded him of Japanese woodcuts. Punctuating his words with kisses, he mumbled into her bare shoulder that he wanted to visit Japan one day.

'But if this war goes on much longer, there won't be much left to see.'

Nancy felt warmth and well-being draining out of her, and turned away, drawing the blanket close, thrusting her face deep into the pillow. She wanted to say, I went there once, I went to Japan and saw nothing. Just the inside of an office, a church, a rickshaw. A small paper house on a hillside and a woman in a white kimono. A child, screaming. A woman who is still there, the unprotected target of our bombs.

She wrote every week to Joey, telling him what she was reading, what music she had heard. She found these letters difficult; censorship made information suspect: even something as bland as a new movie. She held back from describing a trip to the coast, a swim in the ocean, knowing it would make painful reading to someone walled in by barbed-wire fences and watchtowers, living in a wooden hut with bare floors. What would have become of her happy-go-lucky Joey by the time they set him free?

'Hey there,' Charles murmured into her ear, his words muffled by the pillow. 'Come back; you're a long way away.' Tactfully, 'How about supper?'

This was one of the times when she was tempted to tell Charles everything; she had a feeling he would understand. But an unspoken pact had been established: they existed in the here and now, within a bubble of warmth and security. What was outside remained outside.

Were she to say 'I have a son. He's in a prison camp for enemy aliens and I'm sick with worry' — worry for his well-being and, unacknowledged, worry too that he might be drifting away, becoming less her son, indeed someone alien — what could Charles say? Comforting her, he would need to say . . . something. Did he, too, have a son? A daughter? Did he have a wife? He surely had a life. A complicated one.

She twisted back into the circle of his arms, clinging to the warmth of him, swept by the fear of another loss; drawing him into her. They fitted together like a soft jigsaw puzzle, breast, belly, thighs, flesh to flesh, her legs trapping his.

'Later,' she said.

45

Letters from home. On days when a dust storm lashed the barracks and whipped the faces of internees hurrying to mess hall or shower block, Joey, alone in the hut, ran his fingers over the thick, creamy paper Nancy favoured, and pictured her writing at the kitchen table of a narrow house in a street with a dry goods store on the corner where once he had sat on the porch steps and watched shabby men buying sardines and Saltine crackers before trudging on towards the endlessly receding horizon.

'*Dear Joey . . .*'

A letter required a reply. His pen hovered, as usual. There were letters unwritten, that sang their silent words in his mind; revised, refined, endlessly qualified to be ever more precise. These were purely theoretical letters. Head stuff. There were others, written but not posted: jottings, despairing or angry, scribbled, torn up. There were, finally, those Joey completed and entrusted to the collection bin, to the trucks, trains and delivery men. These were the envelopes Nancy opened, the pages she read and reread.

One of these was the brief note that told her he was leaving the camp.

He never intended to enlist. Anger, resentment, a sceptical view of the government's change of heart, all pushed him towards non-involvement. In the hut, late at night endless

337

conversations took place, as they took place in other huts. Kazuo and Taro the smart ones, Ichirō the joker, Joey the oddball. Debating, questioning. What if . . . or if not . . . Would it help to . . . but on the other hand . . .

Afterwards, Joey tried to pinpoint what tipped it for him.

Partly he was doing it for Ben, who had carried a burden of guilt for being the brother too young to go to war, the brother who survived. Partly he was doing it for a whole heap of people who thought they were American until told otherwise; when they suddenly discovered they were enemy aliens. He wanted to peel that label off them: smash the wire fence, yell at the guards, 'Category error! Category error!'

Perversity played its part: he disliked being called a smart-ass who felt he was too clever to be gun fodder. And there was revulsion from his surroundings, a flight from apathy. If he signed, wherever they sent him, he would be out of here. He needed space to breathe; he was twenty years old and his body itched for action.

The decisive moment crept up on him unheralded: in the confines of the hut they were arguing fiercely, Ichirō, pacing and turning; Taro and Kazuo on the floor, backs propped against the wooden wall. Joey, cross-legged on the narrow bed, as always when thinking, had reached for pencils and paper and was scribbling aimlessly — patterns and curlicues, geometrical shapes, boxes within boxes. When he had used up the page, he saw that at the bottom he had drawn a rectangle. In one corner of it was a small

338

square filled with dots, and across the rectangle were scrawled scarlet lines. The star-spangled banner.

The ingredient at the heart of the simmering mix: an unacknowledged need to be part of something. To belong.

★   ★   ★

When he found himself on the train (once again, the sound of wheels on tracks, the locomotive smell of coal fumes, old songs and echoes of his father's journey from disengagement to commitment), he was wryly aware that he was leaving one camp for another, one form of discipline for another, one label for another: student, enemy alien, evacuee, internee, soldier . . . She had it right, the hostile girl who snipped off his hair: he made a habit of categorising people. He was certainly categorising himself.

He had mentioned the haircut episode to Ichirō at the time.

'She was incredibly bad tempered.'

'Oh.' Ichirō looked amused. 'That means she likes you.'

'So what does she do if she *doesn't* like you?'

'She ignores you, of course.'

Joey said sarcastically, 'I guess that's the Japanese way.'

'It's certainly Yasuko's way. She's picky. There are guys all over camp still feel the pain of Yasuko's freeze.'

Yasuko. Now he knew her name.

Before leaving he had searched for her all over

the camp, and catching sight of a slim figure in the distance with shiny, square-cut hair, he had called out, 'Hey, wait!' and turning, Iris had smiled at him, surprised.

He stopped. 'Oh! I thought you were — someone else. Your hair . . . '

'I stopped curling it.'

'Yes.'

'Who did you think I was?'

'Someone.' Oddly reluctant to spill the name, he shrugged. 'It doesn't matter.'

He moved off, then turned and called, 'The hair. It's nice, suits you.'

★　★　★

The train rattled on, the wheels and the track creating their own music, laying down the beat: *Oh the Rock Island Line is a mighty fine line,* escaping slaves sang the words, and in its own way the army, too, was a slave master. The army gave orders and insisted on obedience, punished those who went AWOL, but he had volunteered, hadn't he? No one was making him do this. Surely that made a difference.

46

She sat at her table by the window, a brilliant square of ice-blue winter sky like a blank canvas. Around her, walls of fine reeds embedded in dried pulp conveyed a sense of a room wrapped in grass. Skilled decorators had achieved artful simplicity here, though the marks of time and use had darkened the once pale walls.

Long ago, Suzuki had been impatient with Cho-Cho, urging her to move to something more spacious, a bigger house, set in a garden, at the better end of town.

'You could be closer to us.'

Cho-Cho had the money then; the restaurant was flourishing. But she stayed where she was, like a sea creature safe inside the shell of her little house overlooking the harbour. Later, when the bad times came, when the customers could no longer afford the restaurant and she could no longer afford the staff, and then when the long, drawn-out war was no longer a Chinese affair, but suddenly became World War Two, the little house was once again appropriate. In the fat years she had mocked Henry for his love of tradition — 'Why don't you put in modern heating?' — and he had given his slow, infuriating smile. Now she appreciated the irony of her own situation as she warmed her feet on an old charcoal heater tucked under her desk.

On the desk was a typewriter, and curling out

of it a page half covered with neat black marks. She typed a few words, and paused to look out at the sea, a darker blue beneath the sky. She had been writing these letters for years, all the fleeting thoughts that she might have put into words; love visible. As the page clicked slowly up from the platen, she tapped on. One day, she told herself, he will read this, will perhaps reply.

Kanashimi, Trouble meaning its opposite —

He was never any trouble of course, that was their tender joke. He was *Sachio*, her joy; it was his father who misheard the word and called him Joey.

She plucked the page from the typewriter and laid it with others in the metal box on the desk.

She could see the waterfront, and the road that curved up the hill, going out of sight, then reappearing. Her hands rested in her lap, the wrists thin as a young girl's but at thirty-eight she accepted the finely wrinkled skin, the dark patches on the pale surface, the knuckles large against bony fingers. Her rings had gone long ago; how little a diamond fetches when the market tilts the wrong way. Now her hands were bare of jewels, as they were when she was young. Young. She touched the faint scar on her throat.

She recalled standing by this window as a sailor in a white uniform walked up the hill to the house. Where once she watched, waiting for the unknown in fear, now she dared to dream of a future, unknown; a hope deferred for a lifetime. When the war was over, perhaps, whoever won, the victors and the humbled would come to an arrangement, they always did, and maybe another Pinkerton would find his way to her. She would place the metal box of letters on the low table where once a spinning top had flashed its red and yellow rings, and leave him to read his way through her life.

47

Living through hell was not the worst part; that came later, with recollection. Nobody warned him about the persistence of memory as battle injury.

At the beginning Joey thought of himself as a civilian in uniform. He felt he was an imperfect specimen but somehow doubted that the concept of *wabi-sabi* could be stretched to encompass a flawed warrior.

Gradually he adjusted, was transformed, became a hybrid organism: the soldier, a science fiction creature, part man, part machine. The machine obeyed orders, killed without feeling, fought on even when damaged. The man felt fear, remorse, pain. The man bled. Often he died. But before all that he travelled, crossing the ocean with his regiment, packed tight in an oversized can, from one continent to another.

★ ★ ★

Like new cars off a conveyor belt, men in uniform seem to resemble one another. No longer Tom, Dick or Harry, they are now part of a regiment; they have a rank, a number. The consequence, intended or not, is loss of personal identity, loss of difference. The helmet, the khaki combat gear, the backpack, the boots, blur physical differences to create a unifying portrait:

GI Joe. But this particular batch of soldiers had more in common than the uniform. At embarkation a tired sergeant waved them on board without lifting eyes from clipboard: 'Jap battalion, right?'

Joe had a fleeting urge to disagree; make irritating, hair-splitting, city-boy corrections: wrong, we're *Nisei*, okay, sarge? He could guess the response: 'What the fuck is that? Some kinda fancy name for Nips?' Anyway, the sergeant was right: non-white, segregated, they were 'the jap battalion'. The melding had taken time. He had seen mainlanders and Hawaiians, thrust together, bristle with suspicions: the Hawaiians smarting at perceived snubs from the assimilated mainlanders; the reserved, urban mainlanders resentful of the boisterous islanders who spoke their own pidgin American, laughed a lot, sang songs, played the ukulele and defiantly donned their old grass skirts for fun. To the mainlanders, under the circumstances, fun was not an option.

The battalion filed on board, trim, compact. Many wore glasses. His chosen brothers, although he was the only one who stood out, once again the square peg. Among the others, a familiar figure from Tule Lake: a boy Joe had often seen hunched in a corner, pencil in hand, reading and annotating, lost to his surroundings.

'It's . . . Otishi, right? You always had your head in a book.'

'Yeah. I'd planned to finish my Ph.D.'

How do you make God laugh . . .

Otishi glanced around. 'I guess we've been promoted. From Yellow Peril to soldiers in the service of Uncle Sam: Japs, but *our* Japs.'

There were moments at sea, leaning on the rail of the boat, watching dark water foam into a wake of moonlit lace, when Joe recalled another boat journey, a child peering through the rail at dolphins and a magical green light that danced on the water. *America, Joey! It'll be fun!*

The ship's captain, passing, exchanged a mechanical greeting and, misled by the blond naval haircut, asked Joe where he was from.

'Portland, Oregon, sir.'

The captain nodded. 'Rose festival, right? I hear it used to be quite a sight.'

If Joe had added that he was born in Japan, in Nagasaki, Captain Jensen could have told him, in his soft Southern drawl, that he had spent a few days in the town many years before. But Joe was Government Issue now, bound for Italy; the long cluster of linked islands he once studied on the map were on another page of his life, and he said nothing, so he missed hearing the captain's story about the day he climbed a path high above the harbour in Nagasaki with his senior officer to a house with paper walls and met a woman called Butterfly and a small boy with blond curls.

'Good luck, soldier,' he said and moved on.

★ ★ ★

To Joe every new place provided an opportunity for distraction, for escape. Escaping from what, he had not yet worked out. Exploration was what lay ahead, an activity that filled him with elation, even if Africa had seemed an odd destination for

346

a regiment bound for Europe.

Algeria was not an unfamiliar name: it came into a chapter or two of the textbooks, its aboriginal people hammered by waves of invaders, clinging stubbornly to their culture. Did it all come down to culture in the end, the trading of symbols and exchanging of gifts, language, mode of worship; village elders versus incomers?

Below him, watching the regiment disembark, were the locals, who were both Arab and French. Possibly Arab *or* French?

American and *Japanese* . . . *American* or *Japanese: how do you plead?*

Down the gangplank from the old boat that had earlier carried cargoes of bananas and today brought young men in khaki to a war zone, Joey, now GI Joe, found himself marching into Oran, where the ramparts of a Spanish fort loomed over sun-baked, sandy chaos.

From behind him Otishi attempted a gang-plank lecture — 'Phoenicians, Romans, Vandals — ' the noise of the docks drowned out the rest.

They stepped ashore, disembarking into hostility of various kinds. This was the very edge of Africa, a final step on the way to the war in Europe. But Algeria was part of France, allegiances muddled, death a bullet's range away. Were the Arabs friendly?

'How do they feel about us?' Joe wondered aloud.

'We'll find out!' Eager as a beagle, Otishi was peering about him, matching the past against the present, catching history on the hoof.

But the new soldiers, plucked out of confinement and away from watchtowers and armed guards to flourish their crusading credentials, were not here to learn. Before the friendliness of the Algerians could be tested, there were fresh orders: another boat, another sea voyage, another country.

The pep talks made it clear: they were offering their bodies to defend the free world from the Fascist threat. This fight — they knew because they were repeatedly so informed — was all about democracy and freedom; about the crime of people being deported to concentration camps simply for a word on their papers. How much irony could one situation take?

Otishi, by Joe's side as they tramped from one dockside to another, bemoaned the lack of any marching songs for Nisei:

'*Normal* GIs get to sing as they go; swinging rhythm, great tunes . . .'

Back home, Caruso's sweet tones filled the airwaves — 'Over There!' with the boys roaring back, open-throated, to reassure the world that the Yanks were indeed coming, the boys were on their way, to do the job, to win the war.

Joe sang out, tentatively: 'The *half*-Japs, *half*-Yanks are coming!' He shook his head. 'Doesn't quite have the ring of the original, does it?'

48

In four months Joe aged a decade, the compacted time weighing him down like armour: heavy but not always protective. The bright new soldiers who had sailed from Oran to step ashore in Italy were worn and battered now; uniforms filthy, faces changed, stubble sprouting, eyes dulled, lips dried and cracked. They staggered under the weight of backpacks and weapons, the heavy passing of days, weeks, months.

★　★　★

The first engagement, shocking in its suddenness, lay far behind them. They lived with the knowledge that the closeness of bullets whining and whistling past was not fortuitous, they themselves were the targets.

Earlier on, Nancy had written him letters about Italy. Her friend the Englishman had told her stories about Florence and Pompeii, about the past, about art and music and — bafflingly — wool. Joey had read the letters in what he now saw as the idyll of Tule Lake. None of those pages that spoke of Renaissance frescoes and the Medici, of beauty and elegant intrigue, seemed to play any part in the Italy he saw: a place of shattered trees and bomb craters, ruined villages and dead men; the swollen corpses of horses and cattle sweeping past on a raging, flooded river that rose eighteen feet in ten hours. A river to be crossed, under German fire.

At night, collapsing, they leaned against one another, sharing shelter, a waterproof sheet only partially deflecting the endless rain. Individual foxholes resembled graves: they buried themselves beneath camouflage, a fragile roofing of branches and uprooted undergrowth. Occasionally they enjoyed the luxury of a base in an abandoned farmhouse, huddled round a rough table, candle-ends sending wavering shadows on to the walls as they boiled up powdered coffee with powdered milk. 'Real luxury,' Otishi muttered into his tin mug. 'At least it's not powdered water. Yet.'

The men soon lost their fear of shadowy figures moving around them, not enemy scouts but locals: Italian partisans stealthily passing, or women and children scavenging the military garbage for food.

Scraping cold K-rations from a tin plate one night, Joe saw a small, barefoot girl on the edge of the clearing, watching the scraps of food drop to the ground. He slipped a chocolate Hershey bar into her outstretched, grubby hand. He did not feel generous.

★ ★ ★

By day, jittery, wrenched from uneasy sleep, they plodded on, surrounded by the percussion of bombs, the whine and screech of artillery barrage. The orchestra of war in action. Their thoughts went no further than the next assault, the bullet, the shell, the mortar that could make it their last. There was no context to this, no 'bigger picture'. Survival shrank to the size of a man, the soldier ahead of Joe, crawling ant-like, prodding the ground with his bayonet, checking for mines. So far, they were surviving.

The convoy of armoured trucks and jeeps juddered along rural roads turned to mud and marshland. Bogged down in the slurry, the men found ingenious ways to corduroy the mud-swamped roadway, packing logs and roof tiles, crushed containers and debris crossways to create a solid base for churning wheels. Reaching a crossroads they saw what had been a fine villa behind high gates that were now hanging loose. Ahead lay an impassable bog, surface water shivering in the vibration of the tracks and wheels. From the once-graceful mansion they hauled out a broken bathtub, the remains of some Louis XV chairs, their upholstery shredded; a carved table, fragments of marble statues — all useful for creating a firm surface for military wheels to grip.

Bumping, bouncing, they trundled on. At one village, whose houses were strung out along the route like a broken wall, they slowed down, paused for a few minutes. The place was deserted, but by the roadside, at the village trough, a group of women stood washing clothes. With impassive, peasant endurance, stooped over the trough, grimly dunking and scrubbing, they ignored the looming vehicles and the soldiers. One, straightening up to ease her back, caught

Joe's eye and he sketched a salute, attempted a gesture of generalised goodwill.

Up front the first truck coughed into life. As the convoy moved on, liquid mud flung up by the churning wheels splashed the women and their clothes and they cursed, quietly.

Joe wanted to call out, apologise. But he was learning that soldiers were trained to reverse the evolutionary process: to forget the rules of civilised behaviour, falling back into savagery to protect their minds from the dangers of feeling; just as in other ways they protected their bodies from attack. In war there was no time to apologise.

★　★　★

Here and there were glimpses of what this country had been before the war arrived: stone farmhouses sitting on hilltops, pale oxen grazing in grassland, the spears of cypress trees dark against a blue sky. Wheat fields fat with grain. Olive groves where silver leaves — coins minted by sunlight — hung in the branches. The calm south. In that moment of indrawn breath before an attack, the only noise was the twittering of birds and the sound of a stream as it bounced over smooth boulders; a green and yellow landscape where poppies fluttered scarlet among long grass. Then, shattering the silence, tanks and guns crested the horizon and the sky was blotted out by sulphurous fog, the greens and yellows savagely whipped into a palette of mud, and farmhouses reconstructed, as ruins.

Across the open terrain between the woods and the water, they run crablike, in zigzags, knees bent, leaping, crouching, dropping when a shell explodes, locating the source, firing back. Stumbling on, through air filled with gunfire, confusion, the brief scream of a man as he dies. Close at hand Joe hears the muffled *crump* of a mortar; and for a fraction of time there is a sense of suspended action, as in a car crash, a slow motion collision, before the hit: the thunder, the metallic crunch, the smell and sound of battle.

49

No one had told him it wasn't the enemy you should be afraid of, it was the generals. Your own high command. You could kill the enemy. The generals tell you what to do and you obey them. The generals send you off to die.

And here's where it happens.

The orders are clear; secure the next stretch of ground, the next hill; silence the artillery, cross the river. *Silence* the artillery? The river is fast-moving, treacherous. The Germans are on the high ground, concealed, perfectly placed to pick off men up to their armpits in icy water, attempting the insanity of crossing. Blinded with spray, slithering down the banks, fighting the current, he entrusts himself to the churning flood.

How can something as soft, as formless as water hit you with the force of a blow? Water fights dirty, spiteful, no rules. He loses the contest.

The green fills his lungs; the river engulfs him, the fight is over and he sinks into darkness, the chill dulling all pain. He is aware of a vast sorrowful regret. Then he is dragged from the blackness, hauled from the sucking mouth of the riverbed, is face down on the bank, choking, retching, water streaming off him, an unseen figure punching him repeatedly between the shoulders, screaming, 'Cough, damn you, cough!'

Spewing river water, blinded by mud, Joe is hauled to his feet. He tries to wipe mud from his eyes with mud-caked hands. All around, men are running, yelling, falling, cursing. Smoke envelopes him like a shroud.

He peers, blinking, at his shadowy saviour. 'Otishi?'

'Christ, man, you took your time with the breathing!'

Water dribbles from Joe's mouth and nostrils. His lungs stab and he doubles over, coughing liquid mud, tries to draw breath.

'What happened?'

'Shell. Too close.'

They stagger together up the slope towards the trees, Otishi hauling Joe with him. They are clumsy, climbing with absurdly slow, exaggerated care; boots weighed down with a cladding of yellow mud that covers them head to foot; life-size clay maquettes, only eyes and dark, stretched mouths revealing their humanity.

Later, after dark, they slump alongside the others, waiting for the next morning's push.

Joe says, blearily, 'Otishi, you don't do action stuff. You can't even swim. You just read fucking history. How come — '

'Don't knock history. It teaches you things.'

'How to save a drowning man?'

'Right. Bonaparte's men bent bayonets into hooks to fish enemy bodies out of the Nile — '

'You reckoned if the French could fish — '

'Listen, it worked. To a point. I couldn't bend the goddam bayonet, I kind of harpooned you.

355

So did your life pass before your eyes like they say?'

'Just water.'

For a moment Joe feels again the force of it crushing his lungs. The huge sadness.

'My father drowned.'

He wants to say 'You saved my life', which would sound corny. Moreover it is obvious.

'You were pretty quick there.'

'Just practical. There's nothing theoretical about war; you do what you have to do. And you do it. *Fast*. That's Napoleon again.' Through the mud spattering his face, Otishi's eyes gleam dark, his teeth white.

★ ★ ★

In training camp they were taught the nine principles of war: *objective, offensive, mass, economy of force, manoeuvre, unity of command, security, surprise and simplicity.*

Okay in theory. But as Joe was learning, war is not theoretical. War is a bullet that tears through your arm, the shriek of gunfire blasting your ears, the smell of rotting flesh. Trench foot.

Through the fog, the unrelenting rain, men screamed aloud with the agony of every step. Ankle-deep in quagmire in boots that leaked and split, there was no way to protect infected feet. The burning, the swelling were warnings that came too late: first the deadly numbing, then the real pain, feet turning blue, toes weeping like burst blisters. With luck and dry socks, the swelling subsided. If not, toes twisted like evil growths, spongy and leprous, came away as a man wrenched off his boot. There were amputations. Joe's toes were now stabbing, burning. The swelling would follow. Government-issue combat boots were not made for this bone-chilling, amphibious world.

When Joe stumbled over the dead German soldier half buried in a crater, what he saw first was the dark blood, the tumble of guts. Then he saw the boots. Strong leather. Hobnailed soles. *Waterproof*. Joe measured his foot against the dead man's, squatted and fumbled at laces strong as twine. Inside the boots the dead man's socks were dry; an impossible luxury. Off with his soaking footwear; on with the German's socks and boots, enclosing his feet like a thick skin, supporting, protecting. Unashamed, he felt grateful to the body he had robbed.

He scrambled to his feet, quickening his pace to catch up with the others. Within the boots, he flexed his dry toes.

To Nancy he wrote, *I can't tell you where we are; actually I don't know where we are. Unfortunately, the enemy knows . . . It's raining. It's always raining . . .* '

Afterwards he does the calculations: how much time to obliterate a town; how many bombs to smash a monastery; how long it takes to lose fifty thousand men and at the end gain nothing but the knowledge that it was never necessary? At the time, there *is* no time, just the blind reflex to obey the order. Cassino is pounded into ruin, and high above him Joe sees people fleeing as the monastery dissolves into a torrent of crumbling walls, a stone cascade showering the troops below. Only later, as German paratroopers float down to occupy the shell, does the full irony become clear: they have succeeded in turning a place of sanctuary shielding a couple of hundred civilians into the impregnable fortress the generals had believed it to be.

'Whoever wins,' Otishi commented, 'this will be in a history book one day.'

'You could write it.'

'You kidding? That's for the generals.'

★ ★ ★

The generals give orders. Dog-face soldiers obey, hurling themselves into wall after wall of fire. Acronyms multiply; each day a new SNAFU. Situation Normal, All Fucked Up. Plus FUBAR: Fucked Up Beyond All Repair. Cassino was a FUBAR. The generals themselves inspire a rich, multilingual litany of curses. Gurkhas, Poles, Anzacs, Tommies, Yanks — all have a special word for the gold-braid assholes, the guys who write the memoirs, the bastards.

The Nisei's bastard — *kisama* — was Mark Clark, who sent men to their deaths; the *kisama* who chose the wrong river to cross and the wrong day to cross it.

'What did we do?' Joe hears a mutter from the GI next to him, face down in a foxhole, 'to deserve this shit-head?'

358

Half blinded by mud, they crawl from the foxhole and press on. Jogging clumsily over unexpectedly soft turf, Joe stumbles and glances down: he is trampling the prostrate bodies of dead GIs from the line ahead of him. This is the first time, though not the last, that he throws up. Doubled over, the bile filling his mouth, he retches and runs on, knees bent, dead men underfoot.

Spilled from ripped knapsacks, strewn around the dead like sacrificial offerings, are snapshots, odd socks, bibles, razors, letters from home, all beaten into the ground by the remorseless rain.

How much ground did they cover? A mile? A few yards? Inches? How long would it take to cross the next river, advancing, retreating, aiming and ducking fire as they waded through the swollen water? Nobody knew or cared how far the next hill was — only how long it cost to take it.

In this often perpendicular landscape, wheels were useless. Mules were brought in to carry food, water, guns, ammunition, the wounded. The dead. While the generals gave orders, the officers took their chances with the men, and there came a day when every commander but one of the regiment was dead or injured.

At sunset, following a day of doomed sorties, Joe saw, far off, a line of mules plodding back to mountain base with what appeared to be sacks of grain strung across the saddles. As they came nearer, he saw the mules were laden with bodies.

The mules waited, rain dripping off lowered heads, while dead officers were hauled off the saddles and laid out side by side, a human raft floating on the waterlogged earth. Tired men stood silently by the bodies as though waiting for a service to begin. In due course there would be official recognition; pomp and ceremony. This was the real thing.

One GI crouched awkwardly to pat a sodden shoulder, another touched a dead officer's sleeve. There were muttered obscenities: inarticulate farewells. Joe bent to straighten the torn jacket of a young lieutenant, a Bostonian who had told him yesterday that he planned to come back one day, to see this country properly.

★ ★ ★

It was August when they crossed the Arno, not far from Florence, and coming up over a rise Otishi slapped Joe's sleeve and pointed out a distant shaft of pale stone, slender arches catching the sun: the leaning tower of Pisa. Nobody slackened pace: Pisa, like Florence, was just another dot on the map.

On the outskirts of town villas sheltered, secluded behind walls and iron gates, some set in stone-flagged courtyards. The path of war had swerved here and the street was undamaged. The houses stood shabby and neglected, stucco flaking, shutters hanging crooked from broken hinges. A terracotta urn on a gatepost was cracked, spilling dried earth, dead roots. Evidence of diminished splendour and privilege.

As the convoy penetrated further into the narrow streets, the urban terracing, the damage was all around them: entire houses crushed to rubble, women in dusty black silently picking over the debris, lining up at a wrecked shopfront for bread. Massive walls that had resisted destruction for centuries lay crumbled into chunks of stone. A landscape of defeat.

★ ★ ★

Occasionally they paused at a town where sunshine and Italian girls in summer frocks offered a brief reunion with what seemed like ordinary life. Starving, selling anything that might buy food, survivors welcomed the uniforms, high-born matrons grimly moonlighting as tarts, with a pre-penetration *aperitivo* for officers. GIs got young girls who smiled, offering rounded bodies, a momentary forgetting, a quick fuck in a back room or the park in return for nylons, spare rations, cigarettes and gratitude. Sometimes they got dollars.

There were promises: 'When this is over, Rosina, I'm coming back to find you.'

The definition of comfort can change with circumstances: a flimsy metal seat on the pavement, a rusty cafe table and a glass of sour wine could feel like luxury.

Joe closed his eyes and felt the warmth of the sun sink into his bones. His ribs ached, his feet hurt and there was an unspecific soreness in his guts. He flexed unwilling muscles and stretched out his legs across the pavement, allowed himself to let go, to drift for a moment; but drifting was bad, it allowed unwelcome thoughts to surface. Passing a once-elegant villa earlier, Joe had glimpsed a room empty of furniture, an electric cable hanging from the ceiling where a chandelier had spread its crystal wings. At the window a woman stared, unseeing, into the street. A bare room, a woman alone, waiting. Elsewhere, in another place, were waiting women being ordered to defend their country against the approaching Americans? Arming themselves, barricading their homes — vulnerable structures built not of stone and brick, but of more fragile materials. How do you barricade a structure of paper and wood?

He took another gulp of wine. Not far from vinegar, it still warmed his guts; it gave comfort.

50

Cho-Cho is often hungry, but she is also grateful: at least she is not in Tokyo, where American B-29s have efficiently fire-bombed the city to rubble. Here plants grow and birds sing. But she is hungry, a constant condition.

There is a haiku she recalls with wry nostalgia, written by a woman nearly two hundred years before, but some things don't change — for example, yearnings in a time of shortage.

Once again to be in a world of white rice.
The fragrance of the plums.

White rice! A memory. These days they get by on barley and potatoes; weeds. They gather and grind acorns.

* * *

Official bulletins told them sawdust could usefully supplement flour in a proportion of one to four when making dumplings. Once again they were eating silkworms, harvesting nourishment from sea grasses, trapping snails, frogs, grasshoppers. Fish had vanished. Eggs were but a memory, the hens too scrawny and listless to lay, until they went under the knife, giving up flesh, blood, gizzards, bones. Some said feathers could be stewed.

The government had been bullying them for years. Ministerial orders littered the landscape the way over-ripe fruit had once dropped from trees: one edict prohibited the production and sale of luxury goods, and overnight a whole range of what made life bearable for the well-to-do vanished from the shelves. Cho-Cho folded up her fine silk garments, stroking each one gently as if soothing a child before turning out the light. Then she put them away in a trunk, along with her glove-soft shoes, wrapped in tissue.

'Oh, Suzuki,' she sighed, 'my beautiful French shoes!'

How could she continue to wear them now? Clogs had been designated 'patriotic'; nothing else was seen on the street as people patriotically clacked their way to work on wooden platforms.

She missed her elegant footwear, the sensuous pleasure of fine fabric touching her skin; she felt that in some way she was being punished. Her sense of despondency shocked her: was she then so trivial, so frivolous, that mere lack of luxury was so important? She saw that Suzuki did not grumble; she had not complained even when widowed, but then Suzuki was always so busy, finding creative ways to extend the life of clothes, mending, patching, passing down garments from older to younger siblings; cooking or cleaning or worrying about one or other of her children. Without such distractions, Cho-Cho had only herself to think about, and she saw that solipsism was not comforting at a time like this.

Worse was to come. Offering restaurant menus

above a strictly fixed price could land you in jail; it now cost her more to provide a meal than she could charge a customer. She closed the restaurant.

As the weather sharpened into wintry cold the Nagasaki black market cost of coal rose to almost 50 per cent above the official price. 'And the problem,' as Suzuki pointed out, 'is that you can't find any at the official price.'

Above all, Cho-Cho missed Henry, missed their talks, their arguments, the letters he received from America that had linked her vicariously to her child. After Henry died, Oregon had drifted away like a floating island, not quite real. There had been a note from the American woman, the blonde wife, widow, stepmother. She seemed friendly and Cho-Cho had replied, but then came Pearl Harbor, and information vanished into a void — personal information, anyway. Official information was plentiful: official broadcasts celebrating victories by the Imperial forces and exhorting the populace to work harder, sacrifice more for the glory of the Emperor. There were also detailed accounts of terrible losses by the Americans, and although Cho-Cho knew that America was far from the war zone, she also knew that armies swallowed up young men from farms and peaceful cities and spat them out on to the battlefield. She found herself praying to the Methodist God as well as to Shinto *Kami* without much faith in either.

She was teaching again, instructing the young, running air raid drills, she was a *shisō*, a woman

365

getting by in a man's world, but a man's world was for getting killed in: a boy was safe only until the qualifying birthday, then came military service. She had become one of a grim sisterhood of women whose sons were of an age to take their place in the firing line.

She knew what an American soldier looked like: steel helmet, gun and bayonet, the snarling caricature of the propaganda posters. But she had not learned to hate the enemy: behind the gun, beneath the helmet what she saw was a child with blue eyes. She told herself he would be safer as an American soldier; Henry's books had taught her how the West valued human life; the army would care about its men. A Japanese soldier did not exist as an individual, simply as part of a patriotic force. But any soldier's fate was finely balanced: death or survival, the choice not his to make.

Where would he be sent to face warfare? If he survived, would she see him one day, walking up the path from the harbour, golden and American, like his father?

51

Trundled in boxcars from one combat zone to another, expendable pawns, with new recruits arriving daily to step into dead men's shoes, Nisei GIs were not long-lived.

Now, heading north-west on foot, they seemed always to be climbing, clawing their way through a landscape rising before them like an endless cliff, slogging through France.

★   ★   ★

He was learning that maps are instruments of time. It took three days to cross a river, storm a hill. It took a week to battle their way to and claim the dot on the map which was once a town and was now a place of ruins.

They took La Bruyères, street by street, house by house, room by room. Booby-trapped doors, snipers, mines, the smoke and screech of mortars, crack of gunfire. Men fell as they advanced, gaining a yard, losing it . . . When at nightfall they collapsed, exhausted, Joe saw how many had been lost; some who had become friends lying in the mud alongside fallen Germans, uniforms indistinguishable, caked with clay, dark with blood.

They squatted and slumped, the limping remnants of the 100th and the 442nd snatching a breathing space. The hut-mates of Tule were scattered: Kazuo could be at the bottom of a ditch somewhere along the way; Ichirō was in a field hospital the last time Joe heard.

Pausing to gulp water or chew a soggy chocolate bar, the men swapped bleak jokes, checking the current acceptable level of 'vacation wound', an injury bad enough to get a man away from the front.

'How about death?'

'Death could be good. No way you'll get ordered to advance if you're dead.'

But the gold braid had ways of trumping the blackest joke. Dragging themselves to attention, the men got the message: a battalion of Texas Guard was trapped in the forest nine miles to the east, without food and water, surrounded by Germans.

The general's words were read out, loud and clear.

'Two previous rescue attempts have failed.' Then the punchline. The battalion was to be rescued, 'at all costs'.

At all costs?

Otishi murmured, 'When a Spartan soldier was issued with a shield he was ordered to come back *with* it or *on* it.'

Joe glanced around. 'No shields.'

'Same order.'

★ ★ ★

It took five days and eight hundred casualties to rescue two hundred and eleven men.

The Germans were dug in, camouflaged,

368

waiting. The 442nd hacked its way through frozen undergrowth thick as jungle; machine-gun fire burned through the yellow haze. Progress was yard by yard, snaking forward, belly in the mud. Cresting a low ridge they were exposed for a fatal moment and the mortars erupted. Joe was sent flying by the blast. He rolled, grabbing at exposed roots, undergrowth. Up ahead, through the swirling dust of the explosion, a bloody uniform sprawled, twisted. He crawled closer, chanting the front-line mantra, 'You're okay kid, you'll be okay.' Crouching to drag the wounded man out of the line of fire, he peered into the unconscious, dirt-caked face and saw it was Otishi.

Hold on, you'll be okay kid, hold on; shielding the shattered body with his own, yelling for a stretcher.

He tries to lift the sodden body and *Jesus Christ, oh Christ* — Otishi's helmet tilts and his brains spill down his face and over Joe's hands.

52

Before the war Cho-Cho had cajoled and bullied girls to emerge from their invisibility, take charge of their own lives. She was aware that today's women, sweating in coal mines, steel mills and factories to support the war, looked back yearningly to those inactive years.

She and Suzuki too found comfort in looking back, to the days when Cho-Cho and Henry sparred light-heartedly about tradition and women's rights; when all three lived at ease in the glow of affection, even if Suzuki gave more than she received. Now they were equals, two women alone in different ways, warming hands and feet at a tiny charcoal burner.

They had been lucky, so far, in Nagasaki. While other cities large and small were bombed and burned, they had remained virtually untouched. A recent raid on the shipyards and Mitsubishi works had caused alarm: some of the bombs had hit the hospital and medical school.

A few days later Suzuki trotted up the hill to Cho-Cho. Parents were worried: there might be more raids. They were evacuating children, 'Just in case. Making up groups. I'm taking the girls. Come with us.'

'I'd rather stay here.'

Cho-Cho's small, wood-framed house was across the harbour, further away from the docks, and long ago she had constructed a cellar. She promised to use it. If the planes came, she would be safe in her cellar.

There was an odd sense of waiting: perhaps more raids were on the way. Or perhaps talks were going on, somewhere at the centre of power, and decisions were being weighed. Perhaps — a tentative thought — despite the martial exhortations, peace was being sought. How long could they hold out? How many more would be sacrificed?

Meanwhile, she rolled another sheet of paper into her typewriter and began another letter, to join the rest in the embossed metal box on the desk.

'*My dear Sachio . . .* '

★   ★   ★

On 6 August something unimaginable occurred in Hiroshima. She listened, incredulous, to the reports: this was not an air raid, it was an apocalypse. People began arriving in Nagasaki, fleeing the nightmare, their bodies hideously burned, some blinded, others maimed, barely alive. All over the country leaflets, not bombs, fell from the skies: the American president warned the Japanese people, 'if they do not now accept our terms they may expect a rain of ruin from the air the like of which has never been seen on earth'.

No leaflets were dropped over Nagasaki. Through some bureaucratic error they were not warned. In Nagasaki life went on as usual.

On the morning of 9 August, shortly before

8 a.m., an air-raid warning sounded. Cho-Cho prepared to honour her promise to Suzuki and go down to the cellar, but no planes appeared and half an hour later she heard the siren. All Clear.

She watered plants wilting in the intense heat. She tapped out the last page of a letter to Joey and placed it in the metal storage box. Then she washed some clothes, wrung them out and dropped them into an enamel bowl. Outside the house, even with an overcast sky, they would soon dry.

The time was just coming up to eleven. She stood on the threshold for a moment, watching a bird searching without success for worms. Even worms were in short supply now, put to good use in kitchens. She was preparing to hang up a towel when she heard the sound of an approaching plane. Looking up, she saw two bombers — by now everyone could recognise a B-29. They were some way off, and high, possibly on a reconnaissance flight. As a small statement of defiance she decided she would continue to hang up the clothes. If the planes came lower, she would retreat to the cellar.

She threw the towel over the line and glanced back over her shoulder as a dark, bulky shape dropped from the plane like an egg from a hen. There was thunder. A flash that cracked open the sky. The world roared. Went white.

53

One night when they still had the house and the electric kitchen; when they were doing all right, but doubts of another sort encroached, and she and Ben sat talking, Nancy had said, 'We did the right thing,' touching his hand, 'didn't we, Ben? Joey's happy here. What sort of life would he have had in that place?'

But Ben's reply seemed to be part of a different conversation: 'What must it have been like, for her, knowing nothing of him?'

At the time Nancy had closed her mind to the question. Now, with the wisdom of hindsight, she knows better. How would it have been for her, knowing Joey was out there in the world, growing up, being changed by it, and knowing nothing of him?

He calls himself Joe now, but to her he is still Joey; when she dreams of him, he is the child she remembers — bright-haired, running across a park or splashing towards her through a puddle, after rain, the sun catching the spray.

She cannot control her dreams, just as she cannot control the spasm of her heart as he comes towards her now off the train, a train disgorging soldiers, the platform crowded with mothers and wives, sweethearts and sisters.

His golden curls have gone, brutally shorn; a fine stubble veils his skull and his frame is thin and hard in the military uniform. She can

373

discern scars, scatterings of imperfection: she is aware that the skin of his face is no longer smooth as a peeled egg, the way she remembers it. There is puckering at his eyes, and marks here and there, the aftermath of the lacerations and random injuries of warfare.

She watched the official homecoming on the newsreel in the local cinema: the music playing and flags flying, the President there in the rain to welcome the boys to Washington as heroes, though Nancy wished it could have been not Truman but Roosevelt, her old fallen idol, who had put boys like these — whole families — behind barbed wire at a time of paranoia. That would have had a satisfying irony.

But it's over and here he is, with his unit, so few survivors, so many lost comrades, Japanese American bones sown in foreign fields where death and victory were harvested. The depleted 100th and 442nd, two regiments combined, much decorated, renamed the Purple Heart Battalion now, but she sees no pride in his face; only a long tiredness.

He reaches her and they hug, laughing, the way people do when words seem insufficient. She has to rise on tiptoe, stretch her neck to reach his face, and as she holds him close, another moment brushes her, his arms tight around her neck, a small body clinging — '*This is my mom!*' A moment of frozen time.

Then he releases her, with a grin. 'Hi, Nance.' *Ben's name for her.* She must stop thinking of him as a child.

She recalls words, heard often at services in

church: 'For with much wisdom is much grief, and he that increaseth knowledge increaseth sorrow.' They both have increased knowledge, and in Joey's face she sees the loss of innocence.

And Joe, too, sees the sorrow that comes with knowledge, in the face she lifts to his.

★   ★   ★

When they reached the street, he stood on the sidewalk and stared at Louis and Mary's old house, looked it over, smiling, surprised. In his absence it seemed to have acquired a pleasingly old-fashioned charm.

A passing couple, middle-aged, waved to Nancy from across the street and she waved back, calling out to them that this was her son, Joey, back from the war in Europe. The woman beamed and the man raised his hat, noted the decoration on Joe's breast and called back what a great job the boys had done.

'We're proud of you, son. Welcome home.'

Joe went ahead of Nancy up the stairs — the fifth tread still creaked with that sound like a parrot's squawk, the banister was ridged with wood-grain under his fingertips the way he remembered. He opened the door to his room: it was dust-free and smelled of wax polish and lavender; all his things in place, smooth white sheets on the bed. He felt a squeezing sensation in his chest, an unaccustomed pricking behind his eyes.

'You didn't change a thing.'

He threw his bag on the bed and looked around.

'Funny, I remember it smaller. I've slept in some pretty cramped places since I left here.'

He stretched out on the bed and said again, wonderingly, 'Nothing's changed.'

'You've changed,' she said.

She remembered when he left for the internment camp they embraced and he touched her cheek in a brief gesture of goodbye; smooth fingers, the hand of a boy who spent his days in the classroom or the sunshine, nails clean, skin lightly tanned, faint golden hairs on the back of his wrist. The hand she held in hers now was hard, seemed bigger, the nails ragged, fingers rough. A jagged line like a badly stitched repair ran across the back of his hand, up his arm, a scar where shrapnel had torn the flesh. He too was scarred. For a moment she was unable to speak, swallowing, patting his damaged hand. Finally she asked about France . . .

In the Vosges, he said, like a lecturer offering a statistic, life expectancy was seventeen days . . .

He's screaming for a stretcher for Otishi, man here needs a stretcher. Through the cacophony of guns and obscenities, shouted commands order him on: dead men don't get stretchers. The attack continues. Men stumble as they run, treading the pulpy bodies of the fallen underfoot. And the Texans are rescued; the mission is pronounced a success.

'Tell me about France,' Nancy said, again. He shook his head. He brushed his hand along the line of books above the bed. 'Nance, you

376

remember Whitman: 'I play not marches for accepted victors only — '.' She joined in, her voice chiming with his, ''I play marches for conquer'd and slain persons'.'

'Right. But then he says he plays also for the generals. *The generals?* Assholes like Dahlquist and Mark Clark and MacArthur, who sent men to die while they made notes for their memoirs? March for the *generals?* Shit.'

He had not intended to burden her with these thoughts.

'You know what we dreamed of? Over there? A good cup of coffee.'

'Coming up,' she said.

As he released her hand, he saw she was wearing a ring: a broad band of gold delicately chased and enamelled with dark blue. He touched it lightly.

'I never saw this before.'

'It was a goodbye present. From a friend.'

'Nice.'

She went carefully down the steep staircase. When he had rested, returned to normal life, there would be time to talk about his future: the GI Bill gave men the chance to plan, make choices — a privilege the vets never had.

In the kitchen she slipped the ring from her finger and studied the words engraved on the inside: *Il buon tempo verrà.* The good time will come.

'The ring is old,' Charles had told her. 'I had the words engraved. It's what Shelley had on his Italian ring.'

She had only once broken their pact of

377

inhabiting a bubble sealed from the world's woes: when she received the letter from Joey telling her he had enlisted, was on his way to the Front. She was in tears when Charles arrived and he had comforted her, listening while she wept and talked, not only of Joey in the war zone, but of Ben, the beautiful swimmer who drowned in the scummy waters of the Anacostia.

He produced a folded handkerchief, carefully wiping away her tears.

'We had a march in England a few years ago. Two thousand miles, Jarrow to London; men demanding work. The younger ones are probably at the Front now.'

Charles was rarely direct; his job not spelled out, his explanations oblique, hazy. Things were 'complicated' or 'difficult' in his life, even his departure to do with 'things' that involved the Embassy. Not for discussion. But that day he was different, guiding Nancy through her fears for Joey, reflecting on the problems of a family.

'When they're small, you have small worries — scraped knees, bullying at school. When they grow up . . . ' a vague gesture of helpless anxiety.

He had two daughters. 'One's a Land Girl — helping with the war effort. The other's a nurse. Nice girls.' He reflected for a moment. 'I don't think I know them very well.' A longer silence.

'Their mother . . . ' Nancy noted it was 'their mother' rather than 'my wife'. 'I don't think I know her very well either. It didn't seem to matter too much; we jog along — jogged along, pretty well. I'd say a lot of marriages are like

378

that, a case of jogging along.'

If she were truthful, she and Ben had pretty much jogged along, the brightness of young love tarnished by events.

Charles handed her the tiny box the day he left. He said, 'Read the words. Trust the words.'

Il buon tempo verrà. He could have meant the good times would come when Joey was home from the war. Or he could have meant something quite different.

She made coffee and carried it up the stairs.

★　★　★

Next morning, early, Joe walked down the street and retraced the neighbourhood of his memories. The shadow of a tree that fell across the sidewalk, where as a boy he had jumped the phantom log. The corner where two houses met, their rooftops jostling in ungainly angles, unplanned rivalry. He used to imagine them quarrelling, like Disney cartoon houses, in high, sharp voices, all scowls and sharp elbows.

People passed him, on their way to work, preoccupied, hurrying. The number of cars surprised him, all so shiny. This was a place where the earth was masked by tarmac and concrete. No mud here; even the flower beds looked sifted and clean, composed of some salubrious material. In the morning sunlight plants glowed, washed down by yesterday's rain. Everything looked fresh, unbroken, new. He walked on, easy-paced.

Now and then he came to a halt, stared at a

shopfront or a house window, frowning. At an intersection he passed a news-stand and a front-page story caught his eye. He paused to read a few lines before buying the paper. Then he stood by the door and read the story, slowly, to the end. When he finished, he turned back, away from home, heading for the old town.

★ ★ ★

The slam of the front door shook the building. He strode into the kitchen, startling Nancy.

'Joey?'

He flung down the newspaper with a force that sent it sliding across the tabletop to land on the floor at her feet. She stooped and picked it up.

'What the flaming fuck — ' He took a deep breath.

'Sorry.'

His face was pale, the bones standing out sharply.

'What in hell is going on here? There are signs in shops — 'No Japs served' and rooming-house windows with 'Move on Japs'. The newspaper says State House representatives are trying to stop Japanese Americans from returning to Oregon.' He paused; slowed down.

'I took a walk to the river, to Japan town — '

'Oh!' Nancy broke in, 'it's not — '

'I know: it has a different name now. I called on a couple of families I knew from Tule. One of the sons was with me in France. Their homes had been vandalised, their stuff stolen, smashed

380

up. One of them found their cat hanging from a tree by the front door. Neighbours asked when they planned to *move on*.'

Distraught, Nancy said, 'It's not just this town, Joey. People read the stories — the papers were full of how the Japanese treated their prisoners of war: the torture, the brutality, death marches, executions. There were pictures of a Japanese soldier about to cut off an American boy's head with a Samurai sword. That's what being Japanese means to Americans.'

'But not *these* Japanese; they'd spent their lives here. Why do you think the boys from the camps volunteered? To defend an America that says 'No Japs served'?'

'I promise you it's only a few people who feel like that. A minority.'

'But not an alien minority.'

He had reflected more than once on why his battalion had been chosen to rescue the trapped Texans in France.

'I thought, maybe they sent us in because they knew we wouldn't let anything stop us. They were betting on the *banzai* crap. But now I'm thinking maybe we were sent in because if we failed, if we all bit the dust, well, hell, it's just a bunch of Japs, right . . . '

His head was throbbing, his mouth was dry. He filled a glass with water and drank thirstily. He put down the empty glass and looked around the kitchen as though taking an inventory, touching a mug, a cooking pan, ordinary objects that offered the safety of familiarity. A fork was a fork; these things did not change.

'I didn't know I was Japanese until Roosevelt told me I was. But in Italy I felt things were different: we were all GIs. together, no them and us. We were part of the whole.'

'You're heroes.'

'But they don't serve us in the corner store. Forget the Purple Hearts. What's a hero? Someone who goes in even if he knows he'll be killed? Isn't that a bit Japanese? A bit kamikaze?'

'No,' she said. 'That's courage. Don't put yourself down.'

She noticed he was washing his hands, vigorously, under the running tap, rubbing hard, as though to scrub off the skin. He reached for a kitchen knife, tested the sharp tip against the flesh of his hand, pressing it till the blood welled. He dropped the knife on the worktop and let cold water run over his hand, dripping red into the white sink.

'My guts are twisting up, Nance, I get the feeling I'm being pulled apart. There was a time in history when men were disembowelled, hanged, drawn and quartered for treason, horses dragged bits of their bodies in different directions . . .

'I'm an American, right? I'm also one of those who won't be served in the hardware store down the street; there's no room for *my sort* in those rooming houses with the sign in the window.'

He opened the refrigerator door. The brightly lit interior was filled with food: meat, tomatoes, bread, a jar of jelly, peanut butter. Shelves of plenty. Distractedly he opened and closed the door several times.

382

'Remember when I was a kid I used to ask: does the light go out when you close the door? You used to tell me it did, but I was never sure. People smile at you but when they close their doors do they switch off the smile? You can never know.

'I should never have volunteered. The Stars and Stripes crap? I should've stuck in Tule, behind the barbed wire. Where aliens belong. Some of the guys in the battalion who came home early, they couldn't see their folks right away, you know why? Because their parents were still in detention.'

In the silence he listened to the sound of car wheels going past, the swishing of tyres on wet tarmac.

They had not spoken of Cho-Cho, skirting the subject as though avoiding an open wound. Now he was casting about for words.

'Nagasaki,' he began. When the troops first heard about Hiroshima they were puzzled. A bomb. *One bomb?* They had dropped thousands on Tokyo. Then it became clear that this was not just a bomb, it was a weapon like no other. The statistics were presented reassuringly: they spoke of factories flattened, steelworks, railroads destroyed; the enemy's war machine obliterated.

Three days later the jokily named Fat Man burst its steel belly over Nagasaki. A plutonium bomb. Again the official announcements spoke of factories flattened, Mitsubishi steelworks pulverised. The troops listened to Truman on the army radio, the mild voice, neutral words: docks, factories, railroads, communications . . .

At the time Joe heard nothing of people burning like torches, bleeding, dying. The details emerged later, slipping past MacArthur's censors, smuggled out by the typewriter-toting press the general hated, what he called a fifth column undermining their own countrymen.

What Joe heard at the time and what he learned afterwards had melded in his head, numbing him. Misinformation overload. The atomic plague. The plague 'his' people had visited on 'his' people. And somewhere in there, among the obliterated, or the surviving, was a mother he could no longer visualise.

He said, 'I can't stay here.'

★　★　★

Nancy had heard nothing since the long-ago letter and the snapshot of the woman with pale hands folded in her lap; no word since the Bomb and the surrender. The country had been destroyed; she had seen the newsreels, listened to radio reports of Tokyo firebombed to a desert of ash. Gehenna recreated at Hiroshima and Nagasaki. But the reports spoke of buildings; of concrete and steel. They did not describe the dead or maimed beneath the mushroom cloud. No details of human suffering were offered, only the triumph: an end to the war. She had closed her mind, her eyes, her ears to what that might mean to one faraway person.

She felt dread building inside her; if she spoke or looked at him the tears would spill. She stared at a button on his shirt hanging loose on its thread. She wanted to cry out, don't abandon me! But appalled by her shocking admission of need she pressed her fingers to her lips to prevent such words of weakness from tumbling out.

He took the hand she had pressed to her mouth and held it tightly between his own.

'If it weren't for you, Nance,' he said. And then was unable to continue.

Outside, the sun had been blotted out by heavy clouds seeping rain. Tyres hissed briefly. In a silence between passing cars, she heard him say, 'I have to go back.'

She pulled her hand free and nodded, as though he had announced he needed to fill the car with gas.

'Right.'

She waited, resigned.

'She's probably a statistic,' Joe said. 'But who knows? People did survive.'

He said, without bitterness, 'I've tried to understand, to accept she thought giving me away would give me a better life. But I always come up against a wall. There has to be something more.'

And this, Nancy sees, is what is meant by the moment of truth.

'Listen,' she said. 'That day in Nagasaki . . . '

Weighed down by a guilt that has burdened her for half her life, she no longer has the strength to put up another barrier.

'I talked to her, you were with Ben playing outside the house. I talked and talked. She just listened. And I found the way to get to her. Just me. Your father never knew.

'I'd tried everything: a better future for you, a boy needs a father, all that. She was like stone. Then ... ' Nancy faltered. 'Then I told her I could never have a child. You were Ben's only chance to have a son. I told her how it would finish him, never to be able to care for his only child.

'I said to her, 'You're a young woman, you can rebuild your life, have another child. Ben can't do that. We are in your hands.'' She stopped, took a deep, shaky breath.

★   ★   ★

Joe had wondered, in the past, why Nancy had never produced any children of her own. It must have been hard, he says to her now, to have been aware so young that she could never bear a child. For her to live with that knowledge.

'Ah, but I didn't know, *then*. I did an evil thing. I lied.'

She tries to lick her lips but her dried-out tongue cleaves to the roof of her mouth.

'I told her I was barren and she parted with her most precious treasure. She gave you to me.'

Now was the time to go through the words she knew so well: how she had never forgiven herself. How the Church became enemy territory, God out of reach, how she could no longer pray to be forgiven. But she said none of this.

'And then it turned out to be the truth. We tried for years. I never conceived. My lie became a self-fulfilling prophecy.'

She is shaking as he holds her. Joe is surprised by how small she is, the way her head rests, tired, on his breast. She, who has always been the strong one. He draws her close, rubs his chin gently against her hair.

'Hey, Nance, trust a churchgoing gal to beat up on herself,' he says, and Nancy attempts a shaky laugh, and sobs on his shoulder, in an abandonment of grief and the healing release of an old, enduring sorrow and her long agony of punishment and guilt.

PART FIVE

54

What was he expecting of Tokyo?

The Germans bombed Guernica; the Japanese bombed Chungking; the British bombed Dresden, the Americans Tokyo. Tokyo the last of a terrible line.

On one March night, two hundred and seventy-nine B-29 Superfortress bombers dropped half a million napalm-filled incendiary cylinders on to the city below. Walls of fire trapped people fleeing for their lives and the burning wind sucked them into the consuming flames. Water boiled in the canals, and waves of molten glass poured through the streets. Birds burst into flame in mid-air. Fifteen square miles of the city were flattened; more than 100,000 people were killed; another 40,000 injured, burned. All this Joe knows from what he has heard and read. Now he stands in the place itself.

In Italy he witnessed devastation — helped create it. The ruins of Cassino, the shattered towns and villages, the transforming hand of war. This is something else.

The city has been crushed to ash and cinders, a burnt-out emptiness where houses stood, where people worked and lived and slept. Here and there a concrete structure breaks the rubble surface — a gutted department store, a square stone building topped by a blasted clock tower, a blackened mass that had been a movie theatre;

two twisted metal shafts that once were office blocks.

Joe had one long-gone day driven past a Californian hill-side consumed by fire, blackened, still smoking, the gaunt skeleton of what had been a forest. Tokyo, like that forest, is a graveyard of trees: not one wooden building survived the firestorm, not a dwelling was left standing.

Eerily untouched, the Imperial Palace sits within its moat as though ringed by magical waters. A few yards away he can see the Dai-Ichi insurance building, squat and solid as a fortress; busy with people in uniform coming and going, jeeps lined up outside. This is the American HQ.

He steps through the doorway and enters America. Gleam and polish and comfortable chairs; young bodies encased in crisp khaki come and go in a hurry. There are ceiling lights, desk lamps, shades and chandeliers. The air smells different.

At Reception, he gives his name, presents his papers. Here there is no second glance, no mismatch. Joseph Theodore Pinkerton. Here, he's the right man in the right place.

He is located on a list, identified, tagged, but this time with a difference: now he wears a label that proclaims him a regular guy. One of the gang running the show.

At his desk he is engulfed by checklists, information of every sort: guidelines, schedules, 'categories of suppression'. At the next desk is another uniformed figure surrounded by papers.

Joe calls across: 'These categories. What are we suppressing?'

'They've given us thirty-one topics to be avoided: Criticism of Occupation Forces, Criticism of the United States, Criticism of Allies, black market activities — it's all listed.'

'So basically we're censoring . . . '

'Everything. Yeah. But we're not allowed to mention it. See there, under 'topics to be avoided': References to Censorship.'

★   ★   ★

He walks the streets, charting the ruins as an archaeologist might rebuild a Roman city from its surviving foundations, and he sees that, slowly, life is returning. Here and there the yellow of new planks glows bright against the cindery grey; buildings are rising. From all around comes the sound of dragging footsteps: clogs clattering, boots clanging on metallic residue. People move slowly; they look bewildered. They wear bizarre combinations of clothing: a beaded evening blouse salvaged from wreckage, summer pants, dirndl skirts, torn kimonos, rags reborn as shirts, strips of cloth made from wood pulp which disintegrate in the rain. Young ex-soldiers shuffle past in tattered uniforms, dazed remnants of the Imperial war machine who would have gladly died in action, condemned instead to live.

Water and soap are scarce, which means the normally fastidious locals wander uncaring with dirt-streaked faces, muddy feet, grubby clothing, cracked and gaping boots. Children go barefoot.

By the side of what had been main thoroughfares stalls have sprung up, with anything portable for sale or barter — old war medals, fine leather bags scorched and stiff from flames; here an army greatcoat, there a pair of shoes too fine to wear. One woman beckons Joe over to show him an example of her miraculous refurbishing service: unwanted military helmets refashioned into cooking pots, 'for only seven yen!'

And they shall beat their swords into plowshares and their spears into pruning-hooks: nation shall not lift up sword against nation, neither shall they learn war any more.

As a child in church he had heard the familiar words declaimed, but Isaiah never got round to helmets.

In one broad plaza the crumbling walls are covered with handwritten notices on grubby scraps of paper. He slowly identifies the *kanji* characters, picking out the frequently repeated 'mother' and 'home'. Next to him an elderly man points to a sign, begins to translate, but here is a chance for Joe to practise his Japanese, newly polished from training camp immersion. He reads one message aloud, '*Your brother waits for you.*' And, slowly, from another: '*Your mother waits at sunset each day . . .* '

He too has sent messages, not scrawled on torn paper but carrying the same hope of a response. The letters, via the military grapevine

394

to Nagasaki, have gone to Suzuki, hers the only address he has.

Rain has washed the words away on some notices, the ink blurred as though by tears, the fluttering paper the sound of a thousand unheard voices.

He has been fighting off a sense of horror since he got here; drawn and quartered again, pulled in different directions. Where does he stand in this dead land, the land of his birth, where a smell of burning still rises from the rubble? Where people are starving. Is he among the victors and the generals or is he one of the conquered and slain? Where does he want to be? Where might he be, now, if Nancy had not scooped him up and carried him away?

The streets are crowded with cycle rickshaws, there are carts pulled by horses or oxen. A few taxis powered by charcoal wheeze past, billowing smoke. The city seems enveloped by fog, and people wear improvised mouth masks to ward off the choking fumes. Threading through the traffic, moving fast, bouncing over potholes, are the jeeps of the occupying force. The troops look startlingly bright-faced, healthy, clean.

Further off, gutted factories stand, empty, their broken chimneys smokeless. On the horizon, with a shock of pleasure and surprise, he picks out Mount Fuji, the purple-yellow of a half-ripe plum, a scarf of cloud swirled at its peak, recalling the Hiroshige woodcuts he had pored over in Mr Murakami's hut. This is a sight newly revealed to the city: until they were

395

bombed flat, tall buildings would have hidden Fuji from view.

★ ★ ★

When darkness descends, with no street lamps left standing, acetylene torches from roadside stalls beam lurid brilliance on to the nearest faces; the passing headlamps of Occupation vehicles throw moving silhouettes against the walls as the lights from cars had done long ago when Joey sat on the steps of his grandmother's house and watched the homeless men tramp past, outrun by their shadows.

★ ★ ★

There are hot dog stands run by and for the Eighth Army on corners of the Ginza, where silver coins were once minted. Locals silently watch as GIs grab burgers and orange frankfurters in long bread rolls. They do not beg, they simply stand and watch. This is their town but the hot dog stand is an outpost of America: Japs not served.

Joe knows already that he is not permitted to buy an item and hand it straight over. Nothing pristine can be passed on; first he must take at least a bite, to render the roll 'left-over'. The insensitivity of this repels him, and he finds a way round it: buying a hot dog he breaks it in two and hands half to a grey-haired man, half to the woman by his side.

'*Tsumaranai mono desuga.*'

396

The traditional phrase hardly seems appropriate: the 'trifling thing' he is asking them to accept could be their only food today, but they accept it silently, with a dignified inclination of the head to express their thanks.

★ ★ ★

Everyone knew who was in charge of the Occupation; the picture had gone round the world: the tall US general, relaxed, hands on hips, towering over the defeated Emperor, Hirohito standing blank-eyed, stiff as a doll. A god defeated by a *gaijin*: MacArthur.

Not everyone appreciated the significance of the two flags in the signing of the surrender — also recorded in a photograph. Alongside the Stars and Stripes was the original flag flown by Commodore Perry when he sailed into Edo harbour in 1853 and invited the Japanese to trade with the West — or be blown to bits. There was a touch of ego here: SCAP — the Supreme Commander for the Allied Powers — was not just waving an old flag. Perry was a SCAP kinsman.

For Joe, too, family came into the story: it was an ironic twist of the knife that SCAP, the hero of the hour, should be the murderer, the man who caused his father's death. MacArthur's order to the troops in Washington had sent Ben sinking to the bottom of the river. Here, he had usurped the Emperor, taking on the mantle of a god to bring the nation back to life.

The jeeps bounce past; the GIs see a blond

head and wave at Joe. Otishi told him one night in Italy, as they shared a patch of mud and canvas, that if you stood on a certain corner of the Ginza for twenty minutes you'd be sure to see someone you knew. They had made a pact, sealed with a half-melted Hershey bar, to test the theory one day. *How do you make God laugh?*

Behind him a voice says, 'Well look who's here. The boy with perfect hair.'

She is dressed in what looks like some kind of uniform, eyes concealed by dark glasses, her polished ebony hair longer than he recalls, lipstick scarlet, and she is actually smiling up at him, albeit quizzically, not much more than a curve of the lips. 'Well they say if you stand on this corner — '

Joe says, 'Hi, Yasuko,' trying to sound cool and unsurprised, aware that he is beaming at her idiotically. Understandable, forgivable, surely, to show he is pleased to see a familiar face here in this place of sorrow and numbed pain, but he is prepared for her to be sharp with him.

'What are you doing in Tokyo?'

'I'm writing the new constitution,' she says, and now she does smile. 'Well, I think the idea was I'd make the coffee but I'm lousy at coffee-making, so they're letting me help out in the office. Seeing as I can type and handle statistics and speak the lingo. And since we're giving women the vote. So that's in my favour.' She tilts her head and studies him over the dark lenses.

'We're bringing them democracy, Joey, no inequality based on race or family origin. No

398

unlawful detention. They couldn't set up a Tule Lake here. Doesn't that make you feel proud? Feel *good*? Is my sarcasm too heavy?'

She glances around at the ruined cityscape.

'You know what all this was? Revenge for Pearl Harbor. A case of overkill, would you say?'

Passers-by stare at her, suspicious, some hostile: a Japanese girl, immaculate and elegant with scarlet nails and lips.

'What about you?' she asks. 'Why are you here?'

'I'm with the re-education unit, interpreter stuff — '

'Interpreter! When could you speak Japanese?'

'I did a language course back home. I'm here to do adult teaching. Liaison, they call it.'

'You're a spy, basically.'

'No — '

'It's okay. I am, too. We all are.'

'We?'

'Outsiders. Foreigners. You don't need to be a yellow-haired Yank to be a *gaijin*. You know that. Ask the Koreans. We're all spies, but for different reasons. SCAP and his boys want to find out what makes these people tick, get inside their heads and then change them.'

We, she said.

He has a class to set up: teachers to be introduced to the new constitution, indoctrinated in democracy; she has telegrams to send. They agree to meet later.

He suggests a rendezvous at the Ernie Pyle Theater.

'You mean the Takarazuka. All this renaming,

you're such cultural imperialists.'

You. For a moment she is on the other side of the divide. For a moment he sees the old Yasuko, mouth grim, face stony.

He says hastily, 'We might take in a movie.'

'Why not. Oh, I saw *The Maltese Falcon* again. It's not bad.'

She moves off, calls back over her shoulder, 'That last line you love so much. From Shakespeare? It's a misquotation.'

He watches her go, the slim figure slicing through the shabby crowd, walking fast in her tiny flat shoes. Why was he here? she had asked. He had been devious. He had told her the what, not the why. He had not said: to track down my mother. Paralysed by an undefined fear.

★   ★   ★

Later, they ate dinner in a dimly lit restaurant on the outskirts. Waiters moved between the tables replenishing glasses, removing plates; steaming dishes arrived from the kitchen. Yasuko glanced about, her face shadowed with something resembling grief.

'Yasuko? Are you okay?'

'I hate this place. They make me sick, these people.'

'What people?'

'All of us. We can afford to leave food on our plates when people outside are starving. There's a joke going around: 'What do good parents share with their children? Malnutrition.' I hate myself for being here.'

400

And he learned that Yasuko, too, had been devious, that the why of her presence in Tokyo was to try and reassemble a fragmented family, pay respects to the dead, pull the surviving pieces together.

'I have an uncle. A schoolteacher. He works all hours and he can't feed his family. Black market is a criminal offence, but there's no food, Joe. He may end up killing himself.'

One of her cousins had been an officer in the Emperor's army, present whereabouts unknown.

'My mother hopes he's dead. Traditionally it would, of course, be more honourable to be dead.'

'This morning you said we're spies. I walk around making notes in my head. Today I give them a present of half a hot dog and they respond with a traditional thank-you. But will our presence, our observation, change all that?'

'It could.' She shrugged. 'But don't be too sure. Group harmony versus individuality? The old ways are pretty strong.'

He was unconvinced. 'At SCAP we have these brainstorming sessions. We feel they should be more like us. But when does 'a little more' become too much? How long will it be before the old ways are abandoned, the new world calling payback time? Perhaps we should try to be a little more Japanese.'

'Speak for yourself,' she said.

After that it became easy to tell her the story of his mother and father. Or at least some of the story. She said,

'How come you're still in Tokyo? You should

be hightailing it to Nagasaki.'

'I'm leaving tomorrow on the train. Suzuki will be able to tell me more.'

'Suzuki?'

'My great-uncle's widow.'

'The men in your family surely seem to have had a thing for Japanese women.'

★ ★ ★

They spent the night in a patched and tattered house in the district of the floating world where escape was still possible, where soft girls and loud music blotted out reality for those who could afford black market fantasy. And they, too, floated for a while in tentative exploration until fantasy was abandoned and the force of truth took hold. They stripped each other bare, slippery as eels, her scarlet mouth blurred and swollen, heat fused their bodies, sent the blood coursing between them with a sense of arching, of piercing; an ecstasy of escape.

Wrapped together, the futon thin beneath their bones, they lay watching the sky spin slowly out of darkness through the dirty glass of the window.

They had not slept and now it was almost dawn.

She poured water into a wooden bowl and washed him attentively. He sponged her body clean of sweat and semen.

'You have perfect feet,' he observed, drying her toes, kissing the high, narrow arch. He cupped her small breasts. 'Perfect all over, in fact.'

'You know what they say about the Japanese body: fine from head to hips, then we have these short legs.'

'Perfect,' he said firmly, 'like my hair.' He could tell her now how she had scared him on that first encounter at Tule Lake.

She laughed and said that was her way of dealing with important things: to be stern.

'I was important?'

'Of course. I watched you every day in the mess hall. I spilled stuff down my blouse because I wasn't paying attention to my food.'

'I searched for you, to say goodbye, that last day before I left for the language training camp. I looked all over.'

'I had some kind of bug, and I can tell you that camp hospital was no place for a sick person to be. I made an official complaint but those sons of bitches couldn't care less.'

He felt a vast tenderness for her, for her fierceness; Yasuko was a paper shrew, self-protective. There was no taming to be done here. Disarmed, captivated, he wanted only to try and banish the shadow of pain from her small, questioning face. She looked younger when she laughed.

★ ★ ★

He caught an early train, picking his way through hundreds of blanket-wrapped figures asleep on the station floor, a few hookers hopelessly teetering up and down outside on their cork-soled platform shoes, seams drawn up

403

the backs of tea-stained legs to simulate the stockings they occasionally managed to barter from a friendly GI.

One, with tired eyes and hair tortured into a frizzy bush, called out as Joe passed, 'Hi, kid. You got cheese? Kraft Velveeta?'

He reached into his pocket for a packet of gum and handed it over with a muttered '*Tsumaranai mono desuga.*'

Startled, she responded with an instinctive bow and gabbled phrase of thanks. They exchanged a grin. 'Hey, Johnny,' she called after him, 'you good American. Learning fast!'

55

Again a train heading for an unknown destination. He swayed, lulled by the rhythm, the sound of steel on steel like a fast drum riff, but what old song could he sing this time to the percussion backing of wheels on track?

From the train window he watched the countryside slide past, aware of the smallness of things here. The variety. Tiny streams, delicate trees nodding over chasms, hillsides glittering with waterfalls. No acres of American wheat or prairie grass-lands stretching out unbroken to the flat horizon. With most of the land too mountainous to cultivate, this was farming in miniature, an oddly shaped rice field next to a vegetable patch, ingenious planting, every inch of soil packed tight with crops of one sort and another. What would these people make of the beet fields of America, cultivated so skilfully by the Issei and Nisei, great expanses of dull green stretching for mile after flat mile . . . ?

He was alone in a compartment reserved for Occupation forces, while the rest of the train was crowded with locals — 'indigenous personnel'. Face pressed to the glass he allowed himself to let go, pulled by the train towards an area of pain he had spent a lifetime re-creating, clutching at old memories, fed always by the sense of loss.

And then the letter had arrived, the rug of bereavement had been pulled from under him.

No dead mother after all, just a faraway woman who had divested herself of unwanted ballast and sailed on without the inconvenient child. Or so he had thought, hating the woman, the memory of silk and soft, curved cheek, until Nancy redrew the picture.

★ ★ ★

When, two changes and many hours later, he heard the announcement, the destination named, he felt he was stepping into dream territory.

Nagasaki. Did it really exist?

He got off the train and saw her at the end of the platform: a small, stocky woman with a square face, in a dark robe something between a kimono and a dress. Suzuki.

She trotted up the platform, clogs noisy, and stopped a yard away from him, her expression solemn. She bowed formally, and he did the same. Then, laughing, they found themselves involved in an awkward, shaky hug.

'Welcome to Nagasaki,' she said, in careful English.

'How did you know I'd be on this train?' he asked, in Japanese.

She beamed with relief. 'Ah! So I don't need to try and remember my English.'

She glanced at the train. 'It's the only one today.'

'I was planning to get another message to you once I was here.'

He looked down at the top of her head, the

thinning grey hair, the creased brow. Lines criss-crossed her face; a net spun by time. She was wizened, like a fruit that has dried into age.

He reached into his bag, brought out a traditionally gift-wrapped parcel and handed it to her with a small bow. She bowed, murmuring traditional thanks. A pause.

'I suppose I should call you Joey.'

Her hands fluttered, plucking at her sleeves.

'You must be . . . ' a mental calculation, 'twenty-three. You look . . . more mature.'

He laughed. 'Older, you mean. That's the army. The war.'

There was a pause.

How do you ask the big question — the one too raw, too important, to be incorporated into the pattern of an emotional reunion? It would, Joe felt, be very un-Japanese to blurt it out, splintering the veneer that overlay the cracks in the social façade.

He said, blurting it out, 'She died, didn't she.'

The platform was deserted now and shadowy, their two figures caught in a shaft of sunlight. A breeze, sweeping the track, caught up scraps of waste paper and sent them whirling in the air like dancing butterflies.

'It may comfort you to know that it happened in the moment of the blast. She would not have suffered.'

Would not have suffered? He stared down at her.

She took his arm, as though to prevent him leaving. 'When you see the house, you will understand.'

A cycle rickshaw took them through town, past collapsed and flattened buildings, breached walls and doors that opened on to the emptiness of vanished rooms. The road climbed, leaving the harbour behind.

The natural amphitheatre of the town lay below them now. He could see the shell of the Catholic church standing, blackened, insubstantial, like a sketch for a solid structure, its toppled dome half buried in the ground. A stone bridge spanned the river, its arches reflected in the water like spectacles. Compared with the wasteland of Tokyo, Nagasaki was still recognisably a city.

*　*　*

Suzuki glanced up and caught him staring at the scene, and for a moment she saw it through his eyes: almost, it seemed, Nagasaki had got off lightly. She felt a need to set the record straight.

'Certain buildings, made from concrete and steel, withstood the blast, some protected by the hillside. Traditional dwellings of wood disappeared. Neighbourhoods for a mile around the explosion were completely destroyed. Consumed.'

She touched his arm and pointed to the tall wooden telephone poles that lined the street: he saw that they were scorched on the side facing the explosion.

'Fifty thousand people died that day. Many more, later. Even now it continues: diseased, they sicken.'

The rickshaw creaked on, uphill. Again Suzuki touched Joe's arm, and pointed to a crumbling stone tower set back from the road. Burnt and warped, almost liquefied into its surroundings, a clock face, the twisted hands standing at 11.02.

'The moment of the explosion.'

Later she would tell him how it had been, that day, when she came back.

★　★　★

Settling the girls in their temporary home away from town, further down the coast, she had heard the far-off sound of a plane. She went to the door and looked up, shielding her eyes: the sky was overcast but in a parting of the clouds she saw a distant shape like a dark fish hovering. There was a flash, a glare, brighter than any lightning and then the thunder, a sound so deep it unsettled the ground beneath her feet like the tremor of an earthquake. There was a shift in the air, an onrushing. Then silence.

★　★　★

When Suzuki reached the outskirts, at first she could see nothing, the smoke and the fires too thick. But the boiling wind that hurled people and animals into the air like toys did one thing: it lifted the smoke. And then she saw that the whole area was strewn with corpses and the near-dead. Bodies clogged the river, some flung by the force of the explosion, others who had crawled into the water to try to quench the burning that split and blistered their skin, only to drown. The living stumbled unsteadily through the rubble, reaching out as though blinded; naked, their hair and clothes aflame. Liquid dripped from their hands, as if they had emerged from the river. Puzzlingly, they appeared to be draped in rags. Then she saw that what looked like rags were strips of shredded skin, fluttering from their arms. The liquid dripping from their hands was blood.

★ ★ ★

She would tell Joey none of this; she was not sure she could speak the words. He could read about it in books. Books were already being written, dissertations prepared; artists would paint pictures. The cycle rickshaw was climbing higher, slowly zigzagging towards the house Suzuki had shared with Henry. The rules of hospitality were rigid: Joe must rest after the journey, eat, sip some tea. Then she would take him to the place where he was born, on the other side of the harbour.

Henry's house lay beyond iron gates, square, solid.

'This was the American side of town,' Suzuki told him. 'These houses stood firm on strong foundations.'

She showed him into a large room and disappeared to prepare his refreshment while Joe stood, looking around him at the room, where Nancy's uncle had lived and raised a family and died peacefully before the bombs fell. There was

410

a view over the bay and surrounding hills.

As he turned away from the window he was startled to find a young girl standing in the doorway, watching him.

'You must be Joey.'

'Yes. And you are?'

He spoke in Japanese; she responded in English.

'Mayu. We talked many times about you.'

Of course, she was Henry's daughter, it would be natural for her to speak English, yet there was something ungiving about the tone.

'We?' he asked.

'My mother and I. And Cho-Cho.'

He felt a strange constriction around his heart, not a pain, more an intimation of pain. This child had talked about him with his mother.

'She used to tell us stories. About when she was young.'

He found he was pressing a hand to his chest, easing the not-pain, trying to breathe normally.

He said, 'You know more than I do.'

She nodded. 'Of course. She told us everything.'

Suzuki, pausing in the door with a tray, heard the last phrases. She said rapidly, 'Mayu was a favourite of your mother's. Cho-Cho used to say that when Mayu grew up she would be an example of the Japanese New Woman. Free to control her own life. She would have been so happy that women will have the vote now.'

Suzuki knelt to place the tray on a low table.

'When you have rested after your journey, we will go to your mother's house — '

'What's left of it,' Mayu murmured.

Suzuki, embarrassed, said rapidly, 'Well of course, like everything else, the damage . . . '

This girl was his cousin. He wondered at the chill he sensed, and set out to win her round.

'So my mother must have told you about how she and my father met and got married,' he said.

'That's right,' Mayu said tranquilly. '*So desu ne*. She told us how he rented her. For a while.'

From Suzuki, a small cry as she folded into herself, bowing over the tray of green tea and plate of sweet bean paste dumplings. The girl held Joe in her level glance for a moment, smiled, and left the room.

So here it was, the dirty little secret that was his patrimony. He was descended from a hooker and a sailor looking for a good time in a foreign port. As so often in the past, Joe waited for some spontaneous emotion to seize him. And as in the past he remained empty.

He did not feel betrayed: his life had been built on hypocrisy to maintain a semblance of family respectability, but also with kindness, to protect him. But he could not endure further protection; he wanted information, he wanted the truth. He saw that Suzuki could not be trusted here.

'Is there someone I could talk to, someone else who knew her?'

Suzuki thought for a moment, shaking her head doubtfully.

'So many are no longer with us . . . '

Then she clapped her hands, remembering.

'*Isha!*'

'Doctor? Her doctor?'

'Yes, yes. For many years.'

'Where do I find him?'

★ ★ ★

The building was no more than a wreck; but broken windows had been patched, the door repaired and, inside, the lobby was clean and polished. The waiting room seethed with distress. People perched cautiously on stools, huddled in chairs; some had only the floor. They held themselves carefully, arms bandaged, some with faces swathed in gauze covering. Joe glimpsed skin marked with burns, unhealed sores. The patients made no noise, their pain taken for granted.

Among them, as at Tule, he loomed. But worse, he stood out in his health, his lack of scabs and surgical dressings. Through gaps in the boarded-up window he could see melted metal, blasted walls and a burnt city; the truth that bore out Oppenheimer's words when he witnessed the first explosion of his invention: *Now I am become Death, the destroyer of worlds,* . . .

After just a few minutes he heard his name called out by the receptionist.

He said, protesting, 'Others are before me — '

'You are a visitor; please go through. Dr Sato will see you now.'

Joe paused in the door of the surgery. The thin, grey-haired figure behind the desk rose and bowed.

'Good morning. I hope you didn't have to wait

413

too long.' A trace of American in the delivery.

Joe said, 'I feel bad, coming in ahead of other people. You have a busy day.'

'All days are busy, Pinkerton-san. We have unusual circumstances: my patients all suffer from the same sickness. Bomb poison, they call it; these are among the lucky survivors.' He studied Joe for a moment, silver eyebrows raised questioningly. 'What can I do for you?'

He felt guilty again: taking up a doctor's time while outside the door, the urgent needs of the sick awaited attention.

'I was told — I was hoping you could answer some questions about my mother. About Cho-Cho-san.'

Dr Sato's pale hands shuffled papers on his desk. Questions about Cho-Cho. *A lifeless girl carried in on a stretcher; his first experience of a botched suicide.*

This was not the time to recall that day.

'I knew Cho-Cho-san for many years.'

For a long time she had refused to speak to him except to answer medical enquiries: he formed part of the unwanted rescue team, 'saving' her from her desired end. Gradually she accepted that, welcome or not, a doctor was occasionally needed. Much later, he had become a friend.

There came a day when, formally, tentatively, he had suggested that if he ceased to be her doctor, he could offer her care and attention of a rather more personal nature. She responded impatiently: as a medical expert he was useful to her. As a friend, she valued him.

414

But as a husband? A shake of the head.

Recalling that day he said aloud, '*Ganko-mono*!'

Startled, Joe repeated, 'Stubborn?'

Dr Sato, equally startled, said, 'You understand Japanese. Ah. I meant the word in its positive use: your mother was . . . an independent spirit. I should have said she had *dokuritsushin*.'

He looked across the desk at Joe, searching for words that were safe to use.

'Your mother,' he said. 'At the beginning she was *fujin*, an old-fashioned girl, she followed tradition. Later the traditionalists called her a troublemaker, one of those modern women, trying to be a man, as they put it, attending meetings, marching. But then she changed. Became a businesswoman. She was quite a figure.'

'Did you like her?' It was a loaded question.

The doctor frowned. 'I do not *like* my patients. I offer them my skills.'

'Suzuki tells me she died in the explosion.'

'The blast, yes. It would have been instant.'

'I keep hearing that. But how can you know?'

More shifting of papers on desktop. There were no *right* words here. The doctor gave Joe one of the long, steady looks his patients were familiar with.

'I will avoid euphemism. The blast victims were extinguished. Literally consumed by the heat. Vaporised. As we have no verifiable evidence of an afterlife we cannot know their feelings but, scientifically, there would have been

415

no time to suffer. She will have passed from life to nothingness faster than the human physiology can register.'

★ ★ ★

Outside the doctor's surgery Suzuki waited in the rickshaw, her face closed. The day was not going as she had planned. After the debacle of her daughter's revelation she had attempted not only an apology but an explanation: the Americans had been the enemy, the Americans had dropped the bomb, killed her friends and families of friends. Joe's father was American.

'Mayu decided to punish you. I am sorry.'

'But she was telling the truth.'

'Truth is shapeless. Like water, it can be different things to different people, it can bring life if you drink it or death if you drown. One truth will tell how a tea-house girl took an American sailor into her bed. There's a truth in which an orphan child was sold by one man to another. There's a truth in which a girl saw a golden man walking up the hill towards her and loved him for the whole of her life.'

★ ★ ★

He climbs the winding road from the harbour. In the brilliant sunlight his blond hair is almost white. Even from afar he looks American. He pauses, turns and waits.

Hobbling to catch up with him, Suzuki calls breathlessly, 'It was easier before they rebuilt this

416

as a proper road; I find the surface painful to my feet.' She adds, 'I remember watching your father walk up this hill to the house in his white uniform. He was so handsome.'

What Joe recalls is a tired man, with big hands, hair dulled to a dusty non-colour, who sang along with Bing on the radio.

Listening to her describe the events of that day, dim, blurred like a landscape seen through rain, twisted into so many puzzling shapes in his mind, Joe takes from his pocket the battered spinning top, its paint long ago rubbed off, flakes of red and yellow clinging to the surface. Suzuki glances at the top and exclaims, 'You still have that! The top! I ran down the hill and bought it for your father to give you!'

And here it is again, the unreliable truth. Whose version will it be this time? Are all his memories to be stolen from him, one by one? Surely the top was a present from his mother? How can he remember that so wrong? Is nothing to be trusted?

They are approaching a cluster of buildings when Suzuki says, 'I shall rest here for a few minutes. Please go ahead.'

She points out the remains of the house, and then the path is at his feet — just a few steps to the door with the stone lintel step where he sat. Didn't he? He can recall the cool, hard feel of it beneath his small buttocks. While voices came from the room behind him, he sat here, leaning forward to pick up a snail. He had brought the snail up close, the gleaming slime sticky on his fingers. The waving horns twitched in response to his warm breath. Then someone knocked the snail from his hand, startling him. That must have been his father; he recalls a white sleeve, a tanned wrist with fine gold hairs. What happened next is a jumble. Was that when they took the child's hands and walked him down the hill? When he remembered his spinning top and pulled his hands free, ran back —

The child screaming, tugging, tugging at the woman's white sleeve, so that her hand fell away from her throat, the knife dropped to the floor, the blood flowing . . .

The breath is sucked from his body, and he groans — Suzuki's head twitches as she hears the sound and then she has covered the ground between them and is holding him, the small woman soothing, rocking the muscular young body that is shaking with a grief for so long blanked out.

★   ★   ★

The roof and wooden walls are gone, door blown away. To the right of the doorway one wall survives, damaged by the blast but still standing.

He stares into the shell of the house, into what had been a room, and Suzuki, resting her hand on his arm, fills in the blank places: Henry, who had come running from town, who had rushed his mother to the doctor. How the two of them watched over her. How angry she had been, afterwards.

418

'Henry used to say she never forgave him for saving her life.'

They have spent hours picking their way through the maze of the distant past; the three years of the waiting, when Cho-Cho endlessly repeated, as though invoking a spell, that one fine day Pinkerton would return, sail into the harbour, walk up the hill. Until the long-awaited day arrived, with all that followed.

As Suzuki talked and talked, the silent one, the servant, the observer who had enabled the others to lead their chosen lives, who knew everything and now had someone who was listening, she found herself for the first time playing a central role. And as the words flowed, an unsuspected bitterness went too, leaving her emptied, serene within, as she had always outwardly appeared to be.

When she paused, he had questions and more questions; he mined her for the gold of information.

★ ★ ★

They walked back together down the hill towards the harbour. He told her he would be departing for America when he could get leave, to attend to a couple of things. He tried to explain to Suzuki how much Nancy had suffered, conscience-stricken, for what she did; he recalled something he had learned in his lessons with Mr Murakami: the concept of *honshin* — original truth of heart.

419

'She has listened often to her original heart. I'd like to set her mind at rest.'

She took his arm, allowing him to guide her steps.

'You have your own *giri*. You are a good American son.'

'She's not my mother, but she did everything —'

'We have an old saying.'

'What is it with you people . . . ' He stopped. 'What is it with us, and old sayings?'

'You could call it another form of ancestor worship.'

'And the old saying?'

'*Umi-no-oya-yori sodate no oya.*'

'The ones who care for you are your real parents,' he repeated.

He studied her square, heavy face, not beautiful but pleasing, reassuring. He felt her quietness.

'You and Henry were together a long time.'

'A good, kind man. He was devoted to your mother.' She said no more and Joe was aware of much left unsaid here.

'Thank you.'

Did she know he was thanking her for the years, the caring for Cho-Cho? For peopling the empty places of his past.

'For the spinning top,' he said.

★　★　★

He took the train back to Tokyo, watching the less damaged outskirts give way to rubble as he approached the centre. Everywhere people were

420

at work, rebuilding. Slowly Tokyo would rise from the ashes.

He had thought once that he was American. Later, old, frail ties tugged him in another direction and he saw himself, as though in the last shot of a movie, riding off into the Land of the Rising Sun. But it was too late to put down roots. Here, or anywhere else.

Overhead the birds swept in a dark filigree patterning the sky. When the swallows nest again, Pinkerton told Butterfly, I will return. Suzuki had repeated the words to him with sad amusement.

Wave upon wave, the lacy arrows headed into emptiness. Perhaps the birds could provide his answer: like them he would take off, crossing land and sea, and settle in the chosen place, for a while. And when some inner solstice gave the signal, he would head east — or west, depending on the season.

Yasuko would be busy, ruthlessly organising her fragmented family into shape; goading them back to life, like an irritable sheepdog snapping at their heels. Because they were important. And for once there was something he wanted to hold on to; a need for attachment.

'I'll be back,' he told her as they lay curled together on the shabby futon. She gave him her cool, distanced look, one eyebrow raised:

'I won't count on it.'

'Do,' he said.

★   ★   ★

421

There was much he wanted to do here: walk the spine of this broken bracelet of islands from Okinawa to Hokkaido; rebuild Cho-Cho's house — it was his, Suzuki told him; Cho-Cho had made her arrangements with typical efficiency. Before he left they had surveyed the small strip of blasted wasteland between house and road.

'Maybe if I try very hard I might make a Zen garden.'

She murmured a phrase and he laughed ruefully. 'Not appropriate?'

'She always wanted an American garden.'

'I can't do that.' Mimicking her: 'Not appropriate. D'you think she'd forgive me?'

'It is not question of forgiving. She would see your point of view.'

When they said goodbye she gave him a small metal box, once decorated with elaborate moulding and enamel. It was blackened, the surface rough, like a rash of Braille beneath his fingers; an emblem of enigmatic messages.

'She placed her letters in it, written to you, year after year.'

'Never posted.'

'She hoped one day you would read them and understand maybe a little more.'

Heat had warped the lid. He managed to prise it open and looked into the box: the pages, carbonised in the heat of the explosion curled black and brittle, rustling silkily, like burnt onion skins.

★　★　★

When he had first seen the house from afar, approaching from the path that curved up the hill, it had seemed almost untouched. But close up, it was revealed as a ruined shell. He had stared at this absence of a house, feeling cheated: no trace remained of his mother.

And then Suzuki's fingertips touched his arm, she showed him where to look.

The flash, when it came, in the instant that it consumed Cho-Cho, burned her shape onto the wall. In that second of dazzling light her body shielded the surface behind her and left a perfect silhouette, a shadow that had been a woman. The shadow of a woman with her arms raised above her head, almost as though caught in a dance. But Suzuki knows she would have been hanging up clothes: 'there used to be a line just there'. Pausing, hands raised to the washing line, Cho-Cho had heard the plane and turned to look over her shoulder as the bomb exploded.

He steps closer to the silhouette, so small, the top of her head no higher than his heart. Here she was, his mother: he can see her, the slightness, the curved grace. A flutter at the corner of memory's eye, become an enduring shadow. The sun hangs low in the sky, warming his back. Thrown against the wall his shadow stands next to Cho-Cho's. He stretches out a hand, and his shadow hand moves towards her, but a cloud has inched across the sun and his silhouette vanishes before the shadows meet.

Author's Note and Acknowledgements

My interest in Japan began a long time ago when I visited the country on a writing assignment. I followed up that trip with wide, undisciplined reading — history, fiction, biography . . . Among the many books I am indebted to are works by Lafcadio Hearn, Basil Hall Chamberlain, Donald Richie, Ian Buruma and Meirrion and Susie Harries — all guided my meandering steps. For some years I had a Japanese daughter-in-law.

Outsiders who write about Japan are swimming in dangerous waters. All is nebulous; there are nuances so subtle that every noun, verb, adjective, action — even thought — can prove a hazard, the unwary soon lost and out of their depth. A European writer once described the Japanese language as 'a tool more for withholding and eluding than expressing or stating'. As with the language, so with the culture. Despite taking every possible care, I can only beg indulgence for the sins of imprecision and misprision I will surely have committed.

Butterfly's Shadow is a work of fiction that was inspired by another work of fiction, so I felt my story could be allowed to float free of some limiting narrative restrictions. I updated Pinkerton's arrival in Nagasaki to 1922 — a fictional character stepping into an unknown but real world. Puccini's opera was my springboard: in free-fall, I ventured the question: *what if?* From there, the characters walked free.

I have not consciously distorted or misused known facts, and have striven to keep faith with historical events: the Depression; the plight of World War One veterans; the fate of Japanese Americans following Pearl Harbor (87 per cent lived in California, Oregon and Washington); the part that volunteers from American internment camps played in the Italian and French campaigns; the immediate aftermath of the Nagasaki bomb — all are drawn from fact.

I am aware that Suzuki is not normally a female first name; but, thanks to Puccini, Cho-Cho and her maid Suzuki are such a familiar pair that I was reluctant to change her name.

I did change the name of Pinkerton's American wife because her role in the opera is so slight that she barely exists, whereas in the novel the step-mother has become a central figure. She is *my* Nancy, not the opera's fleetingly glimpsed Kate.

Puccini gave us the music, but the genesis of 'Madame Butterfly' was a process of literary accretion involving writers known and less known: the opera's libretto by Luigi Illica and Giuseppe Giacosa was based partly on Pierre Loti's 1887 novel, *Madame Chrysanthème*, and partly on a short story by John Luther Long, later dramatised by David Belasco. Some researchers have claimed the opera drew on events which actually occurred in Nagasaki in the 1890s.

Friends, family and others knowledgeable in the field have given their time to read the book in progress, and to criticise, contribute and question, among them Simon Richmond, Sarah Richmond, William Rademaekers, Mark Wyndham, Kyoko Tanno, Neil Vickers, Hiromi Dugdale, my peerless agent, Clare Alexander, and long-cherished editor at Chatto, Penelope Hoare.

I also want to thank the British Library, the London Library and my local library in Richmond upon Thames.

In America, Mari Watanabe, Kiyo Endecott and Becky Patchett of the Oregon Nikkei Endowment and Legacy Center helped with research enquiries, as did Scott Daniels, Research Librarian at the Oregon Historical Society, Mary Gallagher, archivist at the Benton County Historical Society and George Edmonton Jr of Oregon State University. Dick Sakurai generously agreed to revisit painful memories to make sure I had kept faith with the facts of Japanese American internment. Any faults that have found their way into the finished book are, of course, my own.

Above all, I want to thank my husband, Theo Richmond. Without his keen eye, patience, challenging scepticism and unflagging encouragement the book would probably never have made it to completion.

Lee Langley
London
January 2010

We do hope that you have enjoyed reading this large print book.

Did you know that all of our titles are available for purchase?

We publish a wide range of high quality large print books including:
Romances, Mysteries, Classics
General Fiction
Non Fiction and Westerns

Special interest titles available in large print are:
The Little Oxford Dictionary
Music Book
Song Book
Hymn Book
Service Book

Also available from us courtesy of Oxford University Press:
Young Readers' Dictionary
(large print edition)
Young Readers' Thesaurus
(large print edition)

For further information or a free brochure, please contact us at:
Ulverscroft Large Print Books Ltd.,
The Green, Bradgate Road, Anstey,
Leicester, LE7 7FU, England.
Tel: (00 44) 0116 236 4325
Fax: (00 44) 0116 234 0205

THE LAKE SHORE LIMITED

Sue Miller

Three years after the death of her brother Gus, Leslie still thinks about what might have been if Gus hadn't got on that plane on September 11th. As she and her husband sit down to watch *The Lake Shore Limited*, a disquietingly autobiographical play written by Gus's former girlfriend Billy, she can't help but wonder if Billy too has been unable to let go of his memory. But does she really know Billy? Meanwhile, Sam, Leslie's friend, finds in the play inescapable echoes of his life and begins to fall for Billy's distinctive, enigmatic beauty.